Cover design by Kirsty-Anne Still @The Pretty Little Design Co.
Editing by Tanya Oemig
Proofreading by Briann Graziano

The Good Girl

Raven Souls MC Book Two

Candice Wright

Also by Candice Wright

APEX TACTICAL SERIES

The Brutal Strike

The Harsh Bite

The Wicked Sting

The Lethal Strike

THE INHERITANCE SERIES

Rewriting Yesterday

In This Moment

The Promise Of Tomorrow

The Complete Inheritance Series Collection

THE UNDERESTIMATED SERIES

The Queen of Carnage: An Underestimated Novel Book One

The Princess of Chaos: An Underestimated Novel Book Two

The Reign of Kings: An Underestimated Novel Book Three

The Heir of Shadows: An Underestimated Novel Book Four

Dulce

Reese

Lollie

Sugar

Raven Souls MC Series

Rest In Pieces

The Good Girl

SHARED WORLD PROJECTS

Hoax Husband: A Hero Club Novel

STANDALONE

Vices and Vows

Sole Survivor

SAME WORLD READING ORDER

"Each individual series can be read as a standalone."

THE QUEEN OF CARNAGE

THE PRINCESS OF CHAOS

RICOCHET

CAUTIOUS (COMING SOON)

THE REIGN OF KINGS

THE HEIR OF SHADOWS

THE CROWN OF FOOLS

THE MERCY OF DEMONS

TAINTED OATHS

TWISTED VOWS

TOXIC WHISPERS

DULCE

REESE

THE THRONE OF LIES

LOLLIE

SUGAR

THE BRUTAL STRIKE

THE HARSH BITE

THE ECHO OF VIOLENCE

THE WICKED STING

THE LETHAL TOUCH

REST IN PIECES

THE GOOD GIRL

Book Description

I grew up as the precocious daughter of a preacher, but death stalked the hallways of my home, tearing my family tree apart and twisting my father's love into something cold and constricting.

Ever the good girl, I remained subservient under his watchful gaze, but each cutting remark and unrealistic expectation forced me to open my eyes and face the truth.

This life was slowly killing me.

At my best friend's urging, I jumped at the chance to stay with her for the summer, having no idea how my life would change after a chance encounter with a dark and brooding biker.

Now, my summer of fun feels a lot like happily ever after, even if the man of my dreams is my father's worst nightmare. But when trouble comes knocking, it won't matter if I'm a sinner or a saint as long as I'm willing to fight dirty for what I want.

They say all's fair in love and war, but nobody told me corruption would taste so sweet.

This book is M/F.

Content Warning:

The Good Girl contains dark elements that some readers may find uncomfortable, including, but not limited to:

• Brief mentions of the death of a child/children (not the main characters)
   • Torture scene (not of the main characters)
   • Brief mention of SA involving a side character
   • Gun violence
   • Breeding kink where the H will give a million excuses as to why he shouldn't wear a condom.
   • Breeding kink where the h pretends to believe him
   • Side Character with Cancer
   • Mentions of child abduction.

Please read with caution. Thank you.

"You have to learn to get up from the table when love is no longer being served."

— Nina Simone

Prologue

Nevaeh

Fifteen years ago

It was my fault. If I hadn't stolen Citi's Barbie and cut off all its hair, she'd still be here.

I wouldn't have been grounded and stuck in my room while a stranger took her from our front yard.

I wouldn't have let them take my sister if I had been there. I would've fought them, kicked them, and bitten them, even though I'm not supposed to bite people, even when I'm mad.

I would've run after her and pulled her from the

1

stranger's car. I would've saved her even if they took me instead.

But I wasn't with her. I was in my room crying and yelling about how much I hated her. But I don't hate her, not even a little bit.

Mom's on her knees screaming as the police try to calm her down. Dad's staring at the wall, and I'm sitting on the bottom stair, trying to figure out what to do.

I look over at my bright yellow raincoat hanging up by the door. The hook next to it, where Citi's pink one usually hangs, is empty.

I stare at my boots under my coat and frown. Should I put them on? It's raining outside—it's been raining all day. If I put them on, I can go look for her. I'm really good at finding things.

And Citlalli's my twin. If anyone's going to find her, it's me.

I stand up and walk over to my boots and decide that I don't like yellow anymore. It's too bright and happy. It makes my stomach hurt to look at them because the color used to make me smile, and now I just want to cry.

I slide my feet inside my boots and stand on the bench to get my coat off the hook.

I pull it on and zip it up before I walk into the living room.

Everything's still the same. Mom's still crying, Daddy's still staring at the wall, and Citi's still gone.

I look at my yellow boots and start to cry, picturing Citi wearing her matching pink ones, running away from the bad man who took her, and trying to find her way back home when it's dark and scary outside.

I walk over to Dad and stand next to him, waiting for him to smile or hug me, but he doesn't notice me.

I look around at all the grown-ups, but none of them look at me or my bright yellow coat.

Did it make me invisible?

I hold my hand up, but I can still see it.

I walk over to one of the police officers and look up at him as he writes something in his notebook.

He looks sad—not like Mom and Dad sad, but still sad.

Sometimes, adults make me feel funny. Like when Mr. Markham, who used to live down the street, watched me. Or when Mr. Jones, the school janitor, brushed up against me.

This man doesn't, though. When he lifts his head to look at me, I see that he has kind eyes. But it seems like it hurts him to see me.

I squeeze my hands tight and look around the room again, finally understanding what I didn't before. It's not that they can't see me. It's that they don't want to because I look exactly like Citi.

I turn back to look at the nice policeman.

"I want to go look for my sister," I say, my voice small and unsure. "I'm really good at finding things, and I know all the places she likes to hide."

"That's really nice of you, miss. But it's dark and wet outside, and I don't want you to get sick."

"I don't want Citi to get sick either. What if she's out in the dark, scared and cold?"

"We have lots of people looking for her, kiddo. It's safer for you here."

I feel angry inside because that's a lie. It's not safe here. If it was, my sister would still be here.

"If she's scared, she'll hide. She won't come out for a stranger. She'd never go with a stranger," I tell him so that he knows she didn't get in a car because someone had candy or a puppy. We're not dumb. We know the rules.

"She knows to trust the police, though, right? She knows this uniform means safety."

I nod, then shake my head because I don't know anymore. I don't know what's safe. Home was safe, but now it's not. What if the same is true for people?

"How about we get you something to drink and a snack while your parents talk to the officers?"

"I'm not hungry or thirsty. I just want my sister." My voice comes out louder than I meant.

"Nevaeh!" Dad yells.

I spin to look at him, stepping back when he stomps toward me with a really angry face.

"Go to your room."

"But—"

He grabs my arm tightly, making me whimper.

"For once in your life, do as you're told. Not everything is about you. If you and your *selfishness* have cost me my—"

"Sir," the nice policeman snaps, stopping him. But it doesn't matter. I'm ten, not five. I know what he was going to say. He knows it's my fault Citi was taken, too.

"Just go to your room. I can't look at you anymore."

He lets me go with a little shove toward the stairs.

The stairs that lead to the bedroom I share with Citi.

I want to argue with him. I want to beg him to let me sleep in their room or on the couch. But he's staring at the wall again.

I walk slowly toward the stairs, my hands sweating, my knees shaking, and my stomach hurting even more than before.

When I reach the bottom step, I stop and look behind me, but nobody sees me—nobody except the nice policeman.

He has a look on his face that I don't understand and won't until years later.

Pity.

I don't know if he knew then how things would turn out—that my childhood would disappear along with Citi.

All I know is that my sister never came back.

The world moved on without us, but inside these walls, we were stuck in a kind of limbo.

I didn't just lose my sister that day. I lost my parents too. And our once-happy home became the place I spent years living with shadows and ghosts.

Prologue II

Havoc

F *ive years ago*

I wipe my oil-stained hands on a rag that's almost as dirty as my skin and take a moment to stare at my bike with pride.

My father left it to me. Unfortunately, he was riding it when he died.

On the plus side, at least he went out doing something he loved.

The downside was that it took me forever to restore it. I'm no mechanic, and working full-time didn't give me much time to work on it, especially with my other club responsibilities. But I did it—and with my own two hands.

"Havoc!"

I turn to see Lola standing with my phone in her hand, her hip cocked, wearing a tiny pair of denim cut-offs that show off her long, tanned legs. Her tits—the ones I bought—are perky and completely bra-free under her white tank, her rosy nipples visible when her cut slips a little.

"It's Khan."

"Shit, thanks, babe."

I jog over and plant a kiss on her lips before taking my cell phone from her and holding it to my ear. I can't help but smile as I watch Lola's ass as she walks away—the cut on her back proudly declaring she's mine.

"Havoc, you there?"

"Yeah, sorry, Prez. What can I do for ya?"

"I need you to come to the clubhouse. Got a situation."

I frown. "What's going on?"

"Just get here. I'll explain when you do."

He hangs up before I can ask anything else.

I sigh and push the bike back into the shed. The test drive will have to wait.

I head inside, grab my bike keys, and look for Lola. I find her in the kitchen making coffee.

"I've gotta head to the clubhouse. I'm not sure when I'll be back, so don't cook. I'll pick something up on the way home or send a prospect over with something for you if I'm running late."

I slide my hands around her hips and pull her back against me, burying my face in her hair and inhaling her perfume.

"That's fine. I'll probably just curl up and watch some TV."

We've been together since high school, and over the last few years, she's transformed from cheerleader to biker babe, trading her soft, youthful glow for an edgy sexiness that has my dick weeping with joy.

She turns and looks up at me.

"Havoc?" Her voice trembles.

"What's wrong?"

She opens her mouth to answer when my phone chimes, probably Khan telling me to hurry up.

She smiles and shakes her head.

"Nothing. It doesn't matter," she says. "Love you."

"Love you too," I tell her, kissing her forehead. I grab my cut off the back of the chair and slide it on. "I'll text you and let you know what's happening."

"Okay, bye," she says softly as I leave.

I pause for a second, something in her voice sounding off. But when my phone chimes again, I decide to talk to my old lady later, after dealing with whatever's going on at the clubhouse.

I climb on my bike and head toward the club. When I pull up, I'm surprised to find the parking area almost empty.

I see my brother's bike and Acid's, Knuckles', and Khan's, but that's it.

I figured whatever the issue was, Khan would bring it to church for all of us to hear. But now, seeing my brother's bike, I wonder if it's personal.

I climb off my bike and head inside, nodding to Knuckles and Acid sitting at the bar. They nod back but continue talking as I head to Khan's office.

As I get closer, I hear raised voices, but I can't make out what's being said. When I reach the door, I knock, and they go silent.

"Come in!" Khan yells, and I open the door.

Khan's sitting behind his desk, running his fingers through his salt-and-pepper hair, making it stick up all over the place. Driller's leaning against the window. His eye's swollen and turning black, and his lip's split and twice its size.

"What the fuck happened?"

"Sit down, Havoc," Khan orders, sounding tired.

I grit my teeth and take a seat.

"Driller ran into some trouble at the tables."

"For fuck's sake." I groan, rubbing my hand over my face. He might be my little brother, but I'm sick of bailing his ass out of trouble. "Don't you ever learn?"

"Fuck you, Havoc. Not everyone can be as perfect as you."

"Enough!" Khan shouts, shutting him up.

"It wasn't the gambling that was the issue," Khan tells me. I barely hold back my snort. I don't know when Khan started burying his head in the sand when it comes to my brother, but it's getting old.

"So he wasn't caught counting cards?" My brother's good with numbers but instead of doing something useful with it he prefers to try his luck at the card tables. He's banned from most casinos, and the ones that let him back in do it because they have no problem breaking his kneecaps if he fucks them over.

"I wasn't counting cards, no matter what that mother-fucker said," Driller yells.

Khan stares at me, ignoring Driller's outburst. "The guy who accused him is currently on life support. Docs aren't sure if he'll ever wake up."

"You stupid fuck. You're already on your second strike. If the cops get a hold of you, that's it, game over."

"That's why I need you to take the fall for him," Khan drops quietly. So quietly, it takes me a second to realize what he just said.

"What the fuck, Khan? No way. I'm not going down for this. And what if the guy dies? I'm not risking a murder charge—"

"The family assured me that no matter what happens, the original plea bargain will hold."

"Plea bargain?" I look at Driller, who's silent for a change, and realize his busted-up face has nothing to do with this, not if there's already a plea bargain on the table.

"How long's this been going on?"

"Five months."

"Five fucking months! And this is the first I'm hearing of this!"

"We hoped to get it thrown out, but the guy in a coma was a candidate for senator, and his father is out for blood."

"So make Driller man up. Sorry, bro, but you're the one who fucked up."

"Oh, and like you're such a fucking saint?" he snaps back.

"Driller, I swear to fucking God, if you don't keep your mouth shut, I'll cut your fucking tongue out," Khan roars before turning back to me. "The plea's for a five-year sentence with the possibility of parole after two years."

"Khan—"

"Death Serpents will only deal with Driller. You know they don't trust anyone after their princess was taken. It took Driller four years to earn their trust, and they aren't interested in anyone else coming in. I asked. Havoc, we need access to that pipeline."

I stare at the man I thought of as a second father, one of my father's best friends, and feel the respect I had for him wither and die.

"So you want me to take the fall for Driller, spend half a decade behind bars, and another however many years out of work—because who the fuck's gonna hire me with a record? And then what?"

"What do you mean?"

"I mean, what the fuck do I get out of this? I'm losing years of my life. Me and Lola are trying for a fucking baby."

"We'll take care of Lola while you're gone. And the club'll pay you a cut to cover any lost income until you can get a job again."

I shake my head and open my mouth to tell him no when his face hardens.

"It's not a request, Havoc. It's an order. I don't like it any more than you do, but it's what's best for the club."

"And if I don't?"

"Then you can kiss the brotherhood goodbye. You'll be kicked out in bad standing, and every club in the country will know not to touch you. You'll be excommunicated."

I stand up, wanting to rip the world apart. This betrayal feels like a knife sticking out of my chest. "If I do this, you never ask me for anything again, and my future with Raven Souls will never be in jeopardy, no matter how things stand between us after this."

"Havoc—" Khan starts, but I turn to look at Driller. "You're dead to me. You don't talk to me, don't look at me, and if you see me, you walk right fucking past me like I'm invisible."

"It doesn't have to be like this, Havoc. Five years is—"

I glare at Khan. "Not mine to serve. I don't see you or any of the others stepping up to serve it."

"None of us look enough like Driller to pull it off."

"Well, aren't I the lucky one?" I snap sarcastically.

"I'm still your president," Khan says, sharply.

"And from now on, that's all you'll ever be, because a friend—a mentor—would never ask this of me. I'll do it, but I need to talk to Lola first."

"Cops are already on their way to pick you up," he tells me, leaning back, daring me to argue. The news hits me like a punch to the gut. "Once you're settled, I'll bring Lola up for a visit. I'll explain everything to her. I won't leave her hanging."

"No, you'll just leave that for me."

Chapter One

Nevaeh

I stare at myself in the mirror, frowning.

After surviving the barbecue, you'd think I'd feel more comfortable going back to the clubhouse. But nope. Maybe it's because I know tonight's party won't be anything like the last one. The thought makes my stomach twist with nerves, and I bite my lip.

Focusing back on my reflection, I sigh. This is as good as it's going to get. The pale pink twin set and the short, pleated skirt don't exactly scream biker party, but I'd feel even more uncomfortable in a pair of tight leather pants and a tube top. More power to those who can pull that off, but that's not me. I have a little belly, thanks to my love of food, and I'm short, with curves—curves that anyone else would flaunt, especially given where I'm going. But I prefer to dress the way I do.

I don't dress to repel people, but I do dress like a pastor's daughter. It's what I am, after all. I think of my sister in her hot pink coat, and how it caught someone's eye and made them take a second look. That niggle has always been in the back of my mind that I could draw the wrong kind of attention, so I spent my formative years trying to blend in instead of standing out. It wasn't until I got older that I realized it wouldn't have mattered what Citi wore that day. A predator doesn't see the wrapping, only the prize.

Still, habits are hard to break and I'll be the first to admit that I use my clothing as a shield.

I sit on the edge of the bed and pull on a pair of black over-the-knee socks before sliding my feet into my patent leather Mary Janes. Pantyhose would have been a better choice, but I hate them. Besides, my feet are always cold, so I either wear socks or carry a pair with me, just in case. Once my shoes are on and buckled, I tie a pink ribbon around my sleek ponytail and add a bit of lip gloss.

I check my watch and curse. I'm going to be late if I don't get a move on. Grabbing my bag from the table, I toss in the essentials: a notebook, pen, lip gloss, phone, and wallet. I hesitate for a moment, looking down at my Kindle before thinking, *why not?* and tossing it in as well. Throwing my bag over my shoulder, I head for the door but stop, remembering that car keys would also be good. I spin around and rush back to the bedroom, grabbing them off the bedside table. I blow out a frustrated breath. At this rate, I'll be a hot, sweaty mess before I even get there.

Making sure that I have everything this time, I finally leave. I lock up and walk over to my car, opening the door and tossing my bag into the passenger seat before climbing in. I close the door, and taking a deep breath, I start the car and head towards the club. After a few miles of silence, I turn on the radio and find a station playing 80s music.

My mom used to love 80s music. I remember dancing around the kitchen with her and my sister with wooden spoons in our hands, using them as microphones as we sang along to Cyndi Lauper and Bonnie Tyler. I'm tempted to change the station, but when "Papa Don't Preach" comes on, I can't help but belt out the lyrics with Madonna.

I slow down when I see the sign for Raven's Nest and turn off the radio as a wave of nerves washes over me. I don't know why—I've been here before, and everyone was friendly to me.

Still, I pull over and sit for a moment, taking a deep breath before looking in the rearview mirror. "Think of all the material you can get for your next book," I tell myself, trying to calm my nerves.

To distract myself, I dig around in my bag and pull out my cell phone to let Amity know I'm just pulling in when I get a notification from SmutFest—the book signing event I told Amity about that tours around the UK. I frown, knowing I didn't sign up for it, even though I would've loved to.

I open the email and start reading, my eyes widening until my eyebrows practically touch my hairline.

Dear Celeste Sky,

I hope this message finds you well. I am reaching out on behalf of SmutFest with an invitation that I hope you'll consider.

Due to an unexpected scheduling conflict, a few of our originally planned authors can no longer attend our upcoming book signing event taking place in London next week. We asked our Facebook followers who they would most like to see instead, and your name came out on top. Given this response, we would be thrilled to invite you to the UK to be a signing author and guest speaker.

We would love to have you, but we understand that this is incredibly late notice. We would, however, be more than willing to cover flights, hotels, and any other related expenses if you'd be interested in joining us.

I shake my head in shock as I continue reading...

The event will provide an opportunity for you to meet your readers, sign copies of your books, and share your inspirations as an author.

Please let me know if this invitation fits with your sched-

ule. If you have any questions, please don't hesitate to contact me.

Thank you for considering this opportunity on such short notice. I look forward to hearing from you.

Warm regards,

Gemma Taylor-Smith

I sit there with my mouth hanging open for a moment before giddiness takes over, making me want to jump out of the car and do a little dance. I hold back, though; the MC probably has cameras out here.

I shove my phone back into my bag and drive carefully down the dirt road until I get to the gate, my excitement over the email overshadowing my nerves. I recognize the prospect at the gate from the last time I was here, but I can't remember his name. He recognizes me too, nodding before opening the gate and waving me through. I park where G had me park before so I don't block anyone's way and turn off the engine.

I grab my bag and climb out, holding my skirt down so I don't flash anyone. I close the door and slide my bag over my shoulder before turning to the prospect.

"Thanks."

"No problem, darlin'," he replies, his eyes taking me in from head to toe. "You trying to cause a riot?"

"Huh?"

"Doesn't matter. Go on up. G and Amity are waiting for you."

"Aye-aye, captain!" I salute him, making his lips twitch as I turn and make my way over to the giant warehouse filled with bikes. I pull the door open and step inside.

"Welcome to Harley Heaven," I mutter to myself, jumping when I hear someone laugh.

"Harley Heaven, huh? I like it." I turn, looking around until I spot the biker crouched near his bike.

"You must be Tinkerbell. I'm Capone," he says, wiping his hands on a rag as he stands to his full height.

"Nice to meet you, Capone." I give him a small wave before pointing to his bike. "Is your bike alright?"

"She is now."

"She?"

"Esmeralda, my favorite girl," he says, patting the bike's seat.

I grin as I step closer to get a better look and see that the gas tank has been painted. Whoever did it did an incredible job. It's covered in flames and black charred roses that look real enough to touch.

"She sure is pretty."

"Isn't she? If you want, I can take you for a ride on her."

Oh boy. Warning, warning. Abort mission. Abort mission!

I've researched enough MCs to know that getting on the back of a bike is usually sacred and reserved for old ladies. Knowing my luck, I'd get on the back of his bike and wake up in Vegas with his ring on my finger, his property patch on my back, and a tattoo on my butt.

Okay, so I might have a teeny, tiny, slightly overactive imagination.

"Umm... that's sweet and all, but—Oh look, is that a squirrel?"

He frowns and turns, and I run out of the warehouse like it's on fire. He calls after me, but I don't stop. I just keep going, running up the stupid slope until I'm out of breath and sweaty all over again.

I slow down and start walking so I don't look like an idiot. I make my way to the saloon, making a mental note not to tell Amity what just happened—even if that means I can't brag about the fact that I just ran. On purpose. And up that stupid slope. She'd be so damn proud. I try to catch my breath. My heart's racing so fast it feels like it's going to burst out of my chest. I just hope they have a defibrillator on hand just in case. I can't believe Amity does this for fun. She's a freaking psycho.

I push open the heavy saloon doors and step inside.

"Pippin!" I hear Amity's voice before she slams into me, wrapping her arms around me. "I thought you might have gotten caught up writing again and forgot," she says as she pulls back and looks at me.

I look down at my watch and see it's only 7:05. I frown and look back up at her.

"I'm five minutes late."

"So I might have missed you," she tells me, and I roll my eyes as we head towards the bar.

"You saw me this morning when we went to the shelter to pick up the kitten."

"Speaking of, are you sure you're okay with us keeping him after we get him back?" She's using the kitten to prank one of the brothers, but the little guy will be coming home with us.

"Of course. He's just a kitten. How much trouble can he really cause?"

She laughs, shaking her head. "Famous last words," she says as an arm's thrown around my shoulders.

"Tinkerbell. You look like my future ex-wife." Toot looks down at me, flashing a charming smile.

"Jaded and sexually frustrated?" I deadpan, making Mac —his actual brother, who's standing behind him—snort.

"Hey now, you never have to doubt my skills. I can make you scream like you've never screamed before."

"Oh, I'm sure you can." I pat his chest and make a face. "But I'm all out of trophies, big guy. Think you can make do with a participation sticker?"

Toot lets me go and growls. "I don't understand you, woman. How can you be immune to all this?" He waves his hands over his body. "I know. Maybe it's because I haven't shown you any of my moves yet."

"I'm scared to ask."

"You're not the only one," Amity mutters beside me.

Toot takes a few steps back before he starts doing a weird dance with a lot of hip thrusting. Or maybe it's some kind of mating ritual. Either way, it looks... interesting.

"Do you need to pee, Toot?"

He throws his hands in the air. "I give up! I'm going to go fuck a bunny to remind myself how virile I am."

"Okay, have fun. Make good choices and remember to wrap it before you tap it." I turn and find both Mac and Amity laughing. "Is anyone here normal?"

"God, I hope not." Mac smirks before heading off into the crowd.

"You can't help yourself, can you?" Amity shakes her head, a grin on her face.

"I don't know what you're talking about," I say with a straight face.

"Let's get a drink," she suggests, and we weave through the crowd towards the bar.

On our way, we get stopped a few times by some of the guys. By the time we finally reach the bar, my throat's so dry, I could really use something to drink. Amity asks for a bottle of water, and the prospect behind the bar grabs one for her before handing me what I assume is a Coke—until I take a mouthful and nearly choke.

I consider giving it back, but then think, *When in Rome...* I don't really drink, but if I go out, I sometimes have a cocktail or a glass of wine—but that's about it. Here, though, I figure I can let loose a little, knowing Amity won't let anything happen to me. I down the whole thing before I chicken out and set the glass back on the bar. Two seconds later, another one appears like magic.

"So, where's G?" I ask, taking a sip of my drink.

"He went to pick up Havoc."

"Ahhh..." I nod, feeling a little warm as my muscles start to relax. Havoc's going to be the next president of Raven Souls, and this is his welcome to the club party.

As we sit at the bar sipping our drinks, the noise in the room increases, and I turn to see what's going on and spot a huge guy with a scowl surrounded by a bunch of people. I'm guessing this is Mr. Soon-to-be President. The man is insanely hot, so I look away before I do something stupid, like faint.

Taking another drink, I start telling Amity about the email, but I can see she's miles away.

"And so they said they'd pay for my flights and accommodation in London if I agreed to be a guest speaker on their panel. All I have to do is go on live TV in my bra and thong." I finish my drink and place the empty glass on the bar, and poof! Another full glass is there.

I smile at the prospect before looking at Amity, who's still nodding along with what I said until my words finally register. "Wait, what?"

"I was wondering if you were listening to me." I throw a coaster at her.

"I'm sorry, I'm just distracted. What were you saying?"

"I saaaid... the people organizing the book signing I told you about have agreed to pay for my flights and accommodation, as long as I agree to be a guest speaker. They've had a few people drop out, and when they asked in their Facebook group who they'd like to fill in, they picked me. How cool is that?" I say excitedly before taking a sip of my drink.

"That's awesome, Pippin. You're going, right?"

I smile at her excitement for me. It feels good to share this with her, but my smile fades when I think about letting her down.

"I promised I'd be your assistant." I look down, swirling the drink in my hand.

She gives me a look. "It's London. You have to do this. You'll regret it if you don't."

"I know, but I'm so damn nervous. I wouldn't even have a passport if it wasn't for you forcing me to get one. I didn't think I'd ever actually use it."

"You'll be fine, but what about people knowing what you look like? You have a pen name for a reason, right?"

"It's not my readers I'm worried about. I don't mind them knowing what I look like or even having pictures taken with me." I take another drink. "The pen name's to keep Dad and his damn congregation off my back. I'm not worried about them being at the convention and discovering my secret, 'cause then they'd have to admit to being at SmutFest." The thought makes me giggle.

Feeling lightheaded, I wonder if I should stop drinking.

But then I see the glass in my hand is magically fully again and decide it would be wasteful to throw it away.

"Good point," Amity says, pulling me out of my thoughts. "These organizers are legit, right? I don't want you getting sold into a slavery ring or something. If I have to jump on a plane and save you, I'll be pissed."

"But you would save me, right?" I bat my lashes at her.

"I'll always save you. You know that." She bumps me with her arm, making me grin.

"You know I'm soooooooo lucky having a superhero as a bestie," I tell her, and she laughs, stealing my drink from my hand. Wait, is she sniffing it? I love her and all, but she's soooo weird.

"How many of these have you had to drink?" she asks me.

I try to count them up in my head, but my brain isn't braining. "Only a few," I tell her because that's a good number. "The very nice prospect keeps filling up my glass when it's empty. The service here really is impeccable. Five stars."

As Amity turns to talk to the prospect, I rest my head on the bar for a moment, feeling dizzy.

"No more alcohol for her. She doesn't normally drink."

I'm about to tell her I'm fine—totally fine—but suddenly I feel so sleepy. I close my eyes and decide to take an emergency nap first instead.

Chapter Two

Nevaeh

Warm lips skim the back of my neck, sending shivers through me as my dream guy wraps his rough hands around me. I sigh, his hard body feeling like a safe haven against mine.

When his hand slips under my top to cup my lace-covered breast, I let out a soft whimper, making him growl in response. His eager fingers tease my nipple, tugging it lightly as he grinds into me. I feel achy and needy, knowing that if this dream ends now, I'll be left needing to find relief with my own fingers.

But instead of fading away, he removes his hand from under my top and slides it down my body, slipping his fingers under my skirt and between my legs, pressing them against the damp lace covering my pussy. His deep rumble of approval washes over me, making my nipples hard and my pussy throb with anticipation.

I might not know what to expect, but I know what I want. I've been dreaming of this ever since I started reading dirty books and touching myself under my cover in the dark of my bedroom. I'd swallow my whimpers and moans, scared of being caught, knowing I'd be branded a harlot—or worse—by my father.

My dream man doesn't give a crap about rules and respectability. He's a sinner, ready to show me heaven by dragging me through hell. When he tugs the lace of my underwear aside, I part my legs a little, inviting him to take what he wants. As he slips a finger inside me, I gasp, the sensation familiar yet foreign and so real that a whisper of doubt begins to swirl in my mind. But then he strokes a place inside that makes me forget everything but the pleasure that builds within me, and I feel myself pushing back into him, his fingers gliding in and out of me with ease. Oh God, this is the best dream ever. I'm so close...

Then the fingers disappear, and I sigh, disappointed. Of course. The dream always ends right before I reach the good part. Why would this time be any different? I think as I feel movement behind me. As the last traces of sleep fade, part of my mind clings to the dream, reluctant to let go and face reality even as awareness sets in.

My skirt is suddenly lifted over my butt, and before I can

figure out what's happening, my underwear is torn from my body, and my eyes snap open.

Clarity slams into me at the same time a huge cock does, stealing my breath and silencing my scream as all the oxygen is forced from my lungs. I whimper as pain throbs deep inside me, my body unaccustomed to anything so big.

"Jesus fuck, you're tight," a voice grits out from behind me. A large, rough hand wraps around my throat, cutting off my ability to speak as he fucks me with sharp, brutal thrusts.

Somewhere in the back of my mind, I know I should be terrified. There's a man inside me, a stranger, stealing my virginity like it's his to claim and not giving a single fuck that he doesn't have permission to take it.

But despite everything, I'm not. How messed up does that make me? Not only am I not scared, I can feel my orgasm tearing toward me at a blinding speed.

"So good. So fucking good," the voice groans as he thrusts into me again and again until he curses and I feel him erupt inside me.

I cry out as I spiral right over the edge with him.

He keeps moving, slower now, gentler, helping me ride through the waves of pleasure. His hand drifts from my throat to my hip before he presses a kiss to the back of my neck and eases out of me.

My heart beats wildly out of control as I feel his cum leaking out and panic sets in. What the holy hell was I thinking? I might have been half asleep for part of it, but why didn't I fight once I was awake? Why didn't I at least beg him to wear a condom?

My head pounds and my stomach churns, reminding me of the alcohol I drank. It probably contributed to this. Everyone makes stupid decisions when they're drunk, right? Still, this was one hell of a mistake. This is why I don't drink. I take a deep breath. I'm never drinking again. I need to make an appointment to get tested and—

I'm pulled back and tucked against his hard body again, like the little spoon to his big one, and my eyes bug out of my head. I've never had sex before, let alone a one-night stand, but isn't this the part where he leaves—or I get kicked out, since I'm just now realizing I'm not in my own bed?

Afraid to open my mouth and ask in case he takes that as an invitation for round two, I stay quiet and will myself to relax until he falls asleep so I can sneak out.

"You smell like vanilla fucking cupcakes," he grumbles, burying his face in my hair and inhaling deeply.

His voice does something funny to my insides, making my stomach clench. Wait, am I attracted to him? No, that can't be true. How is that freaking possible? For all I know, he looks like Sasquatch. But then I remember the way he felt inside me and how he's wrapped around me almost protectively. With that and the gravel effect his voice has on me, two things become glaringly obvious. First, I need to get the heck out of here. And second, somewhere between my first drink and losing my virginity, I went and lost my damn mind.

* * *

It takes forever to slip out of the biker's arms. Inch by inch, I make it to the edge of the bed before easing myself off. I stand for a moment, afraid to move or even breathe in case I wake him. When only his deep breathing fills the room, I blow out a relieved breath.

Looking down, I find what's left of my panties on the floor and snatch them up, feeling my face flame. My heart pounds as I glance around, hoping not to wake him. I spot my phone on the bedside table next to a note. I grab both, my hand trembling as I quickly read the piece of paper.

Hey Pippin, you had too much to drink, so G carried you up here, and we put you to bed. This is one of the spare rooms, so there's no need to worry. There are some pills, water, and your phone on the table.

Text me when you're awake.

Love you,

Amity

No need to worry, my ass. I crumple up the note in my hand and glare at the stupid bed and the stupid biker lying in it, my eyes moving over the ink etched golden skin of his chest.

The sheet covers him from the waist down, but I don't

need X-ray vision to know what he looks like underneath. I have a pretty good imagination, and considering how sore I am, he's definitely not lacking. My eyes travel up to his face, and I suck in a sharp breath.

I've never dated, except for the ridiculous dates my father arranged for me. I never thought I had a type. I just knew what I didn't like (aka the kind of men my father set me up with), but I've always been drawn to large men who look a little rough around the edges. Nothing against pretty boys, there's just something about bigger men that makes me feel.... Ugh. For a writer, I'm terrible at putting my feelings into words.

As I take in Havoc's familiar face—the sharp jaw covered in a five o'clock shadow, his slightly crooked nose with a bump at the bridge telling a story of how many times it's been broken, and his thick blond hair, long on top and shaved at the sides—I realize I do have a type, and it's him. A barbarian-looking beast of a man, like a Viking from one of my books, who wouldn't think twice about taking what he wants. And God help me, he did take what he wanted and I let him. Heck, I'd let him do a whole lot more than that. I'd let him pillage parts of me I'd locked down tight and drop to my knees in servitude. Something tells me there would be war, a battle of wills between us if I ran and he chased me. I'd fight of course, but he'd disarm me, my resistance nothing more than foreplay between us.

This man could make me feel like a queen, but he'd demand everything from me, and I have nothing to give.

I'm a shadow of the girl I used to be. All my emotions are held together with Sticky tape and PVA Glue thanks to the ten-year-old version of me trying to navigate grown up feelings. Now adult me feels out of her depth. And this papier-mâché heart of mine wouldn't stand a chance against a man like him

I shake myself out of my thoughts and hurry over to the door where I saw my bag and shoes just moments ago. I have to leave. Standing here daydreaming is the quickest way to get caught. I grab my bag and shove my phone and the letter inside and slip my shoes on, buckling the straps with shaky hands.

I take one more look at the bed, leaving me feeling hollow inside, and as I turn, I spot my ribbon on the bedside table. I hesitate, and then—because I'm an idiot—I decide to leave it behind. A part of me needs this man to remember me.

Why shouldn't he be haunted by the girl who ghosts him? The thought makes me smile as I quietly slip out of the room and head downstairs. I know I'm somewhere in the club-house; I just don't know where exactly. The last thing I want is for people to see me like this. I feel like there is a neon sign above my head flashing *devirginized*.

Luckily, there's a door at the bottom of the stairs that leads outside. Opening it, I take a deep breath of fresh air and walk around the front of the building and down the dirt road back to my car, not running into anyone on my way.

I spot Hoops at the gate and wonder if the prospects ever sleep. Shrugging, I climb into the car and toss my bag into the passenger seat before he spots me and starts flirting. I start the car and wait for Hoops to let me out. I avoid eye contact and give him a brief wave before I pull out and head straight for the movie set.

All I want to do is curl up in a ball and pretend last night didn't happen. But I know that's not an option. And the closer I get to the set, the more on edge I feel.

Eventually, I pull over. My hands are shaking like crazy as the reality of what happened crashes into me. I had sex—really good sex with a smoking hot biker.

Dear sweet baby Jesus.

Feeling overwhelmed, I pull my phone from my bag to text Amity, deciding to hide out at the diner or the library instead of heading back to the set, when I see the email from SmutFest. Biting my lip, I email the coordinator and accept the invitation. Within moments, my phone pings with a new email from SmutFest thanking me profusely. I scan quickly over the details regarding hotels and tickets, feeling my nerves settle when I see everything is already organized as if they were just waiting for me to say yes.

I blow out a breath. I'm going to London. I can't believe it. I'm a nobody from a small town who has limited life experiences. I've lived more in the last twenty-four hours than I have in the last twenty-four years. That's as terrifying as it is exciting. Is this what Amity feels like when she's doing her crazy stunts?

Shaking my head, my thoughts drift back to last night. I won't be able to hide what happened from Amity for long, so I decide to tell a little white lie to buy myself some time and space to process everything. I'm going to fly out early and hang out in the hotel for a little while. I can deal with it all when I get back. Maybe then I won't feel so out of my depth.

With a plan in mind, I start driving again. Fifteen minutes later, I wave to the security guy as he nods for me to drive through, and I park next to the RV. Amity's standing at the door, waiting for me to get out of the car. I can tell by the look on her face she wants to tease me about last night.

Lord, if only she knew the truth.

I climb out of the car and turn to grab my bag from the passenger seat when a slight breeze has me holding down my skirt, conscious that I'm not wearing underwear.

Closing my door, I walk over to Amity. She must see something on my face because her smirk drops.

"You okay?" she asks. She really is far too observant for my liking.

"Peachy, but I got woken up by a call from the book signing people; they want me to fly out today. A ticket will be waiting for me at the airport when I get there," I tell her, hoping she buys it and doesn't realize that I'm full of crap.

"Oh wow, that's fast. I thought you weren't leaving until next week."

"That was the plan, but they decided to add a meet-and-greet, and they were worried about jet lag, so now that means I need to pack like a crazy person." Lord, I'm going to hell. "What the heck do I wear? I mean, it's London; it rains a lot there, doesn't it?" Asking about the weather is normal, right?

She shrugs. "Who knows? The weather over there's bipolar."

"It doesn't matter; I'll figure it out. I can always pick up a few things while I'm there. Oh God, I'm nervous." *And a liar. And not a virgin*, I think, smoothing my damp hands down my skirt.

She walks over and wraps her arms around me. "Breathe. You're going to have a blast. I'm going to miss you, though. Take a thousand pictures for me."

"I will, I promise. Wow, if my dad knew I was doing this, he'd have a heart attack." Especially if he knew about the big bad biker deflowering me, too. God, I'm gonna be sick.

"He'll get over it. Besides, what he doesn't know won't hurt him."

Blowing out a shaky breath, I nod, tucking my hair behind my ear, feeling like the world's biggest liar, liar, pants on fire.

"I wish I could go with you. If it were just a few weeks later..."

"Nope. Don't you dare feel guilty. I'm the one who said yes to this after I'd already agreed to work for you. If anyone should feel guilty, it's me." And boy, do I feel guilty for so many things.

"How about we both just agree to be guilt-free, then?"

"Deal. And hey, at least you get to rock the RV with Mr. MC for a couple weeks," I joke, trying not to think of another biker boy and his hands.

"Mm-hmm..." she mumbles as we head inside the RV, making me pause my freak-out for a moment.

"What's that supposed to mean? You guys are okay, right?" I ask over my shoulder as we head into the bedroom.

"I'm mad at him right now, but we'll figure it out." She sighs and sits on the bed as I drag my suitcase out from under the bed and start throwing things into it.

"What happened?" I ask. They seemed fine yesterday.

She bites her lip and tells me about waking up alone, finding out he spent the night in her room, that Monica was wearing her helmet on the back of G's bike, and then the angry words they exchanged afterward. I listen to it all while I continue to pack.

Once she's done talking, she gets up and grabs my toiletries from the bathroom. While she does, I sit on the bed and consider my words.

"You know I always have your back. Always. So if you need me to hate G, I will. I'll cut nipple holes in all of his T-shirts and spill a Coke on his keyboard."

She smiles, sitting beside me and leaning her head on my shoulder. "I feel like there's a 'but' coming on."

"*But* I think you overreacted. Could he have made different choices? Sure. But at the end of the day, his job is to keep Monica safe. So if that means checking on her in the middle of the night or having her on the back of his bike, then so be it. It's not like he wants her. Anyone with eyes can see that. Now, with that being said, if her being on the back of his bike bothers you so much, then I think a little revenge is in order. Get bestie number two to give you a ride. Toot seems like he'd have no problem messing with G."

"Great minds think alike," she says. "I told him to ask Havoc to come pick me up. I could tell he wanted to argue when I told him it didn't mean anything, but he couldn't without proving my point."

I flinch at the sound of his name but thankfully she doesn't notice. I swallow down the pang of jealously at the thought of Amity on the back of his bike, knowing I'm being ridiculous. I plaster a smile on my face.

"So devious. It's my second favorite thing about you."

"Really? What's the first?"

"Your excellent taste in best friends, obviously," I tell her.

"Obviously," she says dryly, and I poke her in the ribs, making her laugh.

"Just give him a chance to make it up to you, okay?" I say, giving her a look, and she nods. "Besides, I've heard both angry sex and makeup sex are the best."

"You're not just as short as Yoda; you're as wise as him too."

"I'm tall enough to punch you in the boob," I tell her, and she jumps away from me, laughing.

"I can't believe my little baby is all grown up and..."

"Saving China?" I finish, laughing.

"I was channeling my inner Mushu, yes, but I was going to say—going to London without me."

"As much as I love a Mulan quote, I'm a big girl, Amity. I can handle myself. I know it doesn't seem like it sometimes because I let people walk all over me, but—" She covers my mouth with her hand.

"I know you can. I'm just protective of you. If I didn't think you could handle yourself, I wouldn't let you get on a plane and fly a continent away from me."

She pulls her hand away.

"Alright, I believe you." I pull her to me and hug her tight. For a moment, I consider telling her about Havoc. But when I open my mouth, nothing comes out.

"I've gotta go. I'm supposed to be in wardrobe right now. I just wanted you to know I'm so proud of you, Nevaeh, and I know Citlalli would be too."

"You think so?"

"Absolutely."

After one last hug, Amity leaves, and I finish packing, then take a quick shower. I dry off and get dressed in jeans, a long-sleeved T-shirt, and a flannel. Wearing a skirt makes me think of Havoc slipping his hand under it, and I just can't right now.

I grab my laptop and put it in my bag, pull up the handle on my luggage, and drag it outside. Once I've locked the door of the RV, I take my bags over to my car and load them in. I climb back into the driver's seat and take a deep breath and remind myself that everything is fine. So I slept with a sexy biker and lied to my best friend. It's not a big deal.

Sure, and denial is not just a river in Egypt.

Chapter Three

Havoc

The sunlight pouring into my room wakes me, along with the raging hard-on tenting the sheets.

The smell of sex and cupcakes in the air has me groaning as I roll toward the woman who rocked my fucking world last night, only to find her gone and the bed cold. I sit up and look around, but the room's empty. If I couldn't still smell her, I'd almost believe she was nothing more than a dream.

Cursing, I climb out of bed, hell-bent on finding her. I walk naked to the bathroom and turn on the shower. While I wait for it to heat up, I stare in the mirror, replaying last night in my head.

Blade gave me the key to this room, one of the guest

rooms on the other side of the building, because he knew I'd need some space from the others.

In a severely overcrowded prison, I never had privacy. Fuck, I couldn't even take a shit alone. And the club I'd lived for did that to me. They took everything when they made me take the fall for Driller, then handed over my life to him piece by piece. He took my old lady, knocked her up with the baby that was supposed to be mine, moved into my fucking house, and became the VP while they left me there to rot. Knowing that makes me question everything. My loyalty to the club I believed in was everything—until Khan set it on fire and watched it burn with his ultimatum, which—like an idiot—I took. I should've walked away. I should've taken Lola and started a new life far away, but my pride wouldn't let me. And what exactly did that pride give me in the end?

Nothing but a criminal record and a chip on my shoulder. *And cupcakes.*

My hard cock throbs at the reminder of the woman I found lying in my bed like an X-rated version of Goldilocks.

Sure, there were a few bunnies downstairs who offered me a good time, but none of them were what I wanted. Then I came up here and found the woman that was just right for me. She was fast asleep, curled up on her side with her hands under her cheek and her hair covering most of her face. Even though I wanted to be alone, I found my dick growing hard as my eyes traveled over her body.

At some point, she kicked off the blanket that had been

covering her, revealing a short black skirt and a pink cardigan. There was nothing overly sexy about what she was wearing— until I saw the thigh-high socks and every dirty fantasy I ever had roared to life.

I stripped out of my clothes and climbed in behind her, promising to thank Blade for the gift, knowing he was the only one with access to the room. She might've been a club girl playing dress-up, but I wasn't about to turn down a gift like this.

Everything that happened after that was better than anything I'd ever imagined.

She'd been so fucking tight. She had to be a new bunny. If I had my way, she wouldn't be one for long. I look down at my hard dick as I go to get in the shower and freeze at the sight of the blood.

"What the fuck?"

It takes me a second to realize what I'm looking at. I storm back into the bedroom and rip the blankets from the bed. Sure enough, I find spots of blood on the white cotton.

"She was a virgin," I mutter, a deep possessiveness taking root inside me.

I remake the bed, pulling the blankets back, leaving the bloody sheet exposed like a trophy. Any lingering thoughts of Lola disappear as something shifts inside me. I don't know who this woman is, but I'm going to find her. And when I do, I'm claiming her.

I've already lost five fucking years of my life. I'll be

dammed if I lose another minute. From now on, if I want something, I'll have it. And right now, all I want is a certain cupcake.

I head back into the bathroom and jump in the shower, but I don't wash the blood from my cock. I like knowing it's there, like she branded me and made me hers. As I dry off, I imagine how sore she is today. I'm not a small guy, so there's no way she isn't feeling me with every step she takes. And the caveman in me loves it.

I get dressed and am just pulling on my cut, ready to head down to find Blade, when I spot a pink ribbon on the bedside table. Walking around the bed, I pick it up and hold it to my nose like a fucking psycho and almost convince myself I can smell cupcakes. Some people might think I need therapy, but I don't give a fuck, tying the ribbon around my wrist with a smile. It's the first real smile I've felt since I got here.

I have a lot of shit to still deal with, but now, at least, I've found my reward for all the shit I've been through.

Hours later, I'm ready to kill someone. I can't find Blade anywhere, and nobody else is sober enough to remember a woman who smells like cupcakes. Needing something to do before I explode, I take my bike out, hoping by some miracle I might run into my mystery woman. But after a couple of hours, I head back.

I pull through the gates and into the warehouse, parking and turning off my bike, surprised to see a few brothers gathered around.

"What's going on?"

Midas turns to look at me. "Check out Circus's new artwork."

I climb off my bike and walk over, letting out an impressed whistle. The gas tank has a dark, gothic-looking big top painted on it in grays and purples with blood spattered across it. Standing right in front of the entrance is a little girl holding a raggedy-looking stuffed bear. But she's clearly not just any girl, she's a zombie, judging by the dead eyes and the blood staining her lips.

"That's creepy as fuck. Who—" My cell phone rings, cutting me off. I pull it out of my pocket, glancing at the screen, and answer it when I see it's G.

"G?"

"Havoc!"

"Who is this?" I frown at the woman's voice.

"It's Amity. I need help."

"What happened?" I ask, heading back to my bike, a sense of dread washing over men

"A truck hit us. We both got thrown off G's bike, but G wasn't wearing his helmet, Havoc. And now he's bleeding and won't wake up," she says in a rush, fear clear in her words.

"Where are you?" I ask loud enough to grab the guys'

attention. They all turn to look at me, and I lift my free hand, making a circular motion in the air, signaling for them to round up the others and get ready to ride.

"I don't know. We're in the middle of fucking nowhere," she curses.

"Where were you heading? What did you pass? Think, Amity. I'm on my way, but I need an idea of the direction." I hear her take a breath as I climb on my bike.

"We came from the movie set. We were heading to the Harley shop to get a new helmet. He made me wear his, Havoc. He's hurt because he's so fucking stubborn," she sobs.

"If you had been hurt instead of him, it would've been worse. Trust me. He knew the risks, and he'd do it again, even knowing what would happen. I don't know you, but I don't need to. The way he looks at you says it all. I doubt there's much he wouldn't do for you, and that means risking his life to keep you safe."

"Okay," she whispers.

I pull the phone away slightly and cover the microphone. "It's Amity. She and G were hit by a truck. She doesn't know where they are, but they were on their way to the Harley shop," I tell the men around me. "Probe, go get the truck—we'll need it to bring them and G's bike back."

"You got it." Probe jumps off his bike and runs over to the truck.

"How bad is it?" Hannibal asks, and I remember that he used to be an EMT or something.

"Not sure. G's unconscious. He wasn't wearing a helmet," I tell him, putting the phone back up to my ear as he curses.

"We're on our way. I have a rough idea where you are, but I want you to stay on the line with me, okay? I have Bluetooth in my helmet, so you can just keep talking, and I'll keep riding until I find you," I tell her as I switch to Bluetooth, pulling on my helmet, and firing up my bike.

"Okay, Havoc. Should I have called an ambulance or the police? I didn't know what to do."

"Is he breathing?" I ask.

"Yeah, I... I've got my fingers on his pulse. It's strong and steady. I'm scared to let go in case it stops."

"You're doing good, Amity, real good," I reassure her, tearing out of the warehouse and through the gates, which are already open. Probe must've told the prospect what was happening. "Are you hurt?"

"No, I'm fine," she replies, but I can hear the pain in her voice.

"Alright, you keep your fingers on his pulse. If anything changes—he stops breathing or the bleeding gets worse—I'll call an ambulance for you. You just focus on our boy, okay?"

"I can do that," she says.

I head in the direction I think she is, breaking the speed limit to get to them and not giving a flying fuck.

"Oh, God..."

"Amity, what's going on?"

"They're back."

47

"Who's they?" When she doesn't answer me, I start shouting. "Fucking talk to me, Amity!"

"The truck that ran us off the road. It's heading our way and driving slower than I can walk."

My stomach drops. "Shit. Fuck. Okay, listen to me, Amity. I need you to hide."

"What? No, I'm not leaving G."

"I don't think they're coming back to check on you, honey. I hope to fuck I'm wrong, but—"

"You think they've come back to finish off the job," she chokes out, cutting me off.

"Please, Amity. Hide. Do it for G," I tell her gently.

"No. Fuck you, Havoc. I won't leave him, and you can't make me," she snarls, and I can't help but be impressed by her loyalty.

"They've stopped," she whispers.

I curse, opening the throttle and shifting gears, the engine roaring louder as I push harder to get to her.

"If G doesn't put you over his knee for this, I will," I snap.

"Two of them are coming my way," she says, ignoring what I just said.

"Amity, are you armed?"

"Yes, I have G's gun. You don't think he'd mind me using it, do you?" she asks, her voice sounding odd, making the hairs on my arms stand on end.

"He'd want you to do whatever it takes to keep yourself safe. You hear me, darling? Whatever it takes."

She's quiet for a moment.

"Oh, thank God, it's Raven Souls."

Relief hits me before I stop to think.

Why would it be Raven Souls? If they'd knocked G off his bike, they wouldn't have driven off. And why the fuck are they in the truck—

It hits me then, and I tense, realizing they can't be in the truck because the truck's with us. Probe's driving it.

"I don't recognize them," she whispers as everything starts to click into place.

"Amity," I say, panic and fear rising inside me. If we have the truck, it can't be one of my club brothers. It must be someone from another chapter.

"What's wrong? They're your brothers, right?"

My breathing turns ragged. She doesn't recognize them. She's been around the club enough to know all the brothers. Fuck.

"If you don't recognize them, they're not from the mother chapter. The only new arrival is me. There are no nomads or brothers who have been on runs or helping out at other clubs."

"Okay, but they're still Raven Souls, right?"

I don't say anything.

"Havoc?"

Still nothing.

"Are they friend or foe, Havoc?"

My heart feels like it's being ripped out of my chest. They

must be from my old chapter. They're the closest to us. But why are they here? They had to know they wouldn't be welcome. Plus, Blade said fuck-all about a visit, and I know damn well he would've told me if they were coming.

"Friend or foe, Havoc?" she grits out.

What do I say? Because whatever my answer, there's no going back from this. All I can think is they shouldn't be there. They should have called. And if they knocked Amity and G off their bike, they should have stopped.

"Foe," I snarl.

There's a moment of silence, and then all I hear are gunshots. I roar her name, but she doesn't answer. I floor the bike, going as fast as possible without wiping out, cursing to myself that it's not fast enough.

Finally, the shooting stops, and I pray I'm not too late. Then I hear another gunshot, muffled cursing, and the sound of an engine revving before one last shot rings out, and then... silence.

Seconds later, I see the intersection and spot G's bike on the ground. As I slow down, I notice Amity a few feet away from it. I'm off my bike and running toward her before I even think about it.

She's lying on top of G, using her body to shield him. I slide to a stop beside them and drop to the ground. I lie down on my stomach, my face inches from hers, and reach for the gun in her hand.

"It's okay now, Amity. You kept him safe, and you kept

both of you safe. Now, let me take over, okay? I won't let anything happen to either of you," I tell her softly as she looks at me.

I hear my brothers surrounding us, but I keep my eyes on Amity, who looks as white as a ghost.

"Don't. You'll get your prints on the gun. I don't want you to go back to prison."

After everything she just went through, she's worried about me going back to prison. A man she just met. G's a lucky son of a bitch.

"Shh, don't you worry about that." I offer her a small smile.

"I... I think I killed him," she chokes out, letting go of the gun.

I take it and pass it to Capone before taking her hand. "We need to let Hannibal look at G." She's shaking her head before I even finish, her eyes wide and full of fear.

Hannibal kneels beside us and moves her hair from her face. "I'll take real good care of him, Amity. I promise."

She swallows, looking unsure, but nods. "Okay," she says, and as she starts to move, I reach for her, lifting her into my lap and wrapping my arms around her.

"You did good, sweetheart," I tell her. She buries her face against my neck and falls apart. I don't say anything; I just hold her and let her cry. Her sobs shake her small frame, and my heart breaks for her.

While I take care of Amity, I watch with pride as my

brothers split up and get to work like a well-oiled machine, knowing exactly what needs to be done.

As I murmur words of comfort in Amity's ear, she lifts her head and looks around, taking in the scene. Mac and Toot are helping Hannibal with G, while Midas and Probe check out the guy Amity shot. Crane and Capone are dealing with G's bike, and the rest of the guys are covering us, just in case the other shooter comes back.

"Alright, his vitals are good. Let's get him to the clinic," Hannibal says, and I give him a nod. "Mac, Toot, I want to get him in the truck—nice and gentle. I'll ride in the back with him, just in case."

He looks at Amity, and his eyes soften. "You ride with Havoc. I need space just in case."

She nods but doesn't say anything.

"Good girl. Alright, boys, let's move," Hannibal orders Toot and Mac as Amity sits still in my lap.

Crane walks over to help carry G while Midas drops down in front of us.

"It's Acid—the guy she shot," Midas tells me, making me tense. That dirty motherfucker. "He's alive, but he's bleeding a lot. We'll put him in the back of the truck with the bike." I nod, and then he turns to Amity.

"Let's get you up and back to the clubhouse. You gonna be okay riding?" Midas asks her.

"Let's go," she says, putting on a brave face.

He holds his hand out to her and helps her up. Once she's

standing, I get to my feet and take her hand and walk her to my bike. As I pull my helmet on, I spot Capone walking toward us with G's.

I get on my bike and start it, waiting as Capone slips the helmet over her head and tightens the strap. I watch as he says something to her and squeezes her shoulder before she climbs on the bike behind me and wraps her arms around my waist tightly.

My mind races as I speed back to the clubhouse, thinking about what happened and why. Why would my old club go after G? He's the new VP—that should've kept him safe. And Amity? She could've been killed. What the hell were they thinking?

By the time we pull through the gates at the back of the property, my head is spinning, and I'm no closer to figuring out the reason behind the attack. I head toward the clinic and park. Once I've stopped, Amity climbs off and removes her helmet. I do the same and take hers from her, placing it next to mine on my seat as the others pull in behind us.

When the truck carrying G stops, she moves toward it, but I hold her back. "Give them space, sweetheart. While they get him settled, why don't you tell the rest of us what happened?"

"Okay, but I can do it here, though, right? I don't want to leave him."

"We'll find a quiet spot inside. Come on. Midas, Probe, Capone, you're with me. Hannibal, focus on G. Once he's good, stabilize Acid. I have questions for him." Hannibal nods, and we head inside.

I look around before leading her into the small break room at the back of the building. I pull out a chair for her as Probe grabs a soda from the fridge and cracks it open for her. I sit beside her as she takes a drink, her hand trembling slightly, and wait for the others to sit before I start.

"Alright, I caught most of it. But for the benefit of the others, I'm going to fill them in a little. Then, once you've finished that"—I nod to her soda—"you can tell us the rest, alright?"

"What about Blade?" Capone asks.

"I tried to call him," Amity starts, then clears her throat. "But he didn't answer."

"I called him too and left a message," Probe says shaking his head.

Midas sighs. "Conan has chemo today. Inigo was taking him. King said something about taking Sunshine to visit Alex's grave, so maybe he has Junior."

I blow out a frustrated breath and start telling them what happened. I tell them about the truck hitting Amity and G and how Amity called me. Then I tell them about the truck coming back, before turning to Amity to tell the rest.

"I thought we were safe when they got out of the truck because they were wearing Raven Souls cuts. But I didn't know them."

I clench my jaw, fisting my hands on the table as she looks

at me. "She asked me if they were friend or foe. And I hesitated. I shouldn't have. My answer should've been instant; every instinct I had told me something was wrong," I admit.

"He said 'foe' just as they pulled guns and pointed them at us. I couldn't let them hurt G," Amity says firmly.

"Of course you couldn't," Capone says, reaching over to pat her hand briefly.

"I didn't think. I just aimed and fired. I watched him go down, but I missed the other guy. Then he started shooting, so I covered G with my body and waited to take my next shot. Then I heard your bikes, and I knew everything would be okay. The other guy heard them, too. He started running, so I shot him. I think I hit his leg because he started limping."

"Good job." Probe's angry voice rumbles.

"He got in the truck and took off, but not before firing at me as he drove past. Asshole," she curses, making my lips twitch.

"You think you'd recognize him if I showed you some pictures?" I ask her.

"I think so," she replies, as the door suddenly swings open and slams against the wall, making us all jump.

Hannibal's eyes find mine before he looks at Amity, who walks toward him slowly.

"He's awake, and he's asking for you."

"Oh. That's good," she says quietly, then passes out.

Hannibal catches her before she hits the ground, and the rest of us scramble over to her.

"She hurt?"

"I'll check her out, but it's probably just her body's way of dealing with everything," he says, lifting her into his arms. "I'll take her to G. I'm sure she'll be fine."

"And G?"

"He's lucky. It could have been a lot worse. By the way, Acid's stable. I patched him up and had Circus and Toot take him to the shack. He'll be out of it for a couple of days, so I'd hold off on questioning him."

"Okay. Thanks, Hannibal." I rub my hand down my face, feeling tired all of a sudden.

"Don't mention it." He turns to leave but stops. "You did good today, Havoc. We're lucky to have you." With that, he takes Amity and leaves.

"Midas, go with them."

He nods and follows behind them.

"What now?" Probe asks.

"Now, we do a little digging and find out what the fuck is going on." I blow out a breath.

And to think, this started out as such a good day.

Chapter Four

Nevaeh

B y the time I got to the airport, my head was throbbing so I popped some more pain killers and drank a couple of bottles of water. With a slightly queasy stomach, I avoided eating anything and just hopped on the first plane to London, hoping I'd sleep a chunk of the journey away. Unfortunately, sleep evaded me because my brain wouldn't shut off.

Now, a few hours into the flight, I couldn't pretend what I was doing wasn't for all the wrong reasons. I was running away like a wuss. No, like a chicken. A big ol' yellow-bellied chicken.

I bury my face in my hands, wondering if I left a trail of smoke behind me with how fast I bolted out of there.

At first, I was embarrassed about doing the walk of shame. Now, I'm embarrassed about fleeing the country. I knew I wouldn't be able to keep what happened between me and Havoc a secret for long. I haven't spent much time with the guys, but I know they gossip worse than a bunch of high school girls. That's assuming Havoc even remembers. It never crossed my mind that he might've been just as drunk as I was.

There's a comfort in that, though I'd be lying if I said the ache in my chest was indigestion. My first time might not have gone the way I imagined it, but the thought of being forgotten...

"Ugh, I'm such a drama queen."

"Excuse me?"

I freeze, realizing I just said that out loud, and turn to look at the guy sitting next to me.

"Sorry," I mumble, my face heating.

He smirks at me. In another life, before my vagina had been invaded, I might have felt something. He's a good-looking guy and just rough enough to be my type. He's big and broad with sandy-colored hair. A faint scar runs from his hairline down the side of his face as if someone tried to cut him up, and like Havoc, he's had his nose broken once or twice.

"Dammit, don't think about him."

"Think about who?" the man asks, his pale blue eyes studying me as he waits for an answer, but they don't feel intrusive. They're more curious than anything.

"A man," I reply.

"Ah, well, that explains everything," he teases.

I huff, then open my mouth and everything spills out. "I got drunk, which was stupid because I never drink, and ended up having sex with a strange man."

I slap my hands over my mouth, cutting off the stream of words as my eyes widen to the point where I'm worried an eyeball will pop out and roll down the aisle.

He shakes his head, angling his body toward me. "Honestly, it happens to us all."

"You get drunk and wake up with strange men often?" I ask.

He laughs. "I'm usually the strange man. What can I say? I like women; I just don't want the aggravation of dating one."

"I feel like anything I say now will sound judgy," I admit.

"And are you? Judging me?"

I nod. "Oh yeah, definitely. Not because I think you're a bad person or anything. You can sleep with whoever you want. If it works for you, all the power to you. As long as they know it's just sex and nothing more, I don't see the harm. It just seems so..."

"Slutty?" he drawls.

"Lonely."

He's quiet for a moment, taking me in before holding out his large, scarred hand. "Ambros."

"Nevaeh," I say, slipping my hand into his.

"Nevaeh," he repeats.

"It's 'heaven' spelled backward," I tell him.

"Pretty."

I shrug. I've never really liked it.

"So the guy? Tell me about him."

"What's there to tell?"

"Was he at least good?"

"Umm..." I shift uncomfortably in my seat.

"Come on, you might as well tell me. We still have about three and a half hours to kill. And I'm a man-whore, so no judgment from me."

"It's not that," I say, hesitating before thinking, *screw it.* I'm never going to see him again, and I need to tell someone who won't judge me. Not that I think Amity would. I'm just embarrassed.

I take a deep breath. "I was drunk and passed out. My friend's boyfriend carried me to bed, and..."

"And... please tell me your friend's boyfriend didn't—"

"Oh, no—nothing like that. Amity was with him. G adores Amity. He'd never do anything to mess that up. And if I'm wrong and one day he turns into a colossal creep who would do that kind of thing, I'd tell her all about it after I finished burying his body."

"Okay good, but how do you go from being asleep to—"

"Waking up with a biker inside me?"

He stares at me, speechless.

"I thought I was dreaming. I... um... write books. That's

why I'm on my way to the UK; I'm going to a book signing." I pause, but he just watches me, waiting, so I take a breath and continue. "I don't have much experience, so I read a lot and watch a lot of porn for inspiration."

"You might just be my dream girl," he says.

I giggle. "Yeah, well, that's the thing." I bite my lip. "The books and porn sites don't just inspire my writing; they also inspire my dreams... It usually ends before I get to the good part. Only this time, it didn't."

He's staring at me now like he's never met anyone more fascinating. "So when you said you woke up with a biker inside you, you meant literally."

I nod. "Yeah, but wait, it gets better."

"I can't even begin to imagine how that's even possible."

I narrow my eyes at him. "Are you mocking me?"

"What? No, not even a little bit. You really don't know who I am, do you?"

I frown. "No. Should I?"

"No. And I just realized how arrogant I sounded when I said that. But what I was trying to say is that nobody just talks to me normally anymore. You, little Miss 'heaven spelled backwards,' are a nice change."

"You really are a strange man, Ambros," I tell him.

He smiles and motions for me to continue.

I grip the armrest and lean forward to whisper the rest in his ear. "I was a virgin."

He freezes, and I bite my lip as I pull back and look up at him. His face is a mask of concern.

"Did he hurt you?"

"I was a virgin, so yeah, a little, but..." I let my voice trail off as I look down, embarrassed.

His finger slips under my chin and tilts my head up. "Tell me."

I sigh. If I'm going to tell someone, I might as well tell him. "I liked it. I mean, after I got over the shock and pain. I liked it." I pause for a moment, glancing away before meeting his eyes again. "I think they might've put me in the wrong room, so he probably thought I was there for him."

At his confusion, I explain a little further. "He's part of a motorcycle club, so they have girls there who are happy to warm their beds."

"And you think he mistook you for one of those girls." His eyes move over me before looking up in disbelief.

"I was in his bed, Ambros. Not sitting in a church," I roll my eyes at him.

"So what happened next? Did the fucker kick you out?"

"He held me until we both fell asleep. Then I snuck out... lied to my best friend, jumped on a plane, and left the country," I admit.

He stares at me for a second before throwing his head back and laughing, drawing the attention of those around us.

I slap his chest and cross my arms, slumping back in my

seat with a huff. I wait for his laughter to fade before looking at him.

He wipes a tear from his eye and turns to me with a smile. "Alright, so is there a chance you'll run into this guy again? You said he was a stranger, so..."

"My best friend's dating one of his club brothers, so yeah, I'm going to see him again. But he probably won't remember me."

"Hate to break it to you, sweetheart, but there's no way he's going to forget you."

I frown, confused, but he doesn't elaborate.

"Let me ask you this... if he tracked you down and wanted more, would you be interested?"

I think about Havoc's hands on my body and shiver.

Ambros gives me a knowing look, but it's not as easy as he seems to think.

"It's not that simple."

"Of course it is."

"My father's a pastor."

He grins widely. "The pastor's daughter and a biker?"

"Actually, he's about to become president of the club."

"Of course he is." He shakes his head and chuckles. "You know what, Nevaeh, I've got a good feeling about this."

"You don't know my father, or—" He cuts me off, pressing his finger to my lips.

"You're legal, right?" he asks, taking his finger from my lips.

"Legal to... what? Have sex?" He nods. "Of course I am. I'm twenty-five."

"Then it's none of his business. I understand he might not be happy with the idea of his little girl being with a biker, but it's not his decision. It's yours. Life's short. Tomorrow's a gift, not a guarantee."

He's right. Hell, I know that better than anyone. But still, I'm not the type of girl he's used to. Why would Havoc be interested in me?

"It really doesn't matter anyway, not when he realizes this is what he's getting." I wave a hand over myself.

"All I see is a beautiful, smart, funny woman. And if Mr. President doesn't take his shot, I'll be happy to step in."

My mouth drops open.

"You might want to close your mouth; it's making me think of all the ways I want to fill it."

My mouth snaps closed so quickly, I hear it click.

"Relax, I'm not going to maul you. But you should know you've got options, and most women think I'm a pretty good catch."

"How on earth did you manage to fit that ego of yours on this plane?"

"Let's just say I'm used to carrying big things around."

The rest of the flight flew by—no pun intended—with Ambros keeping me entertained. And by the time we land, I realize I'll be sad to see him go. As we wait for our luggage to arrive, he nudges me and almost sends me flying.

"Thanks for that, Bigfoot."

"Gimmie your phone."

"Why?"

"So I can steal it," he deadpans, holding out his hand. "I wanna know what happens with you and Mr. President."

I unlock my phone and hand it to him. After a few moments, I hear his phone chime, and he hands mine back to me.

"There, now I have your number, and you've got mine. I need to know what happens next."

"Well, what happens next is me surviving my first book signing."

"Book signing? Oh, right. My sister's the same. She's obsessed with this author she's just found. She keeps trying to get me to read the books too, but they aren't really my thing."

"What's the author's name? If they're going to the same signing as me, I might be able to get a book signed for her and send it your way."

"Seriously? She'd love that, and I'd cement myself as her favorite brother."

I laugh. "How many brothers are there?"

"Oh, just me."

I look at him for a second before laughing..

"It's Celeste something."

I freeze.

"Celeste Sky?"

"That's it. I take it you're a fan, too?"

"I mean, I've read all her books."

"Of course you have. What is it with women and book porn?"

"We got tired of real-life men sucking. Fictional men fuck like gods and slay our demons without judgment," I snap, dropping an f-bomb, which is so unlike me. "But it's also so much more than that. It's about finding something we can't get in real life. About exploring your desires, fantasies, and aspects of relationships we can't get or talk about. It's about empowering women. I hate it when people put down romance books, writing them off as just porn."

"Okay, I get it. And since you're looking at me like you might stab me, I'm just going to apologize and beg for your forgiveness." He gives me puppy-dog eyes.

I snort but then sigh. "Whatever. Your sister's right. Maybe you should read one, then you might understand why romance books bring in over a billion dollars a year."

I unzip my carry-on and dig around until I find one of my books. I pull it out and show it to Ambros.

"Oh, I recognize that one. It's on my sister's birthday wish list. I didn't think it was out yet."

"It's not. You got a pen?"

"No." He looks around, then turns back to me. "Hold on,"

he says, and walks over to a guy holding up a handwritten sign not far behind us, coming back with a Sharpie.

I take it from him, pull the cap off with my teeth, and crack open the front of the book. "What's your sister's name?" I ask with the cap still between my teeth.

"Ella. But she'll notice if the autograph doesn't match the others, Nevaeh. It's a nice thought, though."

I ignore him as I write out a message to Ella, not wanting to spell anything wrong, and sign it. Then I hand him the book and put the cap back on the marker just as the guy he took it from looks at him and frowns.

"Hey, aren't you Ambros Deveraux?"

Ambros looks at him before his eyes slowly move to mine, then drop to the book and back up again as all the pieces fall into place. "You're Celeste Sky."

"Yeah, I am. Celeste Sky's my pen name."

"Oh, I need a picture. My sister's going to lose her mind."

"I'll take it," the guy holding the sign says. "Can I get an autograph, too, Ambros? I've been a fan of yours for years."

"Sure, man, no problem."

He hands his phone to the guy and wraps his arm around me. I smile as sign guy takes the picture.

"So, Ambros, what do you do?" I ask him, my curiosity now piqued.

But the sign guy answers, practically bouncing as he hands Ambros back his phone. "He's an MMA fighter. One of the best there is. Man, that fight between you and O'Donnell was insane," he says to Ambros.

"You want me to take your picture?" I ask, amused when Ambros suddenly looks shy.

"Fuck yes, my mates won't believe me otherwise." He hands me his phone, and I take a few pictures before Ambros signs the guy's T-shirt.

I notice the people around us are starting to stare, trying to figure out who we are. Anndd... that's my cue to leave.

"Well, Ambros... it's been fun, but I've gotta go." I hand the phone back and give Ambros a grin. "It was nice to meet you. Thanks for listening."

"Pleasure's all mine, ma'am," he says, tipping his imaginary hat.

I laugh, heading over to grab my suitcase when I see it on the conveyor.

"I'll be checking in to see how it goes," he calls out as I walk away with a wave.

We'll see.

Growing up sheltered, I didn't have many friends and definitely not much interaction with men. Ambros had been so nice, listening to me without judgment and making me feel... I don't know, seen? I want to believe he meant what he said and that he was a nice guy because I could really use someone like him in my life.

I walk through the automatic doors and stand on the sidewalk outside Heathrow and breathe in the London air. I can't believe I'm here. Pulling my suitcase behind me, I wait in line and grab a taxi to my hotel in the West End. Once I've checked in, I head up to my room and collapse on the bed in a heap. It's quiet, just like I wanted it to be. But as I lie here, my mind keeps drifting to a certain biker. After a few minutes, I give up and decide I need to burn off some of this energy. I change into my swimsuit and head to the hotel pool. I swim for an hour, then go back to my room and order room service. Twenty minutes later, my food arrives, and I eat in silence. By the time I'm finished, I can barely keep my eyes open. With a yawn, I pull the blankets back and climb into bed. The moment my head hits the pillow, I'm asleep.

I spend the next week doing all the touristy things. I toured the Tower of London and the British Museum, visited Kensington Palace and Harrods, watch the changing of the guards outside Buckingham Palace, and even checked out Tower Bridge and the London Eye while eating a bunch of amazing food. The portion sizes are bigger than I expected, so it's a good thing I spent my days walking around the city.

By the time the signing rolls around, I realize I've been so busy that I haven't had time to think about anything else.

The signing itself was crazy. Despite my nerves, I loved every moment of it. The first evening was a meet and greet where I got to interact with fellow authors as well as bloggers and influencers who have shared my books far and wide thanks to social media. The meet and greet was a far more intimate arrangement than the actual signing itself which was a full weekend event. It was nothing but organized chaos and as its one of the largest book signing events in the world it felt very much like jumping head first off a cliff but it was worth it. And not nearly as scary as I thought it would be. Getting to meet so many of my readers who were genuinely touched by my words and as protective of my characters as I am meant everything to me and has me itching to get back to writing.

Now that I've survived my first signing, I'm excited to plan out my next one.

"So, how was it?"

I turn to Leah, one of the other authors, whose table's beside mine. "Pretty good. I had no idea how exhausting it would be, though."

She laughs. "Right? You think, 'I'll be sitting all day, how could I possibly get tired?'"

"Yes! Exactly."

"If you're anything like me, this much peopling definitely doesn't help."

"It so doesn't."

She smiles, and I grin as I pack up the last of my things. "You know, since this was a last-minute thing for me, I was worried I wouldn't have enough books or swag. But so many people brought their own stuff for me to sign."

"It's surreal, isn't it?"

"It really is. It also made packing up sooo much easier," I say with a grin.

"Lucky bitch," she says, making me laugh.

"You need help?"

"Nah, I'm good. Hubs will be here any minute, and I'll just load him up like a pack mule."

"Now, why didn't I think of that?" I tease.

A voice over the speakers announces that we have fifteen minutes left to clear out.

"Crap, I better get back to it. It was nice to meet you, Celeste. Hopefully, I'll see you on the circuit again."

"Fingers crossed. And it was nice to meet you too."

After packing up the last of my things and thanking the organizers, I wheel my stuff out and hail a taxi. I'm so ready to get back to the hotel and slip into a hot bath with my Kindle. And I admit, now that everything is over, I feel a little home sick.

After I pay the driver, I head up to the room and open my laptop on a whim to see if there are any earlier flights home. The plan was to rest and sleep for the next two days, but I just want to go home. As luck would have it there is a few seats available tomorrow so I reschedule my flight before I change my mind.

With that done, I hop into action, packing my things for my now stupidly early flight, leaving out only what I'll need in the morning.

I place an order for room service and then head into the bathroom to fill the tub, turning the water to just the right temperature and adding some bubble bath. While it fills, I flick through the TV channels until I find the music stations.

Settling on some soft Jazz, I turn it up loud enough to listen to in the bathroom but not so loud that the neighbors will bang on the wall.

When there's a knock, I let room service in and wait for them to leave before I strip and grab my Kindle, leaving the fruit platter for when I get out.

Walking into the bathroom, I step into the tub and sink under the bubbles.

The break away from home has been just what I needed. It gave me the clarity and space to admit that I may have over-reacted. Besides, there's no way Havoc will remember me, so I worked myself up for nothing.

I settle in with my Kindle and relax. When I feel myself getting sleepy, I get out of the water and dry off. I pull on my PJs and eat some of my fruit, then climb into bed for a few hours of sleep before I have to be at the airport.

Still half asleep when my alarm goes off, I get up, get dressed, and check out, looking more reanimated than alive. When I arrive at the airport, I grab an overpriced orange juice and a breakfast sandwich and wait bleary-eyed for my flight to be called. Once the food kicks in, and I feel somewhat human again, I people watch, imagining what their lives might be like. I spot a bearded man wearing shades in the brightly lit terminal, holding on to an energy drink for dear life.

If he were one of my characters, he would be trying to make it to his wedding on time after being dumped, drunk in the middle of nowhere by his best man after a disastrous batchelor party. The plot twist is that he bumps into the woman he loves right at this airport, only she isn't the woman waiting at the altar for him, but the one who got away. I pull out my notebook and jot down the idea as a giggle snatches my attention. I look up and see a little girl of maybe four or five running ahead of a harried-looking woman, I assume is her mother, hurrying to catch up. The kid plows into my imaginary grooms legs, jolting him out of his daydreams. He reaches for the kid to stop her from falling before his eyes collide with the mother, who apologizes profusely.

I dip my head and grin as I add to the story bubbling in my brain.

The groom takes one look at the woman and sees the one who got away right in front of him like some kind of serendipity before he remembers he's about to marry another. He turns away, focusing on the child. A child who has the exact same eyes that he does.

I jump when I hear my flight being called. I shove my notepad and pen back in my bag before I stand up, throw it over my shoulder, and walk past the groom and his long-lost love. I can't help but chuckle when the kid climbs onto his lap and makes herself comfortable much to the surprise of the adults watching her. Dammit, I'm almost sad to leave and miss seeing how this plays out.

Boarding the plane, I stow my bag and get settled in, slipping on my headphones as I wait for the passengers to board.

The flight home is nothing like the one to London. The person in the seat beside me is a teenage boy who ignores me, so I end up sleeping most of the way. Even though I sleep on the plane, I can't wait to get back home to the RV and curl up for a few hours. I'm not sure when I started to think of the RV as home, but I have—and it is.

Once I finally make it out of the airport, I have to push my way through the crowds of people waiting for their loved ones so I can get my case and not pout over the fact that there is nobody missing me but Amity, assuming G hasn't kept her too distracted with his star-spangled dick. Once I locate my case, I grab it and head out to my car, throwing the case and my bag in the trunk before heading to the movie set. But when I pull up and see the police, I realize something's wrong, and whatever it is, it's bad.

I jump out of the car and grab the first person I can find. "What's going on? What happened?"

"One of the stunt crew got hurt."

"What? Who? How?" I ask, my heart racing.

"I don't know much. I just know it was the girl. I think her name's Amy."

"Amity?"

"That's it. Amity."

"Where is she?"

"I don't know. Probably the hospital." She walks away like she didn't just drop a bomb on my world.

I grab someone else as they pass by, but they refuse to talk to me. Frustrated, I jump in my car and race to the clubhouse, knowing G will know where she is.

I don't pay attention to the prospect that lets me in. I just park and run up to the saloon, praying that she's okay. I can't lose her too.

I burst through the doors and spot G right away. "G!" I yell his name as I run over and crash into him, grabbing his shirt as his arms wrap around me. "Tell me she's okay! Please, God! Tell me she's okay!" I pull back to look up at him. "I got home early and went to the set to see her, but they told me she got hurt, and nobody would tell me anything else!"

"Hey, hey, calm down, Tinkerbell. She's okay, I promise. She's asleep upstairs."

"Really?" I ask, tears streaming down my face. "You promise?"

"I swear it. Come on, I'll take you up to see her."

I nod jerkily, freezing when I hear a familiar voice beside him.

"Vanilla," Havoc groans as he lifts a strand of my hair to smell it.

"You two know each other?" G asks, his eyebrow raising as he looks between us.

"No!" I shout as Havoc moves closer, grinning like a lunatic as he tucks the strand of hair behind my ear.

"Yeah, I know her, G. This is my future wife."

"What the fuck?" G asks.

What the actual... I stare at him, my mouth dropping open in shock.

"Go be with your friend, Cupcake. I'll catch you later."

Before I can say anything, he's gone, leaving me standing there stunned.

"Young lady, I think you've got some splaining to do," G says, doing his best Ricky Ricardo impression. I want to laugh, but instead my shoulders sag.

"Later. For now, I just need to see Amity."

Chapter Five

Havoc

I stand, leaning against the shack, waiting for G. I know he'll turn up at some point. Amity could have died because of these assholes, and after what went down on the movie set, I think the man needs somewhere to channel his anger.

Closing my eyes, I think back to the tiny woman who came tearing into the clubhouse earlier and grin. I can't believe she's here. I'd just about given up on finding her, and then she came strolling into my clubhouse smelling like cupcakes and looking like a sinner's wet dream.

I still remember that night, the memories are so vivid it's like she's right beside me. After years of wading through shit, she's like a breath of fresh fucking air that I so desperately need right now.

Hearing footsteps, I stand up and smirk when G rounds the corner.

"Am I that predictable?"

'No. I just know this is exactly where I'd be if Amity were mine."

He folds his arms across his chest. "You gonna stop me?"

"I'm gonna help you. The way I look at it, both of us have a hell of a lot to gain from watching these fuckers die."

"I think I'm going to like having you as my president," he jokes as he walks inside. I follow behind him, groaning at the smell of shit.

"I'll remind you, you said that," I laugh, knowing we'll likely butt heads somewhere along the way.

We stand next to each other, taking in my two former brothers, who look pitiful, chained, facing each other on opposite walls.

"Acid and Knuckles. Good to see you, brothers. Khan told me you came to welcome me back into the Raven Souls fold."

Acid tries to lift his head but fails. Knuckle's eyes dart my way before they flick to the door. I grin, knowing there is no escape for them.

"Listen, man, it wasn't personal...We were just following orders," Acid says as G walks toward him.

"Oh I don't know about that. It was very fucking personal to me. That was my old lady you almost fucking killed. It was my brain that could have been splattered all over the road." G snarls down at him.

"We thought you were Havoc!" he yells when G presses his boot to Acid's stomach wound. He squeals like a pig before passing out.

I look at G and chuckle.

"He thought you were me?" G frowns.

"Maybe he was drunk." I shrug. "I haven't seen either of them since I was sent to prison. I'm a hell of a lot bigger than the man they remember. I used to be around your size."

"The tattoos," Knuckles mumbles. "We heard he had tattoos."

I shake my head. "So they heard through the grapevine I'd gotten some new ink. And they put two and two together and got forty-six." I summarize.

"That's flimsy as fuck. You're not buying this, right?"

"He always was as dumb as a rock, so I won't rule it out. It's more likely they spotted you and Amity riding past and couldn't miss out on an opportunity to fuck shit up. I don't think they cared who they hit. Maybe they thought you'd kick me to the curb if I brought nothing but trouble. Either way, Acid admitted that they were sent here to take me out. I'll be damned if I know why, though. I'm the one who was fucked over, not the other way around."

"I doubt we'll get the answers we need from these two. They're too far down the food chain to know anything."

"Agreed. So, on that note, there really isn't much need to keep them around. Which one do you want?"

He walks over to Knuckles with a feral grin on his face. "He shot Amity. I want him."

"He's all yours. Might want to take your cut off for this. I have a feeling it's going to get messy."

I stalk over to Acid and wrench his head back, making him whimper. "Not so cocky now, are you? We were brothers once so I'm going to go gentle on you. You know, I almost feel bad. Khan sent you down here to your slaughter, and you're too fucking dumb to realize."

"He trusted us." Acid chokes out.

"You're expendable, you fucking idiot." I shove him back as I release him and walk to the trunk in the corner of the room. I grab a tactical knife and grip it with my teeth as I slip my cut off and hang it on one of the hooks on the wall. I ignore the screaming coming from the other side of the room and focus on Acid, who can't look away from the carnage.

"Fuck you, Havoc. Fuck you." Acid spits as he fights against his restraints, but he has no strength left.

"You don't like seeing what G's doing to Knuckles, huh? Well, let me help you with that." I thrust the blade into his eye, carving into the muscles surrounding it until I can rip the eye out. There is no finesse, and by the time I move to the next, Acid has puked all over himself and passed out. I start whistling a merry tune as I remove the second eye, noting the screams from the other side of the room have stopped.

Once the eyeball pops out, I pick up the other one from the floor where it fell and shove them both into his mouth.

Happy with my work, I contemplate what to remove next when I notice the asshole isn't breathing. I feel for a pulse and curse when I realize the motherfucker is dead.

"You always were a fucking pussy." I spit on him, watching it drip down his face before I turn and walk over to G, who has turned Knuckles into some kind of human jigsaw puzzle.

"Remind me not to piss you off."

He looks over at Acid before cocking an eye at me.

"He dead?"

"Fucker's heart gave out. Pussy. I think it's safe to say Knuckles is gone too."

"Not sure I could find his pulse to check, even if I wanted to," he jokes.

"I've heard of *rest in peace*, but never *rest in pieces*," I say, looking at the carnage.

"I don't envy the prospects cleaning this up."

"If this doesn't break them, they'll stand a good chance of getting patched in."

"Agreed. But I might just sweep up what's left of Knuckles and put him in a sandwich bag or something. Because I'm nice like that."

I laugh, shoving him to the back of the room, where the hose is. "I'll tell you what. I'll sweep him up and get the prospects on the rest of the mess, and you head back to

Amity. It's been a long fucking day, and she might wake up needing you."

He strips down to his boxers and grits his teeth as I spray the hose over him.

"Nevaeh's with her right now, but you're right. I need to be there. I feel like I'm going to crawl out of my skin the longer I'm away from her."

"It's probably gonna feel like that for a while," I warn him as he slips his cut over his damp skin.

"So, Nevaeh? That's her name?"

"Shouldn't you know the name of the woman you're going to marry?"

I glare at him until he sighs.

"Fine, yes, it's Nevaeh. I gotta ask, Havoc. And I'm not trying to be a dick here, but what exactly do you want from her? She's not like Lola. She's a good girl. Hell, her father is a pastor, for God's sake. If you just want someone to fuck, grab a bunny. Nevaeh isn't that girl, and she never will be." He opens the door and walks out before turning to look back at me as I stand in the doorway. "She's Amity's best friend. I know, ultimately, you're going to do what you want, but I'm asking you not to go there. If she gets hurt, it'll hurt Amity. And she's been through enough."

Yeah, that's not going to happen. "And what about what Nevaeh wants?"

"She's a virgin who has next to no life experience. She doesn't know what she wants."

"No, she's not."

"Not what?"

"A virgin."

"She is, Havoc. She wouldn't lie about it. It's not her style."

"I'm not saying she's lying. I'm saying she's not a virgin. Not anymore." I cross my arms over my chest and wait.

"What's that supposed to— Ah, fuck."

He storms off, leaving me grinning. I like G, but nothing, and nobody is going to stand in the way of what I want.

And what I want is the taste of cupcakes on my tongue.

Chapter Six

Nevaeh

Amity fell asleep a few hours ago, and after everything that happened, who could blame her? But I can't sleep. I'm scared that if I do, I'll wake up and find her gone. G left a while ago, so here I am, lying awake, staring at the ceiling.

When I heard that Amity was hurt, I thought I was going to lose it. With all the risks she takes when she's doing her stunts, I never doubt that she'll make it home in one piece. But this reminds me that, for all the jokes I make about her being a superhero, she's just as breakable as the rest of us. And I hate it. Losing Citi destroyed half of me. Losing Amity would finish off what's left of me.

I glance at her. Her hair's fanned out over the pillow, and

she looks so peaceful. But the pink cast resting on the pillow between us is a stark reminder of just how close I came to losing her.

When I hear the door open, I turn and see G walk in. He quietly closes the door behind him and heads toward the bathroom. When he flicks the light on, I see that he's wet and half-naked. Confused, I stare at him until his eyes land on mine in the mirror.

He turns to look at me, leaning back against the counter. "The day you flew out to the UK, a couple guys from Havoc's old club ran me and Amity off the road."

I sit up straight, eyes wide.

"We had a stupid argument about helmets, and she ended up wearing mine, so I wasn't wearing one. It was reckless, and it could've cost me everything," he says, looking at Amity.

"What happened?" I keep my voice low so that I don't wake Amity.

"We were thrown from my bike, and I was knocked unconscious. Amity called Havoc, and he and the guys rode out to get us, but the two guys that hit us came back with guns. I left Amity vulnerable. She was forced to protect us both, and a bullet grazed her leg, but thankfully that was all. The problem is that even though I was out cold, I can't unsee it. Every time I close my eyes..." He shakes his head and blows out a breath. "I've never felt so fucking helpless in my life."

"And then she went over the edge of a cliff. Damn it, G,

you should have called me. I was freaking sightseeing while you and my best friend were hurt."

"She didn't want you to come back. And we were both fine, or I swear she would've called. London was a big deal, and she wanted that for you."

I scrub my hands over my face. I'm so beyond pissed, but I know I probably would've done the same thing. But that doesn't mean I have to be happy about it.

"Fine," I say with a huff, rolling my eyes. "I'll wait until the cast's off before I kick her ass."

His lips twitch. "Appreciated."

"What can I say—I'm awesome like that," I tell him, making him smile.

"So... why do you look like a drowned rat?"

His smile fades at my question. "The guys that ran us off the road were ordered to kill Havoc. But instead, they tried to kill me and the woman I love. I don't give a fuck what happens to me, but I'll be damned if I ever let a motherfucker get away with hurting her."

He lifts his hands and looks at them. "Let's just say, they'll never hurt her again."

He waits for my reaction.

I nod. "Good. You may shower now," I say, dismissing him.

"Yes, ma'am." He chuckles and closes the door.

I lie back down and stare back at the ceiling. He might as well have just told me he killed them. I'm waiting to see if I have a delayed reaction to that, like fear or panic, but I don't. All I feel is relief. Now, what does that say about me?

When the shower turns off, I close my eyes and pretend to sleep. A few minutes later, G comes out of the bathroom and climbs into bed on the other side of Amity. He wraps his arm around her and lets out a contented sigh.

I lie still and listen as his breathing evens out. I wait another thirty minutes to make sure he's asleep before I slip out of bed and slide my shoes on.

I glance down at Amity and G. Seeing her safe in his arms—and knowing what he did tonight to protect her and what he risked going over the cliff to save her—is the only reason I feel comfortable leaving this room.

Grabbing my car key and cell phone from the bedside table where I left them, I slip them into the zippered pocket of my skirt before walking silently to the door. I open it, and creep out, closing it quietly so I don't disturb them. I spin around, ready to sneak out of the compound, when I collide with a wall of muscle. I don't need to look up to know who it is. My body responds to him immediately. He reaches out to steady me, and I look up into the deep, dark eyes of the man I've been trying to forget.

"Hello, Cupcake."

I open my mouth to tell him I'm leaving when he picks me up and tosses me over his shoulder. I let out a surprised squeal as I try to hold my skirt down, but the beast of a man does that for me by covering my ass with one of his giant hands.

"Put me down, you heathen!" I snap, struggling in his hold.

He chuckles, the deep sound vibrating through me, but he doesn't put me down.

"I mean it. Put me down right now, or I'll scream."

"Go ahead, Cupcake, scream all you want, but this is my club, and nobody's going to stop me from claiming what's mine."

Before I can process what he just said, I hear a door opening and closing as he carries me into one of the rooms and gently sets me down.

As soon as my feet hit the floor, I rush to put some distance between us. "Your club? I think Blade might have something to say about that!" I snap, because it's the first thing that comes to mind, even though I know Blade's step-ping down and Havoc's taking his place. But that's not for a while yet, right?

He cocks his head, studying me. "You don't know who I am?"

I want to play dumb, but his name slips out in a barely there whisper. I know he hears it when he growls and steps closer, but stops when I back up.

"You called me yours. I'm not yours. I think you have me confused with someone else." He can't know it was me he slept with. It was dark, and I left before he woke up.

His eyes move over my rainbow-colored skirt and over-sized sweatshirt with a Care Bear on the front, and his lips twitch. "Oh, I'm not confusing you with anyone."

I cross my arms over Funshine, not liking his tone. I should be acting nice so I can lull him into a false sense of security before—wham—I kick him in the balls and make a run for it. But his eyes twinkle like he knows exactly what I'm thinking.

"You must be because I am not your girl," I snap.

He moves so fast I barely have time to breathe before I'm pinned to the wall. "It was my dick you let inside you. My dick your greedy pussy milked dry, and my dick you branded with your blood. So damn fucking straight that makes you mine."

I gasp, but before I can say anything, his mouth's on mine, swallowing my protests. I consider biting his tongue off when he slips it into my mouth. And I'm going to—*any second now.* But as memories of our night together flash through my mind, I can't think of anything else.

Suddenly, he lifts me, and I automatically wrap my legs around his waist. It isn't until I'm flat on my back with Havoc between my thighs that reality comes crashing back in.

I tear my mouth free. "We have to stop."

"We will. In a minute."

His lips trail down my jaw, finding a sensitive spot behind my ear that makes me shiver, and I feel him smile, his arrogance pissing me off as much as it's turning me on.

With that, I shove at his chest, but it's like trying to move a brick wall. "Get off me, you big... big... brute."

He lifts his head and grins, his face transforming completely. My brain goes from *kiss me quick* to *fuck me slow* in an instant, shocking the hell out of me.

"I don't like that you ran from me, baby. Don't do that again, or I'll tie you to my bed."

"Are you insane? No, don't answer that. I already know. Do you need to take your medication or something? Maybe call a priest"

"The only thing wrong with me is that you're wearing too many clothes, and my treatment requires you to wear a lot less."

He drags my skirt up my thighs, revealing my underwear. He looks down and smirks.

I huff, feeling my face flush. If I'd known a boy was going to see my panties today, I probably wouldn't have worn my She-Ra ones.

"Cute, but they've got to go. Therapist's orders."

"You don't have a therapist." I yelp as he grabs my under-wear and tugs them down my legs.

"Sure, I do. To help me deal with my phobia."

He pushes my legs apart, making me yelp again as I try to push him away.

"And what exactly is this so-called phobia that needs you to be down there?" I ask as he settles between my legs.

"Vaginaphobia."

I freeze and look down at him. "That's not a real thing. You just made that up."

He shakes his head. "It's true. I spent a long time around men, and now pussies make me nervous."

Yeah, right. He's totally full of shit.

"Well, you don't look nervous now, so move."

"My therapist recommends exposure therapy."

Before I can roll my eyes, the man's tongue is on me—on me and in me, flicking my clit, then dipping inside me to lick up my arousal.

Dear sweet baby Jesus, I never understood what all the fuss was about, but now I get it. It's like trying to explain how chocolate tastes to someone who's never had it.

Before I realize it, I'm grabbing handfuls of his damp hair, holding him to me. My hips lifting of their own accord, chasing... something. Wanting—no, needing—him closer.

"Come for me, Cupcake. I wanna see if you taste as sweet as you smell."

And after a few more swipes of his tongue, I do, my back arching as he sucks my clit into his mouth.

When I finally catch my breath, I look down and find him grinning up at me, his chin slick with my arousal.

"Well, would you look at that?" he says, his voice full of satisfaction. "I'm cured."

He crawls up my body and kisses me. I taste myself on his

lips. It feels so wrong, but I can't deny that I like it. When he pulls back, he lifts one of his large hands to cup my face, his thumb brushing my cheek.

"This is happening," he says. "You're mine, and I have no problem reminding you of that daily."

"You always take what you want without caring about the consequences?" I whisper.

"When it comes to you, I guess I do."

"I don't even know you. You're just the guy who stole my freaking virginity. What if I was saving myself for marriage?"

I wasn't, but he doesn't need to know that.

He frowns. "You climbed into my bed dressed like a wet dream, Cupcake. And you didn't put up a fight. Fuck, your slick pussy welcomed me in."

"I didn't know it was your bed. G carried me there when I passed out," I tell him. "He thought I'd be safe there."

He leans in until his forehead touches mine. "Did I hurt you?"

I know if I say yes, he'll let me go. But something tells me there's more to this man than I realize, and I might end up doing more harm than I mean to. Besides, it didn't really hurt. It was just... uncomfortable. He's huge, and I'm...well, not.

"Nooo. I just..." I blow out a frustrated breath, not sure how to put what I'm feeling into words. "I'm twenty-five, and I didn't save it to just throw it away like half my friends did when we were teenagers. I wanted it to mean something. I never really got to date, so I held on to it and—"

"And I took it while you were passed out. Fuck." He kisses me softly, then pulls back. "I'm sorry it didn't happen the way you wanted it to. But I'd be lying if I said I regretted it. I've spent the last few years alone. And then there you were, and you smell like cupcakes and fresh starts, and I really need a fresh start right now."

"This will never work, Havoc. You're all that, and I'm just... me. I'm boring. I don't swear. I don't drink, which is why I ended up in this mess in the first place. Heck, I'm a pastor's daughter, for heaven's sake. I won't fit in here."

"Of course you are," he grins before turning serious. "You'll never fit in, Cupcake, because you were born to stand out. I could spend the rest of my life watching you and never get bored."

Yep. He's insane. Figures. The first guy to affect me is a sandwich short of a picnic.

"You need to let me go. Let's just pretend none of this ever happened."

His grip on me tightens. "No. Fuck that. I'm keeping you."

"Keeping me?" I snap. "I'm not a puppy."

He pulls his hand away and runs it through his hair. When he does, I see a nasty-looking burn on his hand. I grab it and turn it over so I can get a better look.

"What happened?"

"Amity went over the cliff, and G went after her. I helped pull them back up."

He says it so calmly. Whereas just the thought of it makes me want to scream.

"You pulled them back up?" I manage to choke out, staring down at his hand. A hand that helped save my best friend's life.

"Of course."

Of course.

Of course.

Of course.

It's such a simple phrase for something so huge.

I press a kiss to the tender part of his palm and hear him suck in a sharp breath. I look up at him. "Thank you."

"I'm going to scare you," he growls, and I jump at his words.

"I'm going to terrify you down to your bones, Cupcake."

"What? Why? I don't understand."

"I know, and I'm sorry. Sorry for every tear I'll make you cry."

"You're right. You are scaring me," I admit, thinking I need to get the heck out of here. I need a change of underwear—and maybe a restraining order.

His nose skims down mine before he pulls back and climbs off the bed. He stands there, holding out his hand. Surprised, I take it, and he helps me off the bed.

"Let me take you for a ride."

"I don't think that's a good idea, Havoc."

"It's just a ride. Come on, say yes."

"I don't know, Havoc. I've never been on a bike before, and I'm definitely not dressed for it."

"Don't say no."

I don't know if it's an order or a plea, but I find myself giving in. "Fine. One ride, but I need to go back to my car first. My luggage is still in the trunk from my trip, and I know I have jeans in there."

"Alright, let's go before everyone else wakes up."

"Wait. Why? What's your hurry?"

"You don't want them asking too many questions, do you?"

"Good point."

I quickly run into the bathroom and clean myself up. When I come out, Havoc's waiting for me exactly where I left him. He takes my hand and holds it tightly. I try to pull it free, but he won't let go. With a sigh, I give up, knowing he'll have to let go eventually.

He leads me out the back, the same way I snuck out after our night together. Just like then, nobody sees us.

When we get to my car, I pop the trunk and dig through my suitcase until I find some jeans, my sneakers, and a pair of panties. Feeling Havoc's watchful eyes on me, I ask him to turn around, and he does, reluctantly. Once he's facing the other way, I quickly pull on my panties and jeans under my skirt. After fastening them, I tug my skirt down and throw it in the back with the rest of my things, then put on my sneakers. Grabbing my phone from my skirt, I shove it in my jeans pocket before shutting the trunk.

"Okay. I'm ready," I say, and he turns back to me.

"The RV is still on set. Not sure if the police have released it or not yet, but I'll call G and find out later. In the meantime, we can drop your car back at the campsite while we ride. If the cops release the RV, it'll save you from coming back here if you don't want to. And if they don't, I'll return you to your car and you can drive back here and crash in one of the spare rooms without anyone knowing you were with me."

"I'm not ashamed to be seen with you, Havoc; I'm just not ready for all the questions and assumptions that come with being seen riding on the back of your bike."

"I know. So you good with this plan?"

"I guess, but I've got my MacBook and other things in the trunk. I don't like the idea of leaving them in the car while nobody's around."

"It'll fit in my saddlebags. We can take it with us."

I sigh because he's not going to let this go. Suck it up, Nevaeh, it's just a bike ride.

He takes my key, opens the door for me, and helps me get in.

"I'll be right behind you," he says, pressing the key into my palm before he closes the door and heads over to his bike.

So what if I watch his ass as he leaves? It's not like it means anything.

I start the car and pull up to the gates and wait for Dice to open them. Once they're open, he nods at me, and I drive through, taking a deep, steadying breath.

There'd been a part of me that was worried Havoc wouldn't let me go. He seemed so obsessed with the idea of us that I was looking for ways to escape. But now, at least, he seems to have calmed down a little.

I check the rearview mirror and see him behind me. I chew my lip, wondering whether going for a ride with him is a smart idea. Maybe him realizing that we have nothing in common will be the best way to move on.

I pull into the lot and park, turning off the engine. I climb out of my car and wait for Havoc's bike to stop before walking over to him.

"I don't have a helmet," I tell him as he pulls his off.

"You can wear mine," he says.

I protest, but he eases it on my head and clips the strap under my chin. "Get on. And watch out for the pipes. They get hot."

I place my hands on his shoulders and use him as leverage as I struggle to swing my leg over the seat. I hold his waist, but he has other ideas. He yanks my arms forward until my front is plastered to his back, and I press my hands to his stomach, feeling one of his cover mine.

"Hold on tight," he yells over the roar of the engine.

I do as he says, and when he takes off, I close my eyes and rest my head against his back.

Riding doesn't scare me, but the thought of crashing does. I have this irrational fear of ending up on life support and my father refusing to pull the plug, given his inability to let go and grieve.

Eventually, I relax and realize I'm enjoying it. I have the strangest urge to stretch my arms out wide to feel the wind rushing over me. Being on a bike like this almost feels like I'm flying.

I'm enjoying myself, but when the temperature drops, I start feeling the cold. Havoc must feel me shivering because he slows down and pulls off the main road onto one lined by trees. It's bumpier, making me hold on tighter, but at least it's not as cold now.

About thirty minutes later, I feel the first drops of rain, and as fun as this has been, I don't want to ride in the rain. When we finally stop, I lift my head and see a pretty little cabin nestled within the trees. It almost looks like something out of a fairy tale.

Havoc climbs off first and holds out his hand to help me off. But my legs feel like jelly, and I'm not sure I can stand up on my own anymore. Havoc must realize the problem because he sweeps me up into his arms and carries me to the cabin.

"What is this place? Do you know who lives here?"

He turns the handle, and the door creaks open.

"Who leaves their door unlocked like that?" I ask in shock.

"There's no one around for miles in any direction. No need to worry about locking doors."

"You've clearly never seen the movie *Cabin in the Woods.*"

Chapter Seven

Havoc

I set her down on her feet and watch as she takes in the cabin. It's not going to win any awards, but it was just what my grandfather needed after my grandmother died. A place where he could live out the rest of his days in peace as he waited until he could join her once more. I find the same peace here that he did. Driller never gave a damn about our grandfather once he retreated from the world. Hell, I don't even think he knows about this place, which works in my favor now. Especially as he would likely have just sold the place like he did my father's bike.

"This might be the most adorable place I've ever seen," she says.

The cabin has an open floor plan downstairs, featuring a

country-style kitchen with aged oak countertops and modern appliances. The living area has an overstuffed sectional facing a huge TV mounted on the wall above the fireplace. Next to the sofa, there's a small end table with a lamp on top, and a colorful rug covers the floor. A round oak dining table and four chairs make up the small dining area off to the side. And a wall of windows runs the length of the cabin, letting in lots of light and making the place feel warm and inviting.

Upstairs, above the kitchen, is the bedroom. There's no wall—just a railing—so you can see the large bed from down here. Beside it, there's a closet, and the bathroom's in the far back corner on the other side.

"Go take a look around."

"I don't want to invade someone's house like that, it's—"

"Mine. My grandfather left it to me when he died."

She turns to look at me, her mouth open to ask something, but she snaps it shut again.

"What?"

"It's none of my business."

"There's nothing you can ask me that's off-limits, unless it's club business."

She bites her lip, looking unsure, before she braces herself. "I heard you were married and lived in another state?"

"That all you heard?"

"That and that you'd been away from the club for five years, I'm assuming you went nomad?"

I evade answering that question for now but have no problem telling her the rest.

"I had an old lady, but we never got married. I wanted to. I just thought we'd have more time, and I wanted to give her the wedding of her dreams. Turns out we had different dreams all along."

"I'm sorry."

I shrug. "I'm not. I'm just glad I found out who she really was before we got married and had kids. It was partly my fault anyway. I think I was in love with who she used to be, not who she became."

She nods before looking back at the room.

"Ah, fuck. We left your laptop in your car. I'll go back and grab it."

"It's okay. I'll come with you. I should probably head back anyway—we've been gone for hours. I didn't realize what time it was."

"No, stay. The wind has really picked up out there and I don't want to risk us both being out on the bike. I'll pick up some food on the way back, we can talk and wait out the storm. Please?" I give her what I hope are my best puppy dog eyes.

It must work because she sighs and gives in. "Fine, but I really can't stay out late, storm or not. I have a deadline I need to meet."

"I'll be quick. I need your car keys so I can grab your stuff." She fishes her key from her pocket and hands it to me.

"Shit, can I borrow your phone too? I forgot mine, and the club might need me."

"Um...sure." She pulls her phone from her back pocket and hands it to me. "My PIN's 07123."

"Thanks. I won't be long. Watch a movie or take a nap or something." I leave before she realizes I'm taking her phone with me.

I slide it into my own pocket, hop on my bike, and head to the nearest grocery store to stock up on some essentials before picking up a couple of pizzas. Once I have everything in my saddle bags, I head back to the campsite.

The light rain turns into a downpour, soaking me through to the skin. I'm colder than a penguin's nutsack by the time I reach Nevaeh's car.

Unhooking the saddle bags, I toss them in the back seat with my cut, before walking around and adjusting the driver's seat and climbing in, not wanting to drive with my knees up around my ears.

Taking both my cell and Nevaeh's from my pockets, I use mine to call Dice.

"Prez?" he answers after the second ring. I hear the sounds of the club in the background before everything goes quiet, indicating he must have left the room.

"Need you to pick up my bike from the campsite and take it back to the clubhouse. There's a spare key in my office in the top drawer of my desk."

"I'm on bar tonight, I'll get one of the club girls to cover me and head over."

"Good. And for fuck sake be careful with it."

I hang up before he can ask any questions, not that he should. Prospects know to keep their mouths shut or they'll never patch in.

Tossing my cell on the passenger seat, I pick Nevaeh's up from my lap and read through the texts between her and Amity to get a feel for how they talk to each other. Next, I check out her other threads for anything useful.

Lou's the one I focus on. After a few minutes of scrolling, I realize she's provided me with the perfect cover. I reread the last few messages.

They loved you! Got a call about you doing another signing in Rome in a few weeks. Given your popularity, they're willing to make space for you.

I can't go anywhere right now. Amity was in an accident.

OMG, is she okay? Is there anything I can do?

Not right now. Thanks, Lou.

. . .

Don't mention it. It's my job, and you're one of my easiest clients. Focus on your friend and maybe write a little to keep yourself distracted.

You know me too well, lol. I'll keep you updated. Thanks again.

So, my girl's some kind of writer, and judging from the messages, she was in London for almost two weeks for a book signing. And they wanted her in Rome. Hmm.

I don't give myself a chance to overthink it—I start typing out a text.

Hey. I hate to drop this on you, but I'm about to board a flight to Rome for another signing. I'll explain everything when I get back. Just know it's a big deal. I wouldn't leave if it wasn't. You've got G, but if anything comes up, message me, and I'll hop on the first flight home.

I love you, and I'll miss you. 🩶

It's weird as fuck texting as someone else, and I know I've just crossed so many lines, but I don't give a fuck. Not when I'm so close to having everything I want.

Starting up the car, I flip the heater on along with the wipers, just as my cell rings.

I reach for it and look at the screen cursing. "G, what's up?"

"Have you seen Nevaeh? She was gone when we woke up, and she just texted Amity. And now Amity's worried."

Fuck. I thought I'd pulled it off, but I guess not.

"Yeah, a couple hours ago, I drove her to the airport in that tin can of hers. She said something about a book signing in Rome. Said she didn't want to go, but I told her to do it. I figured Amity would say the same. She felt guilty as fuck, though."

G sighs. "I thought it might've been my fault."

"Why, what'd you do?" I snap.

"Nothing. Don't worry about it. I'll let Amity know. I'll catch you later."

He hangs up just as Nevaeh's phone chimes.

It's all good. I can't believe you're going to Rome without me, though. Text me when you land. I've missed you like crazy.

I missed you too. I'm so sorry for running out on you like this.

. . .

Don't worry about me. I'll be fine, and my handsome man is more than happy to play doctor for me.

I grimace. That was something I didn't need to know.

Speaking of playing doctor, you should find a hot Italian to play with while you're there.

I narrow my eyes at the phone, not impressed at all.

I'll be working, so probably not. I have to go now. The plane's boarding.

Have fun. No, seriously, have hot, sweaty fun, and then tell me all about it later. I love you.

I need to have a word with that woman. She's a bad influence on Nevaeh.

I put the car in reverse and head back to the cabin thinking all the while about what I'm up against. She's going to fight me, of course she will, but I'm hoping I can fuck her into my way of thinking and stop her from running again. How hard can it be? I know it won't be easy. But where there's a will, there's a way.

When I get back to the cabin, I climb out, shove my phone back in my pocket and turn Nevaeh's off before tossing it in the trunk. I slip my cut on before grabbing the laptop bag and the groceries, leaving the suitcase for now and head on up to the cabin on foot.

The rain has mostly stopped now, but I still look like a drowned rat. I open the door and step inside, panicking for a moment when I don't see her. But when I glance out the window, I spot her sitting on one of the couches on the covered deck, with a blanket around her shoulders. Letting out a relieved breath, I put the groceries away, leaving the pizzas on the counter, before I strip out of my cut and wet hoodie. I jog upstairs and grab a dry henley, slip it on and head outside to join her.

"Hey."

She jumps at the sound of my voice.

"Sorry. I was in my own little world."

"Nothing to be sorry about."

I walk over and sit beside her. She tries to move away, but I don't let her. Instead, I grab her and pull her onto my lap.

"Havoc."

"Cupcake."

"You've got to stop calling me that. I have enough nicknames," she huffs as I bury my nose in her hair.

"You smell like cupcakes." I groan. "Two seconds in your company, and all I want to do is rip your clothes off and taste you. I don't give a fuck what anyone else calls you. Nobody matters but me."

"Arrogant much?"

I nip at her skin with my teeth, making her shiver. "Not arrogant—confident. I know what I want, and I make sure I get it."

"And what do you want?"

"You."

She sighs. "Were you dropped on your head? Because that's the only thing that makes sense." She shifts in my lap to look at me, gasping when she feels my cock harden.

I grip her hips when she tries to move. "Stay right where you are." I thrust against her and watch as her cheeks turn pink and her breathing picks up.

"Havoc, this is a terrible idea."

"Tell me you don't want me."

"I don't—" I cut her off with a kiss, swallowing down her protests. When I pull back and see the glazed look in her eyes, I grin.

"Tell me, if I slipped my fingers inside you, I wouldn't find you wet."

"Nope, I'm dry as the desert. Nice try, though," she replies, not realizing she's grinding down on me.

"Is that right?"

Before she can say anything, I lift her and lay her back on

the couch, yanking her jeans off. The wind has died down, but it's still cool enough out to make her skin pebble with goosebumps. Grabbing her flimsy lace underwear, I tear them from her and shove the scrap in my back pocket. She tries to close her legs, but I use my body to pin her down. With her legs spread wide, I can see how wet she is for me.

"Havoc?" Her voice trembles, and I know exactly how to ease her fears.

I trail two fingers up her inner thigh before thrusting them inside her. She gasps, her back arching as I pull them free and lift them for her to see.

"Looks like your desert's a little moist there, Cupcake," I say, watching the flush spread across her cheeks.

"First of all, never say moist again. And second, I have a medical condition," she snaps defensively.

"Oh really? And what's this condition called?" I ask her with a smirk before I suck my fingers clean.

Her mouth drops open as she watches me.

"Careful, baby," I murmur. "I've been imagining all the things I could do with that mouth of yours. The thought of you on your knees, your lips wrapped around my cock..." I thrust my fingers back inside her, pressing them against the front wall of her pussy while pushing down on her groin.

"Havoc," she gasps, shaking her head, but I'm relentless, thrusting harder and faster. I see the panic in her eyes as she realizes her body's no longer hers—but mine.

"I need to stop. I need the bathroom. I need—"

"You need to let go, Cupcake. I've got you."

"I can't," she sobs, still shaking her head, her body trembling.

"Yes, you can, baby girl. Fuck, you smell so good. It's taking everything in me not to bury my cock deep inside you right now."

She screams, my words pushing her over the edge as she squirts, soaking my hand and the cushion beneath her.

As she comes back down, her eyes go wide in shock and horror. "Did I just..."

"You squirted, Cupcake," I growl as I bend down and wrap my hands around her thighs, lifting her so I can feast on her.

"Havoc!" she shouts as I drink her down. I'm so fucking turned on I'm two seconds away from coming in my pants.

"Such a sweet pussy. Watching you squirt was hot as fuck, but nowhere near as hot as finding the remains of your cherry on my cock."

"Oh, God." She covers her face with her hands, embarrassed, as I sit up and groan in pain. Okay, so I might've exaggerated just a little, but I get the reaction I'm after when she looks at me, worried.

"What's wrong?" she asks, sitting up.

I point to my cock. "I'm so hard it hurts."

"I didn't realize erections were painful," she says, her eyes wide.

I bite back a grin when I realize I can use her inexperience to my advantage. I groan again.

"Oh my God, Havoc, what can I do?"

"Nothing, Cupcake. It'll pass. Unless..."

"Unless what?"

"Unless you want to take care of it for me."

She rolls her eyes. "Havoc, this has already gone too far."

I grimace in fake pain.

She bites her lip. "Fine if it's that bad then feel free to get yourself off?"

"You don't mind?"

She snorts, not realizing she just played right into my hand.

"No, I don't mind."

"Thank fuck. I'm not sure how much more I can handle. You mind laying back down for me, Cupcake? Looking at your slick pussy will have me coming quickly."

She nods, then lays back and spreads her legs a little wider.

"That's my good fucking girl," I growl, freeing my cock. I grip it tight and begin fucking my fist. "Hold your pussy open for me, baby. Let me look at my prize."

Hesitantly, she does as I ask, using her fingers to hold herself open. I take in the sight of her swollen clit and her tight little hole that's begging to be filled and curse, unable to hold myself back. I get up on one knee and move closer to her pussy, my dick so close I can feel the heat of her pussy on my skin.

"I don't think—"

"Not going to fuck you, Cupcake," I grunt. "Just need to come."

I shoot my load all over her pussy, making her jump and gasp in surprise. The sight so fucking erotic that I pull my phone out of my pocket and take a picture of it.

"What the hell? I thought you forgot your phone!" She moves to sit up, but I hold her down.

"I found it in one of my saddle bags," I lie. "Relax. Nobody's seen your pussy but me, and nobody ever will. This is just for me. I'd never compromise you like that."

She narrows her eyes at me as I put my phone on the floor and slide my hand between her legs to distract her. She gasps as I start rubbing her pussy, slipping my finger and my cum inside her.

"Havoc," she says, sounding frustrated.

"Relax, baby. You can't get pregnant if you're not having sex. It's too cold outside the body for sperm to survive."

She cocks her head. "Really?"

"Sure," I grin, pushing more of my cum inside her as I picture her stomach swollen with my kid.

I've crossed so many damn lines today. I clearly left sane and rational back at the clubhouse, because this man right here is completely unhinged. I can't help it. This woman does something to me. I wanna treat her like a queen, but fuck her like a whore.

I barely know her, and with her being best friends with Amity, I should be treading carefully. But I can't. The second this woman's close, my control goes out the fucking window. It's like I'm an addict needing my next hit. And my drug of choice is apparently cupcakes.

I bend down and press a kiss to her stomach before helping her to her feet. "Why don't you jump in the shower and get cleaned up? There are some clothes in the closet up there, so find something comfortable to wear. I'll warm up the pizza and get us something to drink."

She looks up at me, but she doesn't argue as I guide her inside and up the stairs. I show her where the bathroom is and head back downstairs.

I walk over to the kitchen and brace my hands on the counter. Leaning forward, I blow out a steadying breath, telling myself to calm the fuck down. If I don't, I'm gonna end up in that tiny-ass shower up there with her. The urge to fuck her is so goddamn strong I'm not sure I could walk away if she said no. I want to pick her up and slide my cock inside her where it belongs.

I shake my head and look outside.

"I should've fucked her while I had the chance," I mutter. Because once she realizes this is her home until I say otherwise, she won't let me anywhere near her.

Which means I'll have to get creative.

Chapter Eight

Nevaeh

The bathroom's small, and that's saying something coming from me. Heck, it's only a little bigger than the one in the RV, but it has a bath with a shower above it which is one thing the RV doesn't have.

I lean against the cool tiles as the water runs down over me, wondering how I keep letting this happen. The first time, I could blame alcohol. But now?

I'm weak, dammit. So freaking weak.

In my defense I tried to be strong, but the man has magical hands. And just when I thought I was getting control of myself he went and played the 'she's so innocent card' and tried to bullshit me with how painful his erection was and how I couldn't get pregnant having sex outside rubbish. I write sexy books and watch porn like everyone else, for goodness sake. There is a big difference between innocent and naïve. I'd have laughed my head off if the whole thing hadn't turned me on. I'll admit, I'm a little confused by my reaction to it all, but clearly he got off on it as much as I did so I refuse to feel bad about it. I might even see how this thing plays out. As long as I don't have to wear pigtails and call him daddy, it might be fun.

"Ugh no Nevaeh, you're supposed to be resisting him." I mutter to myself. This is what Amity means when she says I'm the trouble maker. I don't agree that I make trouble, but lord knows I find myself in the middle off it far too often.

Damn biker voodoo.

Frustrated, I turn the shower off and climb out. I grab a towel and dry off without looking in the mirror, not wanting to see my reflection and her judgy eyes looking back at me. Wrapping the towel around my body, I make my way to the closet and rummage around until I find a comfy-looking T-shirt and a pair of boxer shorts. The idea of wearing his underwear feels strangely intimate, but since he ripped mine from my body, I really don't have much choice.

I shiver at the memory, and my cheeks heat up as I remember what happened after. I can't believe I squirted. I mean, I've read about it, but I never really thought it was a real thing outside of porn—kind of like those fourteen-inch penises that somehow don't end up sending women to the ER. Or the mythical G-spot that no real-life man can find without a map—and maybe the promise of a participation blow job just for trying.

Now I feel like I've been schooled—in the best and worst ways and I have some awesome ideas to add to my new book, if nothing else. I pause as a thought occurs to me. What if Havoc's the exception to mankind? What if he's just ruined me for all other men? Oh, God, what if I can never have an orgasm again?

"Okay, calm down, Nevaeh," I mutter, realizing that I'm starting to spiral.

At least there's something to put on the "con" list. Sexual contact with the man turns me into a crazy woman.

With a sigh, I put my bra back on and pull the T-shirt on over my head. It falls to just above my knee. Still, that doesn't mean I'm not going to wear the boxers. I pull them on, knowing they'll be too big, but they'll have to do. I don't trust Havoc not to storm the fortress again. The boxers might not stop him, but going with nothing would be like leaving the door wide open for him.

I pause at that analogy and wonder, not for the first time, how I became a writer.

Shaking my head, I take a deep breath and head downstairs, my stomach rumbling at the smell of pizza. I walk silently into the kitchen and watch Havoc as he washes something in the sink.

Every time I look at him, I have to pinch myself to make sure I'm not dreaming. We might not work outside my dreams, but there's no denying the man was created with sex in mind. His body is a work of art—muscles shifting with every movement, and a presence that fills the room. He's gorgeous, but not in a conventional way. He's far too rough around the edges for that. But there's no denying the primal, unfiltered energy the man exudes that would have women around the world lining up to bend over for him.

"Like what you see?" His deep voice makes me jump, and I silently curse myself for not being stealthier.

"I don't know what you're talking about."

"Baby, I could feel your eyes on me. You were staring so hard I'm surprised my pants didn't catch on fire."

I shake my head and look away so he doesn't see me blush. I hear him walk over to me, but I keep my eyes on the fridge magnet, which seems so out of place that I almost ask him where he got it.

"Cupcake, you can stare at me anytime you want. I promise I've never wanted to be objectified more than I do right now."

Despite my best intentions, I feel a grin tug at my lips as I turn to look at him. "You're ridiculous."

"I think you mean sexy." He smiles and picks up the two pizza boxes off the counter. "Table or sofa?"

I glance at the couch and picture us snuggled up together. "Table."

He smirks, like he knows exactly what I'm thinking—he probably does. We walk over to the table, and I sit as Havoc places the pizza boxes down. He pulls a chair out and drags it closer to me before opening the top box and sitting down.

"I wasn't sure what you liked, so I got a plain cheese pizza and a meat lover's."

"I'm not picky. Cheese is fine."

He moves the boxes so they're both open and picks up a slice of cheese pizza, handing it to me before taking a meat one for himself.

"So Amity says you're a writer?"

I frown at him. Amity usually keeps that to herself because she knows I don't like people knowing. But then, with the signing and everything, she probably thought it didn't matter anymore.

"Yeah."

"What do you write?"

"Romance novels."

"Really? I'll have to check them out."

"You read romance?" I cock my brow at that. I can't picture it.

"After being away for years, I learned to appreciate anything I could get my hands on," he admits. That's the second time him being away has been mentioned but he never says he went nomad. It makes me feel like I'm missing something.

"What do you mean when you say you were 'away'?"

He looks at me for a moment. "What did Amity tell you about me?"

"You're from another chapter, and your old lady was a b-word."

He snorts at that. "You can call her a bitch. It's true."

"I don't swear much, and I've never liked that word anyway."

"She slept with my brother and is expecting his kid."

"Okay. She's a bitch," I say, making him laugh. "So when you say 'away,' do you mean metaphorically or that you put distance between you?" I ask, taking a bite of my pizza.

"No, I mean I was locked away in a six-by-eight-foot cell."

I choke on my pizza, and Havoc curses, hitting my back as I cough uncontrollably. When that doesn't help, he grabs a bottle of water from the kitchen and hands it to me.

I swallow a few mouthfuls before looking at him, my eyes watering. "Explain," I rasp out, taking another drink of water.

He rubs his hand through his hair and sighs. "My brother was on his second strike when he got into a fight with someone and put him on life support."

"Okay. What did you do?"

"Nothing."

I scrunch my face, trying to understand what he's saying. But clearly, I don't.

"My president ordered me to take the fall for my brother."

My eyes nearly pop out of my head. "Are you kidding me? That... I... Why would your president do that? Why couldn't your brother serve time when he was the one who committed the crime? Wait! Did the guy survive?"

"Yeah, he woke up and made a full recovery."

"And you served five years for this? Five years that were your brother's to serve? That's crazy!" I shout, unable to hold back my outrage. His lips twitch at my reaction as he waits for me to calm down.

"I'm sorry. Go on," I say, trying to rein in my anger.

"No worries, Cupcake. Anyway, he would've served way more time. It was my first offense. And Khan—the president —he said he needed my brother for some big deal. He straight-up told me that if I didn't take the fall, I'd be kicked out of the club in bad standing, and every other club out there would turn their backs on me. It sounds stupid now, but this is the only life I've ever known. My father was a biker, and his father before him. It's a legacy I wanted to continue with my own kids. But instead, I ended up with a criminal record and an ex-old lady."

"I'm so sorry, Havoc... And I thought my family was messed up."

"I guess my family makes yours look tame, huh?" He chuckles, but I just shift uncomfortably.

He doesn't miss a thing, his face turning serious. "Or not. Talk to me, baby."

I close my eyes and let out a tired sigh. "It's not like it's a secret. Most of the guys at the club already know."

I start picking at the label on the water bottle, avoiding his gaze. "When I was ten, my twin sister was kidnapped from our front yard."

He curses, but I keep my eyes on the label I'm peeling.

"The only suspect was a man called Alan Ellwick, a pedophile who we found out lived nearby. He was killed when the police tried to question him. Apparently, he panicked and pulled a gun, forcing officers to open fire."

"Suicide by cop?"

I shrug. "He was wanted for questioning in another case, too, apparently, so maybe he knew he wasn't walking away this time. I don't know. What I do know is he died, taking all the answers with him. There was nothing for a couple of years. No body, no new witnesses or suspects, and not a single sighting. It's like she just vanished, and we had no choice but to exist without her in this awful state of limbo. Then, out of the blue, someone confessed."

I swallow hard, remembering the wild mix of emotions back then–relief, anger, hope, rage. "His name was Newton Helms. He was serving a four-year sentence for vehicular manslaughter. I thought it was finally over, but he was stabbed and killed inside before police could look into it."

"Did they think it was him?"

"Honestly, I don't know. He had no priors involving kids or violence, but there is always a first time. I tried to find some kind of peace with it all. If he was guilty, then at least his death meant he couldn't hurt any more little girls. Of course, I told myself the same about Alan."

He reaches over and slides his hand over my thigh, giving it a light squeeze.

"I know it's not much, but at least you can draw comfort from the fact they're both dead and likely rotting in hell."

"John Cyrus, Michael Perkins, Alfonso Ramiro, Daniel Waterman."

He frowns at me. "I don't know who they are Cupcake."

"Neither do I, but they all confessed to kidnapping my sister too. Each of them claiming to do unspeakable things to her. Police realized it was some kind of fucked up competition between inmates at various prisons. Nobody knows how they were communicating with each other. No letters or emails were found." I sigh, wondering, not for the first time what makes these animals the way they are.

"In the end people stopped listening to these random confessions and they eventually tapered off. By then the damage was done. My mom just couldn't handle it anymore and slit her wrists. And my dad... well, he couldn't look at me without seeing my sister. He couldn't stand to be near me, but he couldn't let me go either. He was stuck in the past, and I was stuck with him."

"Sounds like we were both in prison. I'm so fucking sorry, baby."

I give him a sad smile before looking back down at my hands. "Part of that's my fault. I gave in because it was easier than fighting with him. He had been through so much. I thought if I could make him happy, maybe he'd go back to being the dad I remembered—the one who loved me, not the one who just tolerated and resented me." A tear slips down my cheek, and I wipe it away.

"You know what's funny, though? People think you should just get over losing someone. That you're supposed to move on, live the life they couldn't, or some crap. What they don't understand is that the pain never goes away. It's always there, a living, breathing thing. You don't get over it—you learn to live with it. You adjust, but you're never the same. You walk with the ghost of your past beside you."

I turn to look at him, surprised to see the look on his face. It's like my pain physically hurts him.

"If I could take it away—"

"I wouldn't let you. The pain reminds me to breathe and that she was real. And even if every breath I take hurts without her, it's one more breath than she'll ever take."

He pushes his chair back and pulls me into his lap, wrapping his arms tightly around me. For a second, I'm not sure what to do. When was the last time someone held me? Amity does, sure, but it's not the same.

"I'm not sure why I told you all of that. Amity is the only person who knows it all. When people ask, we usually give them the simplified version—the pedophile was the main suspect and the cops killed him—end of story. The reality though, is there are so many loose threads that my whole life is just a tangled web of knots I stand no chance of unraveling."

"Thank you for telling me." He murmurs against the top of my head.

Even though I know I'm playing with fire, I slowly relax into his hold, wrapping my arms around him and resting my head on his shoulder, letting his warmth chase away the cold thoughts of my family.

We sit like that for I don't know how long before I lift my head and look at this strange, impossible man. Maybe in another life, if I were another girl, things would have turned out differently.

I kiss his lips, catching him by surprise, and slide off his lap while he's still in shock. "Now, while the weather seems to have calmed down, I think it's time you took me back."

He looks at me with an odd expression, one I can't read, but something about it has the hairs on my arms stand on end.

He gets to his feet and backs me up until I have nowhere else to go. "I didn't know about your sister, but I'm in too deep to back out now."

"What are you talking about?" I ask, frowning.

His nose skims across my cheek before he presses a soft kiss to my forehead. "I'm not going to hurt you, Cupcake. Not now, not ever."

"Havoc, you're freaking me out. What's going on?"

"I've decided I'm keeping you."

I stare at him for a moment before I burst out laughing. But when I see the look on his face, my laughter dies. "You're joking, right?"

"You won't give me a chance."

"Guess I was right not to," I snap, trying to shove him away, but it's like trying to move a mountain; he won't budge.

He trails his hand down and flicks my nipple, which immediately hardens. "Your body knows who it belongs to. I just need your brain to catch up. I'll be good to you, Nevaeh. There'll never be anyone who loves you like I will if you just give me a shot."

"Love? You've known me for half a fucking second."

"I thought you didn't swear," he teases.

"I don't murder people either, but there's a first time for everything."

He doesn't flinch at my threats, grabbing both my wrists and pinning them to the wall above my head. "I like it when you're feisty. I like it when you're sweet. I like it when you come on my cock and say my name."

"Well, you're gonna have to like it from five hundred fifty yards away, because when I get out of here, I'm going to shove a restraining order down your throat."

A grin spreads across his face, and he looks... happy. Honest to God happy when all I want to do is stab him in the eyeball with a pair of scissors.

"Look, if you let me go, I won't say anything. I'll pretend none of this happened. We'll leave and get you some help. Maybe some fancy pills with a name I can't pronounce. And one day, we'll look back on this and laugh."

"I hope so. It'll make one hell of a story to tell our grandkids."

My mouth drops open in shock, which he takes advantage of. His mouth slams down over mine, and his tongue invades my mouth, making my brain short-circuit for a minute before I remember I've basically been kidnapped.

I bite his tongue, hard, tasting blood.

He pulls back and smiles, blood staining his teeth. He looks like a fucking maniac. And even though I don't think he'll hurt me, I wasn't lying when I said I didn't know this guy.

"Havoc, please—"

"I'm going to leave you alone for a little while, give you a chance to get your head around everything. Your laptop bag is beside the couch, but there's no internet. If you get bored, the TV's got satellite. I'll be back tomorrow, and then we'll get started."

"Start what?" I whisper.

"We'll start making you and me an us."

Chapter Nine

Havoc

I grab my cut and hurry out. I call a cab and wait for it on the side of the road before heading back to the club-house. I should be focused on covering my ass, but instead, I can't stop thinking about a tiny, cupcake-smelling woman who looked ready to murder me when she realized I was serious.

Part of me thought she was going to chase after me with a knife as I pulled away, but she just stood there in total shock.

As much as I wanted to stay, I knew we had plenty of shit to deal with here. The guys have handled me taking over as president better than I thought they would, but it'll take time to prove that I'm worthy of the role. Not sure kidnapping

Nevaeh was the way to go, but I couldn't risk her getting away.

I get the driver to drop me off at the turning for the clubhouse. After paying him, I climb out into damp night and slip my cut back on. I walk to the gate, and nod to the prospect as he waves me through before stopping to talk to him for a moment.

"Hoops."

"Yeah, Hav— I mean Prez."

I wave him off. "It'll take a while, and I'm not gonna get pissed if you use my name. I do wanna ask you something, though. You know anyone who might be interested in prospecting? As good as you and Dice are, we need more than two prospects, or we'll burn you out."

"There were three of us, but..." His voice trails off, and I'm not sure why. Whatever went down must have happened before I got here. I'll ask G about it.

"Anyway, yeah, I know a guy who'd be interested. Name's Kieran Knight. I hadn't seen him since high school until a couple of weeks back when I ran into him at the bar. He enlisted and shipped out the day after graduation, but he's back now after being medically discharged thanks to a bomb wrecking his knee. He looked fucking lost. And if there's one thing Ravens are good at, it's collecting lost souls."

I nod. "Invite him to one of the parties and introduce me. I want to get a feel for him. If I think he's okay, I'll let him hang around for a while, see what he thinks, and we'll take it from there."

"Will do. Thanks, Prez."

I slap him on the shoulder before walking up to the warehouse. I spot my bike in its usual place just as Midas stomps in, looking like he's two seconds away from ripping his hair out.

"Problem?" I ask.

He looks my way and shakes his head. "Women. I swear I'll never understand them."

I chuckle. "Not sure we're supposed to."

He sighs before walking over to me.

"You see G and Amity today?"

"No. They're still holed up in their room. But G texted me earlier to let me know they were good, and I know he called down and had Dice bring them up some food."

"Can't say I blame them for hiding out for a little while. They deserve some fucking peace."

"Amen to that," he says as we leave the warehouse and head toward the clubhouse.

"Anything happen while I was gone?"

"Not much. I know the director from the movie called G."

"What did he want?"

"He didn't say much about it in his text. Just that he wanted to check on Amity and to let her know that production has been halted for a week, so everything's been pushed back, including when they'll film here."

"Shit I forgot about that."

"It's not the film crew that bothers me, but the cockroach reporters that will follow them here."

"They can follow them all they want, but they won't be getting through the gate, so it's a moot point."

"Moot point?" He grins. "Got a word-of-the-day calendar in prison, Havoc?"

I snort. "With a smart mouth like that, I can't imagine why you're having woman trouble."

"I didn't say I was having woman trouble. I said I didn't understand them. Big difference."

"You keep telling yourself that," I tell him as we head inside the club.

It's busy when we walk in, but the music's low for a change. People are still on edge after what happened. Even though the asshole responsible is dead, the fact that we came so close to losing not just Amity, but G too, doesn't sit well with any of us.

"Yo, Havoc, where you been?" Circus shouts. I look around and find him at one of the tables with Capone and Kruger.

"Visiting your mom," I yell back, and Kruger laughs as I make my way over, Midas right behind me.

"Anyone see Blade?" I ask when I reach the table.

"He's out back. Everything good?" Capone asks, looking at me.

"Yeah, all good, and thank fuck for that. I think we could all sleep for a week."

"Good luck with that. The movie crew is filming here soon," Crane tells me.

"Apparently, they've been delayed. I'll need to speak to G and find out what's going on."

Rapping my knuckles on the table, I leave Midas with the guys and head out back, finding Blade sitting at one of the tables underneath the large canopy with Sunshine, Inigo, and King.

"Hey, Havoc."

"Sunshine, looking beautiful as ever," I say, giving her a wink as I walk over and take a seat.

"I'd really hate to have to kill my new president right after Blade just handed you the crown and all," Inigo drawls, making me chuckle.

"Are you saying I'm not beautiful, Inigo?" Sunshine asks him, raising an eyebrow.

"I'm saying, if he wants to continue to see beautiful things, then he needs to keep his mouth shut."

I could pull rank, but I let it go.

"How you doing after yesterday?" Blade asks, ignoring Inigo.

"Wasn't me that nearly died."

"Not what I heard," King says, shocking me. Everyone

turns to look at him, but then that's King for you. There is something about him that just commands attention. It's what made him such a formidable president back when he ruled over the Kings of Carnage MC. He's also ex-CIA or FBI, if the rumors are true. He might not be Carnage royalty anymore, and he never officially became a Raven, but both clubs accept him as one of their own, for the most part. He might be getting up there in age, but there's no denying he's always one of the deadliest men in the room.

"Seems to me if Amity or G lost their footing, you were probably going over with them."

There was no probably about it, but I never gave it a thought until afterward. All I cared about was getting them both back on solid ground.

I shrug. "I knew the guys were coming. I wasn't worried." Mostly because I refused to consider the alternative and there was no fucking way I was letting that rope go.

"It was still ballsy. I can see why Blade chose you," King tells me, taking a swig of his beer.

"I'll take that as a compliment coming from you." I nod respectfully before turning back to Blade. "You talk to G today?"

"He called at lunch. Told me about what you two got up to last night." Ah, yes, the slicing and dicing of the traitors who ran Amity and G off the road.

"I figured he would."

"I've gotta stop reading. That sounded way dirtier than it

should've," Sunshine mutters, making Inigo growl. King grins, dropping his head to hide it, while Blade just shakes his head..

"And on that note, I gotta pee. Move it before I cause a flood. It's damp enough out here already." Sunshine nudges Blade, who stands up to let her out.

I smirk as she leaves, turning back to Blade, who's watching me clearly expecting more details.

I lean back and cross my arms over my chest. "You do remember I'm the president now, right? I don't answer to you anymore."

Inigo leans closer and whispers loudly. "That felt good, didn't it?"

"Oh, yeah."

"You're both dicks." Blade huffs.

"I know." I look around, making sure no one's listening, before leaning in and quickly filling them in on what happened.

"I'm surprised you all waited as long as you did to finish them off," King states when I'm done.

I shrug. "Amity could have been killed because of them. G deserved to finish it himself."

"I wasn't sure they'd say anything. Not until they realized no one was coming for them, and that Khan had hung them out to dry," Blade tells him.

"Well, they caved last night. They confirmed that Khan ordered the hit. And apparently, they went after G because they thought he was me. They heard I got tattoos in prison and confused the two of us."

"Were they fucking drunk?" Inigo asks, making me laugh.

"We pretty much said the same thing. Though I was closer to G's size the last time they saw me. I bulked up a lot in prison," I tell him, but he still shakes his head in disbelief.

"I don't get it," King says, and I turn to look at him. "Why now? You were inside for five years, thanks to Khan and your dickhead brother. Not to sound like a prick, but why not have someone take you out while you were inside? Grease a few palms, get a man on the inside with nothing left to lose, and none of us would've been the wiser."

"I think he thought I'd go home, and because I was fresh out of prison, I wouldn't want to rock the boat."

"Rock the boat? Fuck, I'd be more worried you'd set the boat and the clubhouse on fire." King chuckles.

"Because you're thinking logically," Blade grunts, and Inigo laughs.

"Me becoming president of the mother chapter wasn't part of whatever he had planned, that's for damn sure."

"That might've been the trigger," Inigo points out.

"So, what's your plan for that chapter?" Blade asks.

"I have an idea in the works, but for right now, I'm going to do nothing. As long as Khan's playing dumb, so will I. At least on the face of things. Behind the scenes will be a different story, I'll get G to do some digging. I need a lot more information before I declare war on one of our own fucking clubs. What I will say is Khan has to go. I can't let him stay in power. Not after this. Problem is, if we take him out, Driller's the next president. And he's not fit for the job."

"You need someone on the inside," King says, making me look at him.

"No one there's loyal to me."

"Maybe not, but everyone here is," Blade says, and I've gotta admit, it feels pretty fucking good to hear.

I rub my chin as an idea pops into my mind.

"You gonna tell us, or do we need to guess?" Blade snaps, making me stare at him.

"Right, fuck. Not the president anymore," he grumbles, grabbing his beer from the table and downing it.

"One option is sending in a brother in an official capacity — they can't refuse someone from the mother."

"If he's there officially, it'll offer him some protection because they'll know he's gotta check in. I don't know... I can't say I'm sold on it, but it's an option." Blade sighs.

"And someone like Kruger or Hannibal is crazy enough to volunteer for it," Inigo points out. "Any other options?"

"I heard you had another prospect up 'til recently."

"Hicks. We kicked him out after he pulled a gun on Amity and told her to suck him off if she wanted to walk outta here."

I snarl at the thought. Somehow, in such a short time, Amity's become like a little sister to me. The prospect's lucky he's gone, or I'd rip his fucking head off.

"After the beating me and G gave him, there's no way he'd help us out. And even if he offered, I wouldn't trust the bastard," Blade says.

"You don't actually need him," King cuts in, giving me a knowing look. "You just need someone to play him. Someone pissed at this club and looking for a little payback."

"Exactly. I asked Hoops if he knew anyone who might be interested in prospecting. He says he knows a guy fresh out of the military. He was discharged because of a knee injury."

"You wanna send him in as Hicks? We don't even fucking know this guy." Blade shakes his head.

"Sorry about that. I got hungry on the way back." I turn and see Sunshine with a bowl in her hand.

"What'd you get?" I stand to take a look and grimace.

She wraps her arms around her bowl and snarls at me. "Mine."

"Oh, trust me, it's all yours," I tell her, sitting back down.

Happy with my answer, she looks at Blade until he moves, then takes her seat. Once she's settled, King leans over and looks in the bowl.

"What is that?"

"Scrambled eggs, raisins, and hot sauce." She smiles. "It's so good. But without the hot sauce, it'd be weird."

"Sure, that would be weird," I mutter.

"It's better than the Brussels sprouts and chocolate syrup she was into last week," Inigo says.

"You sure she's carrying humans? Because that shit isn't normal." I lean over to ask King.

Sunshine must hear what I said because she turns her head slowly, looking at me like some kind of demonic doll ready to slit my throat.

"You know, I just remembered. I need to take care of a thing." I get up and leave, ignoring their laughter.

Not many things scare me. I've lived through too much, but pregnant women... they're fucking terrifying.

I wonder what Cupcake's gonna be like when she's pregnant.

I stop at the thought. Her getting pregnant right now is a fucking awful idea. But the thought of her round with my baby has my dick ready to punch through my jeans.

For the next couple hours, I hang out with the others, making sure I'm seen even if I'm not mentally here. When midnight strikes, I say my good nights and head out.

I'm only so strong. As much as Cupcake needs space right now, I need to be close to her. I head back to the cabin, parking my bike next to her car so I can grab her suitcase from the trunk. I pick up her phone and turn it on, sending a message to Amity complaining about the cell service. I tell her I've landed safely and that I'll message her in a few days before turning her phone off again, just in case G gets the wild idea to trace it.

I lock the trunk and strap the bag to my bike before riding the rest of the way back to the cabin. The lights are all off when I pull up. I park farther away than before—just in case she comes running out and slashes my tires.

An ominous rumble followed a few moments later but a flash of lightning tells me the earlier rain was just a preview. This must be the storm that was forecast. I had hoped it had passed us by, but I can think of worse things than being holed up here with Nevaeh. Not sure she'll feel the same way though.

Another flash of lighting illuminates the sky but the cabin stays dark and quiet. I climb off my bike and unstrap the suitcase before making my way to the front door. I open it and curse. I don't usually bother locking the place because nobody comes out here—still, there's always a risk. and I won't gamble with Nevaeh's safety. I'll have to get her a key made for when I have to leave so she can lock it. I sure as hell can't leave her with a gun—she's just as likely to shoot me as she is an intruder.

I step inside and close the door behind me, reaching for the light switch as I set the suitcase down on the floor. I flick the light on and freeze. Nevaeh's standing in front of me, with a carving knife in her hand, pointed at my dick.

Chapter Ten

Nevach

They say absence makes the heart grow fonder, and maybe it would have if he'd stayed the fuck away from me. Yet here he is, hours later, and all it's made me want to do is maim the asshole.

"Now, Cupcake, you don't want to hurt me. Put the knife down."

"Hmm... Let me think about that... Nope, I don't think I will. I think you need to take me home before I pull a Lorena Bobbitt on you."

"You might hate me right now, but you like my dick, so maybe aim for my heart instead."

"I would if I thought you had one," I snap.

"Ouch, that hurts, baby. You wound me." He covers his

heart with his hand and grins as a boom of thunder makes me jump.

"It's not funny. I'm mad, Havoc. So beyond mad, mad doesn't even come close to how mad I am."

He takes a step closer, his expression softening. "I get it, Cupcake. And you've got every right to be pissed at me. What I did was fucked up."

I relax a little. "So you'll take me home?"

"I never planned to keep you here forever." He chuckles. "Just long enough for you to fall in love with me. But now I know I'll have to try something else."

Finally, I let out a sigh of relief and drop the knife, letting it crash to the floor before I accidentally cut myself with the damn thing. He picks it up and takes it back to the kitchen, dropping it into the sink.

"I'll just run upstairs to grab a hoodie or something to wear home."

"It's late and it's raining again. It's best if we stay here tonight."

I open my mouth to protest, but he slips off his cut and places it over the arm of the couch.

"The storm is rolling in and I'm exhausted after the last couple of days. I'd never forgive myself if I had an accident and hurt you or someone else."

"Fine." I sigh, lifting my hand and pointing my finger at him. "But we're leaving tomorrow, Havoc. No excuses."

I spin around, stomp upstairs to the bedroom, and climb

into bed. I'd been tossing fitfully when I heard his bike pull up, jumping at every noise or creak the house made. When Havoc walks up and starts getting undressed, I pull the covers up to my chin and tuck them tight around me.

"You can sleep on the couch," I mutter.

He doesn't reply, but I know he heard me. So, I'm not surprised when he ignores me and climbs in behind me, pulling me back into him.

"This isn't the couch, Havoc."

"I sleep with my woman." He buries his face in my hair and sighs, content.

"I am not your woman."

"Yet," he murmurs.

The rain lashes against the windows as I stare at the alarm clock beside the bed and watch as the numbers change from 1:32 to 1:33, then from 1:34 to 1:35. The last twenty-four hours have felt like they were a month long. Part of me wonders if I died in a plane crash on the way to London, and this is all some twisted version of the afterlife. I shift slightly, and his arms tighten around me.

Eventually, his arms loosen, and I know he's asleep. Even though I can pull away now, I stay where I am, trying to figure out exactly where things started to go wrong. After an hour of replaying everything in my mind, it all comes back to one person:

Hoops.

The stupid prospect that got me drunk. If it weren't for

him, I'd still be living my quiet little life as Amity's sidekick, slowly building up the courage to stand up to my dad. But now, because of that man and his stupidly delicious drinks, I'm no longer a virgin, and I've lost most of my self-respect.

The question is: where do I go from here?

What Havoc's proposing is ridiculous. Once he comes to his senses, he'll move on to someone more suitable. I'm okay with that, but I won't be if this goes on much longer. The longer it does, the more I worry that I'll fall for him, only for him to break my heart. And I've had enough heartbreak to last a lifetime.

With my mind racing, and panic flooding my system, I ease out of bed and head downstairs. I flick the light on above the stove so I don't wake up Havoc but freeze when I see his bike keys on the counter. I look up at the bedroom. He told me he'd take me home in the morning, but something tells me it won't be quite that easy.

Sliding my sneakers on, I grab the keys and open the door, wincing when it creaks. I pause, listening for Havoc's footsteps, but when I don't hear them, I slip outside into the rain and carefully close the door behind me.

The rain soaks me before I've taken more than a few steps, the sound of everything else is drowned out under the onslaught of the storm. I have no business being outside in this weather wearing next to nothing but I have to get out of here, even if some part of me rejects the idea.

I make my way down the front steps, tripping on the

bottom one and nearly face-planting. The rain is one thing, but the lack of streetlights makes everything ten times worse.

Once I've righted myself, I slowly head toward the bike, praying I don't step on a snake or something. Now that I've considered that possibility, I can't unthink it.

I breathe a sigh of relief when I reach out and feel the bike under my palm. But then doubt creeps in. There's no way I can ride this thing. My legs aren't long enough to keep it balanced, and it's too noisy. I'd have to wheel it in the dark, far enough away from the cabin, so Havoc doesn't hear me. Let's not forget that I'm not dressed to ride and soaked to the bone.

I tap my chin, trying to come up with a plan.

"Stealing someone's bike is a criminal offense."

I jump at the sound of Havoc shouting, letting out a sound that's somewhere between a dying cat and a mating dolphin as my heart tries to beat out of my chest.

"So is kidnapping but I wasn't stealing it anyway," I lie.

"My mistake. What were you doing then?"

"Admiring it?" It comes out more like a question than I meant it to.

"In the dark?"

"I like the way the moonlight catches it," I tell him, grimacing when I realize it's too cloudy for any moonlight.

"In the rain?"

"It looks pretty when it's wet." Lord I made myself cringe with that one.

I sense him move, but he's quiet—far too quiet for a guy his size to be. I curse when I feel his hand on mine, taking the keys from me. A moment later, his hands are on my T-shirt, pulling it off over my head. I went to bed braless, and now my breasts are completely exposed to the night air.

"What the hell are you doing?" I demand, instinctively lifting my hands to cover my chest, but he grabs my wrists, pinning them at my sides.

"Admiring you in the moonlight, you look so pretty when you're wet," he teases, his voice low and playful before his mouth is on my nipple.

I gasp, squirming against his hold as heat floods my body. The rain pelts down on us, cooling my overheated skin, making me shiver, but I ignore it as he sucks and bites the sensitive bud. When he lets go of my wrists, my hands go to his head, tangling in his wet hair as he moves on to my other nipple, lavishing it with the same attention as the other.

He stands back up and pulls me to him. "You're naked!" I choke out.

"Well, would you look at that? You know what that means, don't you? You're overdressed."

Before I can protest, he yanks my boxer shorts down my legs and spins me around, bending me over his bike. I grab hold of the seat to keep from falling. When I try to stand back up, he leans over me, the hard press of his cock nestled against my ass.

Despite my need to stop this madness, I feel my pussy

growing slick. How can I want this man inside me and want to set him on fire all at the same time?

"Tell me you don't want this, Cupcake," he shouts over the roar of rain as he bends his legs and pushes the tip of his cock inside me.

"I don't—"

He surges into me, cutting off my words and stealing my breath. I don't know how the bike doesn't fall over, but I don't have time to think about it as one of his hands grabs my hip and the other wraps my hair around his fist.

Fuck, this man is huge. Words like *impaled* and *invaded* spring to mind at the bite of pain when he bottoms out, making the pleasure feel so much sweeter as he fucks me hard and deep.

The pounding rain hides the sounds of how wet I am, proof that my head might not be entirely on board, but my vagina is more than happy to ride the big dick express. With every move, Havoc reminds me just who's in control here.

"I don't know if I should let you come," he grunts, thrusting harder. "You were going to leave me."

As crazy as it might seem, I swear I can hear hurt in his voice.

"I wasn't," I lie, desperate to come.

"You promise? You promise you won't leave me?"

"I promise," I shout before I realize he said *won't*—sneaky bastard.

He slides his hand between my legs and strokes my clit,

the pleasure overwhelming. As my back bows and legs shake, the first real tendril of fear wraps around me—not because I think he'd hurt me, but because I'm not sure I'll survive him.

He comes with a roar, triggering my orgasm just as lighting illuminates the night sky. His talented fingers keep working, pushing me until I'm barely holding on and begging for mercy. Only then does he stop.

He picks me up and carries me back inside and straight up to bed. I protest when he lays my soaking wet body down on the bed, but he ignores me. He climbs on the bed with me, yanking the thick comforter over us both. He moves me so I'm laying on top of him, before he nudges his cock back inside me.

"Havoc."

"Tomorrow. I need sleep."

"I need to clean—"

"You sleep with my cock and my cum inside you," he grunts.

Even though I know it's a bad idea, I'm too tired and cold to argue and Havoc is just warm. In the end I give in but the sleep I so desperately need is fleeting. Every time I drift off, I wake up to him fucking me and filling me up again. By the time morning rolls around, I feel sore and swollen.

And still, he fucks me.

"I can't, Havoc, please," I beg, tears falling as he leans over me.

"One more. Just give me one more, Cupcake."

I start to shake, crying out as I come again, sobbing.

"There's my good fucking girl." He kisses me softly as he comes once more.

Too weak to move, he picks me up and carries me into the bathroom, sitting me on the toilet before running me a bath. I don't even have the strength to be embarrassed as I pee. He adds some kind of salt and bubble bath, then disappears, returning with a couple of towels and a glass of water. He places the towels on the counter and hands me the water, which I drink down with shaky hands.

I watch him warily as he grabs some toilet paper and forces my legs apart. I choke on my water and protest, but he ignores me and wipes me before flushing. My face flames with embarrassment as I look away, tears threatening to fall.

Still, without a word, he takes the glass from my hand and sets it on the counter before lifting me into the tub. I bring my knees to my chest and focus on the bubbles. Out of the corner of my eye, I see him grab a cloth and some body wash. When he moves toward me, I suck in a sharp breath.

He hesitates for a second, slipping his finger under my chin and tipping my head back. "Last night was intense. Let me look after you."

I swallow, but I don't say no, afraid my voice might crack. I sit silently as he gently washes me, even taking the time to shampoo my hair before helping me rinse it.

When he's done, he rests his forearms on the edge of the

tub and looks at me. "You tried to run. You tried to leave me," he says softly.

"You kidnapped me, Havoc. Now I want to go home. You told me you'd take me home."

"I can't go back to prison, Nevaeh," he tells me gently, but the weight of his words lands like a punch to the stomach.

"Are you going to kill me?" I whisper.

He looks at me like I'm insane. "I don't fuck dead bodies, and I'm not about to stop fucking you anytime soon. So no, I'm not going to kill you. But I need to know you'll keep your mouth shut about all this when I take you back, and you need to know I won't hurt you. I might spank you if you put yourself in danger, though, but that's only because I need you to think twice before making reckless decisions."

"Like getting on the back of your bike and allowing myself to be kidnapped?" I huff, feeling slightly less terrified now that I know he isn't going to kill me. When he doesn't answer, I back down. "So what happens now?"

He swirls his fingers around in the water before he answers,

"The storm is still raging outside and is set to last for the best part of a week. It's not safe to be out there. You'll stay here with me, and we'll get to know each other."

"For a week?"

"For two."

"Two weeks? I can't stay here for two weeks. Amity will worry."

"I'll talk to Amity. There will be times when I have no choice but to go back to the clubhouse, but it's safer if I don't have to maneuver both of us on these slick roads."

"I get that and I'll agree to a week, but if the storm will have passed by then, there is no reason to stay any longer than that."

"A week isn't enough time Nevaeh. I can't explain why I need you here and I know I sound like a crazy asshole. I just need you to do this for me. I promise that when I'm here, you'll have my full attention—and I expect all yours in return. We'll get to know each other without all the distractions that come with club life. And for the short periods that I'm gone, you can write or read and just relax."

"And once the two weeks are up, you'll take me back?"

He nods.

"Swear it Havoc. If you agree to this and you lie to me and don't let me leave, I'll never trust you again."

"I swear I'll take you back two weeks from today, no matter what."

I sigh, knowing I really don't have a choice.

"Okay, Havoc. I'll stay."

Chapter Eleven

Havoc

Do I feel bad about manipulating her into staying? Fuck no. If the storm hadn't given me the perfect excuse, I'd have found some other reason to keep her here.

After she got out of the tub, I made sure she had everything she'd need for her stay—laptop, notepads, and Kindle. Without the internet, she was limited in what she could do, but it was better than nothing.

For the last five days, I made excuses for my absence at the clubhouse and again, the storm provided me with the perfect out. I filled those days mostly in bed with Nevaeh as we explored every inch of each other's bodies.

Unfortunately, the storm had eased off today. As the club

is on alert, still waiting to see if Khan would make another move, my presence was needed in church so we could run over strategies and contingency plans for the inevitable.

"Anyone have anything else they need to add?" I ask the room of brothers.

"Stefan called," G says, leaning back in his chair.

"Stefan?" Conan asks.

"The director of the movie Amity was working on. He wants to know if we can fit him in next week."

"I thought they were delaying shit because of what happened." Probe frowns. "A week isn't much of a delay."

"Apparently, the studio wants to cash in on all the attention the movie is getting. I guess to them, there is no such thing as bad publicity." G shakes his head

"How does Amity feel about this?"

He shrugs, "You know Amity, nothing much fazes her. Besides, her part in all this is over. Stefan said that they just want to come in and film a few location shots for authenticity. I get the feeling they want out of this place as much as we want them gone."

I blow out a tired sigh, wishing I was back at the cabin.

"With Khan's shit hanging over us, it makes sense to get this over and done with. The last thing we want is for anything to go down when there are camera crews around. All in favor of giving Stefan the go-ahead?"

Everyone votes yes, and with nobody having anything else to add, I end church.

Everyone files out leaving just me and G behind.

"You good?" He asks as I get to my feet.

"Yeah. Why?"

"Haven't seen much of you lately."

"You've been busy with Amity, and I've had shit to deal with."

"Anything I can do?"

I look at the man and shake my head. If he knew what, or should I say who I'd been doing, he'd be pissed. He thinks of Nevaeh as a sister so he was less than impressed when I told him we'd slept together.

"Another week or so, and I'll be back in the game, I might need you to hold down the fort for a little while until then."

"Yeah sure."

I slap him on the back and head out to the bar. I have a quick drink with the guys, then head out again, stopping to pick up a few things before heading back to the cabin.

I hate leaving Nevaeh alone for too long, even though I knew it was necessary. The only way I was able to leave at all was because I knew that nobody knows anything about my grandfather's old place. Hell, I never even told Lola about it or brought her there. Maybe I always knew how this would go down with her and just didn't want to admit it.

As I pull up outside the cabin, I stew on the fact I only have nine days left with her, and she's still holding herself back from me. We've talked some, always sticking to safe topics. But when we fucked, we fucked like it might be our last time. I pray that never happens because I crave this woman more than anything I ever have before.

I take the gifts from my saddlebag and head to the door, as the wind whips around me. Finding it locked; I smile before fumbling in my pocket for the key. I open it and step inside, thankful to be back out of the cold. I find Nevaeh asleep on the couch with a throw blanket over her legs and her laptop open beside her.

Placing the flowers and the books on the counter, I make my way over to the couch and crouch down next to her, staring at her for a moment—fuck, she's beautiful. I trail my fingers across her cheek. She doesn't stir, so I leave her be, knowing it's my fault she's so tired; I've been keeping her awake night and day.

I lift her laptop and carry it over to the table. Kicking off my boots, I scroll through to see what she's been up to and find an open document.

I glance at Nevaeh, then back at the screen. I start reading, and before I know it, I'm lost in the story—getting fucking rock hard when I realize one of the scenes is loosely based off the other night when I fucked her over the bike. Only this time the couple fuck over a balcony during a storm. I look at my girl and smirk. I'm more than happy to be her inspiration.

I leave the laptop open on the table—I don't risk shutting it in case she needs to save her work—and head into the kitchen to find a vase for the flowers. Naturally, I don't have ne. Why would I? I settle on a tall drinking glass and add the flowers to it before setting it on the counter, then get to work making us something to eat.

I open the fridge and grab everything I'll need to make chicken Alfredo. It's been a while since I made it, but it's not something you forget. I liked cooking before I went to prison, but I'd be lying if I said that most of it didn't fall to Lola. There was always some crisis at the clubhouse or with my brother that kept me tied up.

Hearing movement, I turn and see a groggy Nevaeh heading my way. I walk around the counter and grin when she walks right into me. I wrap my arms around her, and she lets out a contented sigh.

"Mmm... You're warm."

"I can turn the temperature up if you're cold," I say, pulling back. I look down at her and see that she's wearing her Care Bear sweatshirt again, this time with a pair of black leggings. On her feet are a pair of fluffy socks with strawberries printed all over them.

"No, I'm okay. It's mostly my feet. Mmm... What are you making? It smells amazing."

"Chicken Alfredo. I thought we could eat and watch a movie. There's a stack of DVDs. Or if you want, we could do something else—the cupboard beside the TV is full of games."

"Sounds good. I'll go look—" She stops talking, staring at something behind me. I turn and see she's spotted the flowers.

"For you," I say, looking back at her.

"Really? Nobody's ever brought me flowers before."

"Good, I like having all your firsts."

She smiles, and I reach behind me to grab the two books I brought, too.

"I don't know if they're the type of books you read or not, but I saw them and thought of you."

She stares at the books in my hand before she looks up at me. "You bought me books?"

"You like to read, right?"

She doesn't say anything, and I'm worried I've messed up somehow, but then she launches herself at me, wrapping her arms around me. Okay, note to self: books are her kryptonite.

"Thank you, Havoc."

"You're welcome, Cupcake." I press a kiss to her forehead and watch as she walks back over to the couch, hugging the books to her chest.

I go back over to the stove, but I'm aware of every move she makes. Once the food's done, I take everything to the table and call Nevaeh over to eat.

"So, how's the book coming along?"

"Good. I'm almost done. I can't remember the last time a book's flowed this easily."

"Maybe I should kidnap you more often."

She glares at me, and I chuckle, taking a bite of my food.

She lifts her fork and groans as she takes a mouthful of food, and fuck, if that doesn't make my cock throb.

"This is so good."

"I'm glad you like it."

We eat in comfortable silence. When she stands to grab the plates, I stop her. "I've got it. You go pick the movie or game. Whatever you want." I smile at the dumbfounded look on her face and carry the dishes to the kitchen.

After I finish washing the dishes and cleaning up the kitchen, I microwave some popcorn and grab a couple of bottles of water from the fridge. Once the popcorn's done, I walk to the couch and sit down next to her, setting the bottles on the table.

"I feel like watching a movie. But we can do games tomorrow, maybe?"

"Whatever you want." I lean back, place the popcorn on my lap, and wrap my arm around her, pulling her so her head rests on my chest. She hits play on the remote and snuggles in closer.

I should've known she was up to something—she was being just a little too sweet. Instead, I'm halfway through *The Notebook* when I realize she played me.

"Enjoying the movie?"

"Sure am," I say, even though I know she's trying to make me suffer.

After *The Notebook*, we watch *How to Lose a Guy in Ten Days* and then *Notting Hill*. I didn't even know I had these DVDs. There must've been a bunch of Lola's in the box I brought here.

I look down to ask if she's done torturing me but find her fast asleep. I watch her for a moment. This—her tucked into me—is what I'm fighting for—these unguarded moments when she gravitates toward me.

I turn off the TV and ease out from underneath her, picking her up and carrying her to bed. She stirs when I take her clothes off but doesn't say anything. She reaches for me, her mouth finding mine in the dark.

I strip out of my own clothes and pull her on top of me, positioning myself at her entrance. I ease myself inside her, slow and steady, until I'm buried completely. Her warmth wraps around me, and for a moment, nothing else matters.

She murmurs something but doesn't move. I run my fingers up and down her back as my eyes drift closed, ever conscious that time is not on my side.

* * *

The next eight days flew by, but something shifted after our movie night. Nevaeh let her guard down. She let me in. And even though I hate talking about myself, I did the same.

We got to know each other during the day, talking and sharing pieces of ourselves, and our nights were spent tangled in each other. But now, on day thirteen, there's this desperation in our lovemaking—like we're trying to hold on to every moment and make every second count. I'm worried it's Nevaeh's way of saying goodbye.

With her head resting on my chest, she trails her fingers

across my skin, tracing my tattoos, teasing the scattering of hair.

She pauses when she reaches the twisted thorns over my heart. "Is that a cupcake?"

I grin, wondering when she would spot it. Most people only notice the thorns, not the tiny cupcake they're protecting.

"I told you, you were meant for me."

"And you got a prison tattoo to mark the occasion huh? You sure know your way to a girls heart," she teases.

I roll her over and tickle her making her laugh and wriggle trying to get free.

"Mercy, mercy!" She gasps as I kiss her.

Pulling back, I tuck her hair behind her ear, so I can memorize every freckle on her face before I roll back over and tug her into my arms.

A comfortable silence settles over the room for a few minutes before she speaks again.

"I like how quiet it is here but it's been weird not having my phone,"

"No signal out here," I repeat what I told her the first time she asked about her phone.

"What did you tell Amity? There's no way she wouldn't freak out about me being out of contact for more than a few days."

I tense, and she feels it. She lifts her head and looks at me.

"Our time here is up, Havoc. You might as well tell me.

You said we were working on trust—no more lies. Not tonight."

I sigh, running a hand through my hair. "Your phone's in the trunk of your car, down the road."

She blinks, and then starts laughing. "My car and phone have been there the whole time?"

"Yeah."

"Of course they have. And is there really no signal here?"

"I mean... it's kinda spotty."

She groans and drops her head.

Taking a breath, I tell her the rest—I tell her about going through her phone, the messages I sent to Amity, pretending to be her, and lying about her being in Rome.

"What am I going to do with you?"

"Stay with me."

She lifts her head back up, and this time, she looks sad.

"We can't stay here forever. We need to go back."

"No, I know. I mean, stay with me outside this place. Be mine, Nevaeh. Think of this as extreme dating if you want to."

"I'm so mad at you right now. I want to scream at you and punch you and kick you and just... urgh."

"I get it," I tell her. I fucked up. I knew it the second I took her, but I just don't regret it.

"The problem is, I'm not just angry anymore."

I stroke her shoulder with my fingertips as she takes a deep breath. "You make me feel things I've only ever read

160

about before. You cook for me, buy me books—*which I do every day*—and you watch chick flicks without complaining. You take care of me, and other than Amity, I'm not sure I can remember the last time someone really did that."

I slide my hand into her hair and pull her down until her lips are a breath from mine. "I dreamed about you when I was in prison. In my heart, I knew Lola and me were over before I ever found out about her and Driller. Aside from the fact she never came to visit, I was already half in love with you, and I wasn't even sure if you were real or a figment of my imagination. Either way, you're the reason I held on. I just didn't know it then."

"What do you mean you dreamed of me? I don't understand."

"I'm not sure I do either," I admit. "I got this tattoo after waking up with the taste of you on my lips and the smell of vanilla cupcakes in the air. I thought I was imagining it. Then I got out, and there you were—in my bed." I brush her hair from her face, letting my fingers linger. "I know this is all new and scary for you, but for me, it feels like I've been waiting a lifetime."

I kiss her softly, pouring everything I'm feeling into it before pulling back. "I need you to be mine because I'm already yours."

A tear slips down her cheek, and she bites her lip. "I'm scared. I know you won't physically hurt me, but..." She swallows hard, her voice trembling. "What about my heart?"

"I can't promise I won't upset you or make you mad, but I will always be careful with your heart."

She groans, squeezing her eyes shut. "I'm going to regret this. I know I am."

I freeze. "You're saying yes?"

"I'm saying yes."

I flip us so she is underneath me, and I can stare down at her. "You're mine."

"I'm yours."

And then I fuck her until she passes out, turning her yes into a promise I won't ever let her break.

Chapter Twelve

Nevaeh

I lied to my best friend. I told her I was sick for most of my trip and spent it in bed. And then, when it came to the signing itself, I told her I was crazy busy and glad to be home and then changed the subject.

I felt crappy lying, but I knew if I told her the truth, not only would she murder Havoc in his sleep, but it would cause problems between Havoc and G.

So, for the almost two weeks we'd been back, I acted like nothing happened, but we didn't hide the looks we kept giving each other. After all, I have to make it believable for when Havoc snaps and kisses me in public. It's going to happen, I can tell. He's been riding the edge of violence for days.

"Look, I just need some air, okay?"

"So go sit outside. You'll find all the air you want," Havoc says.

I step up to him and snarl. "Do not make me hurt you, Havoc. I need to get out of this place for a little while." I pause, taking a deep breath. "I was thinking of going for a drive into town." I lower my voice so only he can hear the rest. "I'm coming back, I promise."

He looks down at me, and for a moment, I swear everyone holds their breath. His lips twitch, then, before I know what's happening, he bends down and kisses me. That damn rat bastard—I should've known. He pulls back, grinning as catcalls ring out around us.

"Hoops!" he yells, not taking his eyes off me.

"Yes, Prez?" Hoops walks out from behind the bar, wiping his hands on a towel.

"Follow my old lady into town. Anything happens to her, and I'll rip your spine out your throat."

"Yes, Prez," he replies without hesitation.

I roll my eyes and sigh. "You just couldn't help yourself, could you?"

"I'm done pretending, and I'm sick and fucking tired of everyone here eye-fucking you. Now they know you're mine, and if I catch them staring again, I'll scoop their eyeballs out and boil them."

"You seriously need therapy."

"Don't need anything but you, Cupcake."

He pulls me in for another kiss, then steps back. "Wait here."

He disappears into his office and comes back holding something. I don't realize what it is until he holds it out for me to see—a cut. The Raven Soul patch is stitched on the back, and underneath it, the words *Property of Havoc*.

"When on earth did you get this made? Amity doesn't even have hers yet."

"Hers came in today with yours. You know me, baby—I don't mess around."

He turns it and holds it so I can slip my arms in. I hesitate for a second, biting my lip. His jaw ticks as he waits. Rejecting him in front of his brothers would be a brutal blow.

Damn it. In for a penny, in for a pound.

"Don't make me regret this."

"Never," he vows, helping me put it on.

The room erupts in cheers, and people come over to offer their congratulations.

"Amity's gonna kill me for not telling her about us and you for making her miss this."

He just shrugs and gives me a quick kiss. "Now go before I change my mind. And be careful. Just because Khan hasn't made a move yet doesn't mean he won't."

"I know." I sigh. "I'm just going to pick up our food."

"Still need you to be careful."

"Yes, Daddy." He gives me a wicked grin, so I cover his

mouth with my hand. I like playing the sweet and naïve virgin with him, but I have my limits.

"No. That's not happening, so get the idea out of your head."

"Ready, Tink?"

I turn to Hoops and sigh. "Nobody's ever going to call me Nevaeh again, are they?"

"Welcome to the club," he says, smiling—until Havoc crosses his arms, and Hoops' smile drops.

"I'll meet you at the gate," Hoops tells me and hurries away.

I hit Havoc's chest. "Was that necessary?"

"What?"

I give him a look. "He didn't do anything."

"He was looking at what's mine," he says, wrapping his arms around me. I roll my eyes.

Crane chuckles as he stand beside us. "Can't blame a guy for looking."

"No, but I can make it so he never looks again."

Crane just laughs, and I pull out of Havoc's arms. "I'm going now. I won't be long."

"Stay safe."

"I will," I reply, hurrying to leave before he changes his mind.

As I step outside, I take a deep lungful of fresh air. Since got back, he's barely let me out of his sight. For someone ɔends a lot of time alone, it's been... well, a lot.

He thinks I'll change my mind and run. I can see it in his eyes every time I look at him. But the thing is, the more time I spend with him, the deeper I fall. Running isn't an option anymore. Honestly, I don't think it ever really was.

Lil and Legs catch up to me as I head down the slope toward the warehouse. "We just wanted to say congrats. I think you're exactly the kind of woman he needs," Legs says, giving me a quick hug.

"She's right," Lil agrees. "I won't lie—I didn't see it at first, but you two just work."

"Well, here's hoping I don't strangle him anytime soon."

Lil laughs. "He's driving you nuts already?"

"He's intense, I get that. But, God, I can pee on my own, dammit. I swear, every time I turn around, he's there."

I look behind me and throw my hands up in the air when I see him watching me from the saloon doors. "Oh, come on!" I say as Legs and Lil laugh.

"Alpha males don't understand the concept of space. They want you where they want you, and that's that."

"Speaking from experience?" I ask.

Legs rolls her eyes. "Midas is the worst of them, but I don't have one of these." She tugs my cut. "So it's a little different for us. He's bossy, but he's not possessive of me because I'm his, it's just a biker thing." She winks, and even though she's joking, I know it hurts her that there isn't something more between them. I can't imagine loving someone who can't see what's right in front of them.

"I better go. Hoops is waiting for me. I'll catch you both later."

"You too. And, Nevaeh..." Finally, someone uses my name. "He might be the top dog, but you're the queen. Make the man work for it," Legs says before slipping her arm through Lil's and turning to head back to the saloon.

I grumble about insufferable men as I head to the diner, cursing Havoc for making me bring a bodyguard and Hoops for being said bodyguard when I'm still mad at him for getting me into this mess in the first place. I've tried to let it go because I'm an adult, and it all worked out in the end, but mentally, I'm still sticking my tongue out at the big stupid-headed asshole.

Not that he's helping change my opinion of him. I just wanted five minutes of peace. Instead, I had to sit there watching Hoops flirt in that noisy-ass bar, of all places. Are five freaking minutes of peace too much to ask for? Well, we're about to find out.

I wonder how long it will take the prospect to realize I've left without him? I guess it depends on if he can pull himself away from the bartender's boobs. I'm sure he'll come looking for me eventually, not wanting to risk Havoc's wrath.

I slow my steps and sigh. I don't want Hoops to get into trouble just because I'm mad. As I pass the alleyway where the dumpsters are, I see a homeless man huddled on the ground with a blanket wrapped around his head and body. It's not too cold today, but it did rain earlier, and I can only imagine that being wet makes it impossible to stay warm.

After a moment of hesitation, I decide that the best way to help him is to grab him something hot to eat. I head inside the diner and smile at the teenager behind the counter. I've seen her here a few times before but have never actually spoken to her.

"Hi, I'm here to pick up my order. It's under 'Havoc'."

"Just give me a second. I'll grab it for you. Anything else?"

"Yeah, do you have any soup or stew? Something I can take to the homeless guy outside?"

"Um, let me just go check."

"Thanks..." I look at the badge on her chest. "Sarah. I appreciate it."

She gives me a smile before disappearing. I look around the diner and spot Conan in one of the booths. I don't know him well, but I do know he's getting treatment for some kind of cancer, so he isn't around the clubhouse much. He's staring down at the table, and I almost decide to leave him alone, but there's something so... sad about the guy that I'm standing beside him before I even realize my feet are moving.

Sensing me there, he looks up, a frown on his face before he recognizes me. "Amity's friend, right?"

I nod. "Nevaeh," I reply, sliding into the booth across from him. "I'm surprised to find you here alone."

He huffs. "I snuck out."

I grin. "Me too."

He takes me in, his eyes moving to my cut before they widen. "And who are you sneaking away from?"

"I should've kept my mouth shut," I mutter before taking a deep breath. "I may or may not have ditched the prospect that's supposed to be watching me."

He doesn't say anything, clearly waiting for more. I groan and close my eyes, dropping my head to bang it on the table.

"Your president is driving me insane," I admit.

"What's Havoc's problem?" He chuckles, picking up the glass of water in front of him and taking a sip.

"I bewitched him with my magical vagina, apparently," I mutter, though clearly not quietly enough because he spits out his water all over the table.

I grab a handful of napkins from the dispenser next to the ketchup and clean up the mess.

"So you and Havoc are official now?"

I narrow my eyes at him. "Why? Are you saying I'm not good enough for him? Wait, how'd you know about me and Havoc?" I ask, surprised.

He blinks, then throws his head back and laughs, drawing the attention of everyone in the diner. "Thanks, I needed that." He grins at me as Sarah walks over.

"Hey, sorry to interrupt. The cook's making some beef stew and biscuits for you."

"Oh, that's perfect. Can I also get a hot chocolate to go

and a bottle of water? And do you have any disposable utensils?"

"Actually, I think we do. I'll throw some in for you."

"Thank you," I say with a smile.

I turn back to Conan, who's looking at me curiously.

"There's a homeless guy outside."

"God save me from women who want to save the world," he mutters to himself. "I'll come with you when you drop off the food."

"It's okay—"

"I'll come with you. I'm sure the guy will appreciate it, but desperate people can make choices they wouldn't normally make. Let's not put him in a situation where he's tempted, or you in one where your good deed goes sideways."

I roll my eyes at the cynic but know better than to argue.

"And FYI, I'm not trying to save the world. I'm just a nice person. What's wrong with that?"

"Nice people get eaten alive in this world. Why'd you sneak away?"

I shake my head at his change of subject and ask a question of my own. "Why did *you* sneak away?"

"I needed a moment to just..." His words trail off.

"Breathe." I finish for him.

"Yeah."

"It's hard trying to be strong for everyone else. I get it. I don't know you, so I don't have a pony invested in this game.

Wait, I don't think that's how the analogy goes, but... oh well, you get what I'm saying."

"Not even a little bit."

"Okay, what I'm trying to say is, if you need someone to talk to, I'm your gal."

I pull out my phone and look at him. "Give me your number."

"What?"

"Your cell phone number?" I say slowly. "Did chemo kill your brain cells, too?"

He huffs before giving me his number. I send him a text and wait for his phone to ping before putting mine away.

He lets out a breath. "Everyone treats me differently now. They don't see my size, or my cut, or my angry glare that only a few months ago would send people running. All they see is cancer."

"Show me the angry glare."

He pauses for a moment before scowling at me.

"Meh, needs a little work." He opens his mouth before closing it again.

"So your hair is a little thin and you have dark circles under your eyes, who cares? I'm sure you're still terrifying to small children and pearl clutching Karen's."

"Do you always say what you think?"

At home I bit my tongue so hard, I'm sure I have scars. Of course, I always made up for it when I was out of the house.

"Pretty much." I lean forward and lower my voice.

"You're entitled to feel however you want, Conan. That's your right. But the way I see it, you've got two options right now: you can be all sad and give up, or you can fight back. And you don't strike me as the kinda guy who would just roll over and welcome death when you've got so much to live for."

"I'm not giving up."

"Good, and I'm serious—if you need someone to talk to, I'm a good listener. I mean, I'll probably interrupt you like a million times and throw out my opinions like glitter, but I'll listen to every word you say and won't repeat it. You can be pissed with me. You can be sad and scared. You can be whatever you can't be around your family."

"Why?"

"Why not?" I shrug, standing up when I see Sarah place a couple of bags on the counter. I walk over and pay, then turn to look at Conan. "Coming?"

He nods, leaving a couple of bills on the table, and walks over. He takes the bags from me despite my protests. "I have cancer, woman. I'm not dying." He scowls, making me laugh.

"I love a man with a sense of humor." I fake swooning.

"Everyone's a comedian these days," he mutters. "Where the fuck's the prospect who's supposed to be watching you?"

"Probably still at The Lookout. He said he needed to talk to the owner but ended up drooling all over the bartender. I got tired of waiting. I told him I needed the bathroom and slipped out the back."

He grumbles something, but I miss it as we make our way

outside. We head toward the alley, and I see the homeless man still in the same spot. The guy lifts his head from his knees as we approach, watching us warily.

He's wearing one of those face masks we all wore during COVID, covering the bottom of his face, but the part I can see is filthy. If I didn't think Havoc would kill me, I'd ask if he wanted a shower and invite him back to the clubhouse.

"Hi. We got you some food."

The guy stares at me in a way that makes me nervous, and I'm glad Conan came with me. I take the bag from the giant behind me and hand it to him.

"Oh, shoot. I forgot the hot chocolate. I'll be right back."

I turn to leave, almost colliding with Sarah, who has the hot chocolate in her hand.

"Oh, you're a gem, thank you."

"You're welcome. I'm glad I caught up with you." Her eyes fall to the homeless guy, and she offers him a smile before heading back to the diner.

I set the cup down next to the guy's leg and stand back up. He doesn't say anything. He tracks my every move, though, his eyes scanning my body and face like he's memorizing every detail.

"Enjoy," I murmur, stepping away from him.

I turn to Conan, who leads me away with his large hand on the small of my back.

"Okay, so you may have been right. The guy creeped me

out. It doesn't mean I shouldn't help though. But thank you for coming with me, big guy."

He chuckles. "Anytime, Nevaeh. Now, let's go find your wayward prospect."

He walks me to the bar, and when we reach the door, he opens it and motions for me to go in first. To my surprise, when I look around, Hoops is still standing in the exact same spot. The girl—and I say that because she looks barely old enough to sell alcohol—laughs at something Hoops says when she sees me approaching.

"Hi, what can I get you?"

"Just a prospect to go, please."

Hoops turns at the sound of my voice, looking confused. He grimaces when he spots Conan behind me and curses when he notices bags of food in his hands.

"Lose something, prospect?" Conan's deep voice rumbles.

"Shit. I thought you were in the bathroom. Why didn't you say something?" Hoops asks me, looking more defeated than mad.

"You were occupied."

"I wasn't occupied."

"You didn't know I was gone until I came back."

He rubs his hand over his face and stands. The bartender's face falls when he leaves without even saying goodbye. I give her an apologetic wave and hurry outside after Conan and Hoops, who are now arguing but shut up when I join them.

"Look, it's not a big deal. Let's just get the food back to the clubhouse."

"It is a—"

"I'm fine, Conan, other than my stomach trying to eat itself. I promise."

He sighs but nods. "Get in."

I salute him and climb in as he puts the bags on the passenger seat.

I buckle up and wait for them to get on their bikes. Conan's is parked at the far side of the lot, which is why we didn't notice it when we pulled in. The diner's parking lot is tiny, so people often end up parking over here. The owners must have some type of deal.

I snap out of my thoughts when I hear Hoops' engine roar to life. I lower my window as he pulls his helmet on.

"I won't say anything. I'm not trying to get you in trouble."

"Not your fault, Tink. I fell down on the job."

He closes the visor on his helmet, ending the conversation.

"Well, okay then," I mutter and follow him home.

Chapter Thirteen

Havoc

Neveah walks in with Conan and Hoops, our food in her hands, just as I'm heading into church.

"Eat without me. I'll reheat mine after."

I signal for Dice to keep an eye on my woman before I head into church, Conan following behind me.

"You're cutting it close," I tell him.

"Your woman distracted me."

I sigh. "She has that effect on people."

I leave him and take my seat at the head of the table, still feeling weird about it.

"Alright, assholes, sit down," I shout as the others filter in.

Once everyone's settled, I begin. "First up: Blade, Conan, King and Inigo are going away for a couple of weeks, so leave them the fuck alone unless they reach out. Honestly, I'm not sure Blade even knows what a vacation is."

Blade flips me off, but he's grinning while he does it.

"As president, I want to say enjoy yourself, Blade. You've more than earned it. But if any of you need us, we're a phone call away. If you go running to Carnage first, though, you'll hurt my feelings."

Inigo chuckles, and Conan just smiles.

"What about Conan's treatments?" Probe asks.

"Just finished my first round, so I have a few weeks off until the next one starts. Can't say I'm looking forward to it. I end up puking more than Sunshine does."

"If fighting were easy, we'd all be soldiers. But if anyone can beat this, it's you."

"Oh, I will. I just hate puking," he complains, making the others murmur sympathetically.

"Where's Hannibal?" Inigo asks.

"He had something important come up." I hold my hand up when they start to argue because you better have a damn good reason to miss church. "Trust me, he's exactly where he needs to be."

"You know what's going on with him?" G asks while the others study me. "He got a call the day Amity and I were run off the road. He hasn't been himself since then."

"It's not my story to tell. Let him figure his shit out and come to you himself. Just be the brothers he's going to need you to be."

"Well, that's not fucking cryptic at all," Circus complains.

"You're all a bunch of nosy bastards. Forget about Hannibal for now. I want to talk about Khan."

"That fucker contact you yet?" Blade leans forward.

"Last night."

Capone snorts. "Took him fucking long enough."

"I expected him to hold out longer. He's pissed. He tried to hide it, but I know that man better than he thinks. He's mad as fuck he's got two men missing. Why? I don't fucking know. He knew he was sacrificing them. Neither Acid or Knuckles were the sharpest tools in the shed, but he was fine losing them if it meant taking me out in the process."

When G looks like he's about to say something, I shake my head. "I know you and Amity were hurt. I'm not taking that away from you, but Khan won't give a fuck about that."

"So what did he say?"

"He congratulated me, threw in a couple backhanded compliments, and a mention or two about Lola's pregnancy and how it's going, obviously knowing Blade would have told me about it."

"That motherfucker," Kruger curses.

"Nah, it was good because I felt nothing hearing it. A couple of months ago, I would've lost my shit. But now?" I shake my head. "Driller's welcome to her."

"Gotta say, I liked Lola when you were with her," Toot says. "But the chemistry between you and Tinkerbell over the last couple of weeks... I only gotta walk past you, and I get a damn boner."

Mac groans and smacks him on the back of the head, and Midas laughs.

"My old lady catches sight of your boner, Toot, and I'll cut it off and feed it to you."

He just grins at me, unapologetically, as I steer the conversation back to Khan. "He wants a sit-down. Didn't say what for, though. He wanted me to ask, but I just didn't give a fuck.

"Still, I can't say I'm not curious. We all know this isn't the last we'll hear from him. I was loyal to Khan for a long fucking time, but that man I swore to serve... he's gone. I don't know this Khan. He's just a shadow of who he used to be. A smart man would walk away while he still can, protect his club, knowing how close he is to losing it. But Khan's not smart anymore. He's digging his heels in. He wants something—I just don't know what."

"He probably thinks he can control you. You went to prison on his orders, remember," Inigo points out.

"It's not something I'll forget," I reply. "It's easy to look back and say it was the wrong move, but I didn't have many other options at the time. Besides..." I spread my arms wide. "I'm the king of the fucking castle now, so it all worked out."

"And that's what's really pissing him off," Mac says. "That despite everything, you managed to one-up him."

"He's acting like a fucking five-year-old, not the president of an MC," Kruger growls.

"You have a plan?" Midas askes.

"I want to set up a meeting, but not here like he wanted. Back at my old club."

Kruger rubs his hands together. "A little salt in the wound? I'm down for that."

"Glad you agree because I want you with me, Kruger. G, you'll hold down the fort here with Hannibal and Midas. I'll take Mac and Toot as well, and Crane. Crane?"

The man who's been quiet this whole time looks up from where he's sitting, and I can see the anger on his face. "It's a sad fucking day...when brothers have to turn on brothers. I thought we'd dealt with all that shit when Bear died. Now Khan's following in the same fucking footsteps. We can't let him get away with what he did to G or our girl Amity."

"And we won't," I tell him. "I want you with me because I'm bringing Nevaeh, and I want someone—specifically you—watching her back."

G whistles. "I still can't believe Tink's your old lady." He shakes his head and huffs.

"You think taking her with you is smart, Havoc? It's gonna get ugly. And if anything happens to Tink, Amity will—"

"Nothing's going to happen to her. I'll talk to Nevaeh first, and if she's against it, I won't force her to go. But I'm hoping we can go and show a united front."

I look to Conan. "Call Carnage and give them a heads up. I'll give Orion a call myself when we get back. I think it's time I spoke with him as the new president anyway and I need to let him know what's going on. It would be just like Khan to fuck with our allies to try and isolate us."

"Shit, I never thought about that," Blade grumbles, rubbing his hand over his face.

I look at Mac and Toot. "I want bugs planted, cameras if possible—anything you can do to get me eyes and ears inside. Kruger, I want you bad-mouthing our former prospect Hicks. That way, if we decide to send someone in pretending to be him, we've already set the stage."

"And anyone you can't stand, Khan's gonna want on his side." Kruger nods in understanding.

"Exactly. Now, if nobody has anything else they need to discuss—"

"Tink," G speaks up.

"You got a problem with her being my old lady?"

"As long as you treat her well, why would I?" He shrugs, but I can tell he's still got his reservations. "My old lady, on the other hand, might have something to say about the fact she missed out on you giving Tink her cut, especially since she was kept in the dark about you two."

I groan. "On a scale of one to ten, how pissed is she?"

"Eleven." I groan again. "But she likes you for her, so that's something."

"He did ride to her rescue when G and Amity crashed," Circus adds.

"Plus, he pulled you and Amity up a fucking cliff. That had to earn him some brownie points, right?" Probe jumps in.

"The man has a point," Inigo says before frowning. "Did I just agree with Probe?"

Probe flips him off.

"Alright, children, can we go now? My woman brought me food, and I'm starving."

Conan looks at me and shakes his head. "Yeah, about that..."

Chapter Fourteen

Nevaeh

"So let me get this straight," Havoc yells at Hoops, making me wince. "You were so busy flirting with the fucking bartender that you didn't even know Nevaeh had left until she came back for you?"

"She said she was going to the bathroom. It's not like I could go in with her," he validly, if stupidly, points out.

Havoc stands up and looms over Hoops, who visibly shrinks into himself. "But you could have waited outside the door for her. You could have clocked the fucking time. If she went to the diner, picked up food, sat and had a conversation with Conan, and then gave food to some homeless guy, she was gone for at least thirty fucking minutes."

"Maybe he thought I was having a poo," I blurt out,

drawing everyone's eye. I feel my cheeks burn, but I also feel awful that Hoops is getting into trouble because of me.

Conan laughs from beside me, but I ignore him.

"I'm sorry, what?" Havoc frowns.

"You know, a poo. They take time. You should know—you take thirty minutes every time you go," I grumble, ignoring the laughter I can hear from behind me.

"You shit in public often?"

I grimace. "Ew no, never. Damm it," I curse, realizing he just caught me out.

"He might have thought I got my period, right?" I glare at Hoops, willing him to play along, but he just looks like he doesn't know if he wants to laugh or cry.

"But you didn't get your period. You snuck out."

"I know that, and you know that, but Hoops doesn't, err didn't. The point is, you should cut him some slack. If he had barged his way in and caught me inserting a vampire's tea bag, you'd have lost your freaking mind."

"A vampire's what now?" Capone asks, choking on a laugh.

"What the fuck is happening? I'm so confused," someone else says among the laughter.

Havoc stalks toward me, his face blank, but I don't miss the look that flashes in his eyes.

"Oops," I whisper, backing up a little.

I don't get far, not with the table behind me.

"Are you trying to tell me how to do my job, Nevaeh?" Uh-oh... he used my name.

"No. I would never do that." I say quickly, shaking my head. "I'm just saying it's not Hoops' fault."

He leans down over me, his nose skimming mine. "So you're saying Hoops didn't do anything wrong, it's all on you?"

"Yes. No—wait, what?"

"Hoops," Havoc calls out without taking his eyes off me. "You're on clean-up duty, which includes the bathrooms, until further notice. You can thank my old lady that you're not being dragged into the ring as well since this is all her fault and all. You should say thank you."

"Thank you, Nevaeh," Hoops shouts.

"I didn't say it was my—"

I squeal when I'm picked up and tossed over his shoulder yet again. A round of whistles follows when they get a glimpse of my underwear before Havoc growls and threatens to rip everyone's eyes out if they don't stop looking at my ass.

"Put me down, you big oaf!" I smack his back as he carries me out of the room and upstairs.

He doesn't say anything to me, which makes me even madder. I try to wiggle free as soon as we are inside his room, but he holds on tight until he sits on the bed and flips me over so I'm lying across his lap.

"Havoc, let me go!"

His hand slides over my panties before he yanks them

down, holding me in place with one hand before, *whack*, he smacks my ass hard with the other.

"You put yourself in danger."

Whack.

"You deliberately left your guard. And got him in trouble."

Whack.

My ass feels like it's on fire, heat radiating across my cheeks.

Whack.

"Do you know what it would do to me if something happened to you?"

Whack.

"I'm sorry, okay! I'm sorry!" I shout, feeling tears drip down my cheeks. I'm not sure why I'm crying. Sure, the spanking stings, but it doesn't hurt, per se. I'm more embarrassed than anything, being treated like a naughty kid."

"Sorry for what, cupcake?"

He smacks me again, making me cry out.

"For everything!" I sob, the words spilling out before I can think. "I'm sorry for leaving my guard, I'm sorry for putting myself in danger, and I'm sorry for hurting you. I didn't think. It won't happen again."

He rubs his hand gently over my ass to soothe it, his thumb slipping between my legs to press against my clit.

"How do you feel?" He asks, like he hasn't noticed I'm wetter than an otter's pocket.

Though, I'll be dammed if I admit it—he'll just use it as an excuse to spank me willy-nilly.

"Sore. Can I get up now?" I ask him, my voice small.

He lifts me off his lap and lays me on the bed on my stomach. "Stay like that for a moment," he orders before walking into the bathroom.

I resist the urge to yank my underwear up and hightail it out of here. It wouldn't matter if I ran—he'd catch me before I even left the room. I've already been kidnapped and spanked. I'm not sure I want to know what he'd do next.

So I stay where I am and wait for him to come back, feeling exposed lying like this— and I don't just mean physically. I jolt when I feel his hands on my ass again, this time rubbing something cool into my overheated skin. I whimper but don't protest.

Once he's done, he eases my underwear down my legs and pulls them off. I turn my head to look at him as he shoves my underwear into his pocket.

"I'm going to need those back."

He bends down and presses his lips to the top of my ass, making me shiver. "Maybe you'll start behaving when you realize the next time I throw you over my shoulder, you won't be flashing your panties."

"Or, maybe you could just stop throwing me over your shoulder."

"Now, why would I do that?"

I roll my eyes—as if he'd let anyone see me exposed like that.

His hand slides up my inner thigh, his fingertips grazing my pussy before they glide over my ass, and he grabs my hips.

"Up on your knees, Cupcake, but keep your chest on the bed."

I do as he asks, feeling my arousal run down my thighs.

"Fucking hell," he growls before I feel his tongue lapping away at me.

I moan, hands fisting the sheets as he holds me in place and tortures me in the best possible way.

Lick after lick, stroke after stroke, he works me over until I'm a quivering mess and my legs are threatening to give out.

"You taste like heaven," he tells me as he shifts behind me, and I hear the sound of his zipper being lowered.

I feel him at my entrance, the tip of his hard cock nudging my clit. He thrusts forward, dragging his length through my wetness, coating himself in my arousal.

"Condom," I manage to gasp as the head of his cock pushes inside me.

"I'll pull out."

"I don't think that—"

My words are cut off as he slams into me, stealing the air from my lungs. Before I can catch my breath, his grip tightens, and he starts fucking me hard and deep.

The world tilts and becomes a dizzying blur of pleasure

and pain as he thrusts inside me as far as he can go over and over.

"That's my good fucking girl," he growls. Pushing me to the edge.

I pant, his words heightening everything. It's too much and not enough all at the same time. I hold on as tight as possible, taking everything he has to give me.

"Tell me you're mine," he demands, his fingers digging into my hips hard enough to leave bruises. A mark of ownership, one I know he'll admire later.

"I'm yours," I whisper, needing to come more than anything.

"Yes, you are. Mine to care for, mine to fuck, mine to protect."

He reaches around me and roughly rubs my clit, driving me wild. One stroke and I'm gasping his name. Two strokes and I'm seeing stars. By the time he thrusts into me hard and pinches my clit, I'm screaming my release, squeezing him hard as he roars my name.

He slams into me, holding himself still for a moment before pulling out and coming all over my ass and pussy.

"You've ruined me, cupcake," he pants. "But fuck me, I've never been so happy to be completely wrecked by someone before."

I feel his fingers at the entrance of my pussy before they slide inside me.

"Havoc," I warn.

"I'm not pushing it in far. I just like knowing my cum's inside you when you're surrounded by other men."

I let him do his thing, feeling myself getting turned on again as his fingers stroke me, working me up until I'm squirming on the bed, my body burning with need. He flips me over and climbs between my legs, lining himself up before thrusting into me again. I'm soaked, a mix of his cum and mine easing his way despite how swollen I am.

He stares into my eyes, his forearms braced on either side of my head, and I melt. The way he looks at me makes me feel seen in a way I never have before. Like I matter. Like without me, he can't breathe. It's both terrifying and exhilarating.

How can this man with so much power make me feel like he'd get down on his knees to worship me if I asked him to?

"You're going to come for me again, aren't you, Cupcake? I wanna feel your pussy strangle my cock, baby girl."

I'm still feeling the aftershock from the last round, so it only takes moments for me to fall over the edge. But there's nothing smooth or easy about it. My back arches as my body locks tight. My brain feels like it's been picked up by a tornado and tossed around so much that I don't know which way is up anymore.

His teeth sink into my nipple as my orgasm consumes me. The sharp bite prolongs the pleasure, intensifying it to the point of being painful. I feel him throb inside me, the pulse of heat as he comes, making no move to pull out.

"Havoc," I chastise, no matter how much I love feeling him come inside me.

"You can't get someone pregnant if you've already come," he murmurs against my throat, knowing what I was going to say.

I bite my lip to hold back my laughter. How does he come up with this crap? At this point, I don't know if he really thinks I'm that dumb or if he just likes toying with me. He kisses me softly before pulling out, and I flush when I notice how wet the bed is.

Before I can move, he takes his cell phone from his pocket and snaps a picture of me. "No way, Havoc. Delete that! You already have one photo; you don't need anymore. I sure as hell don't want pictures of me out there like that."

"I told you, I'd never let anyone see you like this. These are just for me. I have to capture each moment in case one day I forget."

"Forget what?"

He smiles at me, the kind of smile that says he knows something I don't.

Before I can get mad, though, he scoops me up and carries me into the bathroom, where he "helps" me shower. And when I say "helps," I mean he fucks me against the wall.

I gasp out "condom" as he bounces me up and down on his cock. But when he tells me you can't get pregnant in the shower—the good old-fashioned gravity-as-protection method—I give up.

The man is bound and determined to get me pregnant.

By the time we're *finally* cleaned up, dried, and dressed, I just want to climb into bed and sleep for a week. But I also need some girl time away from Havoc and his wonderpenis before chafing becomes an issue.

"You good?"

I turn at the sound of Havoc's voice and see him watching me. "Yeah, just thinking I need to spend some time with Amity."

He looks like he swallowed something funky, but for once, he doesn't complain. Instead, he offers me his hand. I take it, his much larger one swallowing up mine as we head back downstairs.

Havoc stops at the top of the stairs, and I look up at him. "I need to visit my old club. Things are a mess, but we're not ready to make our move yet."

"So you want to go and show them who you've become— make them choke on the fact they made you take the fall, spent five years forgetting you existed, and now you're the one calling the shots, living the dream they never thought you'd have."

Havoc pushes me against the wall, his eyes intense. "Come with me."

"Is your ex gonna be there?"

"Probably."

"You want to show her you upgraded, huh?" I joke.

"I don't give a fuck what Lola thinks. I just want everyone to know what a lucky bastard I am."

"Okay, I'll come. Of course, I will."

His hand slips under my skirt, finding the clean underwear I put on. Damn it, I hoped he wouldn't check.

The smirk on his face grows, and I know I'm in trouble. After the punishment I just received, I can't help but feel like he might just bring out the naughty streak in me more often.

"I told you, no panties."

"Whoops."

He grabs the sides of my panties and rips them from my body like they were tissue paper.

I stare at him open-mouthed. "You're insane."

He kisses me, and I let him, wondering if I'm insane, too. By the time he pulls back, I'm wet again.

I narrow my eyes at him. "You did that on purpose."

"Did what?" He says innocently.

When we get downstairs, I spot Amity sitting at a table with Legs, G, and a couple of other guys who are doodling on her pink cast. She looks up, and the moment she sees me, she jumps up and comes running over, wrapping her arms around me.

Pulling back, she turns to look at Havoc, narrowing her eyes. "G was looking for you."

"Should have checked my vagina; it's where he usually ends up when you can't find him."

Amity snorts as Havoc throws his head back and laughs. I

roll my eyes, link my arm through Amity's good one, and drag her outside.

It's quieter out there, probably because there is a chill in the air and rain is supposed to be heading our way. I don't care; the cool breeze feels like heaven on my overheated skin.

"You look good in your cut," I tell her.

"Why thank you. So do you, even if I'm having trouble wrapping my head around you being Havoc's old lady."

"I can imagine." I sigh, sitting on one of the comfortable sofas.

"But not for the reasons you're probably thinking. I just thought you'd let your father mess with your head, and you'd end up with someone just like him."

I shudder. "I love my dad, and I always will, but I'll never go back to how things were. Having a husband just like him would mean me playing a role I outgrew a long time ago, like an outfit I used to love that just doesn't fit anymore."

She grabs my hand. "There's nothing wrong with wanting to live your own life. I've always supported you stepping out of Citlalli's shadow and following your dreams. I'm happy when you're happy. And even though Havoc's intense, he's a good guy. I won't lie and say your speedy courtship didn't surprise me because it did, but in the best possible way. Just know he won't take your father's shit—and you shouldn't expect him to. I know you like to keep the peace, but Havoc's not that guy."

I groan, burying my face in my hands. "Why do I feel like this will blow up in my face?"

"Maybe it will," she says quietly. "But when the dust settles, I'll still be here, holding your hand every step of the way. And if you let him, so will Havoc."

She and Havoc have developed a bond, so I'm not surprised she's rooting for both of us. My dad, though? He'll hate Havoc on principle. He'll demand that I end things with him, like it's his right to still call the shots in my life. I'm almost twenty-six; I'm not a little kid anymore. He'll tell me Havoc's unworthy of me, but the truth is, I'm not worthy of him.

I'm weak where my father is concerned. I let him walk all over me because I don't like confrontation, so I back down and give in to avoid it. If Havoc knew that side of me he'd spank me for sure. How can the president of a motorcycle club want me as his old lady and expect me to rule beside him if I can't even stand up for myself?

I've been a spectator in my own life for so long that I lost sight of what really matters. Writing has been my only solace, my escape during the quiet moments when Amity was working away and I was alone

I look at Amity, and I can tell she knows exactly what I'm thinking. As much as she'd like to fight my battles for me, this time I have to stand up and fight my own. I have to be the queen Havoc sees me as.

I take a deep breath. "This is gonna suck."

She grins, pride shining in her eyes. "Maybe, but you'll get through it. You're the strongest person I know."

Maybe if I could see myself the way she does, I'd believe her.

Chapter Fifteen

Havoc

The feel of Nevaeh wrapped around me is the only thing keeping me grounded. I didn't think coming back here would hit me this hard, but betrayal's a hell of a lot easier to deal with when you're not forced to face it every day.

As we head through town, I signal the others I pull into the empty lot, and they do. Once I turn the engine off, I lift the visor on my helmet and turn to Nevaeh, lifting hers, too.

She looks at me, her soulful eyes searching mine, and even though I know my expression gives nothing away, she can sense the tension inside me. She lifts her hand and kisses her two fingers before pressing them against my lips. "Whatever happens, you'll still leave the winner."

I grip the bottom of her helmet and pull her closer, leaning my head against hers.

"I've been the winner since you agreed to be mine."

"Stockholm Syndrome at its finest."

"A man's gotta do what a man's gotta do," I say, grinning without an ounce of guilt.

She rolls her eyes at me but doesn't resist when I pull her onto my lap. She wraps her arms around me, letting me soak up her strength. The irony isn't lost on me—the big badass MC president leaning on his old lady. What other brothers haven't figured out yet—we tend to be a bunch of misogynist assholes—is that we might be the fists of the club, but our women are the spine. They're the strength behind our brute force, and the quiet calm in a world of chaos. Anyone mistaking women as a weakness has never loved one. Nothing makes a man feel more like a king than being chosen by the woman he loves. It's knowing they could have anyone they wanted, but she picked you. And when she does, you treat her like the fucking queen she is.

I look at the guys who are silently watching us. "Everyone ready?"

"We've got this, Prez," Toot confirms.

I look to Crane, my orders in my eyes. *Don't let anything happen to my woman.*

"I'll guard her with my life, Havoc," he tells me, dead serious..

I nod, ready to roll. When Nevaeh shifts to move back behind me, I grip her hip to stop her.

"Stay like this. I won't let you fall."

She stares at me for a moment, then rests her head against my shoulder. She wraps her legs tightly around my waist, her arms slipping around my neck.

I grin. Fuck, I love this woman.

My dick stirs between us, but ignore it for now. Asking her to ride my dick while I ride my bike might be taking it a step too far for her anyway.

I start up my bike and tap Nevaeh's thigh so she knows I'm about to pull out, and take off. The clubhouse is only ten miles away, but with Nevaeh wrapped around me, it feels both longer and shorter.

She squirms against me, and I feel my cock throb in response. We're both so fucking turned on, I'm tempted to bend her over the bike once we stop and fuck her like I want to. But as soon as we pull into the lot, I see Driller and Khan standing on the clubhouse steps, waiting for us. A few of the brothers are there, too, trying and failing to act natural.

Reluctantly, I tap Nevaeh again, and as soon as we stop, she loosens her grip on me. I steady her as I lift her off the bike, then climb off after her. Ignoring everyone else, I unclip her helmet and pull it free, watching her shake her hair out. I swallow down a groan as I hang it on the handlebars, then take my helmet and sit it on the seat.

She slips her hand into mine as I look down at her. She

gives me a wink, making me chuckle. Crane moves to her other side, and Kruger flanks me. Toot and Mac take the lead, walking over to Khan and Driller.

"Nice to have you back, Havoc. You look good," Khan says, holding out his hand like if I've been on a fucking vacation, not in prison.

"Khan." I reach over and shake his hand briefly before introducing my girl. "This is Nevaeh, my old lady."

Khan frowns for a second before his eyes move over her face to her cut. I clench my hand, so I don't poke his fucking eyeballs out.

"Not your usual type, Havoc."

"What, loyal?" I snark back. Driller puffs up his chest, but I refuse to acknowledge him.

"You wanted to meet, Khan. So here I am. Are we doing this in the parking lot, or are you going to let me in?"

He looks from me to Driller. I wait for him to say something, but wisely, he keeps his mouth shut. He steps aside and motions for us to go in.

Again, Mac and Toot lead the way, prepared for us to walk into an ambush. But that's not Khan's style. The guy who used to face things head-on is now the kind of prick who would now sneak up behind you and stab you in the back.

Nevaeh doesn't say anything. She sure as fuck doesn't acknowledge Khan. And why would she after his dismissive treatment? Her grip on my hand tightens as I lead her inside. Nostalgia hits me for a moment, but that's all I get. This place isn't home anymore. The woman standing beside me is.

I look around, and the room goes quiet as all eyes turn our way. Ignoring them, I walk over to the bar and nod to the bunny serving. She doesn't look familiar, but her coy smile says she knows exactly who I am.

"I'll take a beer. Nevaeh?"

"Bottled water, please."

The woman rolls her eyes but says nothing as she grabs the drinks before turning to my men to take their orders.

I look down at Nevaeh, who looks at me with a raised eyebrow. "As if I'd drink anything without a sealed lid here," she says, quiet enough for only me to hear.

"Smart girl," I say, pulling her to me and slamming my mouth down on hers. She grips my cut and holds on tight.

I know everyone is watching, I don't give a fuck. Let them see how much better my life is now that I'm out of this place.

I pull back and kiss the tip of her nose. "Let's get this shit over with," I murmur before I feel a slap on my shoulder.

"Let's go talk. You can leave the woman with the others." He nods to the corner, and I see Lola. She's looking straight at me, the pain etched on her face, making me pause for a moment. In another life, I'd have rushed over to her. But the man who once loved her is gone, and she was the one to put the final nail in the coffin. I don't know what fucking game she's playing, but I'm not interested, and I won't let her drag Nevaeh into it.

"You really want to play it this way, Khan? 'Cause I'm not exactly feeling the respect afforded to me as president of the mother chapter."

"Women's issues don't touch us. You know that."

"Women's issues? That's what you're calling it? You want me to send my old lady over to spend time with the whore who swapped me out for my brother while I was serving his sentence?"

"Hey, watch your fucking mouth!" Driller snarls.

"Just speaking the truth, brother. You don't like it, that's not my fucking problem." I turn to Crane and nod.

He steps up beside Nevaeh and wraps his arm around her shoulders. "Come on, Tinkerbell. Let's play pool."

Driller snorts. "You sharing now?"

I turn to look at him, but before I can answer, Nevaeh does. "I was a virgin until Havoc. He was the first man I slept with, and he'll be the last. I'm sure, given who your old lady is, it's a hard concept to follow. But don't tar me with the same brush."

"Shut your—

My hand is around his throat before he can finish that sentence.

"Havoc. Let him go. Your woman was disrespectful. You know they don't mouth off at a patched brother," Khan states firmly.

I squeeze Driller's throat harder before tossing him away and facing Khan. "Nevaeh is my old lady. You disrespected her first, then Driller, more than once. It's her right as my old lady to defend herself. It's just unfortunate that she should have to, and yet, I'm not surprised in the slightest. I'm done playing nice here, Khan. You want to talk, talk. I have better fucking things to do than sit around pandering to you."

"Now you listen to me—" he starts, but I step forward and loom over him, not giving him a fucking inch.

"The next time you point that finger at me, I'll rip it off and shove it up your ass. My days of taking orders from you are over. I outrank you, Khan, in case you've forgotten. I can have you replaced just like that." I snap my fingers as I lean forward and snarl in his face. "Push me. I fucking dare you."

The clubhouse is deadly quiet as if everyone is collectively holding their breath.

An array of emotions play across his face, but he locks it down and pulls himself free from my grip. "It's been a tough time here for us," he states in an attempt to justify his actions. I smell the bullshit all over his breath.

"Then, by all means, let's go to church and hash this out. Kruger, Mac, Toot, let's go." I call out their names and wait for Khan to tell me they can't come. It's on the tip of his tongue. He wants to get me alone. He hasn't realized that bringing them with me is for his safety, not mine. I'm ready to destroy this man. Any respect I had for him died the moment he ordered me to serve Driller's prison sentence.

Khan nods to Driller, who stomps toward church. My

men walk beside me as I follow. I turn and give Nevaeh one last look before I head inside.

Once the door closes, I sit at the table, Mac and Toot flanking me. Kruger sits at the other end to plant a bug, while Khan takes a seat at the head of the table, and Driller sits beside him.

"Aren't any of the other brothers joining us?" Kruger asks, and I wait to hear Khan's answer.

"We want to keep the details as quiet as possible until we know what we're dealing with."

"And what are you dealing with? Why did you call this meeting, Khan?"

"It's Acid and Knuckles…"

"What about them?"

"They're missing."

"If they're missing, it's not like their brothers don't know," Kruger points out.

"They know that Acid and Knuckles went to welcome a brother home and haven't been seen since. I'm trying to make sure we don't stir up any bad blood between our clubs. There'll be some who find it real convenient that two of our brothers disappeared right around the time you got released from prison—especially when you're the only one we can think of with a grudge against us."

I lean back and grin. Amity said this might be a setup to make me look bad, hoping I'd be passed over for the presidency. But it's too fucking late for that.

"And why would I have an issue with the club, Khan?"

Khan sighs and crosses his arms.

"I wish I'd done things differently, but I was out of options. Driller was the only one the Death Serpents would work with, and we needed that deal. We might have the pipeline in our territory, but it means nothing if we can't transport it through Death Serpents' territory."

I wait for him to say something else, but that's it.

"So you think, after spending five years in prison thanks to Driller and you, that I'd finally taste freedom and want to... what? Risk losing it all by taking out Acid and Knuckles? That's what you're getting at, right?"

"Sounds like a stretch to me, Prez. You have Nevaeh. You're the president of the mother chapter, and your men back you one hundred percent. Your life looks pretty fucking golden from where I'm sitting. I can't imagine this club even being on your radar." Toot chimes in

"I fucked a baby into your old lady's cunt. Don't tell me you're not pissed about that," Driller snaps.

Mac tenses beside me, but I keep myself relaxed and adopt a bored expression. "Ex-old lady. But you want my sloppy seconds, go for it. Hell, I should be thanking you. If I'd stuck with Lola, I wouldn't have Nevaeh."

Driller's bitter hatred bubbles up, ready to spill over, but Khan shoots him a look and shakes his head.

"We don't need this. Mistakes were made, but they're in

the past now," Khan says, holding his hands up in a show of peace.

I shake my head. "You expect me to trust you, Khan? Do you trust me after all the shit you did to fuck me over?"

Khan narrows his eyes and stands up, planting his hands on the table as he leans forward. "A good leader leads by example. Come back in ten years and tell me if you still have stars in your fucking eyes. I don't know what Blade was thinking when he picked you, but you'd do well to remember that not everyone agrees with his decision. If things had gone differently, Bear would be sitting here, not you."

Kruger jumps up, knocking his chair over, and pulls his gun, pointing it at Khan as Driller draws his own gun. Before he can so much as twitch, both Mac and Toot have their weapons aimed at his forehead.

"Bear was a traitor and rapist. Are you tellin' me you're siding with that man? Oh, how the mighty have fallen," Kruger snarls.

I stand, and Khan watches me warily. "Tell me, Khan, what were you hoping to achieve with this friendly little chat?"

"I just want to find my men. Your men, too, now that you're president."

"I'm already looking into it. Unfortunately, they didn't leave a trace. And all I've got to go on is your story about how they were coming to welcome me home. The thing is, they never did. Not that I expected it. After all, nobody came to visit me inside either, except Gunther. Even if my brothers had decided I was worth a visit, it sure as shit wouldn't've been Acid and Knuckles. They were never my biggest fans."

"They respected you. You did something good for the club, and they respected that. Respected your sacrifice."

I shake my head, my lips twitching at the man's nerve. "Acid and Knuckles wouldn't give a shit if I was on fire. But if they hated me that much—me, their own club brother—it's safe to assume I've got more enemies. Have you looked into them? Them telling you they were coming to see me was probably a cover."

"No. They went to see you."

"Sorry, Khan, but that's bullshit. But like I said, I've got men on it. We'll figure it out. Now, onto other matters. Since I'm president now, I'll be going around to all the chapters and doing audits. I want to see where we're making money and where we're losing it, and what I can do to help. Also, I'm putting my house on the market. If you want to buy it, let me know by the end of the month."

"That house is on private property," Khan snaps.

Driller growls, "You'd really kick out Lola, knowing she's carrying your niece or nephew?"

"Absofuckinglutely. Move her in with you."

"I don't have a house," he hisses.

"Not my problem. Go steal someone else's. That's what you do, right?"

I turn and head to the door, waiting as Kruger lowers his gun. Once Driller puts his away, Mac and Toot lower theirs.

"I'll be taking Nevaeh to my house, so I suggest you get your old lady out of there before I throw her out myself," I warn Driller before turning to Khan. "I want those files. The sooner I'm done, the sooner I'll be gone."

He shakes his head like he's disappointed in me. "You've changed."

"Thank fuck for that." I laugh and yank the door open. Walking out, I look around for Nevaeh. I find her over at the pool table with Crane standing guard while she hands the guy she's playing his ass.

"You're a fucking shark," he snaps as I walk up behind him.

"And you're a sore loser. Pay up or face the consequences," she tells him.

He lets out a nasally laugh. "Oh yeah? And what might they be?"

"Me," I answer, smirking as he spins around, his face draining white.

"H...Havoc."

"Meet the consequences, jackass," Nevaeh mutters before throwing herself into my arms.

"Hey, baby."

"Cupcake, have you been making the boys cry?"

Chapter Sixteen

Nevach

The guy backed off when he saw Havoc, which made me grin. Havoc clearly isn't the man they remember—everyone looks wary of him.

And honestly, they should be. What they did to him was horrible. Khan forcing him to take the fall for his brother was one thing. His brother being the absolute douchecanoe that he is, is another. But what the rest of them did...

It makes me think of high school when someone's being bullied and everyone just looks the other way. Them not stepping up makes them part of the problem. Their lack of accountability almost makes it seem like it's okay.

Oh, I'm sure they have their excuses. They always do. No one ever wants to admit they're a shitty person.

I wonder what people like that see when they look in the mirror. Does guilt and shame cloud their reflections? Maybe their images are warped and twisted like in a funhouse mirror. It would certainly match their morals, that's for sure.

Not that I'm one to talk about morals. I'm standing outside the house Havoc shared with his ex, feeling almost gleeful that she's been kicked out. It's petty, I know, but it feels like the least she deserves.

I stand beside him, holding his hand, as we look up at the small two-story house. "We can stay in a hotel if you want."

He tightens his grip on my hand and leads me up the steps, past the pretty flower border that someone had spent a lot of time and care nurturing. I can't see Driller doing it. He seems more like a beer-and-a-ball game kind of guy. So, I let go of Havoc's hand and stomp all over the flowers as I walk up to the house, the guys laughing behind us

Yeah, it's childish, but I don't feel guilty about it.

Havoc waits for me by the door, a smile on his face. "How is it you manage to take a shitty day and make it somehow brighter?"

"What can I say? I'm a woman of many talents." I reply, flashing a grin.

He bends down and kisses me. "That you are." He opens the door and leads us inside, taking me straight to the living room.

It's bigger than I thought it would be, with a couple of large, comfy-looking sofas and a huge TV mounted on the wall. A dining table sits at the far end of the room, and just beyond that is a small bookcase with a chair beside it, next to the window that overlooks the backyard.

"Jesus, it looks exactly the same. I thought Driller would have done something to it just to piss me off."

"That probably required effort, and he looks like a lazy pig to me," I grumble.

"You want us to crash here with you, Prez, or get a motel?"

I turn at the sound of Kruger's voice.

"I want you to stay even though it won't be comfortable. I don't trust anyone here but you guys."

"Don't worry about us. We'd only worry if we left anyway," Mac says as he throws himself down onto the sofa.

"Let me go see if I can find some blankets." I pull free from Havoc's hold despite his protest. "I'm not leaving the house. Chill."

Toot laughs. "Only you, Tinkerbell, would tell the president to chill."

"Well, he's not my president," I remind him, calling over my shoulder as I leave the room to their teasing and head upstairs.

The first door opens to a small bathroom, so I don't bother checking it and move on. The next leads to a small room that most people would use as an office, and maybe once upon a time, it had been. Now, the room's empty while the walls are being painted a sunny yellow. It's a special kind of cruel to decorate a room in the house that belongs to your ex for a baby that should have been his.

I close the door harder than necessary, angry at Lola all over again. She didn't say a word to me at the clubhouse, which surprised me. I figured she'd be loud and opinionated, trying to put me in my place, but no. She never even looked at me. She just sat quietly in the corner, pretending she didn't notice me, just like I did to her.

Then again, I have Crane watching me. If she had approached, Crane would have shut her down before she got even a couple of words out.

I walk farther down the hall and open the next door. As soon as it swings wide, I freeze in the doorway, realizing this is the main bedroom.

I don't consider myself a jealous person, or at least I haven't before. Maybe that was because I didn't care enough about someone to stir up those feelings. Now, though, the thought of Lola and Havoc rolling around on that bed once upon a time makes me want to take a knife to the sheets and a match to the wooden bedframe.

It might not be rational. Their relationship was dead long before I came along, but it doesn't stop the twisted thoughts from running through my head. I'm not an idiot. As much of a bitch as she's been, there is no denying how beautiful she is. I could easily picture her and Havoc together. But if she's his type, why the heck is he with me?

I blow out a frustrated sigh, snapping at myself to not be

that girl. The one who compares herself to others just to high-light my flaws.

Looking around the room, I spot a chest at the end of the bed. I walk over and open it, expecting to find blankets, but instead, I find baby clothes—a few plain white onesies, a couple of knitted hats, and a pair of tiny booties. My heart squeezes as I close the lid and move to the dresser to search through the drawers.

I can't imagine what this must feel like for Havoc. Even if all the love between them is gone, it still has to hurt that she cares so little for him that she is now growing his brother's kid.

The drawers and closet don't reveal any blankets either. What I do find is a lack of clothing. Don't get me wrong, there are a few pairs of jeans and some T-shirts, a pair of motor-cycle boots in the closet near the back, a fur-lined winter jacket, and a few thermal shirts. As most of its men's clothing, I assume they belong to Driller.

Either Driller doesn't own a lot of shit, or there is trouble in paradise. That's the thing about the grass looking greener on the other side—people expect it to be the same for them, too. They never think about the work it takes to keep it that way. Without the effort, the green fades, and what once thrived withers and dies.

Part of me feels vindicated that whatever Lola shares with Driller is nothing like she had with Havoc— or what I have with him. But the other part feels sad for the kid. No matter what happens, that baby will still be Havoc's niece or nephew. I don't want them to suffer because the adults in their lives made foolish choices and are now facing the consequences.

Not bothering to figure out where Lola keeps her clothes, I leave the bedroom and head down to the last door and finally find what I'm looking for. There aren't many, but it's better than nothing. I grab the blankets and a couple of pillows from the top shelf before heading back downstairs.

The guys are talking quietly when I walk in, but I don't think they're talking about me, more about the situation and how crappy it is.

"This is all I could find," I say, passing everything to Kruger, who takes it with a wink.

"Don't worry, Tink. This'll do just fine."

I smile. "There isn't much here," I tell them. "And aside from a few baby clothes, they don't seem to be ready for a kid at all."

"I don't give a shit if they're ready or not," Havoc snaps. "They made their bed; they can fucking rot in it for all I care."

I shrug and head into the kitchen, looking through the fridge and cupboards. There isn't much, and despite everything, I'm not comfortable taking food from a pregnant woman. So, I brew a pot of coffee and look through the drawers until I find a bunch of take-out menus. I gather them up and look through them as I fix myself a mug of coffee.

Sitting at the counter, I sip my drink, as the others eventually come in.

"Any more?" Mac asks.

I nod to the coffee pot as Havoc walks over. He picks me up and sits down, placing me in his lap. I sigh and continue to sip my coffee.

"Sorry, I snapped."

"It's fine. I get it. The whole situation is messed-up. I'd be worried if it weren't bothering you. Now, let's focus on the important stuff. Food."

He grins.

"I've narrowed it down to pizza or Chinese," I say, holding up two menus.

He takes them from me. "I remember this place. The pizza tastes like shit."

"Chinese it is then. You guys okay with that?"

Toot grabs the menu from Havoc and looks at me. "You know what you want? I'll phone our orders in, and then me and Mac can ride down and pick it up. I want to check out the locals. Nobody back home minds us in their space 'cause we give back to the community. I want to see what the setup here is like."

Havoc nods. "Good idea. We were never going to win any popularity contests, even before I went to prison. We didn't put nearly as much effort into keeping the peace as the mother chapter does, but they respected us enough to stay out of our business."

"Despite how awful they've all treated Havoc, I don't want to believe that the whole club is rotten," I admit.

"Sometimes one bad apple ruins the whole bunch," Kruger tells me, and as much as I hate it, he's right.

"Alright, tell me what you want," Toot chimes in as he pulls out his cell phone, I assume, to take notes.

I tell him what I want just as my cell phone chimes. I pull it out and see a text from Ambros. Opening it up, I chuckle at the message.

So how's the epic love story going? He fall in love with you yet? Did you fall in love with him? The suspense is killing me. Also, my sister went fucking nuts over the signed book. Thanks again for that. Not sure how I'll top Christmas.

"Who's that?" Havoc asks, reading over my shoulder.

"Ambros. I met him on the plane on my way to London."

He tenses beneath me, his grip on my hips tightening.

"He's been rooting for you and wanted an update. He's hoping we'll find our happily ever after," I say lightly. He relaxes a touch, but I can see he still isn't happy. "His sister's a big fan, so I signed a book for him, and he wanted to thank me again."

"You mean like an autograph?" Crane asks with a frown.

I nod. "Yeah. Trust me, it's weird for me too."

"So you're famous?" He stares at me with an odd look on his face.

"In the book community, yeah, I guess."

"You're famous, and you didn't tell me?" he exclaims, sounding almost hurt, making me cock my head in surprise.

"Kinda pretentious to walk around with a banner saying, *hey, I'm a famous author.*"

"Like fuck it is. I'd walk around naked wearing nothing but a sandwich board, telling everyone who would listen."

"I'm okay with Tinkerbell walking around—" Toot gets cut off by a growling Havoc.

"Finish that sentence and die."

"Touchy motherfucker," Toot grumbles under his breath.

"I can't find you." Crane looks up from his phone and narrows his eyes.

"I'm lying. I'm actually a stripper. My stage name's Heaven Leigh."

"Shit, is that true?"

"No." I shake my head and grin. "I was an escort. It's where I met Havoc. He was a client I used to see in prison for conjugal visits, so imagine our surprise when we bumped into each other at the clubhouse."

He drops his phone as his mouth falls open in shock.

I look back at Havoc and laugh. "Please tell me he's not the brains of the operation."

The guys laugh loudly as I turn back to Crane and give him an innocent smile. I lean forward and wait until he does the same, as if I'm bestowing a big secret on him.

"I met Havoc two weeks after I woke up with him inside me, stealing my virginity in the middle of night. Then he kidnapped me and held me hostage, all in the hopes of making me fall in love with him."

Crane shakes his head and laughs. "Nice try, but I'm not falling for another one of your stories."

Havoc chuckles behind me, burying his face in my hair and I smile.

"Anyway, you won't find me under my real name. Try looking up Celeste Sky."

He bends down to pick his phone up, and I wait while he Googles me. Mac and Toot head toward the door after phoning the restaurant and placing everyone's orders.

"Call in if anything seems off," Havoc tells them.

"Will do," Toot calls back as they leave.

"Holy shit." Crane says, looking at me in shock.

I just grin. "I don't know how to say this, but I'm kind of a big deal."

"And she quotes *Anchorman*," he whispers reverently.

"If you don't stop looking at her like that, Crane, you'll end up with more than stars in your eyes," Havoc warns him.

"I don't suppose I could talk you into sharing, like our former president?" He ducks as Havoc throws my empty mug at him. "So that's a no then?"

"You must have a death wish." Kruger chuckles, picking up the cup, that luckily didn't break, and placing it in the sink.

"Tell me about this Ambros guy."

"I told you, I met him on the plane to London. He was nice."

Havoc growls, and I turn to look at him. "What's your problem?"

"I don't like other men texting you," Havoc grumbles.

"Well, it's a good thing you're not my daddy. I've had it up to here with controlling men, so if you would rather I don't sprinkle arsenic all over your food, you'll learn to trust me and swallow down any accusations your brain might conjure up. I'm not a cheat. I'm not Lola and won't pay for her sins."

I go to climb off his lap, but he grips my hips.

"Not accusing you of anything, cupcake, but I'm a guy. I know what guys see when they look at you, and I'm not okay with that."

"What do you mean? What do they see?"

"Sex."

"You're nuts." I turn to Kruger. "Tell him he's insane."

"Sorry, sweetheart. Those little skirts and red lips? Trust me when I say there isn't a man in the club that hasn't thought about fucking the innocence out of you. There is nothing sexier than a good girl gone bad. We like an angel on her knees with her halo around her ankles."

I have no clue what to say about that, but Havoc is apparently done talking and has chosen violence instead.

He lifts me off his lap before I realize what he's doing. Thankfully, Kruger's figured it out and takes off, Havoc hot on his heels.

"She asked. And you know none of us would touch her now that she's yours."

"Yeah, well, I thought that once before, and look what happened."

"Nevaeh's right. She's not Lola, and we're not this club."

Havoc stops, looking from Kruger to Crane, who is watching everything with a grin, then to me.

"Don't touch him. He's right—he was answering my question." I stand with my hands on my hips and glare at him.

"I don't give a fuck."

"Well, I do. You can't beat up everyone who looks at me, talks to me, or flirts with me."

He stalks toward me.

"Wanna bet?"

Chapter Seventeen

Havoc

I toss her over my shoulder before she can make a run for it and carry her upstairs, ignoring her protests and my brothers laughing. I head down the hall and kick open the door, throwing her on what used to be my bed and reach for the button of her jeans. "What are you doing? I'm not having sex in this bed."

She tries to roll away, but I stop her, yanking the zipper of her pants down before I tug the tight denim over her hips and ass, along with her black panties.

"Havoc!" She spits my name like a curse, but I just grin. She hesitates, seeing the look of sin on my face.

"I'm going to eat you until you scream my name. Then I'm going to fuck you until you can't remember it."

She gasps as I thrust two fingers inside her without warning. She squirms to get free, but with her jeans around her ankles, she's not going anywhere.

"I want you to come all over these sheets," I growl, barely able to hold back.

"Oh God, Havoc, this is so wrong," she moans, her body trembling as I work her over. She's dripping wet now, soaking my fingers and I can't wait another second to be inside her.

I rip my jeans open and pull my cock out. Positioning myself between her legs, I ease my cock inside her before slamming home, her back arching at the intrusion. Gripping both her hands in my hand, I pin them above her head as I thrust into her over and over.

I take her mouth in a brutal kiss, my teeth tugging her lip, my tongue fucking her mouth. My blood's still boiling from what happened downstairs, but when I pull back and look down at her, everything fades away.

Her eyes roll into the back of her head, making me feel like a fucking god. I don't know what it is about this woman, but she has this way of banishing the darkness. I'm never going to be a good man, but holding an angel makes me better. I'll be damned if I do anything that will take me away from her, whether that means in cuffs or a coffin.

I don't want her to find happiness after me. I want her tied so damn tightly to me that not even Death himself could tear us apart. Hell, I'd come back and possess a motherfucker just to keep her. Nevaeh is mine and always will be. There is nothing I won't do to keep her.

"Coming here should have been a nightmare, but you make everything feel like a dream," I tell her when I pull back and stare down into her eyes.

I gentle my thrusts so she can focus on what I'm saying.

"I love you. I've loved you before I even knew who you were. Your smell wrapped around me, and suddenly, I knew I was home. I know you're mad at me for what happened downstairs, but I've lost so much, I can't lose you, too. You're it for me."

I kiss her softly as a tear falls from her eye. I pick up speed and trailing across her jaw, down her neck. When I reach where her shoulder meets her neck, I bite down, needing to mark her like she's marked me.

"Havoc, I'm going to come," she gasps.

I let go of her hands and pull back onto my knees, gripping her hips tightly, so I can watch my cock sliding in and out of her. Using my thumb, I stroke her clit, and she cries out, her hips lifting desperately, chasing her pleasure.

"That's it, cupcake, come for me."

I pinch her clit, and her body tenses, my name falling from her lips in a breathless whisper as she comes hard.

Seeing her come undone for me is all I need to push me over the edge. I pulse inside her before pulling my cock out and coming all over her pussy, my cock still twitching as I stroke her clit.

When I stop coming, I slip my fingers back inside her spasming pussy, rubbing them against her front wall. I know I've found the right spot when she gasps and her eyes roll. I thrust my fingers faster, feeling her body start shaking as I focus on making her lose control.

With my free hand, I start stroking her clit again, never easing up the pressure. She tries to hold back and pull away, too sensitive, but I'm not letting her go until she comes again. I keep going, her head thrashing from side to side. Her legs tremble, and her voice turns hoarse from whispered pleas. I know it won't take long now.

"Let go, Cupcake. I'm not gonna stop until you soak us both."

That's all she needs to hear. She lets go, squirting all over me and the bed, making me grin.

Call it spite, but the thought of Lola and Driller sleeping in the bed I made my woman drench makes something inside me stir with dark satisfaction.

"Oh god. We need to change these sheets. I'm so embarrassed."

"Don't be. You were fucking incredible. And technically, this is my bed. If I want to make you squirt all over it, I will."

She groans, covering her face with her hands. "You're trying to kill me. I just know it."

I chuckle as I get to my feet and strip before scooping her up and carrying her into the bathroom.

I sit her on the counter and pull her pants and underwear off the rest of the way.

"Most people take their clothes off before they have sex, but oh no, not us," she mutters to herself as she lifts her arms for me to take off her shirt.

I pull it over her head and place a quick kiss on her lips. "It's not my fault I can't wait to get inside you," I tell her as I remove her bra.

She rolls her eyes, but I don't miss the grin she tries to hide as she dips her head.

I slide my finger under her chin and tilt her head back. "I meant what I said before. You're it for me. You're my reward for the fucking hell this club put me through. I get that it's a lot, and I'm a little intense sometimes."

She snorts. "You have to admit, this is fast. If you were talking to one of your men, you'd be telling them to slow down, that the woman was a gold digger, or that he was thinking with his penis."

I shake my head. "You can say *dick*, baby. Or better yet, *cock*." I press in closer so she can feel me getting hard again.

She flushes and bites her lip.

"You think G didn't know right away that Amity was it for him?"

She opens her mouth, then closes it, knowing I'm right.

"We could have dated. I—"

"Ran the first chance you got."

Her mouth snaps shut at that.

I tuck her hair behind her ear and rest my forehead against hers. "You're mine, and I'm not letting you run from me again. I don't want you in *my* bed—I want you in *ours*. I want to share a life with you, a home with you. I want to fill your cunt with my cum and your belly with our babies—"

She covers my mouth with her hand.

"I really hate that word," she growls, but the flush of her skin and the speed of her pulse makes a liar out of her.

I lick her hand, making her pull it away. Using her distraction, I slide my fingers through her pussy.

"Well, look at that," I say, lifting my wet fingers. "My good girl's a dirty liar."

She starts to protest, but I cover her mouth with mine, lifting her off the counter and carrying her into the shower, where I fuck her again just to remind her who she belongs to.

She dips her head, ignoring my brothers' grins as she sits curled up in the corner of the couch, eating her reheated Chinese food. When I finally finished fucking her, I let her shower and brought up our bags so she could put on clean clothes. I take in the short, pleated skirt in dark purple and her Rainbow Brite T-shirt and grin. The only thing biker about my woman is the dick she rides.

I focus back on Toot and Mac, who look tense.

"Alright, spill it. I know you wanted us to eat first, but we can all tell how pissed you both are."

Mac sighs. "People are scared. And I'm not talkin' about the kinda scared you'd expect when you have an MC in the area. We"—he nods to Toot—"grew up in a town where a one percent club ran things, and everyone lived in fear of them. That's what this feels like.

"I bumped into a woman when I was coming out of the restroom, and she started bawlin' her fucking eyes out. She was shaking so bad, I thought she was gonna pass out."

"What the fuck? The locals were wary of us, sure, but that makes sense. But fear? That's fucking new. You get anything out of anyone?"

"Talked to the fry cook from the diner on his smoke break. The guy was built like a brick shithouse and looked ready for a fight until he realized we weren't from this chapter and had no clue what was going on. He was happy to spill his guts then. He said the restaurant's a family business that's been here for over fifty years. He started working there ten years ago, back in high school. His uncle runs the place now, but they're thinking of selling and moving, even though they're making a killing."

"Why do I feel like I'm not gonna like this?"

"'Cause you're not. I mentioned your name. Dude remembered you. The whole town was pissed with how things went down—seems they knew the truth."

"I'm not surprised. What happened wasn't my style. Easy to guess something else went down."

"Maybe, but I got the feeling they were getting solid intel from somewhere," Mac adds.

"You mean from the club? But why?"

"Maybe the club wasn't as onboard with things as Khan made it seem. Either way, someone didn't want the town turning on you. Whoever the source was, they're well protected. I couldn't get the name out of him. All he said was you weren't the only one, then he clammed up tighter than a nun's cunt."

"Oh for the love of God, can you all please stop using that word?" Nevaeh complains, lightening the mood as she makes us all laugh.

"I'm sorry, Tinkerbell. Perhaps you'd prefer *lady garden*? Or *petting pearl*," Toot teases her.

She stands up and walks over to where we're sitting at the table. "Don't be mean, or I'll tell Havoc I caught you sniffing my underwear earlier."

It takes a second for my brain to process her words. When it does, all I see is red and all rational thought goes out the window. It isn't until I feel Nevaeh's hands on my face that I snap out of it and realize I have Toot pinned to the floor with my knee pressing against his chest and my hands wrapped around his throat.

"It's okay, Havoc. You can let the mean boy go now."

"Man, she got you good," Crane laughs, clearly enjoying the show.

I release Toot before turning to Nevaeh and burying my face in her hair. "Nobody sniffs your panties but me," I growl.

"Wait, what?" She pushes me away. "Ew, Havoc. Just when I think I've got you housebroken, you go and act like an animal again." she huffs, placing her hands on her hips.

I grin because her attitude is taller than she is. Still on my knees, I grab Nevaeh and pull her closer, her hands flying to my shoulders to stop herself from falling. Once I have her where I want her, I reach under her skirt, ignoring her protests as I grab the lace of her panties and rip them from her body. She stares down at me in shock as I pull my hand free from her skirt, holding my prize. I bring the scrap of fabric to my nose and inhale deeply.

"You're crazy," she hisses quietly.

"There isn't a guy in this room who doesn't wish he were me right now."

She whips her head around, taking in the hungry looks of the others before she flees back to her spot on the sofa.

"You're a lucky bastard." Kruger says with an envious sigh.

Sitting here in the house I once made a home with another woman, after being betrayed by everyone I cared about, I can't help but agree.

"I know," I say before turning to Mac. "Now tell me the rest."

Chapter Eighteen

Nevaeh

"So all those businesses are paying the club for protection?" I ask, later that night, as we're lying in bed.

Havoc's been filling me in on what he and the guys were talking about earlier. I'm actually surprised. Bikers usually keep their women out of club business, but I guess he realizes that if he wants us to be a team, he has to let me in—even if it's just a little.

"It's not unusual," he says, tracing lazy patterns on my back with his fingers. "It means if gangs or punks cause trouble, the club'll step in. But that's not what's happening. People keep calling for help, and all the club did was jack up their protection prices."

"I would've stopped paying if they weren't doing their jobs," I grumble.

"Doesn't work that way," he admits. "The club would've caused trouble to prove a point, then pretend they had nothing to do with it."

"That's pretty childish."

"You're right. It's fucked up, and something that shouldn't be happening," he concedes. "They're not some baby upstarts. They didn't need to sink so low, especially when it's the club's fault the businesses want to bail."

"What else?"

"Huh?"

"I might've stopped listening to you guys, but I saw your face. I know it's more than what you're telling me."

He blows out a frustrated breath, and I can tell he's struggling with whether to tell me or not. I don't say anything. I know I'm overstepping, so I wait. After a few minutes, he finally speaks. "Women have been going missing."

I lift my head to look at him, the crack in the blinds letting enough moonlight in to see the circles under his eyes and how angry he looks.

"What?"

He sighs. "It started with a couple women from a few towns over. Apparently, they came to party at the clubhouse. They never went home, and when people came looking, the club denied they'd ever been there. Then, a few months later, another girl went missing. She said she was going to the

Raven Souls clubhouse to meet a guy, but he swears up and down that she never showed up. He was pissed she stood him up."

"Have any more women gone missing?"

He nods. "Yeah."

"And none of the women have been found?"

He shakes his head. "No, not from what Mac and Toot were told. But I'm gonna get G on it."

"Do you think someone's trying to mess with the club? Like, deliberately pointing fingers in their direction? I mean, they'd make an easy target, especially if people are already mad at them about the extortion thing."

"It's definitely one possibility."

"And the other?"

"There's two. The first, the club's got a brother who's lost his fucking mind. He's taking these girls and getting rid of them when he's done. And the club's either too distracted to notice or are helping him cover his tracks." He swallows. I don't blame him, everything he just said is horrific.

"And the second?" I ask softly, even though I know. I just don't want to put it into words when I can read Havoc's heartbreak as clearly as if it were my own.

"The club's trafficking women."

I deflate under the weight of his words.

"Some clubs deal in the flesh trade. But that's not something the Raven Souls have ever gotten into. Sure, it's been brought up before—there's a hell of a lot of money involved in trafficking—but it's always been shot down."

"But you haven't been a part of this club for a long time, and things change," I say, and he sighs.

"I know. And that's why I can't just ignore it. I can't say none of them would do this shit when they've already proved they're not the men I thought they were. The problem is, what do I do now?"

I rest my head on his chest, tracing my fingers over his tattoos. "You can't let them get away with it."

"I know. I came here to hear what Khan had to say and to find out what the fuck was going on, but now, there are women missing. I need to find out what the fuck happened to them."

"But how? No one here's going to tell you anything. You're not one of them anymore."

"I'm gonna send someone in to find out what the fuck's going on."

I press my lips to his chest, feeling the tension rolling off him. I don't know who he'll send in, but if they get hurt, Havoc's going to blame himself. But if he doesn't do anything and more women go missing... I'm not sure he'll be able to live with himself.

"I know it's not much, but whatever you decide, I'll be right by your side."

He freezes beneath me. "You mean that?" His voice is deeper, almost surprised.

I look up at him and realize that he's done nothing but show me how much he wants me, and I haven't done the same. Though, to be fair, part of me still wonders if this isn't some kind of Stockholm syndrome.

But I guess it doesn't matter anymore, because the thought of walking away from this man hurts my heart. Okay, so he might be a little psycho. And yeah, he's possessive and gets jealous easily. But I've never felt unsafe with him, not even when I was his captive. Okay there was that one time I wondered if he was going to kill me...

I shake my head. "Yeah, I mean it. Turns out there's nowhere else I'd rather be than with you."

He grabs me under my arms and pulls me up his body, kissing me hard.

I tangle my fingers in his hair, holding him close. Kissing Havoc feels like being struck by lightning. My whole-body tingles, stealing my breath and my ability to think clearly.

When he pulls back, my lips feel swollen.

"You tired?"

"No," I answer, feeling my nipples tighten and my pussy clench at the look in his eyes.

"Good, because I want you to climb up here and ride my face."

I bite my lip, feeling self-conscious, but I let it go. If Havoc wants me, he *wants all of me*. There's no judgment in the way his hands run over my body, just heat, raw and unfiltered. But still, I'm not sure how to do this. What if I fall off and sprain my vagina?

"Okay, maybe I'm a little tired," I mutter, because my brain's not firing on all cylinders.

"That's okay; all you have to do is hold on and enjoy the ride."

He lifts me, making me squeal and forcing me to reach for the headboard. He slides down the bed until his nose skims my clit, and I gasp. Havoc yanks me down until I'm basically smothering him.

Suddenly, I imagine the police showing up, asking how he died, and me admitting I suffocated him with my vagina, but I quickly shake it off.

Some things are worth the risk.

I grind against his face as he works my clit, lapping up my arousal like it's his favorite thing in the world. I shift my hips, then jolt when I feel his finger press against my ass.

I shudder, gripping the bedframe tighter. I'm a little scared, but also really curious. He drags his finger lower, dipping it into my pussy before sliding it back to stroke it over my tight hole again. I tense, but he sucks my clit, distracting me. My head falls back, and I gasp as he slides his tongue inside me, stiffening it so it feels like a tiny cock, making me groan as he fucks and licks me with it.

When he moves back to my clit, I know I'm not going to last. Havoc might have the temper of an angry toddler, but he has the oral skills of a god. Lord knows I'm ready to worship at his altar.

I tense, lifting my head as he slips his finger into my ass. A shocked gasp escapes me, my body tightening. My back arches, and I throw my head back, screaming his name as I come hard enough to see stars.

When I come back down to earth, I find myself, once again, lying across his chest.

Unable to lift my head, I grumble, "Go wash your hands."

He laughs but does as I ask, gently rolling me off him. When he comes back, he climbs in behind me and wraps his arms around me tightly.

I sigh, feeling safe and—dare I say it—happy, something I never thought I'd say. Maybe I just needed a chance to really live. Amity gave me a safe place to land and the freedom to spread my wings, but Havoc... He gave me a reason to fly. I've never felt more alive than when I'm with him, even if half the time I'm plotting his demise.

"You love me yet?" he whispers.

"Not yet, but I like you a lot more than I did yesterday," I murmur.

I fall asleep to the sound of his laughter.

Sitting on the back of his bike the next day, I can't find anything to laugh about.

"He's where?" Havoc growls at the biker called Byte, this chapter's equivalent of G.

"Khan and Driller had a meeting with a supplier, but they couldn't reschedule."

"Funny how they never mentioned it yesterday."

Byte shrugs. "I don't get told shit unless they need me."

I frown. It doesn't seem that way at the mother chapter, but maybe that's because G is also the VP.

"Sounds to me like all of you are on a need-to-know basis. Who is the supplier, and what exactly are they supplying?"

Byte looks uncomfortable. "I don't know. It's something the president and VP are working on. They won't bring it to the table until everything is squared away. You know how they are."

"Yeah, Byte, I know how they are. You got the shit I asked Khan for yesterday?"

"He told me to tell you he'll forward it when he returns. He didn't have time to get it ready before he left."

"How convenient," Mac snorts.

"Well, I don't need Khan for this, so it looks like you're up, Byte. Who is the treasurer these days?"

"Elmo."

I nearly choke on my tongue. "Did he say, Elmo?"

Byte narrows his eyes at me, but Havoc barks at him. "Fetch him and bring him to church. We'll meet you there."

"Khan won't be happy—"

"I outrank Khan, Byte. You gonna go against my orders?"

Byte hesitates before shaking his head. "I'll find Elmo."

"Wise choice. Bring your laptop when you join us. I want info, and I'm not leaving without it. And while you're at it, I want anything you have on those missing girls. I've been in town and seen the reaction of town folks around here. We were never going to win a popularity contest, but now you're up for most likely to get stabbed to death. I want to know why, and I don't want to hear any bullshit. As it stands right now, this club is being watched because I don't trust that Khan and Driller have your best interests at heart. If you know something, bring what you have and whoever else you need to. But fuck me around, and I'll add you to the shit list Khan and Driller are on, got it?"

"Got it." He turns and leaves.

"I'm not sure he's got it," I admit, making Crane laugh.

"Well, we'll find out soon enough."

"How about you and me go for ice cream and leave the others to play detective?" Crane asks me when he stops laughing.

Havoc looks at Crane. "Don't let her out of your sight."

Crane gives him a brief nod.

"We can stay," I offer, not wanting him to worry about me.

"No, go get ice cream. Things will get tense here. I want you out of the line of fire."

"Okay, just be careful."

I climb off the bike and walk over to Crane but stop.

"Wait," I say, turning back to Havoc. "Am I allowed to ride on the back of his bike? I remember how mad Amity got when G had Monica on the back of his."

In a couple strides, Havoc's standing in front of me. He takes my hands in his as he looks down at me. "I need you out of here, Cupcake. Your safety trumps everything else."

"Okay," I tell him softly. He lets go of my hands, and I turn, taking Crane's hand and climbing on behind him.

I don't wrap my arms around him like I do Havoc. I grab the sides of his jacket and hold on tight as he starts up his bike and pulls out of the parking lot, away from the clubhouse. I send up a silent prayer that everything goes smoothly because I can't lose him—not now that I'm falling for him.

I remind myself that Havoc's more than capable of handling himself, and he has men with him who'd give their lives to protect him—not that I want it to come to that, of course.

As we ride into town, I take everything in. I can see why people like it here, even if I do prefer our town more.

It's pretty, though. I'll give it that.

But I immediately notice the reaction of the people we pass. The guys were right—there's no missing the look of fear on their faces. I watch as people scurry off the streets into stores they hadn't planned on visiting and as mothers grab their children and hurry away. The ones who don't run just stand and stare. But there are no friendly waves or nods of the head.

My stomach twists. Are we even safe here? They're scared—and they have every right to be. But sometimes, fear makes people act without thinking. It turns into anger, and then, before they know it, the victims become the very people they hate. It's a vicious cycle that I want no part in.

I'm considering whether or not to yank on Crane's jacket to tell him to keep going when he pulls into the parking lot of an old-fashioned ice cream shop. I've never seen anything like it, except for in the movies—and that one time when I was little and my parents took Citi and me to Disney World. I smile at the memory of us waiting in line with my dad and how he laughed when we ordered ice cream from Goofy, who used the whole can of whipped cream on Citi's sundae. That had been a great day and one of the last few memories I have of us happy before everything fell apart.

With a wistful sigh, I shake off the memories and wait for us to stop. Crane holds out his hand for me, which I take gratefully as I climb off. I pull off my helmet, and he takes it from me before climbing off himself.

He looks around, then nods toward the empty picnic tables at the side of the building. "We should probably sit out here. Not sure we'll get much of a warm welcome inside."

"Yeah, you're probably right," I say, glancing at the shop before turning back to him. "I think I should go in by myself."

"No. If anything happens to you, Havoc will kill me."

"They're not scared of me, Crane. They're scared of you. Well, not *you*, but bikers in general. And maybe not all bikers, but Raven Souls for sure." He stares at me as I ramble. "Anyway, you'll be able to see me the whole time through the glass. Plus, I'm armed. Havoc made me wear my gun today." I touch the gun at the small of my back.

"You know how to shoot it?"

I nod.

"You know, shooting a gun and shooting someone are two completely different things, right?"

"Yes, I know, Crane. But I'm not planning on shooting anyone today. I'm just going in to get us ice cream."

He looks at me, not saying anything, and I sigh. "If I have to draw my gun, you'll already be moving toward me. Like I said, you'll be able to watch my every move."

"Are you always this stubborn?"

"I don't know what you're talking about," I flutter my lashes at him.

He sighs, pulling out his wallet.

"I have money."

"Woman."

"Man," I throw back, hands on my hips, making his lips twitch.

"I see Havoc still has some sass to work out of you."

"Do you want me to use you for target practice, Crane?" I ask him sweetly.

He scoffs. "We both know you won't shoot me. You like me. Everyone likes me."

"So modest."

"It's a blessing and a curse," he sighs, and I can't help but laugh.

"Now hurry your cute ass in there and get us some ice cream."

"What kind?"

"Surprise me," he says before heading over to one of the picnic tables. He sits down on the wooden bench and kicks his feet up beside him. I give him a salute, making him chuckle, and head inside.

.

I push the door open. The little bell above it announces my arrival. But I know everyone saw us pull in. The room goes quiet as they all stare at me. Ignoring the urge to squirm, I head straight for the counter. Thankfully, there's no line, so I take a moment to check out the glass case to see what they have.

"Can I help you?" a gruff voice asks.

I look up to find the young woman who'd been standing behind the counter gone and, in her place, a man in his late forties, wearing a white hat and a matching apron. His name tag says Ed, but judging by the scowl on his face, he probably wouldn't be happy if I called him that.

"Can I get a couple of ice creams, please?"

He grunts, so I take that as a yes.

"I'll take one with a single scoop of bubble gum and the other with a scoop of the bourbon and a scoop of vanilla."

Without a word, he turns and starts banging around. Well, okay then. I take a seat at the nearest empty table. Looking outside, I see Crane watching me like a hawk and give him a little wave. He shakes his head and grins as I turn away.

I glance around and see people still watching me. Some quickly look away when they realize I've noticed them, and some glare, while others talk in hushed whispers, disdain clear on their faces.

"You know what kind of man you have out there?" a voice behind me says, making me turn to see an older couple sitting nearby.

The woman grabs the man's arm and hushes him. "Be quiet, David."

He shakes her off. "No, Marjorie. She should know."

"I know exactly what kind of man Crane is. But he's not my man. Havoc is."

That causes the room to buzz.

"Havoc's back?"

The question comes from another table, where an older man sits with two little boys who have ice cream all over their faces. I'm guessing they're his grandkids, but you never know these days.

"Sorta. Havoc's the President of the Mother Chapter of Raven Souls now. He's back to figure out what the heck's going on with his old club. And trust me, he's not happy. I'm guessing some of you know what really happened with Havoc and the club."

"Those bastards shafted Havoc without a second thought," David says, shaking his head.

"He didn't know anyone knew the truth until yesterday. It helps that people didn't think he was guilty."

One of the others in the room clears their throat, drawing my attention. "So, you know what's been going on here since he's been gone?"

"We heard yesterday that girls have been going missing."

Everyone nods, confirming what the cook told Mac and Toot.

I lower my voice, knowing I shouldn't be telling them any of this. Havoc will probably punish me afterward, but something tells me this might be the one chance we have to get the townspeople to help us.

"Havoc wanted to remove Khan and Driller from their positions—"

"And now?" the ice cream guy barks, cutting me off.

"Now we need to find out what happened to the girls first, especially if Khan and Driller are the only ones who know."

The men in the room exchange glances before David speaks. "Marjorie, take the boys home for Jorden. We won't be far behind you."

Marjorie gets up and walks over to the boys covered in ice

cream. She wipes their hands with a paper napkin before taking them outside.

David scans the room and nods at two teen girls in the back. "Becca, Lou, you two should head out too."

"But David, this affects us," Lou protests.

He looks at me, but I shrug. "I think they're old enough to make their own decisions. I've always believed keeping women in the dark 'for their own good' is a load of crap. How can they protect themselves if they don't know what's going on? It's the equivalent of asking us to fight blindfolded."

He sighs and nods. "Okay, girls, you can stay." Looking back at me, he nods to the door.

"Better bring your boy in here."

I take a deep breath and pray that I've done the right thing before standing and heading outside.

Chapter Nineteen

Havoc

I lean back in my seat, watching Byte and Ferris watch Elmo, who's going through everything he's got.

"There's been some discrepancies, and I've brought them up with Khan a few times, but he keeps telling me not to worry."

"When you say discrepancies..."

He sighs and hands me the papers. "Somehow, we're missing close to ten grand every month."

Byte curses, and I lean forward to look over the reports.

"Khan had me stop doing the accounts monthly and instead wanted them done quarterly, then last year wanted them done annually. It makes it harder to track shit because I have more to go through, but I'm a tenacious fucker when I need to be."

"I take it you didn't know about this?" I say, looking up from the papers at the other two men.

"No. I had no fucking idea," Byte growls.

And Ferris just shakes his head.

"If that was me, I'd be pissed and want to know who the fuck took the money."

"So what does that tell you?" Mac asks, already knowing the answer.

Elmo looks like he's been punched in the gut, but Byte's pissed. "That Khan's the one taking it. Son of a bitch."

"Why, though?" Toot asks. "Is he spending it on blow and women?"

"Good question," I say, turning to Byte, Ferris, and Elmo.

The three of them look at each other.

"Look,"—I put the papers down—"I'm not going to sugar-coat it. I don't trust you. How can I, when everyone here was more than happy to let me take the fall?"

"We didn't know," Elmo growls.

"What?"

"None of us knew what the fuck was going on. Khan and Driller weren't saying anything, and Lola was MIA. Khan said you got into trouble but wanted to keep it quiet until you had a plan. We were fucking pissed, honestly. We were your brothers, and you shut us out. It went against every-thing the brotherhood stood for. We didn't know what happened until you were sentenced, and then you refused to see anyone but Gunther. We wanted to visit anyway, but Khan said we should respect your wishes and leave you alone. When we pushed, he ordered us to stay away from you."

"That fucking motherfucker," Kruger snarls.

I don't even know what to say. I should've fucking known.

"That's not what happened, though, is it?" Elmo sighs.

"What exactly did Khan tell you?"

"He said you insisted on taking the fall for Driller to keep him out of prison, and then once you were out, we were never to mention it."

"How fucking convenient," Mac scoffs.

"Khan ordered me to take the fall. Said if I didn't, I'd be kicked out of the club in bad standing. He needed Driller for the Fargo deal, and I was expendable. I was under the impression that you all knew what was going on and agreed and just chose not to visit me when I was locked up. I only found out about Driller and Lola a month before I was released, when Blade came to offer me the president position."

They're all quiet for a moment, like my words hit them harder than they expected. Then, without warning, Byte picks up his chair and throws it across the room.

"Those motherfuckers," he snarls as Mac and Toot jump up and move around the table to restrain him.

"You really didn't know?"

Elmo shakes his head. "I knew something was off, I just

didn't know what." He runs his hands through his hair, looking like he might throw up.

Ferris stares down at the table. He must sense me watching him because he looks up, his jaw tense, fire flashing in his eyes. "I wanna request a transfer."

I suck in a sharp breath.

"Can't stay in a club when there's no trust," Byte adds, shaking off Mac and Toot and heading over to pick up his chair.

"I think a lot of brothers will feel the same way when they find out," Elmo says numbly, still reeling from the shock.

I look at Kruger, who shrugs, before turning to Mac and Toot. They're thinking the same thing I am—can we trust these guys? Five minutes ago, I would've said not a chance. But now...

"I'll be straight with you. I'm still not sure I trust you. A lot's happened. But I get what you're saying. The truth is, Khan's poison, and I'm here to figure out how much of the club he's corrupted."

"I get it," Byte says with a harsh laugh. "I wouldn't fucking trust me either."

Deciding to test the waters, I tap my fingers on the table and steer the conversation to the brothers sent to kill me. "What can you tell me about Acid and Knuckles?"

"They haven't changed, if that's what you're asking. Still have their noses up Khan's ass. But you know Khan—he loves brown-nosers, so it works." Elmo shrugs.

"You know where they are?" Mac asks.

"They went nomad after we heard you were out. Khan said you had some beef with them and thought it'd be better to get them outta the way while you got settled. We didn't know you weren't coming back, though." He snorts.

"As if you'd come back," Ferris mutters, shaking his head. "Fuck me. I can't believe this shit." He sighs.

"Khan told you they went nomad, and that was it?" Toot asks, and they all shake their heads.

"What did Khan tell you was the reason we were coming?"

Byte clenches his fists. "Said you wanted to make peace with Driller and Lola."

Kruger whistles. "The man lies as easily as he breathes."

"None of you thought it was fucking wrong that Lola and Driller were together while her old man was inside?" Mac crosses his arms.

Elmo frowns. "Driller told us you broke up with her when you were sentenced. Said you knew something was going on between him and Lola and didn't want her waiting around."

I huff out a laugh. "And Lola backed that up?"

Elmo sighs. "Lola's changed. She doesn't talk to any of us. Keeps to herself. Only comes around when Driller wants her here."

"Can't say I feel sorry for my cheating ex. She made her bed."

"There was no breakup, was there?"

I give Ferris a look, and he shakes his head.

"Gotta say, though, finding out my brother was banging my old lady and that she was pregnant felt like shit. But knowing they were playing happy families , and none of you blinked... You knew me. You saw us together. Do you honestly think I would've stepped aside for Driller?" I scoff.

At least the three of them have the decency to look ashamed.

"I should really thank them, though. If it wasn't for them hooking up, I wouldn't have Nevaeh."

"I gotta say, Lola and Nevaeh couldn't be more different." Byte grins.

"Yeah, in more fucking ways than you know," I growl, and the smile falls from his face. I sigh. "Look, I can't tell you everything right now—not until I know for sure who I can trust. But you should know—if you back Khan, I'll take you down with him."

I turn to Ferris. "I'm not transferring you—not yet anyway. But if you want to prove your loyalty, I need eyes and ears. I've only been here a day, and I already don't like what I'm hearing."

"The missing girls aren't us, Havoc. I know you have no reason to believe us, but we'd never be involved in that."

"I'm sure you believe that, Elmo. But if you're as clueless as you say, then a lot of shit's already happened right under your nose, and you missed it."

"Taking girls is on another level, though. We'd never miss that," he argues.

"We were called here because of Acid and Knuckles. Khan says he sent them to welcome me home, and now they're missing."

"But that doesn't make sense. Out of all the brothers, those are the last two you'd want to see, not counting Driller." Elmo frowns.

"Exactly. But he sent them, and they did head down my way, but it wasn't to welcome me home. They thought G was me and ran him and his old lady off the road. Almost killed them both. They came back, and when they saw they were still alive, they started shooting. G was unconscious, and Amity threw herself on top of him. She took a bullet protecting him."

When Elmo opens his mouth, I hold up my hand. I'm not going over this shit again. I can still hear Amity's voice, trying to hold herself together in a fucked-up situation she should never have been in.

"Now, Acid and Knuckles aren't missing—G and I showed them our special kind of hospitality after they admitted Khan sent them to kill me."

Mac cuts in, his voice cold. "You breathe a word of this to anyone outside of this room, and I'll come back and kill you all myself. My loyalty is to Havoc. I couldn't give a flying fuck about the rest of you."

"We won't say anything. You have our word," Ferris says.

"I'm guessing you've got a plan, and I know we won't be told shit. I get it. But when this is all over, we'd like a chance to make things right."

I knock on the table before standing. I'm not promising anything. "Give me everything you have here and send the rest to G. I don't care how small or insignificant it seems—I want to know everything. Khan can't stay in power, but if there's a chance he knows anything about the missing women —and they're alive—I won't risk them. I can't take out Khan until I know for sure what happened to them."

"I'll dig too," Byte says. "Now that I know what I'm looking for. Khan told me it wasn't our business, but I don't give a fuck. Even if he's innocent of this, someone out there has them."

"Run everything through G. I want this done clean. We can't afford any mistakes."

"You got it."

I head to the door, and they all follow me. My phone chimes, so I pull it out and see a message from Crane.

On our way back. Your old lady got some of the town folk to talk. You'll want to hear this.

"Change of plans. I need this room. Crane and Nevaeh are on their way back—send them in when they get here."

None of them argue. They leave with a nod and a look of shame that isn't theirs to carry if they were kept in the dark. Once they're gone, I close the door and lean against it as the guys go sit back down.

"Apparently, my old lady got some people in town to talk."

"Of course she did. Her daddy's a preacher. She must've inherited some of his 'confess-your-sins' magic to make people want to spill their guts to her," Toot says with a grin.

"You keep your sins away from my woman, Toot."

His grin turns cocky, but he doesn't say anything.

"You believe them?" Kruger asks, nodding to the door and changing the subject.

"My gut says they're telling the truth. And if they don't know, then my guess is most of the others don't either."

"Not sure you'll have to deal with Khan when they hear the truth. They'll probably handle him themselves. He's made a fucking joke out of all of them."

"On the bright side, I don't think you'll have a problem changing the leadership," Mac says. "I was worried they'd fight for him. But if they lose faith in him when they find out that everything he stands for is a lie—and that he'll turn on them in a heartbeat to suit his needs—they'll vote him out in a second. The only question is, who's gonna take his place?"

"Nobody," I answer. "Not from here, anyway. I want the men to follow the rules and respect their president, but this just shows that following someone blindly isn't the way to go. We're an MC, not a fucking cult. Do you think G won't call me out? Or Midas or Hannibal? Even you three would question my decisions if you felt you needed to. There's a difference between loyalty and stupidity, but these guys are fucking sheep."

"Do you know who you want to fill the role? Because whoever you choose will have a hell of a time. They'll need thick skin. After a betrayal like this, it makes you question everyone. Trust me, we all felt it after what went down with Bear," Kruger states.

"Oh, I know."

He looks at me for a moment before cursing. "Shit, right. Sorry, Havoc. I forgot."

"No worries. But yeah, I have someone in mind. I just don't know if he'll go for it yet. I need to think about it some more. This place needs to be whipped into shape, and the last thing I want to do is put someone in and then have them change their mind six months down the line."

I'm saved from saying anything else when there's a knock on the door. I turn and pull it open.

"Hello, caveman." Nevaeh grins before jumping into my arms.

She wraps her legs around me and holds me tight as I carry her inside. Crane follows us in, and I hear him close the door behind us.

"You okay?" I ask, looking at her.

She lifts her head scrunches her nose. "I think I messed up, and I'm scared you'll be mad."

I brush her hair over her shoulder and sit down with her in my lap. "I can't promise I won't get mad, but I swear I'll never take it out on you. The last thing I want is for you to be scared to tell me things. I'd never hurt you, you hear me?"

I know the others are listening, but I don't give a fuck. The last thing I want is for Nevaeh to be afraid of me.

She nods.

"You won't ignore me, though, right?" she asks softly.

I frown, wondering where this is coming from. "Cupcake, I couldn't ignore you if I tried." I make a mental note to revisit this later, but now's not the time or the place.

"Okay.., so...um...I told them you were planning on getting rid of Khan and Driller." She bites her lips and tenses, but doesn't say anything else.

I look at Crane, who's watching Nevaeh with a soft look. "What happened?" I ask him.

"Folks are scared," he says. "Like Mac and Toot said, and the ones that aren't are pretty fucking pissed. The club basically told the town to fuck off and said the missing girls aren't their problem. When they pointed out that some of the girls were last seen here, they were threatened. Folks want the club gone. There's definitely no love lost there, that's for sure."

"They call the cops?" Kruger asks.

"Not sure if the sheriff's on the club's payroll, but the guy's near retirement and likes to ignore anything that might actually involve work."

"So, no help from him, then."

"If it's the same guy that was here when I left, then no.

Jenkins was a lazy bastard back then. If he'd done any work, he would've known I wasn't guilty."

"He probably knew. He just didn't care."

"Wouldn't surprise me." I sigh. "I want to leave as soon as possible. I don't know which brothers are loyal to the club and which are loyal to Khan."

"I feel like I missed something," Nevaeh says, looking up at me.

"I'll fill you in when we get back home. I want to call church and let everyone know what's going on first." She opens her mouth, but I cut her off before she can say anything. "All I can say is that it seems Khan's been lying and keeping shit to himself. And the brothers we talked to are pissed."

"Do you believe them?"

"My gut says yes, but I won't risk your safety on a feeling."

She smiles softly as she cups my cheek, and I lean down to kiss her just as her phone buzzes. She rolls her eyes, ignoring it, and places a loud kiss on my lips.

I grin down at her before looking over at Crane. "You got a contact? I want to keep them in the loop as much as possible. I don't want them thinking we ignored what they said and bailed."

"I got a couple, yeah. But there's this guy, David. He seems to be their unofficial spokesperson. I'll let him know we're leaving, but we'll be looking into the girls' disappearances and be back."

I nod as Nevaeh's phone goes off again. But before she can pull it out of her pocket, it starts pinging rapidly, making me frown. "What the hell?"

"Relax, caveman," she says, and I chuckle as she pulls out her phone. "It's just a bunch of notifications from Instagram. Let me just look quickly."

I watch, confused, as she checks her phone and freezes. "Fuck."

"What's wrong, baby?" I ask, but her eyes remain glued to the screen.

"Did Tinkerbell just swear? Aww, our baby's all grown up," Toot teases, pretending to wipe a tear from his eye.

Finally, she looks up at me, her face pale, biting her lip. "Looks like my real identity's just been revealed on a much bigger scale than I expected. Oh, God... my dad is going to kill me."

"Nobody's touching you," I tell her. "I'm sure it'll be fine." But even as I say it, her phone continues to ding.

She puts it on silent before closing her eyes in defeat. "Well, the cat's out of the bag now."

"How did it blow up like that? Seems kinda random," Kruger says, frowning.

She shows him a picture on her phone, and he chokes, his eyes widening. He looks at me quickly before I take a look.

It's a photo of Nevaeh at the airport with a huge guy smiling down at her. A surge of jealousy runs through me.

"That's the Ambros you were talking about? Ambros Deveraux?" Kruger asks, his voice filled with shock and awe, grabbing my attention.

Nevaeh nods slowly.

"Why does that name sound familiar?" Crane asks.

"Probably because he's the current UFC heavyweight champion."

I look at Nevaeh, who blushes.

"I think I'm going to start chaining you to the bed."

Chapter Twenty

Nevaeh

The ride home is long and uneventful, giving me way too much time to worry about how my father will react to the news. I'm not naïve enough to think he won't find out, especially with how quickly news spreads online.

My heart hurts at the thought of the upcoming confrontation. I knew it would happen eventually; I just hoped I'd have more time.

When we finally pull into the warehouse and climb off the bikes, I breathe out a sigh of relief, happy to be home. I think the guys feel the same. They follow behind us as Havoc places his hand on the small of my back and guides me through the warehouse toward the saloon.

"You okay?" He asks me once we're outside. "You're quieter than normal."

"Are you saying I'm usually loud?"

"No, but you do like to talk. I'm just not used to seeing you like this. You really are worried about your real name being linked to your pen name, aren't you?"

I sigh. "I shouldn't be. And honestly, once I did a book signing, I knew it was inevitable. People love taking pictures and posting them on social media, but the picture of me and Ambros together runs side by side with one of me taken at the book signing. And as I was tagged as both Nevaeh and Celeste it won't be long before my dad knows."

"It's because of your dad you use a pen name?"

"Yeah, but also because I didn't want the small-minded idiots back home to judge me for writing romance books."

"I would've thought your dad would be proud of you."

"He can't be. He still blames me for what happened to my sister. Besides, in his eyes, romance books promote temptation and undermine the teachings of the church on relationships and marriage."

He wraps his arm around my shoulder and tugs me against him. "He'll get over it. And if he doesn't, he'll lose another daughter and his future grandchildren."

I almost stumble but catch myself. As harsh as it may sound, he's right. If my dad can't accept me for who I am, then he doesn't deserve a place in my life. And as much as it hurts, it also brings with it a wave of relief.

The rest of the way is quiet, and when we step inside the saloon, we're greeted with a warm welcome, which is really nice and feels worlds away from where we've just been, making me smile.

I spot Amity in in the crowd, dressed in her running gear. She grins and waves me over.

"Go see your girl. I need to fill the guys in on what's going on anyway."

"Okay." He kisses my forehead and lets me go. As I walk away, he slaps my ass.

"Ouch." I jump and glare at him over my shoulder

"That little sting means you'll be thinking of me while I'm gone."

"You, sir, have issues."

"Not telling me anything I don't already know, Cupcake," he calls out as he walks away.

I curse him under my breath and head to the table where Amity is standing, rubbing the sting from my ass that's already sore from the ride home. G grins as I approach, knowing exactly why I'm rubbing my ass.

"Don't say a word or I'll twist your nipple." I point at him, and he laughs.

"Wasn't planning on it Tink," he says, still grinning.

"Well good. Havoc wants to talk to you. He's heading to church."

His face turns serious. "Yeah, Mac called ahead. How bad was it really?"

"I honestly don't even know what to say, G. It's bad. Really bad," I warn him.

He sighs before offering Amity a kiss. "Be good," he tells her.

"Like I have a choice," she grumbles, holding up her cast-covered arm. He looks at her skeptically.

"I'll keep her out of trouble, G. I promise." I smile sweetly at him. "Now, go before Havoc has a fit."

He nods, "I love you, baby," he says to Amity, and her face goes soft.

"I love you too."

He gives my shoulder a squeeze and reluctantly heads to church.

I take in her sweat slicked skin encased in tight running shorts and sports bra and shake my head. I love her more than anything, but we couldn't be more different if we tried.

If just wearing underwear isn't an option, Amity likes walking around in skin tight sports gear. I like cute skirts and graphic T-Shirts, but only because PJ's are frowned upon.

She eats clean foods, and I like foods that involve grease, cheese, and lots of refined carbs.

She's also one of those people who exercises a lot—on purpose, for fun. I asked the minister at our church to perform an exorcism on her once because surely she had to be possessed. Nobody willingly gets up before seven a.m. and works out—for fun—except, of course, Amity. I don't hold her disability against her, though. And she doesn't hold the fact that I only run when cake is involved against me.

"I'll keep her out of trouble?" She mocks.

"Hush now. I'm exhausted just looking at you."

She grins. "Then my work here is done. You know, you could join me. You never know, you might enjoy it."

We look at each other for a beat before we dissolve into fits of laughter.

"Oh god, that was a good one."

"How goes the writing? Find any inspiration while you were gone?"

I throw myself in the chair and bang my head on the table, groaning as my sore body protests against the sudden movement.

"That good?" She chuckles as she takes a seat.

I sigh dramatically, wondering what on earth possessed me to become an author, when I could have just as easily run off and joined a circus or become a stripper. Then I remember I can't lift my leg behind my head because I'm allergic to exercise. Ah, a full-circle moment.

"These characters won't listen to me."

"You wrote these characters. Make them listen to you."

"That's not how this works, Amity. They talk all over me, and sometimes, if I'm fortunate, they'll clue me in on what's happening."

"You know, in any other walk of life, if someone said they

heard voices and then went on to argue with them, they'd end up heavily medicated."

"Why do you think I became an author? I can't eat doughnuts if I'm wearing a straitjacket after all."

She chuckles before tossing her now empty bottle into the recycling.

"Alright, enough chit-chat, spill."

I sigh, knowing she was never going to let me stall for long. "I'm not sure what I can and can't say yet."

She frowns at me for a moment before something clicks, and she rolls her eyes. "Not the shit with the other club. I'm talking about your real identity coming out and the stud in the picture. I follow you on Instagram as Nevaeh and as Celeste, remember? You've been popping up all over the place."

I tell her how I met Ambros, the picture, and everything that's happened since it blew up on Instagram.

When I'm finished, she leans over and pinches me.

"Owww. What was that for?" I ask, rubbing my arm.

"Not telling me sooner!"

"I was embarrassed. And you'd just fallen over a cliff; it didn't seem important."

"Okay, fine. I'll let it go...this time. Has your dad called you yet?"

"No, but it's only a matter of time. He might not hear about it for a few days, but he will."

"Well, maybe now's the perfect time to tell him you're not

going home."

"You mean, just tell him everything at once?" She nods. "Right, because what could possibly go wrong?"

She reaches out and grabs my hand. "You've been putting it off long enough. He's expecting you back from Bible camp soon; summer's almost over. You can't hide from him forever." I bite my lip, knowing she's right. "Unless you've changed your mind about staying?"

I know she wants me to stay, and she knows it's what's best for me, but she'd swallow down her disappointment and support me no matter what. She's the one person in my life who's never let me down.

My thoughts keep spinning as I wonder if Havoc will be another. So far, he's proved there isn't much he won't do for me, but will that always be the case? What happens when what I want or need conflicts with the club?

"Don't go looking for problems."

"Huh?"

"I can tell when you're overthinking, Pippin. And I have a feeling it's about Havoc. Forget him for now. I honestly don't think you'll be able to get rid of the man that easily anyway. Right now, this isn't about him or me. It's about you. If you can see yourself going back home and being happy, then I'll support you one hundred percent. But if you know that going back will drain the life out of you, then stay." She squeezes my hand tighter. "I don't want to watch my best friend fade away just for some misguided sense of duty. The only thing I care about is you and your happiness."

"How did I get so lucky" I squeeze her hand back. "And I know you're right. I wasn't joking when I said I wanted to stay. I...I feel like I can breathe here. I love my dad, but there is nothing there for me anymore except ghosts and bad memories."

"It's the right decision, but it won't be easy. He's going to try to manipulate you and guilt you into going home, and if that doesn't work, he'll try to make you feel two inches tall."

I want to argue, but she puts up her hand to stop me, her voice softens. "It's what he always does, Pippin. Time and time again. He takes your love and twists it into something he can use to control you. That's not what love is. And before Havoc came along, I was terrified you'd think that was normal and end up in an abusive relationship."

I feel my eyes well up. "I didn't realize he was doing that." I sigh, wiping away the tears that have fallen. "No, that's a lie. I just didn't want to see it. I've made a million excuses for him, but I refused to see the truth."

We sit in silence for a moment as I try to get my thoughts in order.

"I really was going to tell him I was staying. But I knew he'd be mad. That's why I waited so long. I'm happy here, and I knew he'd ruin it. And now, with my true identity coming out, my dad will find out that I write romance books.

And not even sweet, clean romance, but dirty, bathe-in-holy-water-after-getting-railed-by-the-devil romance."

She snorts.

"And if that wasn't enough, I have to tell him I'm in love with a biker. And not just any biker, but the freaking president."

I lean forward and bang my head on the table. When she doesn't say anything, I look up to see her staring at me

"What?"

"You love him?"

"I mean, I care about him, and I—" I freeze, realizing what I said.

"You love him," she says again, a smile spreading across her face.

My mouth snaps shut, and I look around to make sure no one's paying attention to us before turning back to Amity. "You can't tell him."

"What am I, six? I'm hardly going to hand him a note saying, *"Hey Havoc, my best friend loves you. Will you marry her? Check yes or no."*

"Haha, funny. But seriously, Amity, it's too soon."

"Says who? Love doesn't follow a timeline, Pippin. It happens when you least expect it—no rules, no warning. And trust me, there's no controlling it."

"It's a lot, Amity. He's a lot."

"But is he too much?"

I think of how he pulls me close when we sleep, his arms

wrapped around me like a shield, promising to protect me even in my dreams. Sure, he kidnapped me, but honestly, he's probably the nicest kidnapper on the planet. He fed me, brought me books, and gave me plenty of hot sex—all to win my heart.

He's right when he says I'd run. I flew to the UK in hopes he'd forget me. If he hadn't done what he did, I probably would've run again—only, I might've ended up going home.

"No," I say, shaking my head. "But I'm a mess, Amity. I swear, every time I start processing one thing, another comes along and knocks me off my feet."

"I get it, you know I do, but there are worse things than being loved by a man who'd risk his life to protect you. A guy who looks at you like you're some kind of miracle that he can't quite believe is real. It's the same way G looks at me."

"You two are kind of perfect for each other, though. Havoc and I couldn't be more different."

"You good together in bed?"

I jolt back, not expecting that question. "Uh, yeah, that's definitely not a problem."

"You accept the club, even if that means dealing with a bunch of nosy-ass brothers?"

I think of Crane looking out for me at the ice cream shop, and Conan coming with me to feed the homeless guy, and even Toot driving me crazy, and nod. "Of course, the guys are awesome."

"Then who cares about the rest? I think you're making excuses because you're scared."

"Alright, that's enough out of you, Dr. Phil. If I wanted a well-thought-out, logical argument, I would have asked for one." I mock glare at her, making her grin.

"Gotta make sure you've got your head on straight because Havoc gives off hunter vibes."

"I don't even know what that means."

"It means, Pippin, that if you run home to daddy dearest, Havoc will chase you, and he won't leave without you. Hell, he'd probably fuck you in front of the congregation to prove his point. Can you imagine their reaction? Susan and Brenda would end up with finger cramps from all their pearl-clutching."

I laugh at the image, then swallow and look at her. "I need to call my dad. He should hear it from me first."

She nods. "Want to wait until Havoc is done?"

I shake my head. "No. If I wait, I'll just chicken out. And besides, if my dad makes me cry, Havoc will smash my phone. I just need you."

"You got me."

"This is gonna suck."

"Then it's gonna suck, but we'll get through it."

I pull out my cell phone and unblock my dad's number. My aunt had told him I wouldn't get cell service at Bible camp, but I didn't want to risk it.

I hit the call button and squeeze Amity's hand. I know it

has to hurt, but she doesn't say a thing. Her silent support grounds me as the call connects.

"Nevaeh?"

"Daddy."

* * *

I hang up, feeling sick, and stare down at the scratched surface of the table as I try to swallow around the lump in my throat.

Well, that went better than I hoped it would, but also much worse.

Blowing out a shaky breath, I pull my hand from Amity's and run my fingers though my hair.

"Jesus, you're as white as a sheet. Let me grab you a Coke. The sugar will help."

I nod but don't say anything. My words would be a jumbled mess. I'm so lost in my thoughts that I jump when the glass thumps down in front of me.

"Talk to me, Nevaeh. You're scaring me."

"He told me he was disappointed in me. Shocking, right?" I grab the glass, my hands trembling, and take a sip before placing it back down. "He's disappointed I lied about going to Bible camp. And mad that I involved my aunt."

"But it was your aunt's idea?"

"I know, but I wasn't going to throw her under the bus."

I try to shut out his words, but they keep replaying in my head.

"You act like a slut, and that's how people are going to treat you."

"A biker? Really, Nevaeh, have you no self-respect?"

"Your sister, would never do something like this!"

"You write pornography? That's what you're throwing your life away for?"

"What do you mean you're not coming home?"

"Don't be so ridiculous. You're acting like a petulant child."

I look at Amity and offer her a weak smile. I'm glad I didn't put him on speaker.

"He didn't disown me, so there's that," I joke, but it falls flat.

She wraps her arm around me. "Give him some time to cool off."

"I can give him all the time in the world, but it won't change the fact that I'm not who he wants me to be."

"That's bullshit. Who else are you supposed to be?"

I close my eyes, not wanting to see the look of pity on her face. "Citlalli," I say softly. "I think the only way to make him happy is if I were my sister."

Chapter Twenty-One

Havoc

W e've been back a week, and something's off with Nevaeh. I can't put my finger on it, and she's not sharing, but some of her smiles feel forced, and I've caught her staring off into space with a sad look in her eyes more than once.

I watch her and Amity leave together and head for the restroom. I don't understand why women have to pee in pairs—it's one of life's great mysteries, I guess. Not that I'm complaining. I know as long as Amity and Nevaeh are together, they're safe.

"Alright, spill. What's going on with Tinkerbell? Amity won't tell me shit."

"Neither will Nevaeh. I've tried talking to her, but she just shut me down."

"Amity's the same. It's one of the things they have in common. You think it has to do with her real identity being leaked?"

I want to kick myself as soon as he says it. Of course, that's it. I'm such a dick. I groan, making him chuckle.

"To be fair, you've been out of the game for a while. And with everything going on with Khan and your old club, you've had other things on your mind."

"That's no excuse. Nevaeh should be my priority." I run my hands through my hair before pulling out my wallet and tossing some cash on the table for lunch and a tip.

"I don't have social media," I admit. It wasn't allowed in prison, and honestly, it was probably for the best. It would have reminded me of the millions of people on the outside living their lives while I sat in a cell, regretting my choices.

"I do, hold on. I follow Amity, and I know she follows Tinkerbell. Let me do some digging," he says, pulling out his phone as I glance over at the hall leading to the restrooms.

"Hmm." The sound draws my attention back to him. He's frowning at the screen, his lips pressed tight.

"What is it?"

"Well, Celeste has a lot of followers, and most of them are acting like it's some big deal to know who she is. Some are even hoping she ends up with Ambros, but then romance readers are all about happy endings," he mutters as he scrolls, and I glare at him.

He pauses and looks up at me. "Not that I'd know or anything. Just a wild guess."

"I don't give a fuck what you read, G. I care that half the world wants my girl with another man."

"It's the internet, Havoc—"

"Fuck that. That's my woman," I snap. I'll never be okay with that bullshit. "Set me up an account."

He looks at me warily. "What are you going to do?"

"Kill you if you don't follow my fucking orders for a start," I snarl.

He holds his hands up in surrender. I unlock my phone and hold it out for him. It takes him a few minutes to set it up, using a generic picture of a bike as my profile picture. Once he's done, he shows me how to use it.

When I see the girls walking toward the table, I slide my phone back into my pocket and curse myself for not remembering to ask G about the look on his face earlier.

"Everything okay?" I ask as I stand and pull Nevaeh into my arms.

"Yeah, there was just a line. It's not usually this busy on Wednesday."

Taking her word for it, I ask her if she's ready to leave. When she nods, I take her hand and lead her outside, Amity and G right behind us as we walk toward our bikes.

"Motherfucker." I let go of Nevaeh and stomp toward my

bike. Both tires have been slashed. I curse when I see how deep the slashes are. Whoever the hell did it was not taking any chances.

"G, call one of the prospects and get them to bring some tools and a couple of spare tires from the garage if we don't have any on hand in the warehouse."

"Who the fuck would do this?" Amity curses.

G steps closer, his phone against his ear, as he waits for the prospect to answer.

"Do you think it was someone from your old club?" Nevaeh asks.

"No, 'cause if it was, they'd've cut the brakes. This feels more like an annoyance than a threat."

"I don't like it," G grunts, turning away when his call connects.

"I'm not exactly dancing for fucking joy," I say sharply as Nevaeh slips her hand into mine, instantly calming me.

"Hoops is on his way with tools and the truck to take Amity and Nevaeh back to the clubhouse," G says, wrapping his arms around Amity from behind. "Shouldn't take long to change the tires, but there's no reason for them to wait around."

"I agree."

"I don't mind," Nevaeh tells me softly.

"I know you don't, baby. But you have better things to do than stand around here watching me change tires. Didn't you say you needed to get some writing done today?"

"But I haven't finished procrastinating yet," she whines, making me chuckle.

"The sooner you get started, the sooner you'll be finished," I say as she pouts.

"Thanks for that, Captain Obvious."

"I have a cure for sass," I tell her as I pull her into my arms. "It involves you on your knees and my dick in your throat."

Her skin flushes red as she slaps my chest. "I hate you."

"No, you don't," I say with a smirk.

"Clearly, I need therapy," she grumbles.

"Oral—"

"Finish that sentence and die."

"Have you always been this violent?"

"No, funnily enough, I was sane before you came along. You bring out the crazy in me."

* * *

With the girls heading back to the clubhouse, me and G make quick work of changing the tires.

"I forgot to ask you before, but what was with your reaction to Nevaeh's social media?"

He looks at me and frowns. "Oh, it was nothing. Just a few trolls talking shit. It's just the nature of the beast."

I nod, not sure what to say to that. Social media's blown up since I'd been inside. It's not that it wasn't around before, I just had no interest in it, liking to keep my private life private.

"Alright, but do me a favor and keep an eye on things. I get that this is probably normal, but after what went down with Amity, I want to be extra careful."

He tenses at the reminder but nods, his jaw tightening. After a moment, he blows out a breath. "Let's head back," he says as he starts picking up the tools. "Hoops mentioned that Kieran's coming by in an hour to meet with you. Are you serious about him going undercover at your old club?"

"I want to get a feel for the guy first, but at this point, we have nothing to lose. Khan and Driller haven't been back since I left, and the bugs are up and running, but the room hasn't been used." I run a hand through my hair. "Have any of them contacted you?"

"Yeah, Byte calls me every day. We're working on tracing the missing money. It's taking time, but we'll figure it out."

"Anything on the girls?"

"I've hacked the police files and traced their last known movements. I can see where the cops fucked up. The local sheriff didn't do a fucking thing to follow up on any leads. Honestly, I'm surprised the feds haven't gotten involved. But if girls keep disappearing, it'll only be a matter of time. And the last thing the club needs are the feds poking around, because it won't stop with just that club."

"No, and Khan will make sure we go down with the ship as one last 'fuck you' to me." I rub my hand over my face and my eyes land on the building across the street— and, more importantly, the camera on the side of it. I nod to it. "Think you might be able to see who fucked with my bike?"

"They use our security company so I can look. I don't know if it will have caught anything from that angle, but you never know, we might get lucky."

I sigh. "I won't hold my breath."

We pull through the gates and into the warehouse just as the sky darkens, looking like it's going to pour at any moment.

We park our bikes and climb off.

"That was lucky," G says as we climb off our bikes. "I wasn't looking forward to being caught in the rain today––not that it was even forecasted."

"I swear this fucking weather has a mind of its own. You sticking around to meet this potential prospect?" I ask as we head out of the warehouse.

"Might as well. I'll need to run background on him anyway."

The clubhouse is quiet when we walk through the doors. Most of the tables are empty, and Lil is behind the bar. A couple of old-timers are sitting in the corner, drinking the day away, listening to soft rock on the jukebox.

Our women are nowhere to be seen, so they're either out back or upstairs. As much as I want to find Nevaeh, I know if I do, I'll end up buried deep inside her. And right now, I need to focus. Sometimes, I hate being the president.

We head to the bar and take a seat while we wait.

"Hey guys, what can I get you?"

"Beer for me. You seen Nevaeh, Lil?"

"She went upstairs to work for a bit. Amity is out back with Legs." She looks at G as she says the last part.

He nods. "Thanks, Lil. Can I get a beer, too?"

She grabs two beers from the fridge and hands them to us.

"Everything okay, Lil? Haven't seen you around much lately."

"I've been helping out at the new homeless shelter. There've been a few...issues, but I think they have it under control now."

"Anything we can do to help?"

"Um...I've already given them Capone's number. They've been having trouble with fights and need security. I hope that was okay."

"Yeah, that's more than okay. Hannibal said you thought you'd been followed. Anything more come of that?"

She shakes her head. "Kruger and Circus have been taking turns picking me up. They said they haven't seen anything unusual."

"Good. The shelter—is it for everyone, or just for women?"

"It's for anyone who needs a place to stay, but mostly takes in people with mental health issues that need a little extra help."

I stare at her as she fidgets and bites her lip. "Tell Capone I'm good with him taking the job if he thinks he can make it work and the club will fund it. I don't want people getting hurt if we can help."

She lets out a relieved breath and fights back tears.

"This place means a lot to you?" G asks her softly.

She looks between me and him, looking unsure.

"You won't get any judgment from us," I tell her, holding my hands up.

"After what happened with Bear. I wasn't in a good place," she says gently.

G sucks in a sharp breath but doesn't say anything.

"I couldn't stay here—to sleep, I mean. I kept busy during the day or I was with the guys, but when it was time to sleep, my dreams kept replaying everything that happened like some fucked-up movie stuck on repeat."

"Why didn't you say anything?" G asks, but I can hear the strain in his voice.

"You guys were dealing with enough, and I didn't want to look weak," she says with a shrug. "I'm not stupid. I know I'm replaceable. And what good is a broken whore? If I couldn't do my job, you'd kick me out and—"

"Jesus fuck, Lil. That was never going to happen. I know what you did to protect the others," he tells her, tears and shame appearing in her eyes. "You kept their focus on you and away from everyone else. You sacrificed yourself for them. How could you ever think we'd give up on you when you never gave up on us?"

Watching them, I've realized there's a lot of unresolved tension in this club from what happened. The betrayal, the violence—it's left scars that everyone is dealing with and healing from. I might have my own shit to work through, but I'm not the only one. Everyone here is carrying something. We're just so caught up in our own shit that we don't notice.

"I couldn't take that chance," she whispers as a tear falls down her cheek. G opens his mouth, but Lil continues. "Anyway..." she takes a shaky breath, wiping the tears from her face. "I couldn't afford to stay anywhere other than the clubhouse, so there were days I just slept outside. As strange as it sounds, I actually felt safer doing that than sleeping here. Eventually, I saved enough to buy my car and slept in it for a while.

"A nurse at the hospital told me about her friend. She was a therapist, which I couldn't afford, but she was willing to see me if I worked at the shelter she ran a couple of towns over. So that's what I did. And I think helping out there has helped as much, if not more, than just talking about everything."

Her eyes widen, and I frown.

"Of course, I didn't mention the club or what happened here. I told her something happened when I was in college at a frat party..." Her voice trails off as I reach over the bar and grab the back of her wrist.

"You didn't do anything wrong. I appreciate you keeping our secrets, but if you would've asked, Blade would've found someone for you to talk to and paid them to keep quiet so you could be honest and get it all off your chest."

"But if Blade wanted to know, they would've told him, and what happened is mine to share. Nobody else's." She tugs her arm free.

"You're right," I say eventually, and by the look on her face, she wasn't expecting that.

"Is the new shelter here run by the same person who helped you?" G asks, snapping Lil out of her shock.

She nods. "Yeah. The one she ran before, the building it was in, was torn down for some revitalization project. And there was no other place big enough for her to use, so I suggested she come here, forgetting that I hadn't been completely honest with her."

"I doubt she'll hold it against you. I'm sure plenty of people hold back or tweak shit in therapy."

Her shoulders relax, and she lets out a breath as some of the tension leaves her body. "Thanks. It's been really bothering me," she admits.

"You didn't do anything wrong, Lil," G repeats.

"I'm just a regular whore using her pussy powers for the greater good," she snarks, and I can see a spark of the girl she must have been before everything changed for her.

A cough behind us has Lil dropping her head, humiliation clear in her stance.

"You Havoc?"

I look behind me and see a tall, dark-haired guy in his twenties holding out his hand.

"Kieran?"

"That's me. Hoops said you wanted to talk."

Chapter Twenty-Two

Nevach

The last few days have been busy. Havoc has been with the new prospect, making plans, and I was tying up loose ends with the book I sent off to my editor less than an hour ago.

Now I'm sitting out back, letting the peace and quiet soothe my soul. Of course, as soon as I think that, the silence is broken by a series of loud bangs and shattering glass. I let out a shriek and drop to the floor, hiding underneath the table, unable to see where the noise is coming from. I'm not an idiot. I know what gunfire sounds like. What I don't know is who the target is.

Tears run down my face unchecked as I pray everyone else is safe, too. It isn't until I hear Havoc roar my name that I realize the bullets have stopped. I hear running footsteps as I peek out from under my hiding spot. Havoc looks around frantically for me as the guys try to yank him back.

"For fuck sake, Havoc, it's not safe. The shooter might still be out there."

"Nevaeh," he yells again, ignoring them.

"I'm here," I call out, climbing to my feet, not wanting anyone else out there to get hurt because of me.

He runs to me and scoops me up before carrying me back inside. Despite what happened, it's less chaotic inside than I thought it would be. It's busy, almost a full house, but nobody is running around like a headless chicken. But then I suppose they've faced stuff like this before. That should make me feel more afraid, but I'm comforted by the knowledge that they know what to do in a crisis.

"Nevaeh!"

I turn my head at the sound of Amity's voice just as she barges into us, smacking my arm with her cast. Havoc moves back a step, but instead of complaining, he wraps an arm around Amity and draws her closer as she breathes me in.

"I'm okay. When I heard the first shot, I took cover under the table. Do we know if anyone was hurt?"

"Everyone's fine. The spot they targeted was empty," G answers as Amity pulls back and Havoc lowers me to my feet. He doesn't let me go, though, his large arm wrapping around me and pulling me close to his chest.

"What happened?" Havoc snaps as I sense others drawing nearer.

"You want to do this in church?"

Havoc looks around at everyone. The only people here who aren't brothers are me and Amity.

"Here's fine. Tell me what you know."

"The clinic's alarm went off when a bullet tripped the sensor. I got the notification and checked the cameras. Though I couldn't see the shooter, they were likely just outside the back gates."

"So the property wasn't breached?"

"Not that I could see, but I'd rather get visual confirmation."

"You're thinking it was a sniper."

"Damn right I am."

"Mac, Toot, go check out the back gate. Hannibal, check out the clinic. Take Midas with you to watch your back."

They all nod and disappear without fanfare.

"You said the sensors were tripped. Was the clinic the target?"

G looks at Amity before his eyes come to me, and he shakes his head. "I could be wrong. The camera angle wasn't the best, but it looked like the target was the RV."

It takes a moment for his words to sink in. Amity's RV was her home until she moved in here with G. And technically, it is still mine, even though I spend every night with

Havoc. And now it's been shot up like something out of a fucking movie.

"Did you see how much damage there is?" Amity asks, her voice filled with fury. I reach out and squeeze her hand.

"No. But as soon as the others come back and give us the all-clear, we can go look."

I swallow, my eyes moving around the quiet faces in the room until they fall on the large clock on the wall. It's five minutes past midnight. The witching hour seems fitting for the chaos that just occurred, which is when something else dawns on me.

"What if it was shot up because someone thinks I'm still sleeping there? I mean, if it weren't for Havoc, I would be, especially at this time."

Havoc freezes solid. G curses and grabs Amity, holding her to him before she starts freaking out.

"I'll kill them. I don't care who they fucking are. I'll slaughter them all," she screeches.

I tap Havoc lightly, needing him to let me go, but he's a solid immovable force behind me.

I look at G with pleading eyes and he shuffles closer with Amity. I grab her arm, and as soon as I touch her, she stills. She turns to look at me, her eyes damp with tears, which sets me off.

"Stop crying. I'm fine."

"I'm not crying. I'm allergic to your perfume."

"It's your perfume I'm wearing." I grin.

"I knew I liked it."

She grabs my wrist tightly. "Do not die on me, Pippin. I'm not fucking kidding around here, okay."

"I'm not going anywhere. Have a little faith in me."

She blows out a shuddering breath before nodding. "Okay."

"Okay." I look at G. "Was this what I was like after the whole being thrown off a cliff thing?"

He chuckles. "You might have looked a little unhinged," he admits. Havoc is still not speaking.

People have drifted away a little now to give the illusion of privacy, even though I know they're still tuned into us. I turn in Havoc's hold and look up at my man. I suck in a deep breath at the barely banked fury.

I reach up and cup his face. "Come back to me, Havoc," I murmur softly so that only he can hear me.

His head dips just a fraction so his stormy eyes can stare into mine. "They could have killed you," he grits out.

"But they didn't because they didn't do their homework." That makes me frown. "Anyone from your old club who saw us together knows we are a couple. So either they think we're faking it and know enough to find out I technically live in the RV, or the threat isn't from the club but from somewhere else instead."

I see G step up beside Havoc, a thoughtful look is on his face. He's thinking about what I'm saying, which is just as well because Havoc is stuck on something else.

"You don't live in the RV. You live with me."

"Do I now? And when did you ask me to move in with you?"

"Asking implies you have a choice. The first time you took my cock, you became mine. That means you sleep beside me. That's non-negotiable."

I stare at him, flabbergasted. Looking around for a weapon so I can beat his ass, I come up empty-handed. He seems far too smug. Though I prefer that to the desperation he wore before, I'm not ready for him to reduce me down to property. I'm not opposed to being his as long as he's mine, too. What I don't like is the way he skims the line of doting boyfriend and sexist jackass.

As if sensing the violence inside me, his lips twitch with amusement, which sends my temper from simmer to boiling inferno. Bending down, I slip off my shoe and flip it around so the heel is facing him. I raise it above my head and glare at him.

G sighs, fighting a grin. "I can't let you hit my president, Tinkerbell."

"Why not? He thinks it's okay to slap my ass if he thinks I'm in the wrong. I'm just returning the favor."

I ignore the laughter in the room as Havoc unfolds his arms and lets them hang loosely at his side. I roll my eyes when I realize he has a giant hard-on.

"You want to spank him?" G chuckles.

"I want to knock some sense into him," I hiss.

Havoc uses my distraction to make his move. I expected him to toss me over his shoulder, as that seems to be his signature move. Instead, he leans down and kisses me, and I forget why I was mad with him to begin with.

"I want you to live with me," he murmurs against my lips. "Move in here officially, and we'll look for somewhere we both like."

"Okay."

He grins and resumes kissing me. I swear my IQ falls faster than my panties when this man gets his hands on me. He just tricked me into giving in, but it's hard to resist when I want the same things he does. He may not be everyone's dream man, but he's mine, no matter how much I like to pretend otherwise.

He pulls away when there is a commotion behind us. With a sigh, I find myself once more tucked within the cradle of Havoc's arms as Mac and Toot approach, grim-faced, with Hannibal and Midas behind them.

"There is no damage to the perimeter fence. Unless someone scaled it and got in and out without being seen, then my guess is we're looking at a sniper," Mac tells them, coming to the same conclusion G and Havoc have.

"Amity jumped the fence once, though, right?"

Amity grins. "Not everyone is as good as me."

"Thank fuck," Havoc mutters. "The clinic?" he asks Hannibal.

"There is no damage. Nobody has been inside, either.

The alarm was still on when we entered. The RV took most of the damage," he admits softly.

I sigh. "I guess we better see what we're dealing with."

"In the morning. I'd rather err on the side of caution. It will be impossible to spot a sniper in the dark until it's too late. I will send the prospects out to patrol the area so I need someone on the gate."

"I'll do it," Crane offers.

Havoc nods. "G, contact Byte. See if anything suspicious has gone down on their end."

"Want me to message Kieran too?"

He shakes his head. "No. I told him we wouldn't unless it were an emergency. I don't want to risk blowing his cover. He'll contact us if he finds anything."

"Alright. Come on, Amity. I might as well get some rest. I have a feeling it will be a rough few days."

She walks over and gives me a quick hug. "It's just stuff. We can replace anything we need to. We can't replace each other." She's right, of course. Nobody knows that better than us.

"Everyone's alright. We were lucky," I agree.

G leads her away as Havoc walks us to the closest table and sits down, tugging me into his lap.

"You don't want to get some rest?"

"I need to talk to the guys."

"Want me to give you some space?"

"No, stay. I'm not ready to let you out of my sight just yet."

"Okay."

"Here you go, Tinkerbell." Toot offers me my shoe, which I must have dropped mid-kiss.

I should probably be embarrassed, but I'm too tired to care. Instead, after thanking him, I drop it to the floor and kick off the other before straddling Havoc and tucking my head against his neck. He relaxes further under my submission, his talented fingers trailing up and down my spine in a soothing gesture.

I let them talk everything through, not paying a lick of attention as I start to drift off. I'm glad it was the RV they targeted. If they'd noticed me alone on the deck, would they have targeted me instead? I can only imagine Havoc's anguish if I were killed, and maybe that's the point. I might be the target, but Havoc is the prize.

Thank God none of the girls were out there with me. I would have never forgiven myself if they got hurt.

I bolt upright, almost clipping Havoc's chin with my head. "The girls. Legs, Lil, and the others. Has anyone spoken to them?" I ask turning to face the table.

I see something dawn on Midas's face, something that looks an awful lot like regret. Before he can act on it, Kruger answers, "Legs and Lil were at the pawn shop. I grabbed them and sent them upstairs. The rest of the girls are in the kitchen."

"Oh, thank God. I couldn't bear it if something happened to them. Not after everything they've already been through."

"They didn't make an attempt anywhere else. They were never in danger," Midas says. Something tells me it's to absolve himself of his guilt.

"No, thankfully Legs decided not to go to the clinic because she's feeling better," I say sarcastically, even though she'd have never been there at this time of night.

"She's sick?" Midas sits upright.

"She's had that sickness bug that's been going around. Doesn't she work for you? Haven't you noticed?"

He mumbles something and storms off.

"That man needs high fiving in the face with a chair," I snarl before settling back down against Havoc's chest.

"It's been a long night, cupcake. Why don't you rest a little and when we're finished here, we'll head on up to bed. We can check in on the girls if you want first."

"Okay," I agree on a whisper, my eyes already drifting closed.

Chapter Twenty-Three

Havoc

An hour later, long after Nevaeh passed out in my lap, we finally decide to call it a night.

As Crane and Kruger stand up to leave, G walks through the door, heading toward us.

His eyes turn gentle when they spot Nevaeh. "She okay?"

"Yeah. Once the shock wore off, she fell asleep. Amity?"

"Same."

As G takes a seat, Kruger and Crane look at me, silently asking if I want them to stay.

"Might as well hear what G has to say."

They retake their seats and wait for G to start. "Byte says there has been nothing that stood out on his end today, until about an hour ago when Khan and Driller walked into the clubhouse as if they didn't just bail on everyone."

"The timing can't be a coincidence." Crane shakes his head.

"Well, it couldn't have been them personally. They wouldn't have had time to shoot up the RV and make it back. But that doesn't mean that Khan didn't put someone else up to it."

"I asked Byte about that. He said their only sniper is Hachette, and he's on a run to the Tainted Saints MC."

"And what business do they have with them? We might not be affiliated with them, but they've always kept to themselves."

"I didn't ask, but I can find out. Maybe the fact that we have no ties to them makes Khan think we won't check the intel."

"That would be a stupid mistake to make. But if the Tainted Saints are in some alliance with them, I have to assume they'll lie for him. I'll call Bishop, the president, in the morning and feel him out. Could be he's under the impression that Khan speaks for me, and I'd like to debase him of that notion."

"You meet Bishop before?"

"A couple of times. Once at Sturgis and once as a courtesy when they set up shop just outside our territory. The guy didn't give much away, but he didn't set off any red flags."

"So we have Hachette as our prime suspect, doing Khan's bidding. Anyone else it might be?" Hannibal, who has been mostly quiet since the attack, asks.

"I've been monitoring Nevaeh's social media presence since her real identity was revealed," G jumps in, making me tense.

"You think it could be a crazed fan?"

"I told you before that trolls are something everyone with an online presence has to deal with. People in the public eye, like Nevaeh, however, have it ten times worse. But the thing about trolls is that they're only powerful behind their keyboards. That's usually the case, anyway. But every walk of life has a crazy or two in it, and there are two that I'm watching right now that make the hairs on the back of my neck stand on end, mostly because they are posting on Nevaeh's personal page, not Celeste's."

"Do you know who they are?"

"No, they have usernames, and their accounts are locked down tight, so it might be worth involving the police. But as it stands right now, there have been no direct threats made, just a lot of backward and forward comments about what they want to do to Nevaeh if they see her and how they're mad she tricked them."

"It's a big leap to make nasty comments behind a screen then to come here and start shooting at the clubhouse. Besides, how would they even know where she is?"

G looks at me, and I wince.

"Oh-oh, what did you do?" Crane sighs.

I open my mouth to explain myself but close it again when I realize I don't want to admit that I was a jealous asshole.

G doesn't have the same issue, though. "Havoc here decided to make a social media account. Mostly it's pics of him doing whatever the fuck he does, shirtless." He rolls his eyes at me. "The rest are photos of him and Nevaeh looking all loved up. He, of course, follows Nevaeh, not Celeste and tags her in them all." He roll his eyes.

I groan realizing my mistake. "It never dawned on me to follow Celeste Sky because I don't think of her as that."

"It wouldn't have mattered anyway. People already know Nevaeh is Celeste and clearly she isn't bothered as she hasn't commented back. Unless she hasn't noticed. Either way, in plenty, you're wearing your cut, which marks you as president and shows the club name. Wouldn't take much sleuthing to track us down."

"Shit, this is my fault."

"No, I won't rule it out as a possibility, but it doesn't quite fit. For starters, none of her fans knew about the RV. Both Amity and Nevaeh are very careful about what they post. Anything too personal, like family or where they are living, has always been under wraps. Even on their personal accounts. This feels a lot like it was done by someone with a least a little information about Nevaeh. Information that could only really have come from someone observing the club. If it were someone from here they'd know nobody was really living in the RV anymore."

I relax a touch thankful that we don't have a traitor in house again.

Nevaeh stirs in my lap, so I hold tighter.

"Take her up to bed. I'm heading back now to join Amity. Nothing we can do tonight."

I nod and agree, saying goodnight to everyone as I lift Nevaeh and hold her to my chest. I think over what G said. Though I'm not convinced it's a crazed fan who shot up the trailer, I can't deny that my jealousy might have naively painted a target on her back.

Hearing arguing, I turn when I get to the top of the stairs just as the noise cuts off. I see Midas pin Legs to the wall and start kissing her. Leaving them to figure out their own shit, I take Nevaeh to our room and lay her on the bed so I can strip off. Once I'm done, I gently undress her before climbing in beside her.

I tug the covers up over us and roll her into my arms so her face is on my chest. Something settles in me with her touch, just like it always does. Tonight could have been so much fucking worse. But somehow, despite it all, everyone is safe. And Nevaeh is in my arms, exactly where she's supposed to be.

* * *

Rapid knocking on the door wakes me the next morning. When I glance over and see the alarm clock, I realize it's actually closer to lunchtime than dawn. I guess that happens when I toss and turn all fucking night worrying some motherfucker is going to come steal my girl out from under me. My dreams were filled with blood and death, so much so that I swear I can still smell the coppery tang of it in the air.

"Havoc, we've got an issue." Circus's voice rings out.

I slip out from Nevaeh's hold as she stirs and hurry to the door, not giving a fuck about my nakedness.

I yank the door open. "What is it?"

"Cops at the gate and some dude claiming to be Tinkerbell's father."

"Shit. Give us five to get dressed, and we'll be down."

"Alright, I'll stall them for now."

"Don't let them in. If they don't have a warrant, they can wait where they are."

"I look like I was born yesterday?"

I glare at him until he sighs and nods.

"I'm on it."

I close the door as he leaves and turn back to the bed. Nevaeh looks at me with wide eyes, the sheet pulled up to her chin like some kind of protective barrier. I hate it because it hides her luscious tits. Even though my dick stirs, I know he'll have to wait.

"Did Circus just say my father is here? Here, like at the clubhouse, here?"

"That's what the guy said. Whether he is or not, I don't know. Get dressed, cupcake. Let's go find out what's going on."

She jumps up, her movements jerky and uncoordinated. Her thoughts are undoubtedly on her father and not getting dressed. I stalk over to her and gently grip her arms.

"Take a deep breath for me, cupcake."

She takes a shaky one before blowing it out.

"Good girl. I know this has thrown you, but I need you to keep it together for a minute and tell me what to expect. You've always been pretty close-lipped about your dad. At first, I thought it was the MC you had an issue with. Maybe you were ashamed, but I know that's not it now. Is it me?"

She shocks the shit out of both of us when she slaps me across the face. It's not a hard slap, but the shock of it renders us both mute for a moment.

"Don't you ever say that again. If I should be ashamed of anyone, it's me. I mean, what the hell do I have to offer you when my own father can't even love me? I'm ashamed that you're going to see where I come from. I hate that you're going to hear the vile words he'll spew at me. I don't want to look at the brothers because I know I'll see pity in their eyes. I'm embarrassed, okay? I was embarrassed that I stayed for as long as I did and tried so hard to get him to love me. I—"

I yank her to me, wrap my arms around her, and press her

face against my chest. Her tears make my skin slick, but I don't move. I don't tell her to calm down or offer her false platitudes. Something tells me this has been brewing for a long time, and I just accidentally kicked the hornet's nest.

Once she's calmed down a little, I pull back and tip her head up so she can look at me. Her skin is flushed, her eyes puffy and red, and her cheeks streaked with tears, yet she has never looked more beautiful than she does right now.

She always puts on a brave face, and don't get me wrong —she is brave. But I've seen the glimpse she has kept hidden from me, especially over the last week. The moments of vulnerability she's too scared to show me in case I use them against her. As much as I wanted to force her to talk to me, I knew my usual bulldozer routine could do some permanent damage, so I waited for her to come to me.

I just didn't realize it would all come to a head like this.

"There is nothing unlovable about you, Nevaeh. I fell head over dick the second I slid inside you. I didn't know what you looked like, didn't know what you sounded like beyond those sexy little moans of yours, but I knew what you felt like. You felt like mine. Like I'd paid my penance, and you were my reward. Every time I learned something new about you, I fell in love all over again. But even without me...even if you'd never walked into my life, you had Amity. She doesn't love many people. I know that. But you, you own a piece of her heart that she will never take back. You saw what she was like downstairs when she realized you might be a target. She nearly lost her damned mind, and that's because the thought of losing you would break something inside her. You are not unlovable. You're unforgettable, and that's what your father's problem is. He wants to forget because then the pain will fade away. "

"He doesn't want to forget. He wants to live in the past. I wish he'd forget. Then, we might finally be able to move on. My sister's death, though, has left him in some messed-up time loop."

"He wants to forget you, Nevaeh," I tell her softly. "Because you're a direct reminder of all his failings. He wants a do-over so he can get everything right this time, but you're not playing by his rules. You're not the puppet he hoped you would be. And even if you were, I still don't think it would be enough. He's looking for perfection in broken places."

She sighs, and I can tell she's still not convinced that the problem isn't her. I let her go so we could both get dressed, but I kept my eyes on her. She's quiet, but she looks steady once more.

Once she's done, she looks at me and blows out a steadying breath. "I'm ready."

"No matter what happens today, nothing will change how I feel about you. Nothing he can say or do will ever make me walk away from you. I'm afraid, cupcake, that you're stuck with me."

"That might just be the best thing I've ever heard."

I kiss her gently before taking her hand and leading her

downstairs. Mac and Toot are there waiting. A few others are milling around, mostly minding their own business, but I see them look at Nevaeh, checking her over to make sure she's okay. It makes me feel proud to be the president of this club. I don't think I realized just how fucked-up my old club was until I came here and saw what a functioning family was supposed to look like.

"We'll walk you down. G and Circus are keeping an eye on things. I sent Dice and Hoops to get some sleep. They've been on duty all night," Mac tells me. I nod and give Nevaeh's hand a squeeze.

"You should probably know...Amity is there too."

"Ah, crap," Nevaeh curses, making Toot snort.

"Don't worry, she's holding her own," Mac reassures her.

"Oh, it's not Amity I'm worried about. She's protective of me. If my father talks crap about me, and he will, Amity will lose her mind. She has bit her tongue for a long time to keep the peace, but she will only let so much slide."

"I told you she loves you," I murmur, making her look up at me and roll her eyes, but I don't miss the small smile on her lips.

By the time we get to the warehouse holding the bikes, we can hear raised voices. I feel Nevaeh tense again. I rub my thumb over the back of her hand in a soothing gesture. "This is why you've been quiet all week, isn't it?"

"I called him when my identity was leaked. I told him the truth about everything. It didn't go well."

She pulls back her shoulders and lifts her head proudly, her game face on for all to see. "I'm done letting him make me feel small just to make himself feel better. I'm ready to tell him a few home truths, face to face. It's time."

"Okay, cupcake. Let's do this. You take the lead, and I'll have your back."

Chapter Twenty-Four

Nevaeh

I walk through the warehouse toward the sound of my father's voice and feel the fear and trepidation melt away. He might be the king of the castle back home, but here, I'm the queen.

When I walk into the sun, I stand beside Amity. G on her left, stands guard with his hand on her hip, and Circus stands beside them.

"Nevaeh, I've come to take you home," my father snaps when he sees me.

"I am home, Daddy. I'm more at home here than I've ever been anywhere else before."

He flinches but stands straighter. The look in his eyes,

which I'm all too familiar with, prepares me to brace before he flings words like barbed wire at me.

"You are not of sound mind. Amity was always a bad influence on you, and now that she's shacked up with a biker, she expects you to do the same. Well, not on my watch. I refuse to let you whore yourself out—"

"I'm not on your watch. Not anymore. I haven't been for a long time. You may have observed me, but only in the same way a scientist studies a bug. You thought if you did things differently with me, you could...what? Make me into the perfect daughter? You could make me into Citi?"

"Don't you say her name," he spits.

"Why? She was my sister. You act like you're the only one who lost her, but I lost her too. She was mine more than she was yours. She was my twin, for goodness sake. I felt like I'd lost half my soul. You were supposed to help me. You should have held me, grieved with me, and loved me harder. But you left me, too. Where were you when I needed you?"

"I was looking for your sister," he roars.

"I know, and I get it. But while you were out chasing ghosts, you forgot about raising the little girl you still had at home."

"It was your fault that—"

Havoc growls, knowing precisely what my father is about to say. But I shake my head, feeling sorry for him.

"I was a child. I was not responsible for Citi's disappearance, and shame on you for blaming me. Should I have blamed you for sending her outside to play alone? Should I have blamed Mom, who got stuck in her soap opera and didn't check on Citi enough? Maybe I should blame the cops. Or the justice system in general. Lord knows I'm angry enough to blame all of you. But I didn't because the only person to blame is the man who took her.

"Miss?" one of the police officers calls out to me after silence descends.

I look toward the man and wait for him to continue.

"I'm Officer Pauly. This is Officer Jacobs. We are here because it is believed you're being kept here against your will." He says it evenly, but I can tell he's figured out that not everything is what it seems.

I look back at my dad and cross my arms over my chest, letting my anger blanket the wounds his words have caused. "Really? That's what you told them?" I shake my head, disappointed. "As you can see, officers, not only am I healthy, I'm of sound mind, if you discount how pissed I am."

"Nevaeh," my father snaps at my language.

"Don't. You don't get to parent me now, not after everything you've done."

I blow out a steadying breath and draw comfort from Havoc, who rests his hand on my shoulder in a show of solidarity.

"I'm sorry you were forced to come out here, officers. Wasting police time is not something I'm okay with. That being said, I understand you checking up on me, and I thank you for it. I can assure you, though, that I'm happy here."

"Ridiculous. You will get your things and come home, or you'll never be welcome back again."

I fist my hands and bite back the vicious retort I feel on the back of my tongue. I'm better than that, and I refuse to let him bait me into making me the same kind of bitter and twisted human he is.

"Your house stopped being my home a long time ago. I'm done arguing with you. I love you, Daddy, but I don't like you very much right now. I hate that someone came and stole my sister and broke what was once a happy family apart. I hate that after all these years, you still give him the power to do it over and over again. Citi is gone, but I'm still here. One day, I hope we can find a way to live with the memories that haunt us. But right now?" I shake my head. "I can't give you any more pieces of me just so you can discard the parts that don't matter to you. You take me as I am, or don't take me at all."

He opens his mouth, but I hold my hand up and stop him. "Not today. You're not ready, and honestly, neither am I. You need to grieve for Citi. Find a way to move forward. Nobody is asking you to forget her, but you can't change what's happened."

"Don't you think I know that?" he snaps, the look of anguish ravaging my insides until I feel torn apart. "I can't move on, Nevaeh. How does someone move on from that?

You don't get it. She might have been your sister, but she was my baby girl," he chokes as tears slip down his cheeks.

"I was your baby girl, too. You still had me. That's the part I don't understand. Citi might have been taken, but you ignored me to the point where I thought I was invisible. I get that you were hurt, but you don't have the market cornered on grief. You lost your daughter. I lost my twin. I lost my whole damn family. And now, after years of emotional abuse, you come here and try to take my new family from me too? No. Hell no."

"I think it's time for you to leave." Havoc takes over when he feels me shaking beneath his fingers.

"Who are you to tell me?" My father's snarl is cut off, but Havoc's quiet but firm voice remains.

"I'm the man who loves her. I'm the man who wipes her tears, who makes her laugh, supports her, and protects her. I'll never look at those things as anything less than the gifts they are because taking care of your daughter is my privilege. I'm going to marry her one day. God willing, we'll have babies together and maybe even grandchildren. I pray we never have to deal with what you did. I can't even imagine your pain, but I would never leave my other children to fight the currents of sorrow while letting myself drown in it."

"Go home, Dad. Go pray to a god you don't even believe in anymore. Lie to your reflection and curse my existence if that's what you need. There is no place for me there anymore anyway."

"I think it's time to leave, sir," Officer Jacobs states.

"You're making a mistake," my father tells me, his eyes locked on mine.

"Your house is not a home. It's a shrine. Until you can see the difference, I think you should stay away," Amity tells my dad gently, making him wince. He takes a final look at me before storming off.

The two officers, who look a little uncomfortable, offer their apologies.

"I'm sure he told you a really good story. He's a pastor. If there is one thing he's good at, it's telling tales that draw you in and make you believe." I sigh.

"We'll follow him to make sure he leaves anyway. I'd rather we keep the peace than have to deal with any issues," Officer Pauly says.

"We won't be opening the gate for him, so there will be no issues on our end. The only time we'll call you is if he turns up and refuses to leave," Havoc warns them.

The other cop looks from me to Havoc, his eyes narrowed with suspicion.

"This is not one of those times where I'm saying something to distract you from the truth. I'm not hurt, battered, or bruised. I'm not a sex slave or a drug addict or whatever the heck else you might be thinking. And honestly, I'm starting to feel a little offended that you're judging these people—people you don't know—because of the cuts they're wearing. Imagine if I did the same thing to police officers, because lord knows there are enough corrupt ones around."

His partner says something to him. His words are urgent but too damn quiet for me to hear. "Thank you for your time," he says before they both turn and leave.

I relax against Havoc, feeling as if my strings have been cut.

"I'm so proud of you," Amity says, rushing over to hug me.

I feel emotionally wrung out, but there is something to be said about the sense of empowerment when you find the courage to stand up for yourself. It doesn't undo the pain his words caused, but they would have hurt regardless. You can't stand in front of a man who sharpens his words like knives and not expect to get cut. Standing up for myself was a way to limit the damage and help me heal faster.

"It was time. It doesn't make it feel any less crappy, but I couldn't hide from him forever. I think I have Havoc to thank for that."

I look at him over my shoulder.

"What did I do?"

"Made me realize that if I'm strong enough to stand up to you, then I'm strong enough to stand up to him."

"Parents always feel larger than life because we spent our childhoods looking up to them both physically and emotionally."

"Plus, they're supposed to be our heroes, when truth be

told, parents are often the ones that fuck us up the most," G adds, reaching over to ruffle my hair the way an annoying big brother would. I growl at him, making him grin, but secretly, I love it. I don't think I truly realized how lonely I was until I found myself here, surrounded by people who don't know the meaning of *personal space*. They love fast and hard, and with everything they have. And the best part, they never let go.

I retreat to our room to lick my wounds and lose myself in a book.

I must doze off because the sound of my stomach rumbling jolts me awake.

Standing up, I feel a blanket slip from my shoulders. I frown and look around, knowing I didn't cover myself up. Spotting a note, I pick it up and scan it.

Pippin,

I checked your pulse because I couldn't tell if you were in a deep sleep or a coma. The good news is you're still alive; the bad news is you missed out on my awesome company.

If you have not risen from your grave by the morning, I shall attempt to reanimate you with coffee and pastries. Oh and take a shower and brush your teeth. You stink.

"I really need new friends."

I head to the bathroom, take care of business, wash my hands and brush my teeth before staring in the mirror.

When I came upstairs, I wanted comfort, so I changed out of my clothes for a onesie with little pumpkins all over it. I know I should change. No self-respecting old lady would walk around the clubhouse in a onesie, but I just can't be bothered. I think the confrontation with my father has taken more out of me than I realized.

Shrugging, I tug the hood up for the full effect and own it. It's not like Havoc is going to break up with me because of my love for all things fall. It's not like it's covered in dinosaurs. That one is still in the closet.

I head toward the stairs. Now that I'm out of the sound-proof room, the noise from downstairs is slowly filtering up to me. The soft sound of Fleetwood Mac drifts from the juke-box, along with animated talking and laughter.

I make my way through the crowd to the bar. Most people ignore me until Toot turns and catches sight of me. His eyes rove over my body before they light with laughter.

"Well, hello, pumpkin."

I groan. "No more nicknames. I have so many I can hardly keep track. Have you seen Havoc?"

He points to one of the sofas on the far side of the room. I can see Havoc leaning back with one ankle hooked over his knee as he sips his beer and listens to something Midas says to him. I move toward him, but Toot steps in front of me. I think he's going to stop me for a minute until I realize he's clearing the way for me. One of the many drawbacks of being short is that getting smushed in a crowd is far too easy.

Gripping the back of Toot's T-shirt, I let him lead me across the room before letting go and moving around him. Havoc's eyes land on mine right away before they fall on my onesie.

"Can I just say, your outfit is adorable?" Toot teases me. Midas grins, checking me out.

I roll my eyes as I move toward Havoc. "What are the other girls wearing, Toot?"

I turn to see him frown. "I don't know."

"But you'll remember me, right?" I wink.

He chuckles. "Sneaky. I like it, though you're hardly forgettable in those little skirts you like to—"

"Toot," Havoc snaps.

I sigh, turning to Havoc, who has his back to the wall. I reach up to lower my zipper. I flash him my naked breasts for a few seconds before I tug the zipper back up into place.

Turning, I see Toot staring at me in shock as Midas roars with laughter. "It's always the quiet ones."

Neither of them could see anything, but I guess they both knew what I was doing.

"Easy access and I don't see Havoc complaining."

"Lucky son of a bitch," Toot curses before turning around and storming off.

Grinning, I climb onto Havoc's lap, sucking in a sharp breath when I feel how hard he is beneath me.

"Behave," he whispers in my ear when I start to wiggle. "I'm two seconds away from bending you over the back of this sofa and showing my men exactly what's underneath this onesie."

I take a few moments to regulate my breathing. His words sure as heck don't help with that at all. Eventually, I lift my head, my eyes colliding with his.

"I'm hungry. I came down for food."

"And almost caused a riot." Midas laughs.

"I think it would take more than a pair of boobs to cause a riot in this place."

"Clearly, you've underestimated your tits," he grins.

"I will kill you, Midas," Havoc warns him.

Before Midas can answer back, Havoc's cell phone rings. He grabs it from the pocket inside his cut. No name comes up on the screen, just a number, but I feel Havoc tense.

"I've gotta take this."

He eases me off his lap, leaving me with Midas.

"So, pumpkins?"

"You gotta problem with that?"

"No, ma'am" he tells me with a grin.

"That's what I thought."

Chapter Twenty-Five

Havoc

I answer the call once I know I'm alone. "Yeah."

"They're up to something. I don't know what. I'm treated like any other prospect for now. They're careful what they say, unless they are making jokes at your club's expense to see how I react."

"You safe to talk?"

"Filling up at the gas station a couple of miles away."

"Alright. Tell me what your gut feeling is. Do I need to pull you out?"

"No, they've given me no indication I've been made. I'm good to stay. The top two are definitely up to something." He avoids saying Khan and Driller's names, which is smart even if he is alone.

"I've heard they've become a secretive pair anyway, dealing in things and keeping the others separate from it all."

"Yeah, I noticed that, and even I know that's not how it usually works. Most of the others don't bat an eye over it, so I guess it is the norm for them. Though in the last few days, there seems to have been a bit of a shift."

"What do you mean *shift?*"

"There is more of a divide present than I noticed before. I'm unsure if that's new or if they just aren't hiding it anymore, but it's there. I won't name names, not here, not now, but the top two appear to have fewer allies than I think they realize."

"Can't say I'm surprised. Clearly, they're making decisions that are best for them, not for the club. On a side note, the bugs we placed aren't getting shit. We get the odd, innocuous conversation every now and then, but that's it. Haven't heard them call church once."

"They had church yesterday."

I sigh. "They're using a jammer. I don't know if they found the bugs and left them there so we wouldn't notice, or if they're being extra cautious. But either way, they're useless to us now."

"Sorry, I don't have more for you. Just...watch your backs. I have a bad feeling. I'm just not sure what it's about."

"I'll talk to the guys. Stay safe. If it even looks like someone is onto you, bail."

"Will do."

Kieran hangs up, so I slip my cell back into my pocket and take a second to think over what he said. None of it is new information, but it's interesting to hear about the divide. It means what Byte, Ferris, and Elmo said wasn't just for effect. It gives me hope that I won't have to wipe out the whole club —not that I'd ever be able to fully trust them again.

Hannibal walks out of the restroom as I turn to head back inside. He looks at me, asking a question with no words.

"Nothing new yet, other than the fact he has a bad feeling and the suspicion they're using jammers to mess with the bugs we planted."

"They made us?"

"Not necessarily. It could be a precaution, especially if they think there are people in the club who are no longer loyal to them. They won't want anyone to catch them out if they are doing shady deals."

He grunts as he walks beside me.

"You think any more about what I asked?"

He tenses but doesn't answer.

"I know you got a lot going on, but don't take too long to figure shit out. I need you. So does she."

He freezes solid, so I move past him and leave him alone for a moment. I walk back to where Nevaeh sits with Midas and scoop her up, making her screech.

"You scared me." She smacks my arm.

"Such a jumpy little thing. Let's get you some food before you get hangry."

I carry her to the kitchen and sit her on the counter while I rummage in the fridge for some food. "Got the fixings for sandwiches, leftover pizza, or lasagna."

"Lasagna, please."

I plate her a portion and heat it as a couple of club bunnies walk in and head our way.

Kiki twirls her hair. "Hey, Havoc."

"You need something?"

She bats her eyes at me. "We just haven't spent any time with you, that's all."

"Why would I spend time with you?" I frown.

Nevaeh chuckles as I stare at them and wait for them to answer.

Stacey drops her voice. "What Kiki is trying to say is, we can show you a real good time."

I look at Nevaeh, the frown still on my face.

She shakes her head and grins. "She means sex, honey. She's offering you the free use of her vagina. I think all of them are."

"Pass," I reply, getting back to the food.

"You haven't tried us yet. We'll let you do things to us that will blow your mind." Macy purrs like a cat. I'm not sure if that's supposed to be sexy. If it is, it didn't work.

I put the food on the plate and carry it to Nevaeh, ignoring them.

"I think he's good, ladies. But thanks for the offer."

Nevaeh offers them a smile, clearly not offended at all. I'm not sure I'd be as calm if a man—

My hands fist, so I let the thought go before I punch something.

Kiki pipes up. "He's only with you because you're the first pussy he fell into since he got out of jail. He'll get bored. There is nothing you can give him that I can't."

Nevaeh stands up to her full height, which still makes her the shortest person in the room. Even so, the girls take a wary step back.

"I gave him my virginity. Can any of you give him that? Why would he trade in a custom, made-to-fit model with all the bells and whistles that's only had him as an owner for someone who has been ridden more times than the subway and by just as many passengers? I guess you could give him an STD. That's something I can't give him. Honey? You feel like downgrading?"

"Fuck no."

"You bitch," Stacey snaps.

"You walk in here and try to sleep with my man, and I'm the bitch?" Nevaeh's voice is pitched low, but I can hear the barely concealed violence in it.

"I was more than nice to you before you took things too far. If you want to stay, I suggest you shut your mouth and learn to read the room. Because if there is one thing I know, it's that Havoc is loyal to this club and to me. We are the only things that matter to him. You're nothing. If you disappeared tomorrow, Havoc wouldn't lose a wink of sleep." Nevaeh leans forward and smiles. It's cold and cruel and makes my dick go rock hard.

"Fun thing about being a writer? I get to research lots of interesting facts. Like the best way to kill someone and dispose of their body. Push your luck again, and we'll see just how effective my research is."

They back up, visibly shocked. All of them hurry to leave, but I stop them. "You're new. I'm new. You don't know me any more than I know you, so I'll give you one chance to take what my old lady said on board. If you approach her or me again with anything related to my fucking you, I'll kick you out so fast your head will spin. My cock belongs to Nevaeh. It's as simple as that."

"I'll give you a little bit of advice because I'm nice like that," Nevaeh adds with a smile. "Don't pull this shit with G and Amity. I might have hit your pride, but she'll hit your face."

She waves as they leave before sitting back down and yanking the lasagna closer to her. She digs in, her eyes closing briefly as she shoves a forkful of food into her mouth. "Mmm...so good."

"If you want to finish that, you'd better stop making those noises."

"If you don't speak to me until I'm finished, I'll give you a blowjob and let you come all over my boobs."

I stare at her for a second, surprised that it came out of her mouth.

She shrugs and gives me an innocent look. "Let's just say I'm feeling the need to mark my territory. But first, I need sustenance."

I sit in the chair opposite her and grab the table.

"Havoc? You okay?" she teases.

"Eat fast," I grunt, making her laugh.

Chapter Twenty-Six

Nevaeh

"So, there's a pop-up signing a couple of towns over. It's at a large bookstore, and a few local authors are attending."

"Okay?"

"I've been invited to go, and as it's not far and my real identity is out now, I can't see the harm. I love meeting fans and other authors. It reminds me why I do what I do. Writing can get lonely sometimes."

He leans back and looks at me as I chew my lip. "You know you don't need my permission, right? But I need you protected, so I won't let you go alone."

I beam a huge smile his way before diving into his arms.

"I'm not your father, cupcake. You're not a prisoner. That said, I'm coming with you, so don't even argue. When is it?"

"Wouldn't dream of it. It's at the end of next week. They pop up all over the country and always last minute. I guess it's a way to keep the crowds small."

"As long as I'm beside you, you'll be safe anyway. We'll bring a second for backup, but if the event is small, then I can't see the point of having a large team going with us."

"No, and I think that would probably be an issue anyway. You're an intimidating bunch. You'll scare my readers away."

"Please. They love me."

I tilt my head and frown. "And how would you know that, Mr. President?"

He curses. "My testicles are urging me to lie right now," he mutters before he presses his forehead against mine. "I may or may not have posted photos of us together on my social media."

"You have social media? Huh."

"You're making me feel old."

I laugh. "It's not that. It's just out of character. It's akin to imagining Hannibal at a knitting club."

He chuckles at that.

Unlucky for him, though, my thoughts are taking root. I cross my arms over my chest. "What did you do, caveman?"

He pulls his phone out and opens the app before handing it over to me. "Nothing bad. I made the mistake of tagging your personal account instead of Celeste's, but I've fixed that now G pointed out my mistake. I didn't mean to cause issues. I'm just proud of you, that's all. What's wrong with that?"

I soften before leaning forward and giving him a kiss. "Nothing at all. It feels really good, actually. Unfortunately for you, I'm getting better at reading between the lines. Something tells me you are proud of me, but that's not all there is to it."

I scroll through his phone, laughing and sighing at the pictures of us together. Pulling out my own phone, I look through my social media. I've been avoiding it for weeks. I can only imagine the number of tags and messages I've missed.

My eyes widen as I see just how popular Havoc is with my readers. I put both phones down on the table. "You're right. They love you. I'm kind of worried now that you might need security yourself. You've caused quite a stir. Perhaps I should make you one of my cover models."

"You write romance books. Not sure many readers would be interested in a biker like me."

I blink and grin at his naivety. "Oh, you poor misguided fool."

He glances at me in confusion. I smile sweetly and decide to let him find out the hard way. I'll have to see if I can bribe whoever he brings with us to take photos and capture the moment he realizes how much readers like men just like him.

His cell phone rings before he can ask me what I'm thinking, making him groan. "Can't a man spend some fucking time with his old lady without every man and his dog trying to interrupt him?" he mutters to himself.

"Yeah?" he answers. He frowns, his eyes widening a fraction before he responds. "I'll be right there."

He disconnects the call and turns to me. "There is someone at the gate that wants to talk to you."

Now it's my turn to groan. "My father?"

"No. My ex."

The shock of that statement must be evident on my face.

"Stay here, and I'll go deal with her."

"Not a chance in hell," I tell him, standing up and brushing the crumbs from my lap.

I smooth down my skirt and straighten up my cardigan. I'm not vain, or at least no more than most people, but going up against Lola makes my insecurities flare. She might be many things, but ugly is not one of them.

Still, Havoc is mine, and if she thinks she can come waltzing in here and make some kind of play for him, she has another thing coming.

"Maybe we should build a moat, add some crocodiles and a drawbridge or something," I mumble, making Havoc laugh.

"How can I be pissed off and yet still laugh?"

"Mental health issues?"

He grins and kisses me hard, leaving me unstable on my feet.

"Come on. Let's get this over with." He takes my hand and walks me down to the gate for another confrontation.

I notice a few others hovering around, eager to see what's happening without trying to appear too eager. I roll my eyes. I swear bikers are worse than a bunch of school girls.

When we walk through the warehouse holding hands, it shows solidarity and ownership. Lola might have had Havoc first, but she threw him away. I won't make the same mistake because I know exactly what kind of treasure he is.

When we walk through, we find the gates already open. Dice is standing in front of Lola, so we can't see her properly until Havoc calls Dice's name. Dice turns at the sound of Havoc's voice before stepping away.

We get our first good look at her. She seems smaller than I remember, and I don't mean height-wise. I'm tiny, hence the stupid nicknames, but my attitude is far bigger than I am. Lola might be taller than me by a good half a foot, but she's giving off the air of someone trying to make themselves look small.

She is wearing a Yankees ball cap with a pair of oversized sunglasses. Dressed in a pair of ripped jeans and a sweatshirt two sizes too big for her and hiding her bump, she looks more like a teenager than an old lady and far more vulnerable. I don't like it one bit. I can't tell if it's genuine or a ploy to bring out Havoc's protective instincts.

"Why are you here, Lola? I have nothing to say to you," Havoc tells her. His voice, usually filled with warmth for me, is stone cold.

She flinches, and I can't say I blame her. I would, too.

Having anger turned your way is one thing—at least there is feeling in anger. Indifference is worse. Knowing someone who used to love you feels nothing at all for you anymore hurts worse. I know that feeling all too well.

"I came to warn you. Khan and Driller are planning something." She slides her hand protectively over her stomach as she swallows.

"Aren't they always? Besides, shouldn't you be beside your old man, cheering him on?" Havoc asks.

His words hit like barbs. Her head jerks back as if she can physically feel them lash against her skin.

"You don't know me, Havoc. You never did, or you'd never have asked me that." Her voice cracks as she speaks, but I'm too busy focusing on her face. Her glasses slipped when she jerked back, letting my eye catch what she was hiding.

"You're right, I don't know you. The woman I loved was a fucking lie. Go home, Lola. You've caused enough damage."

I let go of his hand while he was distracted and walked toward her.

He calls my name when he realizes what I'm doing but doesn't try to stop me. I step in front of her and see how tense she is. She braces herself as if waiting for a blow. I never thought I'd feel a wave of pity for this woman, but as I reach up and slide the glasses off her face and reveal deep purple bruising, I remind myself that nothing in life is ever black and white.

Chapter Twenty-Seven

Havoc

"What the fuck?"

I storm toward them. I don't touch Lola, but I don't need to, to know how tender her eye must feel. That's when I register her clothes. Preppy or biker chic, Lola has never been a jeans and sweatshirt kind of woman. She took pride in her appearance—something that her mother, who was once a former beauty queen, drummed into her.

"Who did this?"

"Who do you think?"

The air between us becomes thick with tension. It's on the tip of my tongue to snarl at her about facing the consequences of her actions, but I swallow it down. "He hit you anywhere else?"

"You believe me?" She looks surprised.

I shrug. "I don't care if you're lying to me or not, but Driller never did know how to take care of his toys."

She flinches away from us both so hard she almost stumbles.

"Lola, do you need to see a doctor?" Nevaeh asks her softly.

Lola looks at me. The betrayal etched into her face would have once brought me to my knees. But not now. Not after everything.

"Lola, think about the baby. Do you need to see a doctor?" Nevaeh presses.

Lola looks to her and sucks in a shuddering breath. Her eyes are glassy with tears, but she fights them back. "If I go to the hospital. It will only make it worse. We'll be okay. Nugget is moving around, so he's fine."

I pull out my phone and dial Hannibal. When he answers, I start talking before he asks questions. "Head to the clinic. I'm bringing someone in for you to look at." I hang up as Lola shakes her head.

"I have to go before they notice I'm missing."

"We have a clinic here onsite, Lola. It won't be much longer. Wouldn't you rather know for sure the baby is okay before you go?" Nevaeh soothes her like she would a wounded animal.

I can see she's going to refuse, so I shake my head. "For once in your fucking life, stop being selfish and let Hannibal check you over. Don't worry. He'll get you out of here as soon as possible."

"Havoc." Nevaeh scowls at me.

Stepping in front of me, she reaches out tentatively and gently takes Lola's hand. "Look, I don't know you. You don't know me. The history between you two is just that, history. Right now, all that matters is getting you and your baby checked out. I promise nothing will happen to either of you while you're here."

Lola's eyes slip closed momentarily before one lone tear slips down her cheek. Her shoulders sag in defeat. "Okay."

"Okay, good. You okay to walk?"

"I'm fine," she murmurs, not that any of us are convinced. But if she wants to walk, I won't fight her on it.

I turn to Dice, who has been watching us curiously. "Lock the gates and watch yourself. Driller might come looking for her, and he won't give a shit about starting trouble. Don't let anyone in unless they are a part of this chapter until I tell you otherwise, got it?"

"Yes, Prez," he answers. I slap him on the shoulder before turning. I watch Nevaeh lead Lola up through the warehouse.

"You think she's here to spy?" Midas asks as he slips out of the shadows.

"It's likely. She has no ties to this club, and we already

know she has no trouble shooting me in the back. I don't doubt Driller hit her. He's always had issues, and they were reaching fever point when I went to prison. I can only imagine how out of fucking control he is now."

"What's the plan?"

"Right now? To let Hannibal look her over and see what he says."

He nods but doesn't say anything else. We both follow after the women, through the warehouse and up the slope. We walk in silence, keeping a little distance between us and them. If anyone can get anything out of her, it will be Nevaeh. Assuming she doesn't verbally slap her first.

"I'll head to the saloon and let everyone know what's going on so they don't bother you for a bit."

"Thanks, Midas."

I start to move but Midas says my name.

"I know how you feel about her. I'd be the same way, but that baby? None of this is their fault. Driller might very well beat that baby out of her. Can you live with that? Whatever happened between you and her, that kid is still your niece or nephew."

"I know, Midas. But that doesn't change the fact that it should have been my son or daughter. I might not want her anymore, but it's not easy to forget everything she took from me."

"And if she had stood beside you, you wouldn't have

Nevaeh. Think carefully before you let regrets cloud the fact that you won in the end. Not to mention, you and Nevaeh will make beautiful babies. As long as they look like their mama," he teases, though I don't miss the tightening around his eyes. I'm not the only one who would have had kids now if the fates had been kinder.

I think about Nevaeh and know everything worked out exactly how it was supposed to.

"I hear you, Midas. Let G know what's going on. See if he can get hold of Byte. Find out if anything is going on their end. I spoke to Kieran, and he knows something is brewing. He doesn't know what. Prospects aren't privy to much information, as you know. The bugs are a no-go. It seems they have a jammer. We need to get ourselves prepared for the worst, just in case. I'll be fucking damned if I let them catch us with our asses out."

"You thinking lockdown?"

"Not yet. Besides, sometimes having everyone in one spot is the worst idea." I take a step away before I remember something else. "Get hold of Blade and fill him in on everything. He knows most of it, but tell him and the others to be vigilant. Blade was the one who made me president. He might be just as much of a target as I am."

"I'll call him after I've caught G up."

I nod and jog to the clinic.

When I walk in, it's quiet. I head toward the treatment

room and stop when I see Nevaeh in one of the blue plastic chairs.

"I thought you'd be in there with her."

"Hannibal asked her if she wanted privacy, and here I am. Can't say I blame her."

I grab the door handle, but she stops me.

"No. I know you're the big bad president, but you don't need to be in there with her while she's vulnerable. Hannibal will tell you everything you want to know afterward."

I manage to stop myself from blurting out that I've seen it all before, realizing how bad that would sound. "Fine. She must really not like you if she's willing to be alone in there with Hannibal."

"I have the man who used to be hers. I get your smile, your heart, and your time. And having been on the receiving end of it all, I know how powerful it is to be loved by you. Seeing us together will make that void you left behind feel like a chasm."

I shrug. "She walked away. And now that I have you, I'm glad she did." I yank her into my arms and kiss her soundly.

She leans into me, grabbing my cut and holding me to her. I pick her up so I don't get a crick in my neck and urge her to wrap her legs around me. I feel the heat of her pussy through the denim of my jeans. Sliding my hand under her ass, my fingers just slip under the edge of her panties when the door opens. Hannibal steps out—the damn cock blocker.

Nevaeh pulls back to look at him, wriggling until I put

her down. I glare at Hannibal, who gives me a knowing smirk before he turns serious.

"She should see her OB/GYN."

"Not sure that's an option right now. I could force her, but I don't think that's the way to go here."

He sighs and wipes his hand over his face. "Probably not."

"How is she? Is the baby okay?" Nevaeh asks.

Hannibal looks at her with a soft expression before turning those eyes on me. I can read him clearly. He's telling me I've got a good one here, not to fuck it up. I give him a nod because I'm well aware of what I have.

"We're lucky we have an ultrasound."

"Why do we have an ultrasound anyway?" Nevaeh questions with a frown.

"One of the old timers lost a bet, which resulted in them stealing one. Don't ask." Hannibal shakes his head. "Baby looks good. He's not hugely active, but that's mostly because he has little room left to maneuver. Obstetrics is not my area of expertise, but by all accounts he looks healthy, if a little small for his gestation."

"He?"

"Oh yeah, it's a boy. Lola already knows, apparently, but she hasn't told Driller and wants it kept that way."

"Not like I'm going to sit down with that motherfucker any time soon."

"And Lola?"

Hannibal turns back to Nevaeh. "She was more than

happy for me to check on the baby, but she wouldn't let me give her a full exam. From what I could see, there are more bruises, both old and new, on her arms and chest, including what looked like a bite mark. She shut down any questions that weren't baby-related. But if you're asking me if I think Driller has made her his current punching bag, then the answer is yes."

I wipe my hand over my face, wondering how it all came to this. "She came here to give us a warning. Told me that Khan and Driller are planning something."

"Nothing we didn't already know."

"Midas asked me if she's been sent here as a spy."

"What do you think?"

I look at the door that hides Lola from us and shrug. "She's done a lot of shit I wouldn't have thought her capable of."

"You think she took a beating so it would make us more sympathetic to her and let her through the gate?" Nevaeh looks at me in shock.

"Nothing would surprise me anymore. But Driller wouldn't have given her a choice either way if that was the plan he and Khan had devised."

"She cares about the baby. That much was obvious, and it's not an act," Hannibal states. "I don't think there is much she wouldn't do to protect him."

"Like stab us all in the back."

"Not sure, given her current state, she feels any loyalty to anyone in Raven Souls, but I'm with Hannibal. I don't think she'd put her baby in danger if she could help it," Nevaeh says.

"She's in danger just being with Driller."

"And would he let her go if she ran?"

I shut my mouth, which is an answer in itself. I look at Hannibal, knowing he can read the questions in my eyes.

"Fuck. Fine, I accept."

"Accept what?" Nevaeh looks between us.

Hannibal is focused on me. "I'll do it. But I'll take her back with me and make her my old lady. Call it fucking spoils of war for all I care, but I might need her in the long run if I can't get shit sorted out with Millie."

I fold my arms over my chest.

"She'll be protected with me from any of the club members."

I don't say anything, waiting him out. He throws up his hands. "I won't hurt her either. Happy?"

"Ecstatic."

"She can stay with me until this is over. I'll make sure she doesn't say shit."

"I'll let you break the news then."

I take Nevaeh's hand and lead her out, even as she tries to resist.

"Hold on a freaking second. What just happened?"

I wait until we're outside before I stop and press her against the wall. "When I remove Khan and Driller from their positions, Hannibal is going to take over as the president."

"What?"

"He's a scary motherfucker who people will think twice about crossing."

"How does Lola play into this? And who the heck is Millie?"

I bend down and press my forehead against hers. "You can't say anything to anyone, not even Amity."

She huffs but nods.

"Lola won't last five seconds without protection of some kind. Taking out Driller might save her from him, but it won't save her or her son from the enemies he's made. And knowing Driller, he's made many."

"So if the club's new president makes her his old lady, she'll be protected by the club."

"Exactly."

She blows out an incredulous breath. "And Lola doesn't even get a say in this?"

"She decided to take her chances with Driller. She's lucky Hannibal is offering her a way out at all. It won't be easy, though. She fucked me over while I was in prison. People will remember that."

"What a mess. Is it weird that I feel sorry for her?"

"No. You're a good person, Nevaeh. There's nothing wrong with that. Plus, like it or not, that kid is my nephew. He deserves a chance regardless of who his parents are."

She nods before looking up at me. "So, who is Millie?"

I hesitate for a moment, knowing it's not my secret to tell. But Nevaeh won't say anything, and this particular secret will come out eventually.

"Millie is Hannibal's daughter."

Chapter Twenty-Eight

Nevaeh

I kept quiet about Hannibal having a daughter. Even if I wanted to say something, the shock rendered me mute. I can't picture it, and I'm too much of a chickenshit to bring it up with the man himself. Not that he's been around much.

I haven't seen Lola since the day she arrived last week, so my guess is he's keeping busy with her.

The only thing I do know is that after agreeing to be the new president of Havoc's old chapter, church had been called every day to discuss the future for both clubs. I'm not privy to all the details, but I noticed Amity looking at me with wide eyes after G pulled her into the corner and whispered in her ear for five minutes. When she came to tell me that Hannibal is going to be president, I noticed she didn't mention Millie, so I keep that to myself, admitting that I already knew the rest.

"What happened to *hoes before bros?*"

"I'm one rung above a virgin. I haven't reached hoe status yet."

"Good point." She nods, eyeing my plate of food. I take a bite of my burger before sliding the plate toward her.

"Fries before, guys?"

She takes a handful with a grin. "Works for me."

"I don't know why you didn't just order yourself a side of fries to go with your salad."

"I'm filming a commercial next week, remember?"

"You could eat fries every day for a week, and you'd still be in better shape than anyone in here."

"You're a bad influence on me, Pippin."

I use my finger to draw an invisible halo around my head while batting my lashes at her. She throws a ketchup-covered fry at me, hitting my cheek. I peel it off and eat it because, hello, it's a fry.

"What time are you leaving anyway?"

I wipe the sauce from my face before I look at my watch. "In an hour. The plan was originally to travel there and back tomorrow, the day of the signing. But Havoc decided last minute that we might as well go early and stay overnight so we don't run into any delays."

"Aww, sweet."

"Hmm..."

"What do you mean hmmm? The man is taking you away for a night of dirty shenanigans, and you're complaining?"

"I'm not complaining. Have you seen my man? My point is that being here doesn't exactly stop the shenanigans. Biker, remember? He wouldn't think twice about doing me over the pool table if he thought I'd let him. Until he realized everyone could see me, he'd get all snarly."

"Sounds like Havoc." She grins.

"It's not that, though. He's just been...not off but...I don't know how to explain it. Like he's planning something, maybe?"

She doesn't dismiss me like I'm nuts. She thinks about it, a small crease between her eyebrows.

"Hmm..."

"See, that's what I said."

"Maybe it's just everything with the other club. Plus, G told me there was a break-in at The Lookout a few days ago. Someone showed up wearing a Ravens cut. If it wasn't for the fact that Jimmy is friendly with the club and comfortable calling Havoc to find out what the fuck is going on, we could have had the police at our door."

"You're probably right. It all feels so childish after the shootout. A part of me almost hopes they make their move already. I'm tired of waiting for the other shoe to drop."

"I hear you. We've barely recovered from the crap with

my stalker, and now this. I must be getting old because all I want is some peace and quiet."

"I'm surprised we haven't taken the offensive."

"Being the mother chapter means we are held to a higher standard. The other clubs have to see that we're not overreacting or overstepping. We have a whole lot of hearsay right now and not a whole lot of proof. Can't take out the top two members without concrete evidence, not without turning the other clubs against us."

I lean back and rub my food baby as I let her words sink in. "I guess you're right. That reminds me, did you get things sorted with the insurance company?"

"Eventually, yes."

After taking in the damage the RV had sustained, Amity decided to scrap it and get a regular car now that we were both living with our men anyway.

"They tried stalling and calling my bluff. But I have special insurance on account of it not just being my home but often on a movie set where weird things can happen. No point paying premium dollars for something like that if they're going to be dicks. Anyway, I managed to persuade them it was in their interests to just write me the damn check and be done with it. And finally, they agreed."

"Good, that's one less thing to worry about."

A loud whisper has us both looking up to see G waving for Amity to join him.

"Looks like I've been summoned." She rolls her eyes.

"Not that I'm complaining. I'm so ready to get this thing off." She waves the cast around. "I'll see you when you get back tomorrow. Bring me back some swag."

"Will do."

She gives me a quick hug before heading over to join him. With a groan, I get to my feet and stretch.

Feeling a little sick, I walk to the bar and get a bottle of water from Dice, who is working there today. I unscrew the cap and take a sip of the cool liquid before holding it to my head.

Legs comes and sits beside me with a frown on her face. "You okay?"

"Think I over ate. Though saying that, I've felt sick on and off for the last few days."

She presses her hand to my forehead. "You don't feel hot. Any other symptoms?"

"Just being tired. But then things have been hectic as hell around here."

She looks at me oddly before taking my hand and urging me to accompany her.

"Where are we going? I'm leaving for the signing soon."

"This won't take long."

I stare at her, bemused, and let her to lead me into the clinic. She lets go of my hand and rummages in one of the drawers for a moment before dragging me to the restroom.

"Okay take this and go pee on it."

I look down at the pregnancy test in my hand and blink.

"Think about it. You've been feeling sick and tired, and something tells me the last thing on Havoc's mind when he's with you is protection. You tend to make him love dumb. It's cute and kind of sickening."

"Hey now." I laugh, taking the pregnancy test when she presses it against my chest.

"Off you go."

"While Havoc appears to have somewhat of a breeding kink, he clearly doesn't realize that inexperienced doesn't mean uninformed. I'm on the pill, and I haven't missed one. I'm not pregnant."

"When was your last period?"

"I can't remember. But before you say anything, my periods are always irregular."

"The pill is not foolproof. Take the damn test, woman."

"I'm not taking the test."

She grabs another one and pulls me into the restroom. Before I know what she's doing, she pulls down her under-wear, sits on the toilet, and rips open the packaging with her teeth. She maneuvers herself until she can pee on the stick before my brain comes online again, and I turn around.

"See, it's that simple."

"If I agree to take the test, will you leave me to pee in peace?"

"You'll do it?"

"Uh-huh. Mostly because I'm scared you'll pin me down and tickle me until I pee so you can do the test for me."

She chuckles before flushing the toilet and shuffling around me so she can squeeze out the door.

I shake my head and pee to the sound of Legs washing her hands.

"How the heck did you make this look so easy?" I grumble, only just missing peeing on my hand.

"I'm bendy."

I walk out of the stall and place the test on the counter beside hers. I wash my hands and lean against the wall.

"Says you have to wait for three minutes."

"I told you, I'm not pregnant. My stomach always acts up when I'm stressed out. With everything going down with the other club and my dad, I swear my head is ready to explode."

"Well, if you're right, then this will just be a tiny blip you can forget about. But it's better safe than sorry."

"Yeah, I guess."

She's quiet for a minute before she grins. "So Havoc has a breeding kink, huh?"

I cover my face and groan. "The man is ridiculous. I've heard everything from 'you can't get pregnant standing up' to 'you can't get pregnant in the bath because the water is too hot.' I'm not sure if I'm supposed to be insulted or amused that he thinks he's pulling the wool over my eyes."

"Why not just tell him you're on the pill?"

"Now, where's the fun in that?"

She shakes her head and chuckles. "Sounds like he might not be the only one with a breeding kink."

I feel my face flush and swiftly change the subject. "Amity tells me you've found a place?"

"Yeah. I've put a deposit down, and I'm just waiting for all the checks to come back. Then I can move in. The previous tenant had to relocate in a hurry due to a sick family member needing help, so they're looking to get someone in as soon as possible."

"Oh, I'm happy you found somewhere. You'll invite me over, right? I'm nosy and don't want you to forget us when you leave."

"Fat chance of that. For now, I'll still be working at the pawn shop." Her smile drops at the mention of that.

"Things still not right with you and Midas?" I venture.

"It's complicated."

"It always is."

She looks at her watch before reaching for the test, her eyes widening before she grins.

"Ha, I told you you were pregnant." She shoves the test in my face before doing a little jig. "I'm so happy for you. I get to be honorary aunt, right?"

I stare down at the two pink lines and swallow.

"Nevaeh?"

"This isn't my test Legs. It's yours."

She looks at me like I'm joking, but the grin slips off her face when she sees my expression. She snatches the test from me and stares at it in shock for a minute before she tosses it on the counter. She grabs the remaining unopened ones she dumped on the counter when she dragged me in. She carries them to the toilet and closes the door.

I stand there, not knowing what the hell to say. I double-check my actual test and blow out a relieved breath that mine is negative, even though I knew it would be. I chew my lip and wait for Legs to come out. When the toilet flushes and she still doesn't come out, I realize she's staying there while she waits for the results.

Five minutes later, still nothing.

I walk into the adjacent stall, climb onto the toilet seat, and stand on tiptoes so I can look over.

Legs is on the floor with her knees pulled up to her chest. Her eyes are laser-focused on the test in her hand. Her hand is shaking so much I'm surprised she can see what it says.

"Legs?"

She looks up at me in a daze. "I'm pregnant?" It sounds like a question, even though the proof is in front of her.

"It looks that way. Maybe we should make a doctor's appointment just to make sure."

She nods mutely as her eyes fill with tears.

"Let's get you out of here, okay?"

"Okay."

I climb down and hurry around to her door, tapping it lightly. I hear her moving before the door opens.

Legs is called legs for a reason. She towers over me, and her legs are where most of her height comes from. But that doesn't stop her from throwing herself into my arms.

I steady myself so we don't end up back on the floor. "It's gonna be okay, Legs. You'll see." I soothe her as I lead her to the counter.

I reach behind me and turn on the water. She lets me go as I reach for a handful of paper towels. I dampen them and use them to wipe her face free of mascara.

"What am I gonna do?"

"You're going to take a deep breath and blow it out for me."

She does as I ask, her chest hitching for a minute before she calms a little.

"First things first. Let's make you a doctor's appointment. Everything else can wait until after that."

She nods. "Doctor. Okay, I can do that."

"You want me to come with you?"

She nods rapidly, another tear slipping free. "Yes. I...I..."

"Take another breath, Legs. If you faint, you'll squish me like a bug."

She laughs but does as I ask. "I'm okay. I'm just in shock, I think. It's taking everything in me not to do another test. My eyes know what they saw, but my head just refuses to believe it."

"I get that, I do. But beyond the shock, what's your gut telling you?"

She thinks about it for a moment before a wobbly smile lights up her face. "I get to be a mom?"

Jesus, now I feel myself tearing up. "Yeah, Legs. You get to be a mom," I tell her softly.

"What if I mess up?"

"All parents mess up. Nobody is perfect, trust me. All you have to do is love your kid and be there for them. Everything else will fall into place. I know you, Legs, and you have a lot of love to give."

"Thank you."

"Can I ask who the dad is?"

She blows out a shaky breath. "That's not something I can answer right now."

"Okay, no pressure. Just know I'm here for whatever. You'll get no judgment from me."

She reaches out and squeezes my hand. "I think I'm going to make that call and then go lie down for a bit."

"Sounds like a plan. I better go and find Havoc before he comes looking for me."

She slips two tests into the back pocket of her jeans—I assume they're the positive ones—before throwing the empty boxes and my negative one in the trash.

"Do I look like I've been crying?"

"Yes. If anyone asks, we talked about you moving out, and we both got teary."

"That will work."

"Would being pregnant maybe change your plans?"

She shakes her head. "No. I don't want my kids to know who I am until they are old enough to understand the choices I made and why. By then, hopefully, it will all be ancient history."

I wish I knew the right thing to say here, but I'm at a loss, so I say nothing. I walk beside her as we head back to the saloon, each of us lost in thought. She leaves me to head the back way up to her room.

I look around and wonder how this is all going to play out. There has been something brewing below the surface between Legs and Midas for ages. Anyone with eyes can see it. Whatever is going on between them hasn't changed Legs' status. He hasn't made her his old lady, therefore, she still has to play her bunny role. I think that's why she has been so adamant about leaving. She's in love with a man who can't see that being a bunny is what she does, not who she is. And now, he might have lost the best thing that could have happened to him. After all, I don't need to know who the father is to know who it isn't. Midas can't have kids. Something tells me finding out she is pregnant is going to make him lose his mind.

"There you are. You ready to go?"

I shake out of my thoughts as Havoc wraps his arms around me, and nod against his chest.

"Alright. Dice is driving the truck up with your books and

shit. He'll meet us at the hotel. There anything else you need to grab?"

"Just my jacket."

"Then let's get this show on the road."

"I hope you know what you're getting yourself into."

"I'm the president of an MC, cupcake. I think I can handle a book signing."

Chapter Twenty-Nine

Havoc

"Jesus Christ," I curse as I spin.

Nevaeh laughs her ass off beside me as a woman in her eighties gives me a wink.

"She just pinched my ass."

"Us book girls are a bunch of thirsty bitches. Plus, it's a great ass."

"You just swore. It's like I don't even know you anymore." I sit down, mostly so my ass is safe from snatch-and-grab grannies, and look around the room.

This is the first time all day that there hasn't been a line of people waiting for Nevaeh's autograph. I knew she was an author, but I don't think I truly understood what that meant in terms of fandom until I came here and watched grown adults lose their minds over seeing her. I've been fighting off the urge to scream *mine* all day. I almost got into a fight with a guy who ripped off his T-shirt and asked her to sign his chest so he could get it tattooed.

"I did try to warn you. Most authors I know are pretty introverted. But this, this is our Mecca, and these are our people. Romance readers are a community like nothing you've seen before. I've never met most of these people, yet they're all my friends. Social media has its benefits. In this case, it's building friendships with people where the oceans between us mean nothing."

"And this is small?"

"Compared to some venues, yes."

I look at her and watch her smile. She looks happy, but it's more than that. She looks relaxed in her own skin. Here, none of her history matters. Nobody cares about her sister or her dad. All they care about are the stories and characters she creates.

"Hello, Nevaeh."

We both turn at the sound of her name and see a tall, thin man wearing a three-piece suit and a fedora. He's wearing dark sunglasses and has a thick beard and mustache, which would make it hard to distinguish his age if it weren't for the paper-thin skin of his hands dotted with liver spots.

"Hello. Do you want me to sign that for you?" Nevaeh reaches for the book he's holding, but when she grabs it, he holds onto it for a little longer than necessary.

She brushes it off, clearly used to fans of all ages being a little odd, but I'm not sure I'll ever get used to it.

"Who shall I make it out to?"

"Jasper," he says so low that I have to lean in a little to hear him.

She writes his name and a little quote before signing her name with a flourish and handing it back. He stares down at it for a moment before he's nudged out of the way by two giggling women who Nevaeh seems to recognize. She jumps up and rounds the table to give them both brief hugs.

"Laura, Jo, this is Havoc, Havoc, this is Laura and Jo, the organizers."

Jo fans her face as she stares at me. "You lucky bitch."

This makes Nevaeh and Laura dissolve into laughter. Seriously, these women are all insane. I look for the old guy, hoping for some kind of solidarity, but he disappears into the crowd.

"We won't keep you; we're just stopping by the tables to see if anyone needs anything." Laura smiles.

"That's sweet, but we're good."

"That's what we like to hear. I have some books for you to sign later if you can squeeze me in." Jo adds.

"I'll make room for you, don't worry."

I wait for them to leave before I lean closer and kiss her lightly. "I think there might be a witch or two in your family tree because the second you sat down, there was magic in the air."

"Oh, really. And are you under my spell, Mr. President?"

"Fuck yes. I'm your biggest fan."

"Want me to sign your chest?" she teases.

I grab her hand and slide it under the table and onto my hard cock. "I've got something you can sign."

"Oh my gosh, you guys are so cute together. Can I get a photo?"

Nevaeh grins against my lips before she turns to look at a young girl standing in front of the table, bouncing on her heels in excitement.

"Of course. Want me to sign something first?" She squeezes my legs, letting me know she's buying me time for my cock to go down.

"Oh, thank you, that would be great. Can you make it out to Katie?"

"Absolutely."

She hands Nevaeh a scrapbook. Nevaeh signs with a flourish before handing it back.

The girl then hands it to me. "Would you sign it too?"

"Me?" I ask, confused.

She blushes and nods. I take the pen from her, ignoring Nevaeh, who chuckles beside me.

"You're so handsome. Are you going to be on the next cover? Squeal, I'm so excited."

I hand the pen and book back to her, bemused as Nevaeh stands up and tugs me around the table so we can have our photo taken.

Once the girl says goodbye and we're alone again, I lean into Nevaeh. "Did she say squeal? I feel so fucking old. Not to mention violated. Did you see the way she looked at me?"

"Well, sir, you are mighty easy on the eyes."

"I don't think I've ever blushed in my fucking life until I came here."

That sets her off. She laughs, catching the attention of those around us, who start snapping pictures. A guy walks toward us with a grin on his face, snagging some of the attention away from me and Nevaeh.

There is something familiar about him, but I can't figure out why until Nevaeh spots him. "Ambros. What are you doing here?"

The MMA fighter?

"My sister heard you were going to be here from a friend, and she insisted I bring her. She's just exchanging bracelets with someone. I swear it's like a Taylor Swift concert or something."

"You a Swiftie, Ambros?" Nevaeh teases as she stands up and moves around the table to hug him. I hook my finger in the waistband of her skirt and stop her.

"Nothing sexier than a woman with confidence and the talent to back it up. Hell yeah, I'm a Swiftie."

His eyes move to me. He holds out his hand for me to shake. "I'm guessing you're Mr. Cherry Popper?"

"These books are heavy, Ambros. Don't make me knock you out with one," Nevaeh warns him as I laugh.

I stand up and shake his hand. "Havoc."

"Ambros. Nice to meet you. Glad you guys worked it out. Guess I'm more like my sister than I realized because I'm a sucker for a happy ending too."

"Are you talking about me again?" A pretty brunette walks up to Ambros and elbows him before her eyes land on Nevaeh, and she freezes. "You're Celeste Sky," she whispers reverently.

"Oh boy," Ambros mutters, sounding amused.

"I've read everything you've ever written. You're my favorite author. I can't believe it's you. I must be dreaming. Somebody pinch me."

Ambros obliges her.

She smacks him in the chest. "Ass, that hurt."

"Just snapping you out of it. You got a little crazy there."

"I did not, right?" She looks at me. I can't help but laugh.

"It's the eyes. I half expected you to tackle her to the ground."

"Don't listen to him. I'm always happy to meet a fan, and honestly, I'm worse. You should have seen me when I met Winter James a few years back. I swear I forgot the English language entirely and just made a series of grunting sounds. I might have even cried a little. It was bad."

"I met her once, too. She was really nice, though I found it hard to concentrate with all her men there." She fans herself.

I look to Nevaeh, having no clue who Winter James is.

"She's an author from the UK. She currently has a sexy harem of men. They own an exclusive nightclub in London, I believe."

I narrow my eyes at her so she doesn't get any funny ideas.

She taps my chest and laughs. "One man is more than enough for me." She turns to the woman. "I have a friend who has a biker harem. One of them used to be the president of Raven Souls before Havoc took over."

"Oooh, biker MC trumps nightclub moguls. Suits are sexy, but bikers..." She trails off, looking embarrassed when she remembers I'm standing there, too.

"Don't mind me, I agree. Bikers are better."

Ambros groans. "Please don't encourage her. You're happily married, Ella, remember?"

"Happily married and in love with a dozen book boyfriends. It's the best of both words."

She opens her mouth to say something to Nevaeh when the sound of gunfire rips through the room. I throw myself at Neveah and take her to the floor.

The sound of screaming and shattered glass ring out around us as I shove Nevaeh under the table, knowing the tablecloth will hide her. A second later, Ella is shoved under from the other side.

"Stay here," I bark at them both before crawling around the side of the table, bumping into Ambros.

"What the fuck is happening?"

"Don't know. I've got a prospect outside, though, and a brother on the far side of the room." I pull out my cell and text Dice and Capone to head my way.

"You armed?" he asks me as I shove my cell phone away.

"No. Funny enough, I didn't think I'd need a gun at a fucking book signing."

"Shit."

I spot Kate, the girl who just took her photo with us, lying on the floor crying with what looks like a bullet wound on the leg.

"Fuck. Gotta move these people out of the way. They're sitting ducks."

Ambros looks around and nods. We both move, keeping low. I scoop the girl up and move her behind one of the overturned tables. I run back out to grab another as Ambros moves past me with someone in his arms. Most people have hidden, so it doesn't take us long to get the rest of the people out of the way.

Capone drops down next to me with Dice in his arms.

"Oh fuck." I rip Dice's prospect cut open and see a bullet hole in his stomach. His gray T-shirt beneath is rapidly turning red.

"Hachette," Dice spits out.

"You sure?"

"Him and four others," he murmurs before he passes out.

I look at Capone. I must have fire in my eyes because he swallows hard.

"Keep pressure on his wound. I gotta check on Nevaeh." I turn to Ambros. "Call an ambulance. Tell them there are multiple casualties."

He nods and yanks out his phone as I crawl back to Nevaeh with my phone in my hand. Once I'm out of sight of the others, I fire off a text.

Go time.

I delete it.

I lift the tablecloth and find Nevaeh leaning over Ella. "You guys okay?"

"She's bleeding. I think a bullet winged her arm."

"Here, let me see. Ella, you okay?"

"I think so." Her voice comes out shaky.

"Help me tug her out this way, Nevaeh. Stay behind the table. They might have stopped firing, but that doesn't mean they're gone."

"They?"

"Sounded like more than one gun firing," I answer smoothly.

Once we get Ella out, I check her arm and agree with Nevaeh. "Just a graze. Doesn't mean it won't hurt like a moth-erfucker, but you'll be fine, I promise."

"Okay, that's good. And I get a cool story out of it right?"

"Right."

"Ella?" Ambros skids across the floor to land next to his sister.

"She's fine. A bullet clipped her arm, but the bleeding has almost stopped already."

"Jesus fuck, you just took ten years off my life. I didn't think. I shoved you under the table. I should have checked that you were okay first. I should have—"

"Done exactly what you did. Don't second guess yourself now," I tell him.

He takes a deep breath before blowing it out, gently tugging his sister to lean against him. I turn to Nevaeh, who is as pale as a ghost.

"Dice is hurt. I've gotta get back to him."

"What? I'm coming."

Stay here—"

"Fuck that. Where is he?"

I snarl, but don't waste time arguing. I drag her across the room to where Dice and Capone are.

"How's he doing?"

"Still breathing, but stomach wounds are not good. Too many things to damage."

Nevaeh moves so she can lift Dice's head onto her lap. She runs her fingers across his forehead, looking up at me with tears running down her face.

"He's a fighter, Nevaeh. He won't give up easily."

She nods and looks down at him, murmuring soft words meant only for Dice. I crawl over to the girl with the leg wound and yank the tablecloth off the nearest table. A man is pressing his hands to the wound, but blood is pumping out between his fingers.

"Need to make a tourniquet. It looks like they hit an artery." He moves back and holds her as I wrap the tablecloth around her upper thigh and pull it tight. She cries out, clutching onto the other guy. "Sorry, sweetheart. I need to slow the bleeding down." I tie it as tight as possible and hope the ambulances arrive soon.

"You good with her while I check on the others?" I ask the guy.

"Yeah, I've got her." I slap his shoulder and get to my feet, surveying the room.

I had a feeling Khan might tail us here. I knew someone had been watching us. I knew there'd be eyes on Nevaeh. She was too much of a temptation. A way to hurt me that they would take pleasure in. What I didn't expect was for them to shoot up a fucking bookstore to get to us. This kind of massacre will make front-page news. What the fuck was Khan thinking?

I scrub my hand over my face as I hear the sound of sirens in the distance. Doesn't matter what the intention was, shit like this can't happen. It won't just bring the spotlight to their club. If anyone sees them and notices their cuts, it will bring unwanted attention to all of us. If there was ever a doubt before, it's gone now.

Khan has to die.

Chapter Thirty

Nevaeh

It's hours later before the police let us leave. I refuse to go home until we have more news on Dice, which is why I'm sitting in the hospital waiting room and sipping crappy coffee as Havoc paces back and forth while he talks on his phone.

I tune him out, needing to stay in my little bubble of safety for a bit longer. A place where my readers aren't being shot at and where a man I care about isn't fighting for his life.

"You okay, Tinkerbell?" Capone asks from beside me.

I look at him. His T-shirt is covered in Dice's blood, and a smear of it across his cheek has me swallowing down bile.

"No, Capone. I don't think I am. I don't think I'll be okay until Dice wakes up."

He reaches over and takes my hand, squeezing it.

"Is this my fault?"

"Fuck no. How can this be your fault?"

"Because I knew there was a chance that the trouble with the club might follow us, and I came anyway," I tell him quietly so nobody will overhear us.

"Nobody could have predicted this. This isn't the work of a man going off the rails, Nevaeh. This is the work of a madman."

I sigh and look down at my hands. Hands that stroked Dice as he lay bleeding out on the floor. Hands that just hours before signed an autograph for a girl who might never wake up. I don't try to stop my tears. I let them run down my face and drip from my chin.

Capone curses before he takes my coffee and wraps his free arm around me. I bury my head against his chest and sob until I'm picked up, and I find myself surrounded by Havoc's scent. It calms me a little, making me feel safer.

"I've got you, baby. Let it all out."

And so I do. Because if I don't get it out, it will rip me to pieces.

I must doze off because when I come too, I hear Amity's voice. I lift my head and find her and G sitting beside me where I'm curled up on Havoc's lap.

"They hurt Dice," I tell her softly.

"I know." She tucks my hair behind my ear, her eyes

puffy from crying. Neither of us says anything after that. What's there to say?

And so we sit, waiting in limbo, preparing for bad news while praying for a miracle. The waiting room fills up around us as people come to wait for news and offer their silent support.

Finally, after what feels like days, a voice clears behind us. "Family of Dalton Jones?"

Havoc gets to his feet before gently easing me to mine. He takes my hand, this time drawing strength from me.

"He's an orphan. He grew up in the system. We're the only family he's got."

This makes more tears fall, but I keep quiet.

The doctor looks at me before sighing. "Mr. Jones was incredibly lucky. The bullet clipped his liver and caused some internal bleeding, which we managed to get under control. He lost a lot of blood, but miraculously, the bullet missed his bowel, which is what I was initially worried about. It's early, but barring an infection, if he makes it through the next forty-eight hours, then I expect him to make a full recovery."

My legs buckle with relief. Havoc catches me before I fall, holding me tightly to him.

"Thanks, doc."

"There was a girl. She was shot in the leg. Havoc was the one who helped her."

"You put the tourniquet on her?"

Havoc nods.

"You saved her life. I can't tell you anything else, but she's alive, and that's thanks to you."

My breath rushes out of me in relief.

"Go home and get some rest. Mr. Jones won't be up for any visitors for a while yet. I will make sure someone calls you if anything changes."

"Thanks again," Havoc tells him before he walks away. "Thank fuck."

Happy laughs and tears now replace the earlier sadness. There is still worry, naturally, but for now, we've been given a reprieve.

"Midas, Circus, I want you two to stay and keep an eye on things."

"You got it, Prez," Circus answers.

"Amity, you come on G's bike?"

"Yeah."

"You up for driving the truck Dice drove here home? I know it's a beast, but if you can handle the RV—"

"No, I've got it. Is it at the hotel still?"

"Yeah. We loaded it up before we checked out this morning. Get the keys from Capone."

"What about the stuff from the venue?" G asks.

I shake my head, thinking about the books and swag I had on display. "Just leave it. I can't go back there."

"I can get it. I have my car." Lil offers.

"I'll go with her," Toot says, wrapping his arm around her shoulder and kissing her temple.

"Everyone else, head back. I'm calling church. I'll fill the rest of you in when you get back. Any questions?"

When nobody says anything, Havoc leads me outside to his bike. He straps my helmet on and lifts me onto the bike before slipping his own helmet on. He stands there for a moment with his helmet pressed against mine. I feel him swallowing down his rage before he climbs on and takes us home.

The ride home is a somber one. So far, everyone has pulled through, but this could have all gone differently. We lost track of Ambros and his sister when the cops were questioning us, so I make a mental note to call him later to make sure they got home okay. I'm not sure I'd have ever forgiven myself if that bullet had done more than graze her. I close my eyes and try to shut out the images flashing in my brain, but it's impossible to think about anything else.

By the time we pull into the compound, I'm so exhausted I'm not sure I can climb off the bike. Havoc helps me and removes my helmet before taking off his own. He wraps his hand around mine and leads us up to the saloon, the others falling in behind us. None of us speak. There will be enough of that to come. For now, the quiet of the night offers comfort from the loudness of the hospital and the chaos of my mind.

When we walk in, Havoc stops dead, making me look up. Standing in front of us are Blade, Inigo, and Conan.

"It's done," Blade answers Havoc's unspoken question, which makes him relax.

"I've called church so you can fill everyone in," Havoc tells him before stepping forward and giving the man a one-armed hug.

Conan steps up to me. I have to tip my head all the way back to see his face.

"Rough day, Tinkerbell?"

I try to smile, but it comes out strained.

He tugs me free of Havoc's hold and pulls me in for a hug. We must look ridiculous together, but it's impossible not to feel safe when a literal giant is wrapped around you. "How about I sit with you while everyone else goes to church?"

I nod. Part of me just wants to crawl into bed but I don't trust my brain to let me fall asleep.

Conan lets me go so I can look at Havoc. Havoc moves into me, kissing me until I'm breathless before pulling back and pressing his lips to my forehead.

"Stay with Conan. I'll fill you in on what you need to know once we're done."

"Alright."

"Make sure she gets something to eat. She hasn't had anything all day."

"I've got her, Havoc. Don't worry."

I don't bother telling either of them that food is the last thing on my mind.

When Havoc steps back, Inigo steps forward and kisses

my head before following Havoc into church. Blade says my name softly before he swipes a tear from my face. Hell, I didn't even realize I was crying again.

"Everything is going to be okay. Trust your man. Trust the club."

"I do."

He nods before quickly hugging me and turning me into Conan's arms. Conan leads me over to one of the sofas at the far end of the room. He urges me to sit as the rest of the brothers follow Havoc. A handful of club girls hover near the bar, looking unsure of what to do. The rest of the room is empty.

"Where's Hoops?"

"He's on the gate tonight."

"Does he know that Dice is okay?"

"He knows. G messaged us all."

"Good. I know they're friends," I tell him, fiddling with the sleeve of my T-shirt.

"Is Sunshine here?"

"She and Alex are staying at Carnage for now. And before you ask, Legs is at the clinic."

I sit up straight. "Is she okay?"

"She's fine. She's keeping her eye on Crane, who took a bullet to the shoulder."

"Crane? But he didn't come with us. I don't understand."

He studies me for a moment. "Tell you what, let's get

some food into you, and I'll tell you what I can. Havoc can fill in the rest."

"Okay," I agree. I know I'm missing something big.

I trail him into the kitchen and sit quietly at the counter while he makes me a sandwich and a large mug of hot chocolate. The sandwich tastes like sawdust, but I swallow it anyway, knowing I need to eat. The hot chocolate works wonders, though, shaking the residual chill from my bones left behind by the shock.

"Okay, now tell me what's happening." He leans over the counter, his face looking tired, his eyes rimmed with circles. "Sit with me first. You look ready to fall over. How are you feeling?"

"I'm tired, but I'm always tired. It is what it is. Chemo is every bit as fun as I expected it to be, but doctors are optimistic, and that's enough for me right now."

He pours himself a coffee before sitting beside me.

"The shootout here was a turning point for Havoc. He knew they'd keep coming until they got what they wanted. The damage to the RV was proof they wanted you either dead or in their hands and wishing you were. That they failed the first time would piss Khan off enough to send a stronger message the next time.

"Havoc knew they'd follow us to the signing?" My stomach sinks at the thought.

"He didn't think they'd open fire like that. How could he? None of us could have predicted that. He suspected they'd split their defenses and send a couple of people to try and snatch you and a couple here to cause trouble, distract Havoc, and keep him off his game. We didn't expect Khan to recklessly try and take out as many people as possible."

I take a moment to absorb his words. My immediate reaction is to get angry—at Khan for being such a psychotic bastard and at Havoc for not telling me it was too dangerous to go. I could have stayed home, and all those people would have been safe.

I breathe deeply, try to push through the anger and look at the other angle. I could get mad at Havoc, but that's only deflecting. I knew it was possible that trouble could follow us. I'm not dumb, so I don't get to pretend now to make myself feel better. Like everyone else, I had no clue Khan would take things this far. Staying home might have been an option, but then the gunfight could have happened here. We might have fared better, but then maybe we wouldn't have. Maybe more people would have been hurt or even killed. People I know. People I care about.

I shake my head. There is nothing simple about this. It is a nasty mess left behind to wade through.

"Havoc called us in. If the club was being watched, nobody would be looking at us since we'd been away for a while. We were in Khan's territory, waiting for the call. Crane and Kruger were sent out to join us, but as a way to draw attention."

"Because if the focus was on them, nobody was looking at you," I summarize.

"Exactly. We were able to get into place without being detected. The mother chapter was put on a soft lockdown. Everyone here knew an attack was possible, and they were ready."

"Instead, the attack happened at the book signing."

He nods. "It was one of those unpredictable variables that we just had to roll with."

I run my hand through my hair, feeling sick when I consider how much worse this could have been. And though it doesn't feel like it right now, I know I'll look back and feel how lucky we were.

"G messaged Byte and Kieran to let him know what would happen. They got everyone to safety except for Khan and Driller, who were once again taking a private meeting."

"That was risky. Khan has his supporters—" I laugh when it dawns on me. "He sent his supporters out to do his dirty work. He knew the others wouldn't do it because you don't mess with the mother chapter."

"Exactly. So we can thank Khan for making that part easy on us. We now know exactly who was on his side."

I nod. At least there was some good to come from it. "What aren't you telling me?"

"You Havoc's old lady?"

"You know I am."

"I'm asking because if you have any doubts, I'll take what I know to the grave."

"I have doubts about everything, Conan. But not about Havoc. He might have gone about showing me he loved me in the most unconventional way, but he's never hidden how he felt about me. He's never kept me a secret or downplayed what I am to him or to his brothers, even when I know I'm as far away as you can get from the regular biker chicks."

"I think you fit in more than you realize." He smirks.

"My point is, I'm always on Havoc's side, and I'll never do anything to hurt him."

"Good. He deserves that." He looks around to make sure we're still alone before leaning closer. "After the shootout, he sent us a message that put us in play. We were ordered to capture Khan and wait for the rest of the men who took part in the shootout to return—one of them being Hachette, the sniper who shot up the RV. We took those who came back the second they were inside the gates. They tried to kill innocent people, Nevaeh. They didn't deserve to wear Raven Souls cuts. I had no problem watching them die in them."

He says nothing else, waiting for my reaction. I'm not sure what I'm supposed to say. I'm not scared of how they were dealt with. I'm more scared that I feel nothing but satisfaction over it.

"You said some came here? What happened to them?"

"We were ready for them. Nobody on our side was hurt. We took them out as soon as they opened fire."

I let out a shaky breath. "And Khan?"

He shakes his head. "Khan held all the answers about the missing girls and money, that's why we planned to bring him back here, but when we went to retrieve him from his cell, we found him dead with his throat slit."

"Oh shit."

"Exactly," he sighs.

Even though we needed answers from Khan, I can't help but feel relieved that he's gone. I relax then, not realizing how tense I was until now. "So it's over?"

"Not quite."

I look up at him and frown. "I don't understand. Khan is dead. Hannibal is taking over, and the rest of the traitors are dead. How can it not be over?"

"Because one got away."

"What? Who?"

"My brother."

I whirl around at the sound of Havoc's voice. "Driller escaped?"

He nods, looking tired.

I jump off my chair and hurry over to him. "You think he'll come here to carry out Khan's last wishes?"

"He won't know he's not president by default just yet. Soon, though, he'll know that not only is Hannibal about to be president, but his old lady and kid also belong to him. That's gonna piss him off. In his eyes, Lola is his property. He won't accept Hannibal's claim on her."

"He'll go after them first?"

"That's my guess. Oh, he'll come for me. He won't ever let sleeping dogs lie. But his own club just turned their back on him and are ready to swear in someone else into a position he assumed would be his. Lola will be his primary target, especially while she's pregnant. Then, it will be his club. We'll be an afterthought in the grand scheme of things, but that doesn't mean we can get complacent. Rats have a tendency to turn up when you least expect it."

Chapter Thirty-One

Havoc

I glance around the room; glad I left Nevaeh back at the compound despite her arguing with me. Things might have calmed down a little since Khan and the traitors were killed, but there is far too much unrest within this club for me to feel comfortable bringing her here.

I look around at all the familiar faces as Hannibal stands beside me with his face blank. Lola stands just in front of him, her head down. His hands rest on her shoulders as if waiting for her to run.

"Khan is dead. Driller is a marked man, and everyone else who thought it was acceptable to open fire on innocent civilians are also gone. What Khan did to this club was fucked-up, but none of you noticed. Or if you did, you let it slide. How it got this far, I don't know, but it won't be happening again. Not on my watch. Initially, I thought about disbanding this chapter altogether. The locals detest you. I'd be doing them a favor," I point out, ignoring the protests. My gaze falls on Elmo, Byte, and Ferris, who are also standing at the side of the room quietly watching.

"Then I came here and realized there are good brothers here. Some of you just lost your way." The room quiets more.

"Hannibal is going to be your new president. I'm sure those who don't know him have heard of his reputation. I dare you to fuck with him."

"I won't be letting shit fly, so if you don't want to get this club back to where it should be, then leave now. There's the door. Nobody will stop you, but this is the only shot you get. If you stay, you're agreeing to me being your president. You're agreeing to abide by my rules and do as I ask to make this club formidable once more," Hannibal warns them.

"How come you're making an outsider president?" someone calls from the back of the room.

"Because I don't think any of you are up to the job."

"And you think you're the right person to make that decision?" Someone snorts but shuts up when they realize nobody is joining in.

"I honestly don't give a shit what any of you think, but I'll remind you just this once. I'm the President of the Mother Chapter of Raven Souls. Either learn respect, or I'm burning this club to the ground. I do not give a fuck. I owe you nothing."

"The fact he's giving this club a second chance is more than you deserve, but by all means, piss the boss off. See how that works out for you." Hannibal laughs, a cold, cruel sound that has people stepping back.

"We hear you, Havoc." Elmo steps forward. "There is a lot of shit you don't know. Shit I've only just found out about. I'll tell you everything later, but you need to know that Khan was a traitor to us all. He didn't deserve to wear the Raven Souls patch. Every word out of his mouth was a fucking lie. I've been investigating him since Havoc was last here."

Shuffling and surprise in the crowd now.

"Khan was embezzling money from the club. I found an offshore account in his name with just over a million dollars in it. I've also found direct ties to him and at least half of the missing girls."

"Oh shit," someone curses. I hear a couple of women crying, but I ignore it. The openly angry faces now look shell-shocked.

"Driller was working directly with Khan. I don't know if he knew about the money. It seems unlikely because he'd have demanded a share of his own. But money was never Driller's motivation. He's a bully and a narcissist." Out of the corner of my eye, I see Lola flinch.

"He is the loose end right now. He is considered an enemy of the club. If any of you offer him safe harbor, you'll answer to Hannibal. And if there is anything left of you, you'll answer to me."

"What about Lola? She's carrying his kid. He'll come back for her."

Hannibal squeezes Lola's shoulders. "Lola is mine." His hand slides down to cover her belly. "This baby is mine. If Driller comes for either of them, I'll gut him like a fish before I show him how I got my name."

Nobody argues. It looks like they do have some common sense between them, after all.

"I'll pick who I want on the cabinet at a later date. I need to talk to you all first and see who I think will work best where. The only exception is Byte. I'm making you my VP. You know this club, the brothers, and the town. You get the delightful job of being my voice of reason." He grins at Byte, who nods.

"If that's what you need. I've stood by for too long and watched as Khan took the club I loved and turned it into something I barely recognize. If Hannibal says he can bring us back to glory, I'll happily stand beside him."

"Good." I turn to Hannibal and clap him on the shoulder. "Good luck, brother. Remember, I'm only a phone call away."

My eyes drop to the woman in his grip. "Lola."

She looks up at me. Her expression is pained.

"We're never going to be friends, not after what you did. But I can let bygones be bygones if you treat Hannibal better than you did me."

Her eyes flood with tears, but she doesn't answer.

"Don't worry about me, Havoc. Lola knows exactly what I'll do to her if she crosses me."

I swallow down my retort. Hannibal might be a psycho in his own right, but I have enough faith in him that he won't push things too far. Besides, Lola's alternative is Driller, and he won't settle for mind games. He beat her black and blue for the fun of it.

I turn, wanting to get home to Nevaeh. Dice is coming home today, and something tells me she might smother him if I don't rein her in. I say my goodbyes and leave. Hoops, who was waiting with the bikes, joins me as I pull out. It's a cautionary move. Until Driller is found, I don't want anyone riding alone.

We ride straight through, not stopping until we reach the gates of the compound. Kieran, who now goes by Powers thanks to his stint as a spy, opens them for us, waving us through. I stop and wait for him to close the gate behind us.

I lift my visor and wait for him to approach. "You settling in okay?"

"Nevaeh got me set up and made sure I knew where everything was."

"Good. Hannibal wants you to call him if anything you think he should know comes to mind."

"No worries."

"Thank you for what you did for the club."

"I don't feel like I did much at all," he admits, but I shake my head.

"You were my eyes and ears when I couldn't be there myself, and Inigo told me how you played backup for them. I'm glad to have you here as a prospect. I think you'll be an asset to the club."

"Thank you, sir. I won't let you down."

I nod and ride into the warehouse before heading to the clinic. I laugh when, through the open window, I hear Dice trying to argue with Nevaeh.

"I swear to you, I'm fine."

"I know you are, but I'm going to make sure it stays that way. Now, do you need anything else? Some water or some ice chips? Here, let me just—

"Woman, if you fluff my pillows once more, I might voluntarily slip into a coma just to get some peace."

I push the door open and walk in to find Nevaeh with her hands on her hips, glaring down at Dice, who gives me a relieved look when he sees me in the doorway.

"Please tell me you've come to rescue me."

Nevaeh spins around when she realizes someone is behind her. "Oh hey, Havoc. I'm just making sure Dice is okay."

"Looks to me like you're tucking him in. You sure you don't want to read him a story next?" I tease but shut up when I see hurt flash across her features.

"I'm sorry, I'll go."

"Hey now." I wrap my hand around her waist to stop her from leaving. "I'm just teasing, and so is Dice. We both know you care about him and that you're worried. But you have to let the man get some rest. He'll let us know if something is wrong, right?" I look at Dice, who nods.

"I'm not going to do anything to jeopardize my recovery, Tink. I promise."

She groans. "Not you, too."

Dice grins. "I can't help it if the name fits. Besides, when you were shaking your head and tapping your foot at me, you really did remind me of an angry fairy."

Nevaeh rolls her eyes, but her lips twitch. "Alright, I'll leave you alone. I know I'm hovering. I'm just happy you're home. I'll make sure your apartment is ready and stocked for you, though Hannibal says you need to stay here for the next few days. A traveling medic is coming in to check on you. If you're really good, I'll ask one of the bunnies to play nursemaid for you."

"This is why you're my favorite," Dice whispers, his eyes slipping closed.

"Come on, let's give him some peace. I'll get one of the girls to come keep an eye on him."

"Okay."

I lead her over to the saloon, nodding to Circus and Capone, who pass us as we walk in.

"How did it go?" Circus questions.

"Better than I expected. There are a few disgruntled

brothers, but none of them are stupid enough to go up against Hannibal."

"Damn straight."

"Either of you seen Lil?"

"She's playing pool with Kruger."

"Alright, thanks, man." I lead Nevaeh over to the pool table and watch for a second as they wrap up the game. Lil kicks Kruger's ass, much to his annoyance.

"What can I do for you, Prez?" he grunts at me.

"I'm actually here to ask Lil a favor. You mind sitting with Dice for a bit? He's asleep now, but with Hannibal gone he's alone over there."

"I don't mind. I'll take my Kindle over and some snacks. Don't worry, I'll look after him."

"Thanks, darlin'."

I see G waving me down. "You okay here for a minute? Looks like G wants me for something."

"Sure. I want to see how Amity's shoot went anyway. Come find me when you're done."

She heads off to find Amity as I walk over to G, who nods to my office. I don't say anything until he closes the door behind him.

"What's up?"

"Two things. I managed to pull some footage from that camera the day your tires were slashed."

He holds his phone out for me to see. From the angle of the camera, you can't get a clear shot of the bike, but you can see a man on his own and a couple holding hands as they walk past where it was parked. One of them might have seen something. "I vaguely recognize the homeless looking guy as the one who I sometimes see hanging around the diner. I not sure about the couple though."

"The blond guy is Clem Abbot. He's a realtor who is relativity new to the area. The red-haired woman is Angela Hannigan. She's a barfly with a reputation of going home with anyone who buys her drinks. Clem is married, but not to Angela so whoever we send to question them should keep in mind that they're likely to lie to save their own skin."

"I'll send Toot. I have a feeling; he'll get what he needs out of Angela at the very least. That's assuming they saw anything at all. I figured it was a long shot anyway. What else?"

"The comments on Nevaeh's social media posts are getting worse. They've used the shooting as a way to draw others to their cause."

"Her personal page?"

He nods.

"How bad is it?"

"It's only a handful of people and one ringleader, one of the guys I was already watching. They are pretty much saying Nevaeh is the reason that so many people got hurt at the signing. They're saying she should kill herself and other nasty shit. The ringleader mentioned what he would do to her when he gets his hands on her. Then went on some rant about making them pay for fucking everything up."

"Them?"

"You, Dice and Capone? Each of you were photographed at the event and seen arriving with Nevaeh. The only other them could mean the shooters. But as there were no credible witnesses, nobody has linked them back to Raven Souls. Not to mention, how would he know it was a them and not a solo shooter?"

"Unless he was there at the signing." I rub my hand over my face.

"Might be time to call the cops in on this one. Nevaeh is too high profile, and the comments are already gaining traction. People who were at the signing have come to both Nevaeh's defense and yours. There is even a photo doing the rounds of you carrying the girl who was shot in the leg to safety. Most people are backing Nevaeh and you, but that seems to only make this small group even more pissed."

"Nevaeh see any of this, you know?"

"I swiped her phone and disabled her social media apps so they won't open for her. Once she notices, she'll get me to look at it and I have to turn them back on. I just wanted to give you a heads up so you can tell me how you want me to deal with it."

"Can you trace who these assholes are?"

"Maybe. It depends on what kind of setup they have. Average Joes do little to hide their online presence. Someone with more knowledge might use a VPN, but I'll see what I can do."

"Do your digging first. If I need to call the police, I will. But they're unlikely to do much unless there is a real possibility of a threat to Nevaeh's safety. For all we know, these people could live halfway across the world and be all bark and no bite."

"I hear you. Leave it with me, and I'll see what I can find. Just make sure she has eyes on her wherever she goes."

"With Driller on the loose still, that's a given."

"Any signs of him making an appearance yet?"

"I told Hannibal he could stay in my house. It makes sense, as Lola was still living there. He told me the place had been trashed, so Driller has been back at some point."

"We figured Lola would be first on his list."

I shrug. "All he did was ruin the baby stuff and shit belonging to Lola. He's acting like a fucking toddler that had his favorite toy taken from him."

"I guess, in a way, he has."

I walk to the mini fridge and pull out two beers before offering him one. "With Hannibal gone, we need a medic, a nurse, or even a doctor on hand. Know anyone that might be interested or who owes us a favor?"

He taps his fingers on the desk as he considers. "Lil is the first one who comes to mind."

"Lil?"

"Yeah, she was studying to be a nurse when all that shit

went down with Bear. She dropped out when she only had a couple of months left until she qualified."

"Shit, seriously? Think she'd consider going back if we foot the bill?"

"I don't know. Something happened with her, something more than she's told us. You didn't know the old Lil, but this version is a ghost of the woman she used to be."

I take a sip of my beer and think about it. "It's been almost six years. If something more happened and she is still shut down and not letting anyone in, then maybe we need to push her a little."

"And what if we break her, Havoc? She put herself between Bear and his cronies and saved the old ladies and kids who were here at the time. And do you know how they thanked her? They left. They left her here with all their demons and moved on with their lives. None of them keep in touch. I doubt they even spare a thought for the woman who protected them. That's what changed the dynamic around here. There was always a division between bunnies and the old ladies, which is in most clubs. But when Bear turned on us, those of us who stayed worked together, brother and sister, side by side. They're good girls for the most part, though I worry some of the newer ones want to mess with the status quo."

"Yeah, I had a run-in with them myself. Nevaeh put them in their place, and I reminded them that I won't take their shit. If they push, I'll toss them out on their asses. But back to Lil. If I ask her in such a way—"

"You mean guilting her because we don't have anyone with medical training anymore?"

"Tomatoes, to-mah-toes, but yeah. If I force her hand a little, think she'd do it? Or will she run? I want to force her to start living again, not retreat to the corner."

He thinks it over. "I think she needs something more than what she has now. It's one of the reasons she volunteers at the shelter. She might be scared to take the leap, so perhaps a push is exactly what she needs. Just tread carefully."

"Careful is my middle name."

He chokes on his beer.

I flip him off, grinning. "How did Amity's commercial go?"

"Good. Though she still finds it weird playing herself."

"I can see why they'd want her, though. After the publicity generated by the movie and the fall out of the stalker, people were impressed with Amity and her grace under fire. If anyone should be marketing a clothing line for female rock climbers, it should be the woman who managed to survive being thrown off one."

He grits his teeth.

"Sorry, man, that was shitty of me."

"Why? It's true. My nightmares aside, she deserves this, and they're paying her a crazy amount of money to be their spokesperson. People love a champion they can get behind. Amity has overcome more than most to get to where she is, and she did it herself through sheer hard work and determination. I'm proud as fuck."

A knock at the door interrupts us. "Come in," I yell.

Blade pokes his head in. "Still weird as fuck knocking," he grumbles as he walks in. "Just wanted to let you know we're heading out. Sunshine's not been feeling great, and Conan has reached his limit. Not that the stubborn fuck will admit it."

"Thank you for coming when I called."

"You're the president now. You get to make all the shitty choices. But for what it's worth, I'd have done the same. Felt pretty cool to be the one to come in and play badass for a change," he admits, making me laugh.

"Probably not what you had in mind when you said you needed a vacation."

"No, but we've got plenty of time before the baby gets here to take it easy."

"That you have. Now go spend some time with your old lady."

"Yes, Prez." He winks at me before leaving.

"He's right, it's weird as fuck." G laughs, making me grin.

"It was the right choice for him to step down. I think he'd have started resenting the club if he'd stayed."

"I know. As much as it pissed me off in the beginning, I agree. Just don't tell Blade I said that."

"Your secret's safe with me."

Chapter Thirty-Two

Nevaeh

"I felt ridiculous."

"Why?" I frown as Amity takes a drink of her water with her cast-free hand.

"I'm used to doing my own stunts. Some of those are pretty crazy."

"Trust me, I'm aware." I nearly had a heart attack the first time I saw her jumping off a moving horse.

"I've worked in some amazing locations and in front of green screens, and none of it bothered me because it wasn't about me."

"Ah. And now your face is going to be everywhere."

"Exactly. Me. I'm used to lending my body and skills to

actresses, but I never planned to be in front of the camera as the star. What was I thinking? I'm not an actress. I'm—"

"A real-life action hero. Nobody says you need to use this as a stepping stone into actress territory. You played yourself in the campaign, after all. You're not selling a lie or playing a character. You're inspiring a generation of young girls to be extraordinary."

She sighs, picking at the label of the bottle. "I feel like an imposter."

"Ah, yes, imposter syndrome. I know this feeling well." I lean across the table and squish her cheeks. "Repeat after me. I, Amity Hollis, am a badass. Everyone who meets me wants to be me or be with me."

"I'm not saying that." Her words come out muffled as her face is squished.

"Say it!" I order.

She grumbles, but reluctantly repeats my words.

"Good. Now remember that. Hell, woman, you have a very famous sports brand wanting to sponsor you. You'll get all the free sportswear you could ever want, *and for the running on purpose, yoga at the butt crack of dawn, I can bench press my best friend kind of woman you are*, that's gotta be the closest you can get to an orgasm without G."

She chuckles, but because of her squished lips, she spits on my cheek.

"Ugh, gross. You're supposed to be giving me the news, not the weather." I let her go and wipe my face.

"I don't get that excited about exercising."

I just look at her. She caves first, of course.

"Fine, I get a little bit excited. And okay, I can't pretend free sportswear won't make me a little giddy. My ass looks great in gym wear."

"Your ass looks great in everything. It's almost enough to make me switch teams. But don't worry, your ass is safe from me. I prefer sandwiches to tacos."

She frowns. "That doesn't make sense."

"Of course it does."

"If you said you preferred hot dogs to tacos, I'd get it, but not a sandwich." She takes another sip of water.

"Clearly, you've never had a footlong."

She sprays water all over my face. I sit there for a moment, water dripping from my chin, before we both dissolve into fits of giggles.

"I'm never going to look at Havoc the same way again," she gasps once she manages to catch her breath.

"Please try. The man's ego is big enough already."

"I can't help it. And you're so little. How are you not bow-legged?"

I sigh, knowing I have nobody to blame but myself for opening my mouth. Her eyes look down my body and pause on my crotch area, making me regret not tucking my chair under the table.

"Please stop staring at my vagina."

"I can't help it. I'm picturing that time I tried to charge

my iPhone, only I had the cable backward. I was trying to squeeze the fat end into the tiny hole."

I dead stare at her. "There is something very wrong with you."

"I know," she admits, banging her head on the table.

"Though now that you mention it, I've thought this a time or two, picturing Sunshine with Conan."

"Right?"

"What are you two talking about?" Probe asks as he drops down into the seat next to mine.

"Slot machines," I tell him, making Amity choke again.

"Huh?"

"You ever have the wrong kind of coin, and you try to shove it in any way?" she asks him.

"Only if I'm desperate," he replies, making me and Amity crack up again. "Why do I feel like we're not talking about slot machines?"

"Because you have a dirty mind, Probe."

"Well, thank you." He nods graciously. "You ladies want to make s'mores with me?"

"S'mores? Really?"

He shrugs. "I've got the fire pit going. Might as well."

"I love s'mores. You've got yourself a deal."

"Excellent. I get the two prettiest ladies all to myself." He does an evil laugh as he stands. "I'll grab the stuff and meet you outside. You might want to grab a blanket. It's a little chilly."

When he walks away, I look at Amity and smile. "You think these guys realize they're breaking every stereotype we had about bikers?"

She focuses on something over my shoulder, so I turn and see Crane walking across the room with his kitten perched on his shoulder.

"I rest my case."

"He does love his pussy."

"Ew, yuk. Come on. I've got a couple of throws on my bed. We can grab those." I get to my feet and head upstairs, Amity just behind me. I unlock the door and push it open.

Amity walks past me and sits on the edge of the bed before she flops backward. "So this is where the magic happens."

I snicker at her. "You're so weird."

I walk over to the desk Havoc had set up for me and click on my emails. "Give me a few seconds. I'm waiting to see if the signing people message me. They were nice and all about what happened, but I don't see myself getting invited back any time soon, which is just as well, I guess."

"It wasn't your fault, Pippin."

"Logically, I know that. But logic and guilt are like a divorced couple who can't stand to be in the same room as each other."

I click on my latest email and scan it over before my legs turn to jelly, and then I have to sit.

"Shit, what's wrong?" She jumps off the bed and reads the email as I try to wrap my head around what I just read.

"Holy shit, Nevaeh. They want to turn one of your books into a movie." She reads it again, mumbling some words out loud so I catch snippets over the white noise sound in my head. "...option for rest of series, exclusive rights... adaptation..."

I shake my head and try to focus on Amity.

"This is big, Pippin. This studio does not mess around."

"You worked for them before?"

"Once. You have to do this. You know you do."

"I don't know. Writing a book is one thing, but a movie is something else altogether. What if it sucks?"

"What if it doesn't? Come on, you gave me a big speech downstairs about not letting chances pass us by and having no regrets."

"I didn't say anything like that."

"Huh, funny, that's what I heard. They want a meeting. Go, see what they have to say, and keep an open mind."

"A movie, huh?"

"A movie," she agrees before she laughs and tugs me to my feet.

We do a little dance we made up in the third grade that involves far too much hip wiggling before we end up jumping up and down on the bed.

"And they say fantasies can't live up to the reality." Havoc's amused voice drifts into the room.

We both stop and look at the door where G and Havoc are standing, looking amused.

"Please don't stop on our account. I'm enjoying the show." G winks.

Amity tosses a pillow at him, making me chuckle.

"What's got you all excited anyway?"

"We're going to have s'mores with Probe," I tell Havoc as he walks closer.

"A studio wants to turn one of Pippin's books into a movie," Amity yells.

"Really?" Havoc looks at me. I bite my lip and nod, unsure of his reaction. The last time he was on a movie set, everything went boobs up.

"Fucking hell, cupcake, that's amazing."

I jump and launch myself at him, knowing he'll catch me, and he does. I wrap myself around him as his hands slide under my ass.

"I'm so fucking proud of you, baby."

I stare into his eyes and feel like Alice falling down a rabbit hole. There may be danger ahead and a million hurdles to overcome, but this man and his crazy ways make it all worth it.

"I love you."

Every time I say those words to him, he gets a look on his face like he can't quite believe it's true.

"If you don't want a show, get the fuck out."

Amity squeals as G tosses her over his shoulder.

"But s'mores," I protest.

"You can have your dessert after I have mine." He lowers me to the bed, leaning over me to kiss me senselessly.

By the time he pulls back, I'm a horny mess of need. He slips down my body before sliding his hands under the hem of my dress and pushing it up to my hips, exposing my basic white cotton panties.

He presses his nose against them and breathes me in as I squirm. "If you knew the power you have over me," he murmurs mostly to himself.

It's funny he thinks I have power over him because he only has to look at me, and I start leaking like a broken faucet. It's a pain in the butt. I'm just hoping radical exposure therapy will mean I'll build up some kind of resistance over the years. Because if I don't, I'm going to be screwed in every sense of the word.

He tugs my underwear down my legs and slips them free, shoving them into the pocket inside his cut. I open my mouth to snap at him for stealing yet another pair of panties when he dips his head and sucks my clit into his mouth.

Now, I can't say I'm proud of the noises coming out of my mouth. Anyone passing by might think I'm either possessed or in need of medical attention. Maybe the last part is true because my body responds to him as if he owns it, taking control and turning me into a sex doll.

"Such a pretty pussy and all mine."

He dips his tongue inside me as my eyes roll into the back

of my head. I grab his hair with both hands and hold him against me. He looks up at me from between my legs, the devil in his eyes as he fucks me to hell and back with his talented tongue. He doesn't slow down, doesn't relent even when I thrash my head and arch my hips, a classic sign that I'm about to fall over the edge. I come with a scream, his name on my lips, as he drinks me down like his favorite whiskey.

He presses a kiss to my pubic bone before his hands move to slowly unfasten the path of buttons that lead up to my chest. He takes his time. There is no rushing for this president of mine. Sometimes, it's a blessing, giving me a moment to catch my breath. Other times, it's a curse, edging me to the point of hysteria before he lets me come.

As each button opens, more of my skin is revealed, making Havoc's eyes blaze like molten lava. Once the dress is completely open, he tugs the lace of my bra down, freeing my breasts. He flicks one of my erect nipples with his tongue, making me gasp.

"That feel good?"

I nod.

"Words, cupcake. Tell me what you want."

"I want you inside me."

"You want me to fuck you, baby?"

"Yesss," I hiss as he bites down on my nipple.

"Say fuck."

"Fuck."

He hums in satisfaction. "Say, suck."

"Suck."

"Tell me you want to suck my cock."

"I want to suck your cock."

"My good girl with a dirty mouth."

He moves his hand between us, fumbling with his jeans as he frees himself. I feel him there, hot and hard, at my entrance.

"Condom."

He flips us, so I'm on top. I gasp as he positions himself once more, and I easily slip him inside me. By the time my ass is resting on his thighs, and I'm taken him all from root to tip, I'm stuffed so full I can barely breathe.

"Can't get pregnant when you're on top," he manages to get out as I find my balance.

I refrain from rolling my eyes just as I start to move, ripping a curse from him as his large hands grip my hips. Turnabout's fair play, so I fuck him slowly until I feel his whole-body tense. Then I speed up, fucking him hard and fast, feeling the tingle of my own orgasm approaching again.

"Fucking hell, you take my cock so well. That's it, baby, ride me fast. Use my cock to get yourself off."

He reaches up and pinches my nipple. I throw my head back and moan, feeling my pussy fluttering around his cock. With a savage snarl, his hands return to my hips, his grip tightening to the point of pain as he uses his strength to move me just how he wants me to move.

I lean down over him, my hair falling over his face as I bite his ear lobe. "Let go, Havoc. Fill me with your cum."

He thrusts up, sinking his cock into me as far as it will go before I feel him explode inside me. His orgasm triggers mine, his pleasure turning me on almost as much as my own. I collapse over him, my body trembling over his as we ride out the last of the tremors fused together.

Once I feel like I can speak, I lift my head and give him a lazy smile. "I'm going to have to be careful where I say 'I love you' if your answer is to fuck me into oblivion each time."

"I don't see you complaining. You like my cock inside you," he replies with that cocky ease that comes from a man who knows how to please his woman.

"I do, though I'm not sure I'd feel the same if we were in the supermarket or doctor's office."

"Nobody would care. Everyone's been inside a pussy one way or another before."

"Not mine."

He makes a noise that can only be described as purring, like the cat that got the cream. "No, your pussy is reserved for only me."

"Just as well. I'm not sure after having that thing parked inside me, I'd notice if anything smaller pulled up."

He chuckles, making his cock move inside me. We both groan.

I feel him start to harden again, so I scramble off him. "You promised me s'mores." I waggle my finger at him, but his eyes are on my pussy. Or, more importantly, his cum leaking out of me.

I slip my fingers between my legs and coat them in his cum before I lift them to my mouth and lick them clean. "Yum. Now, are you going to feed me or what?"

He climbs off the bed, his hand stroking his now-hard cock as his free hand presses down on my shoulder. "Oh, I'm going to feed you, cupcake. Get down on your knees and open your mouth."

And just like that, s'mores are forgotten.

Chapter Thirty-Three

Havoc

"Someone at the gate to see you and Nevaeh."

I groan. "Not again. Neveah's not here. She's got a meeting with her agent and the studio execs interested in buying the rights to her books."

"Ah, I didn't realize that was today," Midas states before frowning. "I thought you were going with her."

"Probe's with her. I was supposed to take her, but I had a couple of meetings. First one was with Bishop, who denies any knowledge of Khan's plans, and the other was with Hannibal. He FaceTimed me to give me the lowdown on what's happening up there. An anonymous sender mailed a ledger to Hannibal. The postmark is local but they don't have much else to go on. Byte and G are going over it. It's all in code, but we think if we can crack it, it will tell us what happened to all those girls." I stand up and head toward the door.

"Who's at the gate anyway? Please tell me it's not Nevaeh's father. I don't trust myself not to lay him out cold without Nevaeh acting as a buffer."

"No. Dude says he's a friend. Wouldn't give his name until I produced you or Nevaeh."

"Right, because that's not suspicious at all."

Midas laughs and follows me out. We walk down to the front gate. Walking through the warehouse, I nod to Kruger, who is tinkering with his bike, and head out the other side.

I'm not sure who I was expecting, but it sure as shit wasn't Ambros.

"Oh, thank fuck. I had this awful feeling that I had come to the wrong club. I remembered you had a beef with them at the last minute." He shakes his head as I nod for Powers to open the gate.

"Come on in. The problem with the other club isn't such a big issue anymore," I tell him, not giving anything away. "Midas, this is Ambros, Ambros, Midas. Ambros is the UFC champion Nevaeh met on the plane to the UK. He was at the bookstore shootout with his sister."

"Ah, shit, man. Sorry you got caught up in that. Is your sister okay?" Midas shakes his hand.

"She's pissed someone tried to shoot her favorite author. I swear I don't understand women at all."

Midas snickers. "That makes two of us."

"What brings you out here anyway?"

He sighs and runs his fingers through his hair. "Two things, actually, if you've got time."

"Just finished up a meeting, and Nevaeh's not here, so yeah, I've got time." I indicate for him to walk with us. We pass through the warehouse and head up the slope to the saloon.

"This place is cool as fuck."

"We get that a lot."

"I bet."

"Is what you have to say private, or can Midas stick around?"

"No, that's fine. Look, I'm not sure how much you follow Nevaeh online, but there is a group of people that, since the shooting, have taken things to the extreme. I've noticed most of its contained to her personal page, but its spilled over onto her Celeste one and even mine. People are tagging me to see my reactions. Mostly I ignore the trolls, but some of the shit they're saying is setting off every fucking instinct I have."

I sigh. "I know. I have my VP, who happens to be my tech guy, on it. I don't know if they're a threat or just a bunch of chickenshit trolls, but Nevaeh hasn't been alone since the shootout, much to her annoyance."

"Thank fuck. I wasn't sure if it was connected to the shootout. And honestly, I didn't know how hip bikers were with social media, so I took a chance that you'd listen."

"Why did you come here, really? I'm not doubting the reason you came. I just think there's more to it."

He's quiet for a moment, gathering his thoughts. "The day I met Nevaeh, she treated me like a regular person. She had no clue who I was, and when she did, it made no difference to her."

"Sounds like my old lady."

"I've spent a lot of time around people. You live and work in the public eye, and there is no avoiding it, but none of them cared about anything beyond what I could do for them. The only person I trust one hundred percent is my sister, and she's dying."

I stop for a second and look at him. His face is drawn and tired looking, the kind of tiredness that has nothing to do with a lack of sleep and everything to do with life wearing you down.

"The bullet—"

"Really did only graze her arm. It's not that. My sister has acute lymphoblastic leukemia. She went into remission, and we thought she'd beaten it, but then she got sick again last year. Not that you'd know to look at her. She's refused any more treatment. She's made peace with her death, but I'm not there yet. I don't think I ever will be."

He rubs a hand over his face. I look at Midas and nod for him to leave us for a moment. I start walking again, knowing Ambros will follow me.

"How long?" I ask him gently.

"Docs say around three months. I retired from fighting so I could spend as much time with her as possible. Fighting all seems so pointless now anyway."

I get it. Why fight when you have nothing left to fight for?

"When she's gone—" He coughs and starts again. "Dad died in a boating accident when we were kids. Mom got COVID and died during the height of the pandemic."

I get it now. Like a lot of brothers here, he'll have no one left. Being cast adrift can do strange things to a man. Grief doesn't care how strong you are. It cripples gods and mortals alike.

"I came to see if you needed more prospects."

"As a matter of fact, I do. But maybe hang around for a while and see if it's really what you want. Once you're in, you don't get to back out because you've changed your mind."

"I know. I just need something to keep going for."

"Why here? Why us?"

"Nevaeh."

I tense, but he just shakes his head at me.

"I'm not gonna lie and say I'm not attracted to her. I have eyes. I see the same thing you do—most of your men will see it, too. There is an innate lightness about her. At first, I thought it was naivete. A mix of innocence and inexperience. And maybe that does play a part, but—"

"It's the fire."

"Yes. She doesn't hide her pain very well. I don't know what happened to her, I didn't ask, but I know it was bad. If grief were a cut, she'd still be bleeding. But she's still here. Still holding on and carrying on with a smile and kindness that I rarely see in people. She's this tiny little dot, and I'm convinced she's stronger than both of us."

"And you'd be right. She's also mine. There will never be a time when that's open for discussion. If you touch her, I will cut off your hands."

"I don't poach. And even if I did, that woman is so in love with you I could walk in front of her naked, and she wouldn't even notice."

"Let's not test that theory," I reply dryly.

"Oh, no worries there. I'd rather not have my balls ripped off."

I shake my head and chuckle. "Alright, Ambros, why don't you come meet some of the brothers? You staying local?"

"My sister and her husband live only a few towns over. I've been crashing in their guesthouse. I have money for my own place, but I usually move around too much to settle on a home base. Until now."

"If you want to crash, we have a couple of empty spaces we can put you in."

"I'll keep that in mind, thanks."

I push the doors of the saloon open with Ambros on my heels.

"Jesus, it's like stepping onto a movie set."

I chuckle, stopping only when I see G heading my way.

"I was looking for you. Got something you might want to see." He looks from me to Ambros. "I know you." He pauses while his brain whirls before he clicks his fingers. "Ambros Deveraux. UFC champ."

"That's me." He holds his hand for G to shake.

"This is G, my VP."

"Nice to meet you."

"Ambros came to warn us about Nevaeh's social media presence. He's also thinking about prospecting."

"Sweet. I think you'll be a good fit around here." He turns to me. "What I want to talk to you about is the trolls, actually. You got a sec?"

"Yeah. You mind if I bring Ambros in? He might have a different take on things as he's used to dealing with fans."

"Fine by me."

"Ambros?"

"Not sure how much help I can give you, but yeah, whatever you need."

We walk into my office. I sit behind my desk while Ambros and G take the two chairs in front of it. G takes his laptop from the bag slung over his shoulder. He sits it on his lap and taps away on it.

"So do you follow Nevaeh or Celeste Sky?" I ask Ambros as he takes in the office.

"Both now. In the beginning I just followed Celeste. I didn't want to draw attention to her real identity. I mean she kept it hidden for a reason right? After the photo of us together went viral, it didn't seem to matter anymore."

"I think the buzz of you and her died down the second our illustrious leader decided to publicly claim her." G rolls his eyes.

Ambros smirks. "I did notice a few topless shots of you on your bike coming up on my feed. I was starting to think going topless was a requirement of joining."

"Your virtue is safe here, pretty boy. Besides, the prez has quite his own following now. Ten thousand the last time I looked."

"Oh, I bet he does." Ambros grins.

I narrow my eyes and look at him.

"Of course, I've been doing the whole topless thing a lot longer than you," he jokes. I assume he means promotional pics where he's just wearing shorts. "Before you know it, you'll have ninety thousand followers too."

G looks at Ambros. "You have ninety thousand followers? Who the fuck are you, Selena Gomez?"

Ambros laughs. "Not even close. She's got around five hundred million."

"Really? Well fuck a duck. I can't imagine that many people interested in my life," he swears before he sits the laptop on the edge of the desk. "Okay, out of the dozen or so people who were the most vocal, three live across the globe. One is sixteen, living in Australia, and attending high school. I have two in Europe—Germany and Sweden, to be precise.

Both are married and live normal lives, from what I can gather from their profiles. These ones feel more like sheep who like to follow a leader. They don't start the chaos but have no problem reveling in it."

"You'll always find those. Someone will say something, and you'll get ten more jump on the bandwagon, and before you know it, they've gone viral. Most of the time, it's all for show so they can get their five minutes of fame."

"Who wants to be famous for being an asshole?"

"Some people have made a living out of it."

"What about the others?"

"I've managed to dismiss most of them as trolls instead of a threat. I have six left on the list. John Cyrus is a trucker who drives all over the country, delivering beer. He has a record for domestic violence. His ex-wife filed for divorce after his last stint in prison and walked away with nothing—her choice by the looks of things. The only thing she took was the dog. He still has the house they shared in Tampa but spends eighty percent of his time on the road."

"Wait, you're tracking these guys through their social media?" Ambros sounds surprised.

"I'm protecting my president's old lady from potential threats," G tells him.

"I'm not judging. I'm just conscious about what I post."

"Honestly, it's not that hard to hack into someone's life. People say plenty without even realizing it."

"You think this guy is a threat?"

"He says some nasty shit about Nevaeh in his posts and has the potential to be a problem, but only if the circumstances are right."

"Like?"

"If she were handed to him on a silver platter. He won't miss an opportunity, but he won't go out of his way to seek her out either."

"Alright, who stands out?"

"I've circled two. The other four all have criminal records. These two, I couldn't find anything on. Their social media is locked down tight. In fact they have virtually no social media presence beyond what they posts about your girl. I searched, and there are five Newton Helms in a two-hundred-mile radius of here and eight Alan Ellwick's. And none of them fit with the other four unless you count the dead guys."

I pause. "What did you say?"

"There was an Alan Ellwick and a Newton Helms who would have fit but they're"—

"Dead." I finish for him, spinning the laptop around so I can check out the other names.

"Alfonso Ramiro, Michael Perkins, Daniel Waterman. Fuck me."

"You know these guys?"

"No, but I recognise their names."

G sits forward. "Talk to me Havoc."

"Run those six names against Nevaeh Dillon," I tell him.

G types the names in before he freezes. "Motherfucker."

"What is it?" Ambros leans closer.

"Alan was the man suspected of abducting Nevaeh's sister. He was killed by cops during his arrest. The other five all admitted at different times over the years to murdering Nevaeh's sister.

"What the fuck?" Ambros curses.

G does some fast typing before he looks up at me. "John, Alfonso, Michael and Daniel are all still alive and kicking but Daniel and Alfonso are still in prison."

"Where they won't have access to social media. It's not them posting."

Ambros frowns. "What if it's one guy, posting as all of them?"

"But why? This goes beyond trolling. Posting as people who could have murdered and raped her sister is messed up." G questions.

"He found out the worst thing that happened to her, and he's using those names to taunt her?" I snarl. "Who the fuck does that? Call Probe. Tell him to bring Nevaeh straight home once the meeting wraps up."

G pulls out his cell phone and dials.

"Is there anything I can do?" Ambros asks quietly.

"No. I just need to find out who this motherfucker is. I don't want Nevaeh reliving this shit because some whack job has a hard-on for her."

"He's not answering," G tells me.

I pull out my cell phone and dial Nevaeh. It rings and rings, but she doesn't pick up.

"Maybe she's still in her meeting," G says as he redials Probe.

I look at the time and shake my head. "Meeting should have finished ten minutes ago. Can you track either of their phones?"

"Hold on." He types quickly before he looks up. "Probe isn't transmitting. Must be dead because he wouldn't switch it off. Nevaeh's is on, though, and it says she's still at the building where the meeting is being held."

I stand up and head to the door.

"Where are you going?"

"I'm going to wait for her to come out, and then I'm going to escort her home. At least if she's with me, I know she's safe."

"Her phone says she is exactly where she's supposed to be."

"I call bullshit because if she were where she's supposed to be, she'd be with me." I turn the handle and walk out.

"That man has it bad." I hear Ambros laugh.

"You have no idea," G mutters. "Come on, you might as well witness crazy in action."

Chapter Thirty-Four

Nevaeh

I walk out of the meeting in somewhat of a daze with Lou, my agent, beside me.

"That went well—exceedingly well. We could negotiate for more, but if anything, they are offering more than I would have thought," Lou tells me.

"You think I should take the deal?"

"I think I flew out here to make sure you weren't getting shafted because you might be my client, but you're also my friend. You're not gonna get a deal better than that. I don't know who has a hard-on for you, but someone does. If you want to see your book become a movie, this is it. It really doesn't get better than this."

I look up at her smiling face. Her dark skin practically glows with excitement.

"You have time to think about it, but my advice is not to take too long. Deals like this come along once in a lifetime."

"Take it."

"Really? You're sure?"

I chuckle. "I thought you were trying to talk me into it."

"Oh, I am, but I want you to be one hundred percent sure."

"I'm ninety-ninety percent sure."

"Works for me. My flight is due soon, so I'll email them from the airport to let them know you're accepting their offer."

She wraps her arms around me and gives me a squeeze. "I'm so excited for you. This is going to be amazing. I can see it now."

I blow out a nervous breath. "I hope you're right. Just don't expect me to do a bunch of talk shows or press junkets. I'm not that girl."

She waves me off. "Leave me to work my magic. We'll figure something out." She looks at her watch. "Shoot, I really do need to go."

"Go. I'll be fine. I'll wait here until my ride gets back. He must have grabbed a coffee."

"You sure? I'd give you a ride, but I might miss my flight."

"I'll be fine. Besides, I think Havoc would have a meltdown if I slipped my guard for the day and wandered back into the clubhouse without him."

"The feminist in me wants to tear apart everything you just said, but the other part of me wants to stab you with my knitting needle and take the man for myself. Not sure what it says about me."

"That maybe you should leave knitting to people without psychopathic tendencies."

"No, that can't be right." She grins before crossing the parking lot and climbing into the rental she parked a few down from my car.

She lowers the window and calls my name as I look around for Probe.

"I'm proud of you, honey."

"You just remember that the next time you want me to do something and I say no," I yell back, making her laugh as she pulls away.

I shake my head and pull out my cell phone, firing off a text to Probe. I can see his bike, so I know he hasn't gone far, but Havoc won't be happy if he finds out he left me, even if it's to use the bathroom.

I read messages and fiddle with my phone for a bit, but I curse when I see that I still can't access Instagram or Facebook. I will have to get G to look at it. I wander over to my car, figuring I might as well wait inside where I can sit and run the AC. Besides, it's safer in there, and I'm pretty sure I have a cereal bar in the glove box. I didn't eat before the meeting because I was too nervous. Now I'm starving.

Heading toward my car, I keep my eyes peeled for anything unusual, but all seems quiet. I unlock the car and lean in to place the bag on the seat when I'm grabbed from behind. I freeze for a second and curse the universe because I did everything right, and I'm still being punished.

I drop the bag as I fight against him. A glancing blow with my elbow to his gut makes him loosen his hold. Too close to the car to get in and lock the door before he grabs me, I take off running in the other direction, across the parking lot, hoping someone will see me and help. I run down the side of a car before spinning around, using the car as a barricade between us.

"Help!" I scream at the top of my voice, hoping it will deter him. But when Driller comes into view, I know there is nothing I can say or do that will stop him. The set expression is the same one Havoc gets when he's made up his mind about something.

"You won't get away with this. Havoc will kill you," I snap at him as I keep moving, feinting one way and running the other. But it's quiet here today, and too few cars are in the lot to offer me protection.

I need to stay out of the way long enough for Probe to return. I throw caution to the wind and sprint as fast as I can to the next row of cars in the lot. I'm running in heels, but I'm fueled by terror. Even so, Driller tackles me to the ground like a linebacker, knocking the air out of me and bashing my head against the concrete. I feel my body burn in places where the skin has ripped away. I try to scream as he pins me to the ground, but I can't get enough air into my lungs.

He grins down at me maniacally, grinding himself against me. Tears slip down my face when I realize he's hard. My struggling is getting him off. Finally, I manage to take a breath, but when I feel the snick of a knife pressing against my throat, I know screaming is not an option.

"You keep your pretty mouth shut, and I'll take it easy on you."

He drags the knife up my neck to my chin before he traces it over my lips. I can tell the blade is small and narrow, but this close, he'll still do some serious damage. I don't move, too scared to try anything. If I were Amity, I'd have him in a fucking headlock by now instead of whimpering underneath him like a coward.

"My brother always was a fucking dumbass. This is why he should never been made president. He fucking tricked his way into that role and cheated me out of mine. He thinks I'm just going to let that go?"

My eyes flit around, looking for something, anything that will help.

He presses the knife against the corner of my eye before he lifts it and licks away my tear. The knife is back at my throat before I can process the fact he didn't gouge my eye out when he had the chance.

421

"If you're looking for your guard today, don't bother. He won't be coming to rescue anyone anytime soon." He grins before dipping his head and covering my mouth with his.

I resist the urge to bite his tongue off, just waiting for a chance where I can make a run for it. He has to let his guard down sometime.

"You killed him?" I feel my heart crack at the thought of Probe being gone. I should have known something was wrong when he wasn't outside waiting for me.

Stupid Nevaeh.

"He really has no idea what to do with a woman when he has one, does he? Fucking idiot. Let me guess. He thought I'd go after Lola first, right? After all, she's my old lady, carrying my baby and all that shit." He laughs, and it makes the hairs on my arms stand on end.

"She doesn't matter. She never did. I took her because I could, but Havoc did more damage to her than I ever did. He was supposed to love her, yet he never questioned her actions. All that time together, and he just accepted that she jumped from him to me." He shakes his head as my blood runs cold. "So insecure she changed her whole world to fit his, and then he was gone, leaving her all alone."

"What did you do?" I whisper, not wanting to know but at the same time needing the truth.

"I didn't give her a choice. I beat that bastard's baby right out of her before replacing it with mine. If it's anything like me, it will rip her apart during labor." He laughs gleefully.

My eyes slip closed, and I cry for a woman I disliked on principle only weeks ago.

"Now I'm going to ruin you and leave you for my brother to find. I do so like breaking his toys. Be interesting if he'll want you once I've been inside you. History says he'll walk away after all."

His free hand slips under the hem of my shirt and I thank God I wore pants instead of a skirt today. I try to wiggle away, but the hand with the knife presses a little harder against my skin. I reach up instinctively and wrap my hand around his fist, trying to stop him, but his strength is no match for mine.

"I'm gonna enjoy making you scream my name."

His fingers reach for the button of my pants just as a figure steps up behind him. I feel my eyes widen as I stare into my father's horrified eyes moments before he brings a rock down on the back of Driller's head.

Driller collapses over me, his hand going slack over the knife. I cry out when it nicks my skin. I slip the knife from his hand into mine as I try to wiggle out from under him. He groans above me as my father rolls him off me.

"Run!" my father yells.

I grip the knife, realizing belatedly it's one of those switchblade things, and get to my knees.

"Get up, Nevaeh. Get in the car and get out of here now!" He yanks me to my feet, then lets me go when there is a scuffle behind me.

My head is swimming, and I know I'm more of a liability

here than a help. I flip the blade closed, shove it in my pocket, and run to my car, knowing my phone is in my bag. The door is still open, and my bag is sitting on the passenger seat. I jump in and slam the door, flipping the lock into place before reaching for the bag with shaking hands.

I freeze when I remember dropping the bag in the parking lot, scattering the contents on the ground. Before I can do anything, a rope is around my neck, pulling me back against the car seat.

There's movement behind me as I tear at the rope with my fingers, ripping my nails in a blind panic. A click sounds, making me freeze. I've been around guns enough to know what a safety being removed sounds like. The rope loosens a fraction, just enough for me to drag in some air, but the press of the gun to my temple guarantees compliance.

"Back in my day, everyone knew to check the back seat. That's what's wrong with this generation."

Says the man with a fucking gun.

"Put your hands on the wheel and drive. I'll tell you where to go. If you try anything funny, I'll blow your brains all over the dashboard."

"Okay," I whisper, knowing nodding my head might not be such a wise move.

He's already put the keys in the ignition, so I start the car and move toward the exit. My father looks toward us, the rock still in his hand. His eyes flash with relief when he sees me, but they quickly shift to horror when he sees whoever is in the backseat. He starts running toward me, yelling my name.

"If you stop, I'll shoot him. Head west toward the highway."

I do as he asks, ignoring my dad, my tears, and my panic. I focus only on surviving.

The window opens a crack in the back. I look in the rearview mirror and see the figure wearing a hoodie covering their face, tossing my phone out the window. There goes my hope of G tracking it.

I swallow down the urge to puke and focus on the road. I'll get my chance to make a run for it. I just have to bide my time. The pen knife burns a hole in my pocket, but I know if I try to use it now, I'll be dead before I can even stop the car. I don't allow myself to think about all the things that can go wrong. I've done enough research to know that being taken to a secondary location is the worst thing a kidnapper can do.

The rope scratches the skin of my neck, rubbing it raw, but I don't dare take my hands off the wheel.

"Take a left here and keep to the speed limit."

I do as he asks, wondering when Havoc will know something is wrong. I told him what time the meeting was supposed to finish. It let out a little earlier than I thought, but by now, he would assume I was on my way home. When I don't make it back, he'll call. And when he cannot reach me or Probe, he'll come look for me.

When he knows something is wrong, he'll have G dig and

see what he can find. Surely, in this age of CCTV, there are a dozen cameras around that caught my kidnapper on camera. All G would need is one clear shot to identify him. Once he has that, he'll dig until he knows everything down to his underwear size. They'll find me, and Havoc will come for me guns blazing. That's not a doubt in my mind. The question is, will he find me in time?

I turn when he tells me to, taking a side road that is far quieter than the one we just left. I swallow and keep going, taking in everything I can around me—things that can be used to trace back to this location, things I could tell the cops if I survive.

I think of my dad. I have no idea what he was doing there today. I didn't even know he was still in town. Our relationship might be a mess right now, but the look in his eyes when he realized what was happening to me will haunt me forever.

How will he get over this when he barely survived the first time? Every nightmare he had is coming true all over again.

"Turn off here."

I make the turn onto a bumpy dirt road. The panic threatens to claw at my insides when I realize we're getting closer to our destination. The road is longer than I anticipated. It takes twenty minutes before a house comes into view. A lone structure that looks like a family farmhouse, not the place where I'll likely end up dead.

"Who are you? Why are you doing this?"

Make yourself more human to him, Nevaeh.

I need to make him see me as a person, not an object.

"Pull over here and get out. Try anything stupid, and I'll kill you. Don't make me do that, Nevaeh. That's not what I want."

I stop the car and swallow. "What do you want?" I whisper, scared of the answer.

I open the door and slip my hand into my pocket, fingering the knife as I flip it open and slip it into my sleeve. The sharp point presses to my wrist as I bend to keep the knife from slipping free.

I close the door as he climbs out and use the move to put me closer to him. With his gun, he can kill me wherever I am. With this knife, I need to be closer. I lock my legs to stop them from trembling.

He climbs out, gun pointed at me, and hoodie pulled low over his head. He closes his door and the slam makes me jump. Covering me with the gun, he uses his teeth to pull the glove from his free hand. I close my eyes for a moment when his hand reaches out almost reverently to trail over my cheek.

I open them when I realize his skin feels papery and rough. A glance at his hand shows aged skin covered in liver spots. The hoodie threw me. This man is much older than I thought.

"The missing piece, finally," he murmurs, pleasure clear in his voice. He lets me go and lowers his hoodie.

He's much taller than me. Too tall for me to reach

anywhere important. I'm not sure the knife is big enough to do much damage to his chest, and his stomach is covered with the baggy hoodie.

My writer's brain tells me to go for the femoral artery, and before I can second guess myself, I let the knife slip fully into my hand. I grasp it tightly, ready to make my move when I get a good look at his face.

His cold eyes belong to the homeless man from outside the diner.

The liver-spotted hands belong to the man from the book signing.

But it's more than that. Now that I can see all of him, I realize I know him.

He smiles that creepy smile that always made me uncomfortable as a kid. "Mr. Markham?"

"Hello, little one."

I stumble in shock but use it to get myself into position. He reaches out to steady me, lowering the gun instinctually. I use my momentum and stab the knife as hard as I can into his inner thigh, leaving it embedded in his leg. I can only pray I hit my intended target.

He drops to the ground with a bellow. I don't hang around, not while he still has the gun clutched in his hand.

I take off running, heading for the back of the house as he fires the first shot. I know I won't make it into the woods before he shoots me, not unless he bleeds out. Clearly, I'm not that lucky.

I need a weapon and somewhere to hide. I run up to the door and yank it open. I make it halfway down a long hallway when I notice a figure standing at the other end.

My hand covers my mouth as the ghost takes me in and does the same.

"Citlalli?"

"Nevaeh? Oh my god, what are you doing here?"

I stand frozen on the spot as I take in her white, threadbare dress and bare feet. Around her too-thin ankle, a metal cuff and a chain limit her movements.

"Oh god, I thought you were dead," I whisper, tears running down my face.

She stumbles toward me. "I'm not dreaming—you're really here?"

I swipe my hand across my cheeks and run toward her, wrapping her tightly in my arms as she sobs. Pulling back, I cup her face with my hands. "We need to get out of here."

The sound of gunfire makes us both jump. What little color she has in her gaunt face drains away.

"You can't be here. He'll kill you."

"I'm not leaving without you, Citi."

"You have to. Please just go."

The gun fires again, splintering the wood of the door. Citi screams and runs.

"Citi, wait!" I run up the stairs after her, trying not to trip over the chain that trails behind her. I know she's scared, but I have to make her see reason.

All those thoughts fly out of my head when I find her in one of the bedrooms with a little girl in her arms.

She looks around four or five, but it's hard to tell with her face buried against Citi's shoulder. It's the color of her hair that has my stomach churning. It's the exact shade and color as mine—as Citi's.

"Oh, Jesus." It's all right there, the evidence that my sister's been violated in the worst possible way. She's been held captive all this time, of course, she's been raped. I can't—

More gunfire snaps me out of my horror. She cradles her child protectively. I don't know if it is from me or Mr. Markham, but I know Citi will fight tooth and bone to protect her.

"I have a niece?"

"I won't let him hurt her. He can do what he wants to me, but I won't let him hurt her."

"He'll have to go through me first," I tell her with a snarl.

Another shot rings out, followed quickly by another.

I was too young to save Citi before, but I'm not a kid anymore. I'm an old lady to the president of the Raven Souls MC. I'll die before I let him near my sister or niece.

"Stay here."

I hear the gun click as he shoots, followed by two more clicks. I smile. He's out of bullets.

"You can't go out there, Nevaeh. He'll kill you."

"Not if I kill him first."

"There are no weapons here. He took everything and then used Star to make me comply."

"Everything's a weapon with the right intent."

I look around the sparsely decorated room and find nothing I can use, but when I look up, I spot the oak curtain pole, which looks exactly like the one we have back home. I push the bed until it's under the window and reach up to unhook it. I unscrew the wide ends of the pole before I grab the curtains and yank hard until the pole slips out of the grip holding it up. I step back to avoid getting hit on the head and quickly slide the fabric from the pole.

"Yes," I hiss, seeing it is the same—which means it's not one pole, it's two solid pieces that screw together in the middle. I quickly unscrew the two pieces as a voice calls up the stairs.

"If you don't come down here now, I'll set fire to the house and watch you all burn." I can hear the anger in his voice, but it's laced with pain. Good. There is more where that came from.

Once I have the pieces unscrewed, I have sections of wood a little longer than a baseball bat. It might not be the best weapon, but it's better than nothing.

I turn to Citi, who is still holding her daughter. Gathering the curtain fabric, I hurry over to her and use the material to tie the kid to her. It's not perfect, but at least it will leave Citi with free hands.

"Take this." I hand her half the pole before stepping in front of her.

"You stay here unless I tell you to move. If he comes for you, give him hell. He's an old man now, Citi, and you have a daughter who needs you to fight."

She nods rapidly. I can see how weak she is. Lack of food and exercise have taken their toll on her. But she's not a quitter, and a mother's love has given birth to miracles before.

"You're being very naughty. I'll count down from five, and if you're not down here by the time I get to one, someone's going to die."

"Fine by me." I push all my fear down and let my anger blanket it. My sister and niece need me. There is no place for fear here.

I step out into the hallways and head to the stairs.

"Four."

I make my way down them quietly, his counting working to my advantage because I can judge how close he is.

"Three."

I make it to the second to last step and take a deep breath, gripping the pole like a bat.

"Two."

Hurrying down the last step, I round the corner with the pole raised above my head. I skid to a halt when I find him standing in the kitchen with the knife still sticking out of his leg. In one of his hands is a gas can, in the other is a zippo.

"I'm so disappointed in your behavior."

"That sounds like a you problem, you selfish fuck. You kidnapped my sister. You kept her all these fucking years when we all thought she was dead!" I yell.

"I love her," he roars at me.

"She was just a little girl, and you raped her," I whisper.

"She was always meant to be mine. I saw the way she looked at me, the same way you did. It was supposed to be both of you. A perfect set, but your fucking father kept you from me."

I feel physically sick as all the what-ifs press down on me. "Alan Ellwick was––"

"Easy to point the finger at," he cuts me off. "A few choice words to the right people, and everyone came running with their pitchforks. He was an old adversary of mine. Always trying to one-up me, but I got the last laugh, didn't I?"

I tighten my grip on the pole, poised and ready to strike.

"I was going to come back for you, but your father wouldn't let you out of his sight. In the end, I got a sick sort of pleasure out of messing with him. I spent some time inside, you know, before I moved to your street. It wasn't for anything bad—fraud is barely a crime these days—but it did enable me to meet some interesting characters. Newton Helms, now he was fun to play with. Such a simple mind to manipulate. He was the first player in my game of '*Guess who took Citlalli.*' I visited others over the years and got them to play, too. It was fun watching the police scratch their heads."

"Why bother with the game at all? Nobody knew you had her. You were home free."

"Because I could. Because it messed your mother up so bad she killed herself, and I got to watch from the sidelines as your father fell apart," he smiles gleefully.

I swallow down bile, taking a step closer. "You watched us?"

"We moved around a lot, I didn't want to arouse any suspicion with the neighbors, but I always came back to check up on you. Imagine my fucking surprise when I came back, and you were not there," he snarls.

I shuffle forward a little more as he continues to rant.

"It didn't take me long to track you down. I was going to bring you home with me finally, but then you had to give away what was mine to a dirty fucking biker." He spits out.

I take another step closer. "Give me the key to Citi's shackle. I'm taking her out of this hellhole."

"You're not taking her anywhere. You're both mine now. You'd do well to remember that."

"News flash, asshole. I'm not ten anymore, and I'm not afraid of you."

I close the distance between us, channeling every ounce of rage and indignation I feel rushing through my bloodstream. I swing the pole just as he flips the zippo, and a flame sparks to life.

Chapter Thirty-Five

Havoc

I pull up to the building where the meeting is taking place and see cops and an ambulance in the parking lot.

I'm off the bike and running before it's even a conscious thought. "Nevaeh!" I yell, catching the attention of the nearest police officer, whose hand moves to his holstered gun.

"He took her," a voice shouts. I turn toward it and see Nevaeh's dad sitting on the curb with a paramedic fussing over him. He waves them away and struggles to get to his feet.

"Sir, sit down. I need to speak to you further," a cop tells him.

"Why? You're not listening to a word I'm saying." He

hurries over to me. I can see a nasty cut above his eye, which explains the blood running down his face.

"Where's Nevaeh?" I snarl at him, feeling G step up beside me.

"I've been following her to try to get her to listen to me, but when I saw her today, there was a man on top of her, hurting her." He grips his hair, his eyes going to the ground near a row of cars where paramedics are working on someone else.

It takes me a second to realize the bloody mess is Driller. "What happened?"

"I couldn't let him hurt her, so I hit him with the rock. I told her to get in her car, and she did. I thought she was safe, but he was in the back seat waiting for her. He had a gun to her head— made her drive away. I tried to catch them." He grabs my cut. "You have to find her. Please, God, find my daughter. I can't do this again."

I gently pry his hands away. "Who was in the car? Who took her?"

"Jasper."

"Who the fuck is Jasper?" G questions.

"He's flatlining. We've gotta go now!"

I look toward ambulances at the shout and already know who they're working on. There is no way Probe would let anyone take Nevaeh unless he was unconscious.

"I'll call the clubhouse." G steps back as I focus on Nevaeh's dad.

"Who is Jasper?"

"Jasper Markham. My old neighbor. He lived on our street for a couple of years. He moved away just before..." his voice drifts off as something dawns on his face.

"Oh god. He made Nevaeh uncomfortable. She told us that. She told the police when they asked her questions, so many fucking questions. But he'd left six months before, so they put him to the bottom of the pile. They had a suspect to focus on, but then Alan was shot and— Oh god, how did we get it so wrong?"

"Mr. Dillion—" a cop starts, but he shuts up when the man in question glares at him.

"My daughter is in the hands of a monster, and all you want to do is talk."

He pulls out his cell phone, taps on something, and hands it to me. "They wouldn't listen, but you must."

I take the phone and look down at it as G steps closer. "You put a tracker on the car?".

He nods as the cop barks something, but I ignore him and stare at Nevaeh's father.

"I'll find her, I promise."

I turn and run with G right beside me. Cops are shouting at us to stop, but I don't think they'd shoot us in the back. Ignoring my bike, I run for Ambros, who is sitting in his Corvette on the phone.

I yank the door open and climb in. G slips into the back. "Go before they stop us."

Ambros drops his phone and does as I ask without hesitation. "Where are we going?"

I pass the cell phone to G, who starts giving directions.

Pulling out my own phone, I call Midas.

"Prez? G called. I've got Circus and Capone on the way to the hospital right now. Any news on Nevaeh?"

"Her dad put a tracker on her car. We're following it right now."

"Jesus, I can't even be pissed. Tell me what you need?"

"Keep Amity contained. Get the club lawyer down to the precinct in Flemington for Nevaeh's dad. He saved her from Driller. We owe him."

"On it. I'll call now. Want me to send some guys your way?"

"No, we're heading closer to Hannibal's chapter. I'm calling him next."

"Keep me posted."

He hangs up, so I dial Hannibal. It rings and rings for what feels like forever, until finally, a female voice answers.

"Hello?"

"Lola, put Hannibal on the phone now."

"He's in the shower."

"I don't give fuck. Your ex-fuck piece just attacked my old lady. You get Hannibal on the phone right now, or I'll hold you accountable for whatever happens to her," I growl.

A few minutes later, Hannibal answers. "What the fuck did you say to my old lady?"

"Nevaeh's been kidnapped. We're tracking her, but I could use some help, and you're closer."

"Fuck. I'm leaving now. Just tell me where to go."

"G will text you directions." I hang up and rub my hand over my face. "Do we know who the fuck this guy is and what he wants with Nevaeh?" Ambros asks.

"He was her neighbor when she was a kid. It's possible he was the one who kidnapped her sister."

"Fucking hell, you're serious? Wait, could this be the guy trolling her? It can't be a coincidence."

I look back at G furiously typing away on his cell phone.

"Motherfucker. In 1989, Alan Ellwick and Jasper Markham were cellmates. Ellwick did three years for aggravated sexual assault and spent the end of his sentence in the infirmary after he was attacked. Guess who saved him?"

"Markham. And what's the betting Markham felt like Ellwick owed him for it?"

"Who's Ellwick?" Ambros asks.

"The guy they thought kidnapped Nevaeh's sister. Cops killed him when he resisted arrest."

Ambros taps his fingers on the wheel. "You think this Markham guy was the one who fingered Ellwick for the abduction?"

"Without a doubt, he had priors that included raping a twelve-year-old girl. The only reason he walked free was thanks to a technicality. Ellwick was the perfect suspect to keep the police busy, and in doing so, Markham slipped right under their radar," G answers.

"What was Markham in prison for?"

He taps away on his cell before he replies. "He served twenty-two months of a three-year sentence for fraud. He had no priors involving violence or any kind of sexual abuse. He hid his proclivities

well."

"The best kind of predators do," I growl.

"I don't get it. This Markham guy sounds like a pedophile, but Nevaeh isn't a little girl anymore. Why would he want her?" Ambros frowns, looking over at me briefly before returning his focus to the road.

"Maybe it's because she looks like her sister. Maybe he has a thing for twins," G says.

Ambros hisses. "Her twin?"

I run my fingers through my hair. "It's been fifteen years, why now?"

"It's because of me." Ambros hits the steering wheel. "The photo of me and her outed her real identity. Before that, she used a pen name and lived a quiet and sheltered life."

"This Jasper guy knew who she was all along and where to find her." I point out.

G sits forward. "Until she moved here. Maybe that's it. If he's always known where she was, it would have tripped his trigger to find her gone. And when he does find her, she's not the pure preacher's daughter anymore—she's tangled up with an MC."

I close my eyes, remembering Nevaeh in our bed with that just fucked look on her face. I picture her smile from the day of the book signing, how happy she was and—

My eyes snap open. "He was at the signing. He walked right up to her and introduced himself as Jasper. I thought he was odd, but..." I let my words drift off.

"Nobody could have predicted this Havoc," Ambros says quietly.

But I should have. It's my job to protect her, and right now, she's on her fucking own. *Fight for me, baby. I'm coming for you, but you gotta fight for me, fight for us.*

I listen to G give Ambros directions, but I keep my mind on Nevaeh. I refuse to believe that she won't come home. I know her, even terrified she'll fight to get back to me.

I fist my hands, trying to keep my own fear at bay. If I give into it, I'll tear this car apart with my bare hands. If I lose her, I'm done. I won't live in a world where Nevaeh doesn't exist. If she dies, I'll follow her. Some might think that's the coward's way out, but they have no idea the hell I'll rain down if I stay. I won't stop until the streets run with blood and there is nobody left alive to remember her. All the memories left will be mine and mine alone.

I think of G and Amity, the club, and all the people who love Nevaeh—it wouldn't be enough to stop me. Is a monster born or made? I've never weighed in on that, but I know now that losing Nevaeh will make me into a monster. I've always been fair. I might skirt the laws of morality to suit my needs, but I've never crossed any lines I couldn't live with— *Until Nevaeh.*

There isn't anything I won't do for her, any line I won't cross, or law I won't break. I'd sacrifice everyone, friend and foe alike, as long as I got to keep her.

"Turn left here."

I tune back into what's going on around me and find us on a long dirt road. I sit up and look around, seeing nothing but trees on either side of us.

"We might need to bail out and do the rest on foot," G says, but I shake my head.

I think about the house I took Nevaeh to and how far off the beaten track it is. "Not sure how long this road is. Stay on it for now. I don't want to leave the car and find we have ten miles to run. Time is not our friend right now."

After fifteen minutes, I knew I had made the right call. When the trees start to thin, I see the outline of a house in the distance. "Now we bail. How far out is Hannibal?"

"Seven minutes. He's on the path behind us. Should hear him soon," G answers.

"I'm not waiting. Seven minutes might not seem like much to us, but it's plenty of time to kill someone. Hands around her throat would take no longer than five minutes, a gunshot, seconds."

"We don't know what we're walking into, Havoc. We should wait for backup, in case—"

I turn and look at G. Whatever he sees on my face shuts him up.

"You went over a cliff for your woman. This is my cliff. Don't expect me to stand back because I'm the president. I'll take off my cut right now and shove it down your throat."

I get out of the car, pull out my gun, and ready myself. "G, go around the back. I'll take the front. Ambros, you armed?"

"No, but I know how to fight."

"I won't order you to stay in the car, but don't get killed. My old lady likes you, and she'll get pissed."

I move toward the house, focusing on keeping low until I reach the front door. I wait until G rounds the back before I grab the handle. A shout from inside has me abandoning caution. I burst through the door and follow the sounds of a scuffle down a long hallway.

"Go. I'll watch your back," Ambros says from behind me.

I dimly note that I can hear bikes approaching but don't slow down until I reach the kitchen.

It takes a second for me to process the scene. Nevaeh is pressed against the kitchen counter with a bat of some kind in her hand. She's soaking wet and oblivious to me; her focus is all on the man, who is a few feet in front of her. He doesn't look good. He's standing in a pool of blood and clinging to the island to keep himself upright. As I move into the room, I realize it's the Zippo in his hand that has Nevaeh held in place.

That's when I smell it--gasoline. And Nevaeh's soaked in it.

I run, barreling toward the man. He turns to look at me at the last second, but he's too late to stop a 220-pound pissed-off man. I close my fist over the lighter and take him to the ground. The flame goes out the second I close my hand over it. I throw the Zippo aside as his head bounces off the tile, but that's not enough for me. I pull back and hit him in the face.

"Mine. Mine. Mine," he yells as blood coats his teeth.

"Wrong, asshole. She's mine." I rain down punch after punch, reveling in his pain until his screams fade and his face resembles hamburger meat. And even then, I don't stop, not until I feel hands on my arms, pulling me away. I fight them, ripping at the body in front of me, needing to be sure he's dead.

Hannibal's voice penetrates the fog. "Havoc, Tinkerbell needs you."

I whip my head around and find her still in the same spot, her hands over her mouth, tears dripping down her face.

Shit, fuck. And now she knows the truth about what kind of man I am without her around to leash the madness. There is a reason I earned the name Havoc, after all.

I climb to my feet, ignoring Hannibal and Ferris beside him, and take a step toward Nevaeh. "Nevaeh baby, come here."

She doesn't react, her eyes on the body on the floor.

"Cupcake."

Her head snaps up, her eyes widening a fraction before she runs and collides with me, sobbing against my chest.

I pick her up and wrap my arms around her. "I've got you now, cupcake, no one is going to hurt you."

A cry sounds out, and Nevaeh freezes, then yanks herself from me. She runs out into the hallway before taking the stairs two at a time. I'm hot on her heels as she spills into a bedroom where G is crouched near the door, trying to make himself look smaller.

Nevaeh rushes past him. "Citi, it's okay. This is my family."

My eyes jump to the woman when Nevaeh says her name. I see the frail-looking version of Nevaeh staring back at me and feel bile in the back of my throat.

"Holy fuck," Ambros says behind me. He squeezes past me, and since he doesn't have a cut and looks a fraction less intimidating than the rest of us, I let him pass.

G moves close to me as he stands. "He had her sister the whole time. I don't even know what to say. Nobody was looking for her, Havoc. Everyone thought she was dead."

And I bet there were times when she wished she were.

"I promise you; they won't hurt you or Star, Citi. But we need to get out of here now," Nevaeh tells her. As I move closer, I realize she has a kid strapped to her chest and a wooden rod in her hands like Nevaeh had downstairs.

445

"He'll come for me, Nevaeh. He always comes when I run. That's why he chains me up."

My eyes slip closed as I picture a kid escaping into the woods only to be dragged back time and time again.

"He's dead, darling." I lift my bloody hands for her to see. "I killed him myself."

She stares at me for a minute. "Do you promise?" There is something so childlike about her question that it hurts my fucking chest to answer.

"I swear it."

She drops the rod with a sob. Nevaeh runs over to her, Ambros hot on her heels. When Citi's legs give out, he catches her.

The loud clank of chains brings my attention to her ankle and the shackle on it. I turn and walk out of the room before I lose my shit again. I jog down to the kitchen and round the counter. I stalk over to the body and lift my leg before stomping on his face.

"Havoc?"

I pause, my breath wheezing in and out of my chest as I look at Hannibal and Ferris. "Nevaeh's sister is upstairs with a shackle around her ankle and a child, I suspect is hers, strapped to her chest."

"He kidnapped Nevaeh's sister too?" Ferris questions confused, but Hannibal just looks shocked because he knows the full story.

"Yeah, Ferris. Fifteen years ago."

His mouth snaps shut as a look of horror passes over his face.

"I need to find the key," I say, bending down to rummage in the dead man's pockets. I come up empty.

"Let me go look. I can pick most locks," Hannibal says.

"Just go careful. She's terrified."

He nods and heads up.

"We need to burn this place to the ground," Ferris snarls.

"Yeah, but we need to check on the sister first to see if there is anything she needs from here."

"I'll go see what kind of accelerants I can find and rig the place." He leaves, so I take a second to get myself together before I head back up.

Nevaeh is standing near her sister, who is still in Ambros' lap. She has her arms wrapped around herself as she watches Hannibal use his lock pick on the shackle. I walk up behind her and wrap my arms around her tightly, lending her my strength.

"Probe?" she whispers to me.

"No news yet, but Circus and Capone are with him."

"My dad? He fought off Driller, who was trying to—"

"Shh...your dad is fine. A couple of scrapes and bruises, but he'll live. I don't know about Driller, and right now, I don't care. I've got the club lawyer on his way to your dad to make sure he doesn't get railroaded. He was the one who recognized who had you."

"He creeped me out when I was little, but nobody ever

listens to a kid. I feel sick, Havoc. He had her all this time, and we gave up on her."

"You didn't. You didn't know."

"But I should have. I'm her twin, for god's sake."

I turn her into my arms and hold her while she cries. "We have her now. We're going to help her heal."

"Got it," Hannibal says triumphantly.

Ambros scoops Citi up into his arms, kid and all. "Let's get you out of here," he tells her softly.

I take Nevaeh's hand and move closer. "We're going to burn this place down. Is there anything you need or want before it blows?"

Citi looks down at the little girl who hasn't spoken a word since we entered. "I have everything I need," she tells me, stroking the little girl's hair.

"Okay then. Let's get the hell out of here."

G takes the lead, followed by Ambros, me, and Nevaeh, and then, Hannibal brings up the rear. When we get outside, Hannibal breaks off to talk to Ferris. Ambros lowers Citi gently to her feet.

"Let me help," Nevaeh tells her softly as she helps untie the material wrapped around her. Once it's free, the little girl looks at Nevaeh over Citi's shoulder.

"Hey, Star. I'm your auntie."

Star looks from Nevaeh to her mom, who nods with a soft, tired smile. When Star reaches for Nevaeh, a tear runs down her face as she gently takes her from her mom. Star lays her head on Nevaeh's shoulder and slips her thumb into her mouth.

"I need to do something before we go," Citi says, looking at her daughter and sister.

"I've got her. Do whatever you need to do."

She nods before walking away. I nod to Ambros, who follows behind her.

I press a kiss to Nevaeh's temple. "You okay?"

"No, but I will be." Nevaeh adjusts Star, who's eyes flutter. "She's heavier than she looks."

"I can take her." I dip down so the kid can see me.

"Star, this is Uncle Havoc. Do you think he could carry you?" Nevaeh asks her gently.

She thinks about it for a moment before she reaches for me. I tuck her against my chest, her head under my chin. Her curls tickle my jaw, but I don't care. When she settles, I relax along with her.

Nevaeh turns to walk around the back of the house. "I'm going to check on my sister."

Not ready to have her out of my sight yet, I follow her. When we round the corner, Ambros stops Neveah from going any farther. I'm ready to snap at him for touching her when I catch a look at the ravaged expression on his face. I glance from him to Citi, who is sitting in the middle of the grass, a dozen or so feet away, surrounded by wildflowers.

"What's she doing?" Nevaeh asks as Hannibal and Ferris join us. Ferris nods to let me know the house is ready to burn.

Ambros casts a look my way, warning me that what he's about to say will hurt Nevaeh. I move closer until she can feel the heat of me behind her.

"Ambros?" she whispers, bracing herself. "What's my sister doing?"

"She's saying goodbye to the rest of her children."

Chapter Thirty-Six

Nevaeh

Amity comes barreling into the room, slamming the door into the wall, a wild look of panic on her face until her eyes land on mine.

She takes in a deep, shuddering breath before she crumples to the floor and sobs.

G is behind her in seconds, scooping her up and carrying her to the bed where I'm sitting.

"I'm okay, Amity, I promise." Physically at least. Emotionally, I feel like I've been put through the wringer.

"Yeah, well I'm not," she snaps through her tears. "You could have been killed and I couldn't get to you. Midas had me locked down, but I swear Pippin, I'd have come—"

I cover her mouth with my hand, muffling the rest of her words.

"I know you would have Amity, but I didn't want you near that asshole any more than the guys did, and you know Midas was just following orders.

She turns her head to glare at Havoc, who is sitting in the chair beside my bed, but he just crosses his arms and scowls at her.

"I wasn't risking you too."

She opens her mouth to argue, but I squeeze her hand.

"He's the president, Amity. He's the one who has to make the tough calls. He didn't know if he was going to walk in there and find me dead. He would never put you in that situation, and I'd never want him to."

Her shoulders drop, some of her anger draining away. "I get it. I don't like it, but I get it," she whispers before she moves to lay down in the bed beside me.

G sits in the free chair and watches us both while Havoc remains by my side, silently guarding me.

"Citi's really alive?"

I nod, feeling myself choke up. "She's been through hell and back, Amity. I can't even wrap my head around how he had her all this time. The things he must have done..." I choke out as Amity pulls me into her arms, and we cry together.

As glad as I am to have her home, safe and sound, there's a part of me that wishes she'd died all those years ago. Not because I'm cruel, but because I'd give anything to have spared her the years of torment and abuse. I don't know what to say or do. How do you move on from something like this?

"She survived all this time Pippin. That tells you just how strong she is. I'm not sure I could have done it. Fuck I'm in awe of her. Giving up would have been so fucking easy, but to live?" She shakes her head. "She's a fucking warrior."

"She really is. And you should see Star, Amity. She looks just like we did at that age."

"Who's sitting with them?"

"Ambros and Hannibal. I think she feels safe with them because they helped her get free."

"Hannibal? Not many people can say they feel safe with him. It's that dead-eyed glare of his that gives me the heebie-jeebies."

My lips twitch at that. "I'm telling him you said that."

She shrugs. "He won't care. He lives to freak people out."

"Knock knock,"

"Speak of the devil," Amity mutters as Hannibal walks into the room.

"Hey Tink, how you feeling?"

"Honestly, I'm fine. I'm just waiting for the doctor to discharge me."

"That's good. You had us all worried for a minute there."

"I had myself worried," I admit. "How's my sister doing?"

"She's asleep right now, so's the kid. Your father just turned up, but Ambros is sticking with her." I nod and feel Amity squeeze me a little tighter.

"Any news on Probe?" Havoc sits forward at my question.

"I just passed the doctor. He's out of surgery, but the next twenty-four hours will be touch and go. Have a little faith in him, Tink. The man is too fucking stubborn to die on anything other than his terms."

"I know," I whisper. It doesn't stop me from feeling helpless.

"I'm going to head out now if you don't need me, keep me updated about Probe."

Havoc stands and holds out his hand for Hannibal to shake "Thank you."

"No thanks necessary. You know that."

He offers me a wink before heading for the door, stopping when I call his name.

"Hannibal?"

He turns to look over his shoulder at me. I try to tell him about Driller and what he said about Lola, but snap my mouth shut. If Lola wanted him to know, she'd have told him.

"Take care of yourself."

He stares at me for a moment before answering softly. "You too, Tink."

I watch him leave before turning to look at Havoc. It might not be my place to tell Hannibal, but Havoc is a whole different matter. My loyalties lie with this man. Am I worried it will change things between us? No, I know he loves me. I feel it wrapped around me like a child's safety blanket. No matter how this plays out, he'll still be mine, and I'll still be his.

That doesn't mean I'm not a little wary about how the dynamic might change between him and Lola. I push my own insecurities aside because this isn't about me. I just hope that when Havoc realizes Lola isn't the villain here, that she doesn't become the one that got away.

Havoc leans forward and grabs my hand. "What's wrong?"

I shake my head and offer him a small smile. There is a time and place for this conversation and this isn't it. "Nothing. I just want to go home."

He bends his head and kisses the back of my hand as a doctor walks in with a smile on her face.

"Sorry for the long wait. It's been a crazy couple of days. The full moon makes everyone go a little nuts."

"I'll forgive you for anything if you tell me I can go home."

She chuckles. "Then I have good news."

I sigh in relief as I half listen to some signs and symptoms to watch for. I know Havoc will be paying attention to every word, so I let my mind drift to my sister and Star and what their futures might look like now they're free.

"How's my sister doing?" I ask once she's finished talking. She gives me a sad look that makes me swallow.

"I'm not her doctor, but I've been briefed so I could let you know that she's doing okay. She'll need to stay here for a while longer yet. She's severely malnourished and needs treatment for an infection. Her daughter, though, will be ready to go home tomorrow. We'd just like to keep her in overnight for observation."

I fight back my tears and take a deep breath. Amity sits up beside me and leans her head on my shoulder in solidarity. "She can stay with us. If Citi is okay with that, I mean. Right?" I ask Havoc, who squeezes my thigh.

"Of course. She's family."

Family. I've got my family back. I feel myself start to shake before the first sob slips free. And then I find myself in the middle of a Havoc and Amity sandwich with a side of G and he wraps his hand around mine, making me cry harder.

✳ ✳ ✳

I'm greeted with hugs and well wishes when we get home which sets me off again.

"I'm getting really sick of crying," I sniff as Havoc takes a couple of tissues from a box someone tosses at him.

He holds them to my nose. "Blow."

I don't even question if it's weird or not, too emotionally wrung out to sweat the small stuff. Besides, it feels good to be taken care of.

I settle in his lap and look around the room, seeing that most people have moved away to give us some space. Amity walks over with G, who has a tray of drinks in his hand. He slides them onto the table before they both take a seat. Amity passes me a coke before taking a bottle of water for herself.

"We need to get a room sorted for Star. I'm just not sure where to put her. Most of them are soundproof, which is great for not disturbing her, but what if she cries?" Amity bites her lip.

"What about the apartment above the clinic? It's got two bedrooms, so the three of you could move in there, and that way, Star won't see or hear anything she shouldn't," G suggests.

"I didn't even realize there was an apartment above the clinic," I admit and see Amity shake her head.

"Me either."

"It's mostly used during lockdown. We can get the bunnies to give it a clean. Me and Amity can go into town and grab some shit for Star. I have no idea what a little girl might need, but I'm sure we can figure it out between us."

"Sounds like a plan." Havoc agrees, calling over Lil, who gives me another hug.

"Can you round up a couple of girls and get them to clean the apartment above the clinic? We're going to be moving in there temporarily with Nevaeh's niece."

"Of course. Leave it with me, and I'll get it sorted." She hurries off, heading straight for the circle of bunnies near the pool table.

"I can make a list of what Star might need. Any chance I can see the apartment first though?"

G nods before getting to his feet. "Let's do it now before the bunnies descend."

I climb off Havoc's lap and wait for him to get to his feet, knowing there is no way he won't join us. Amity walks around the table and links her arm through mine, leading me out the back as the guys follow behind us.

"I'm thinking we need some pretty bedding and cozy sleepwear," she muses.

"Definitely. She'll need a week's worth of clothes too. We can always grab more if we need to. Get something for her to play with, some books, maybe a teddy or two." I take a deep breath before I let the sadness overwhelm me. I have no idea what Star likes. I don't even know if she knows. Judging by what little she had in that house, I'm not sure she's had the chance to be a kid.

Raised voices snap me out of my thoughts. I look to see what's happening and find Legs walking around the side of the building with a cardboard box in her hands, tears streaming down her face.

Amity pulls away from me and jogs over to her just as Midas rounds the corner. "Don't come back, Legs. We have fresh meat. Don't need to bother with lying bitches like you."

"Hey," I yell at him.

"Stay out of this, Nevaeh. This has nothing to do with you."

"Legs is my friend, and you don't get to speak to her that way."

"Huh. Typical. I guess sluts like to stick together."

He is so focused on me that he doesn't notice Havoc beside him until he punches him in the face and puts him on his ass.

"Please get me out of here," Legs begs Amity. I can see how hard she's shaking as she tries to put on a brave face.

Amity looks at me. I nod and move toward them both. I grab the box from her and let Amity wrap her arm around Legs' shoulder as she leads her away from Midas, who now has a furious G and Havoc circling him.

I'm too pissed to walk away, though. Instead, I storm over to Midas, ready to kick the asshat as he lay on the ground, but Havoc catches me.

"How fucking dare you. You know what? I'm sick to death of your sanctimonious bullshit."

"She was sleeping around, and now she's fucking pregnant—"

"And? She's not your old lady, Midas. She's not good enough for you, remember? She was doing her job. Bunnies don't get to stay unless they fuck the brothers. You know this. And still, you did nothing but set expectations she couldn't reach. You set her up to fail. You're pathetic. One day, you're going to wake up and realize what you did, and by then, it will be too late. I hope regret keeps you warm at night, Midas."

I spin in Havoc's arms to look at G. "Can you and Amity take Legs home? She's in no state to drive."

"Absolutely. I need to get away from the smell of bullshit anyway," he snarls down at Midas before walking over to me and relieving me of Legs' box. He heads over to Legs, and says something to her that I can't hear, but she nods rapidly and lets Amity lead her down the hill. She glances back at me briefly, her eyes filled with so much heartache that it makes my chest hurt and makes me want to kick Midas in the dick. I watch until they are out of sight before whirling on Midas again.

"You just lost the best thing that ever happened to you, and you're too much of a dick to even realize it."

He gets to his feet, wiping blood from his mouth, his gaze warily on Havoc, which is smart. If he didn't have his hands wrapped around me, I know they'd be wrapped around Midas' throat. I can feel his anger pulsing through him like a living, breathing entity ready to strip the skin from Midas' bones.

"You don't get it." I hear the pain beneath his anger, but I'm too far gone to care.

"You're right, I don't. From what I can tell, you want kids, and you can't biologically have them. That sucks, Midas, it really does, but there are other ways to be a father. Look at Hannibal. He considers Lola's baby his too." I sigh and move to step toward him, but Havoc is having none of it.

"Don't move," he growls at me. "If I let you go, I'll kill him."

I close my eyes for a moment and take a deep breath

before focusing on Midas once more. "You need to figure out what it is you want—what's important to you. You can't play with people's hearts like that."

"I didn't..." his voice drifts off as he drops his head.

"You did, and you know it. Lie to me all you want, but don't lie to yourself. She loves you Midas, and she hates herself because of it. Why do you think she's leaving? You've called all the shots and held all the power, but that positive pregnancy test changed everything. Now she has someone in her life she loves more than you. You better figure out real quick if you can accept that because if you can't, you need to let her go."

I tug Havoc, who, after a moment of resistance, lets me drag him toward the clinic—my mind on Legs. No matter what, she'll be okay. She'll have the baby she always wanted. If Midas doesn't get his head out of his ass, she'll find a man who'll love her and her kid—Midas will be nothing but a memory. And one day, when he wakes up—and he will—he'll come back for her and see the perfect life she made for herself. The one he could have had if he'd fought for her instead of throwing her away.

Lord, won't there be fireworks when that happens?

Epilogue

Nevach

I hug my sister gently, scared I'll hurt her if I squeeze any harder.

"I'm not ready to let you go," I admit. My stomach feels like it's full of rocks.

She pulls back and looks at me. "You built a life here. If I had what you do, you'd have to break my hands to tear me away from it."

"But I just got you back," I cry.

"You can come visit me whenever you want."

I nod, knowing I'm supposed to be the brave one here.

"I'd stay, but I'm not strong enough yet. I don't know if I'll ever be. I need time to heal. There is so much that I don't know or understand." She hugs herself.

I feel Havoc step up behind me. He has a sleeping Star in his arms. They've bonded over the last few weeks after we took Star home with us.

"You are stronger than you realize, Citi. I know grown men who couldn't survive what you have. You take all the time you need, and we'll be here whenever you need us. We're not going anywhere."

Citi's eyes fall on her daughter. "She loves you."

"She's an easy kid to love, just like her mama."

He moves around me and kisses Citi's forehead before walking past her to where my father's car is. My dad opens the door so Havoc can put Star in the car seat. I watch my dad, who almost had a heart attack when I returned safe and sound and with my sister in tow.

Amity steps up to Citi and gently takes her hand. "It won't be easy. In fact, this is going to be hard as fuck. But it's far from the hardest thing you've done."

I think about the mass grave Jasper buried each of Citi's babies in because they were boys and he only wanted girls. No, she's already survived the worst. She would survive this, too.

"I love you." I reach out and take her other hand, giving it a squeeze.

"I love you too." She looks at Amity. "Thank you for taking care of her."

"You don't have to thank me for that. Look after yourself okay, and don't be a stranger."

Citi gives her a small smile, before releasing her hand and taking my other one.

"I'm going to call you so much you'll be sick of me," I warn her,

"Never."

We stare at each other for a moment, two pieces of the same puzzle finally finding their way to each other, only to find that one piece has been so damaged it doesn't fit the way it used to anymore. In many ways, the Citi I knew is gone, but that doesn't mean I don't love this version just as much.

She rests her forehead against mine for a minute before she lets go of my hands and takes a step back. With a quick smile, she turns and walks toward the car, pausing when she sees Ambros. As our new prospect, he watches her from his spot at the gate. She walks over to him, keeping a little distance between them.

I look away, giving them the illusion of privacy as my dad heads my way. He stops before me, looking like he's aged ten years in two weeks.

He twists his hands together as tears fill his eyes. "I'm sorry. I'm so goddamn sorry, Nevaeh."

"Daddy," I whisper and step into his embrace. I try to hold it together, but it's impossible with his tears soaking through my shirt.

I don't know if we'll ever have the relationship I hoped for, but I wouldn't be here at all if he hadn't saved me from Driller. In the end, his love for me won out. We might never be what we could have been, but the pain that usually accompanies that thought isn't there anymore. I love him. He loves me, and right now, that's enough.

He pulls back and cups my face, his thumbs swiping over my cheeks. "Be safe."

"I will. Besides, these guys have my back."

"They do, don't they?" He gives me a sad smile before he steps back.

He walks backward for a few minutes, neither of us willing to look away. Havoc steps up beside him. My dad holds out his hand to him, and Havoc shakes it.

Walking over to me, Havoc pulls me to his side and holds me to him as my dad gets in the driver's seat. My dad waits for Citi, who waves at Ambros before climbing into the passenger side. She turns to me once she is strapped in and presses her hand to the glass. I hold mine up to her and bite my lip to keep my tears at bay.

I could go home with her for a while and we could spend some time together, helping each other heal, but that's not what she needs right now. I need to let her breathe, or I'll choke the rest of her will to live out of her.

"She'll be okay."

"I know. I just wish there was more I could do."

"I don't like feeling helpless any more than you do, but Citi needs to take these next few steps on her own."

I turn into him, slipping my arms around his waist, and breathe him in. "Thank you."

"For what?"

"For coming for me, for loving me, for not giving up on me. I could go on."

"I have time."

I pinch him, making him chuckle.

His fingers slide under my chin and tip my head back. "I will always come for you. If I couldn't ride, I'd walk. If I couldn't walk, I'd crawl. Nothing would stop me from reaching you."

He kisses me gently before pulling back when Amity nudges my side. "You okay?"

I nod and sigh. "I'm hanging in there."

She reaches over and squeezes my shoulder. "Good."

G walks out of the warehouse, and when he sees Amity with us he heads over. "You ready?"

Amity groans. "As I'll ever be." She looks at me when I frown. "It's our turn to amuse Probe."

I grin, knowing the man has been going stir-crazy since he woke up, and he's driving everyone nuts in the process. I'm just glad he's okay.

I wait until they're gone before turning back to Havoc. Time to rip off the Band-Aid.

"I need to talk to you about Lola."

"Not right now."

"You said that the last time I mentioned her, but this is important, Havoc."

He stares at me for a moment, his jaw tight, before he nods and takes my hand. "Let's take a walk."

I don't say anything until we've put a little distance between us and the clubhouse.

When we come across the remains of a fallen tree, Havoc puts his hands around my waist and lifts me up onto the trunk.

He leans into me. "Okay talk."

I grip the front of his cut and consider my words, but the truth is, there is no way to say this.

"Driller said something to me."

"He's in a coma now, Cupcake. The second that changes, he's a dead man. He won't hurt you again." And I know he'll lose no sleep over it, even though Driller's his brother.

"I'm not worried about me." I blow out a frustrated breath. "God, this is hard."

"Whatever it is, you can tell me. It changes nothing."

I reach up and cup his jaw, feeling tears prick my eyes. "No, Havoc, it changes everything."

I kiss him, pouring everything I am, everything I feel into it, anchoring him to me before I pull back.

"Driller raped Lola," I blurt out.

His eyes close, his shoulders drop as he presses in closer. "I want to say I'm shocked, but I'm not. How can I be? I just don't understand what she saw in him in the first place. They were never friends. She acted as though she hated him when we were together."

I swallow, realizing he's not getting it. "She did hate him. She does. She never chose him over you, Havoc. He took her." My words settle around us, freezing the air as if the universe is holding its breath.

His eyes fly to mine as understanding dawns. He shoves away from me. "No. I would have known. Someone would have told me."

I don't say anything; I just watch and wait as everything falls into place.

He roars, pulling back his fist and punching the trunk of the tree, splitting his knuckles open. I reach for his hand and hold on tight, feeling him shake with rage beneath my touch.

"She should have told me. Why didn't she tell me?" He whispers, looking lost.

"I don't know Havoc."

His hands move to my hips, yanking me to him as I wrap my arms around him.

"I need to talk to her."

"Yeah, I think you do."

"Driller could have been messing with you."

"He could have. He wanted to scare me." But I don't think he was lying, not about this.

"Oh fuck, Nevaeh, what did I do?"

I close my eyes and try to absorb some of his pain.

"Nothing is ever black and white, Havoc. You didn't know."

He sighs and lifts his head, kissing me urgently before whispering against my lips.

"I'll call Hannibal and arrange for a visit. You'll come with me?"

"Of course. We'll deal with this together like we do everything."

"Fuck, I love you."

I feel that knot of worry unfurl inside me. We'll be okay as long as we have each other.

"Good, because I love you too."

Acknowledgments

Kirsty-Anne Still – For my awesome cover.

Tanya Oemig – My incredible editor - AKA miracle worker. I'm so grateful to have you on my team. You're amazing and I adore you.

Briann Graziano – Proofreader extraordinaire and natural-born word ninja.

Stacey, Mallory, Marie, and Thais – you girls are the bomb diggity. Thanks for sprinting with me and for talking me off the ledge when needed.

Julia Murray — my amazing PA, friend and book whore-der.

Jamie Mott, Jennifer Ratzel, Amanda Eastling, Andrea Torrent, Sarah-Louise Graham, Darcie Fisher, Liselot Holloway, Kathryn Barr, and Gemma Louise Poulton– you all went above and beyond to help me get this book ready for the masses. Thank you, thank you, thank you.

My kids– for being epic human beings. Remember, I want the fancy kind of retirement home, okay?

My OH – for feeding me when I forget and for giving me

moral support when I'm running on nothing but caffeine and sarcasm.

My Candi Shoppers– you are the best readers group a girl could have. I love you more than muppet porn.

My readers – You guys are everything to me. I am in awe of the love and support I have received. Thanks for taking a chance on me and on each of the books that I write.

Remember, If you enjoyed it, please leave a review.

About the Author

Candice is a romance writer who lives in the UK with her long-suffering partner and her three slightly unhinged children. As an avid reader herself, you will often find her curled up with a book from one of her favorite authors, drinking her body weight in coffee.

Printed in Dunstable, United Kingdom